Hot and Heavy

ITALIAN STALLIONS
BOOK FIVE

MARI CARR

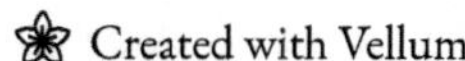 Created with Vellum

Hot and Heavy

What's better than one sexy protector? Two.

Hazel knows she's in serious trouble when her shady uncle threatens to implicate her in his crimes. When two police officers show up at her apartment, she's forced to flee Boston in the dead of night. Philadelphia feels like a big enough place to hide...until the seedy motel she's staying in burns down.

Kayden and Aldo's protector instincts rise to the surface after they spot a shivering redhead standing alone at the scene of a fire. Discovering everything she owned was destroyed, the sexy cop and charming firefighter offer her a place to stay.

None of them can resist their instant, scorching attraction to each other. The three give new meaning to the term "hot and heavy." Aldo and Kayden want more...hell, they want it all. But Hazel is in too deep, and as her lies begin to unravel, she's caught between a rock and a hard place.

Especially when the past catches up to her. Unless she puts her fears aside and offers Aldo and Kayden the one thing she's never given before—her trust—she stands to lose everything.

Chapter One

"I don't understand."

"Hazel. We could understand Grandma misplacing a couple of things, but too many of her possessions have gone missing over the past month or two. Expensive possessions."

Hazel gazed over Annabel's shoulder to where Mrs. Maloney sat on the couch. She kept trying to catch the elderly woman's eye, but Mrs. Maloney was either avoiding her or—more likely—completely unaware of what her granddaughter was accusing Hazel of.

"I've never taken anything from this house," Hazel said. "I would never steal from Mrs. Maloney."

After working for three years as Mrs. Maloney's in-home nurse, she was hurt by Annabel's accusation. The family had always trusted her, praised her work, and sworn up and down they couldn't live without her. Over the years, she'd begun to feel closer to the Maloneys than she did to her own fucked-up family, which wasn't really saying much. Because while kind, the Maloney family had always treated her as an employee—a valued one, but still basically the hired help.

Annabel's brother, Jeremiah, sighed, making it perfectly clear he thought Hazel was lying. Of the two Maloney siblings, Hazel had always been partial to Jeremiah, who was far more laid-back than his uptight sister. None of that easygoing attitude was present now. Right now, he looked pissed.

"Grandma's engagement ring is gone," he said.

A knot formed in Hazel's stomach, another in her throat. How could she defend herself against their accusations?

Jeremiah had been dating a lovely woman, Emily, for the last year, and he'd confided in Hazel a couple of weeks earlier that he planned to pop the question. He'd told Hazel that Mrs. Maloney's ring would pass to him for his future bride.

"You knew I was planning to ask Emily to marry me. You knew that ring was mine."

"What are you saying?" Hazel blinked rapidly to beat back the tears. There was no way in hell she was going to cry in front of these two, lest they took that as a sign of guilt.

"You knew your chance to steal it was running out," Jeremiah sneered at her, a look of pure derision written on his face.

"I didn't steal the ring. I didn't steal anything." Hazel looked at Mrs. Maloney again, praying the dear woman was in a lucid state. "Mrs. Maloney, I—"

"Don't you dare talk to her," Annabel interrupted angrily.

Mrs. Maloney's gaze lifted, and Hazel knew in an instant any hope of help was gone. Mrs. Maloney was suffering from dementia, her moments of clarity growing less and less with each passing month.

When she was first diagnosed, Mrs. Maloney had flat-out refused to move to a nursing home, insistent that she would die in the same house where she was born. Mrs. Maloney had been a powerhouse in those early days, so as a compromise—and since the family knew they wouldn't win the argument—she'd agreed to a private nurse. Hazel had been hired, and for three years, she'd worked six days a week—Fridays her only day off—from eight in the morning until six in the evening, taking care of her beloved employer.

For the first year, she'd been more companion than nurse

because Mrs. Maloney hadn't required much care. The hours had been a lot more than the elderly woman had needed that year, probably too much, but Hazel had agreed to them because this house was infinitely better than the shithole she called home, and because she'd loved spending time with Mrs. Maloney.

Unfortunately, Mrs. Maloney's mental state had declined more rapidly this past year, so the family had begun taking turns staying with her at night and covering for Hazel on her day off. Many days, Hazel hung around until eight or nine, waiting for that evening's relative to arrive.

"Annabel," Hazel started again, though one look told her the judge and jury had already decided her fate. "I swear to you, I have never taken anything from your grandmother."

Annabel sniffed. "The silver was here three months ago. We used it for Grandma's birthday dinner. And Jeremiah saw Grandma's ring not two weeks ago when he came by to tell her he was going to propose. The only reason he didn't take it that day was because he was on his way out of town for business and didn't want to run the risk of losing it. You are the only person outside the family with a key to the house, with access to Grandma's things. If not you, then who?"

Hazel didn't have an answer to that. Because the Maloneys were a very tight-knit, close family—no addicts, no assholes, no one who wasn't well-off in their own right. Hazel had gotten to know all of them very well, and she couldn't think of a single family member who would steal from their much-loved matriarch.

So...

How could she defend herself when she couldn't suggest a more likely suspect? Hazel didn't have a clue where Mrs. Maloney's things could have gone. While her mind was fading and Hazel could certainly claim that because of the dementia, she'd begun squirreling things away, the woman was never alone. Unless, perhaps...she was getting up at night?

As if he could read where her thoughts had gone, Jeremiah

added, "We searched the house from top to bottom yesterday. The entire family was here, and we left no stone unturned."

Yesterday was Hazel's day off. It appeared the Maloneys had been busy, building their case against her.

Annabel held up a notebook and began rattling off a list of missing items, all of them expensive things—like the jewelry and silverware—that would also be small enough to carry out in her backpack.

"Several pieces of the missing jewelry were family heirlooms," Annabel said, her voice breaking at the end, unshed tears filling her eyes.

Annabel's crying was almost Hazel's undoing, and she swallowed hard, fighting not to fall completely apart.

Jeremiah placed a comforting hand on his sister's shoulder, the gentle gesture in direct contrast to the pure venom in his eyes as he looked at Hazel.

"We want it all back," Jeremiah said.

Hazel had no response to that. If she knew where it was, she would give it to them in a heartbeat, but she wasn't lying to them. "I don't have it."

Jeremiah scowled. "So you already sold it? To who?"

Hazel hated how thin, how shaky her voice was when she replied. "I didn't t-take it."

Annabel turned away from her, a wobbly breath escaping. Clearly, her anger was fading in the face of hopelessness. Hazel could only assume they'd expected her to crumble and confess.

Jeremiah took the notebook from his sister, waving it furiously in Hazel's face. "Bring it all back and we won't call the cops."

Shit.

No.

Hazel closed her eyes, searching desperately for some answer, some reply that would convince them she didn't do what they were accusing her of.

If they called the cops...

She knew how that would end. Because Hazel's family wasn't unknown to the Boston Police Department. There was no way in hell the cops would believe Hazel Walsh over the Maloneys, given the fact Hazel's dad, Danny, was currently serving a life sentence after a bank robbery gone bad.

God. It had gone as bad as one could go. Because in his attempt to outrun the law, he'd killed two of the police officers in pursuit.

To make matters worse, Hazel's uncle Dennis had also been in on the robbery, though he'd been captured just prior to the shooting. It was the only thing that had saved him from that same life sentence for murder.

Add to that, her mom's countless arrests for petty theft, shoplifting, and assault—she had major anger management issues —and the Walsh family was pretty much a household name as far as the Boston cops were concerned, and there was no love lost.

If the Maloneys followed through on their threat, well, while they had no evidence, Hazel didn't want to test the theory that the cops wouldn't still find some way to pin it on her.

"I would bring it back if I had it." Hazel was aware she'd lost this battle before she'd even stepped foot in the house this morning. She cleared her throat, then swiped away the stray tear she hated the second it started to fall. "But I swear to you, I didn't take anything. I wouldn't steal from Mrs. Maloney. I love her."

Annabel had turned back around but refused to look her in the eye. Instead, she shook her head. "I can't believe you would do this to her. To *us*."

"You're fired." Jeremiah held his hand out. "Give me back the key. And if you've made copies, you might as well throw them away. I'm changing all the locks the second your lying ass is out of here."

Hazel fought to take Mrs. Maloney's house key off the key chain, her shaking hands making the task difficult. Finally working it loose, she handed it to him, her gaze on the floor.

She'd spent her entire life fighting to overcome her family's name and reputation, always keeping herself on the side of right, never breaking a rule, never giving anyone a chance to accuse her of wrongdoing.

A lifetime of being as close to perfect as possible, and it had all been for nothing.

She glanced up at the sound of paper ripping, taking the page Jeremiah shoved into her hand.

"There's the list of what's missing. We want it back."

She didn't bother to repeat herself, to tell him once again that she couldn't help him recover what was lost.

Instead, she gave up the fight. Glancing once more at Mrs. Maloney, she longed to be able to go to the woman, to hug her, to reassure her she hadn't done what they were accusing her of, and to say goodbye.

It was obvious from the way Annabel stood in front of her grandmother, they'd never let Hazel get close.

She swallowed heavily and turned toward the door, anguish pulsing through her with each step, as she realized this was the last time she'd ever be in this house she'd come to love.

"I mean it, Hazel. Don't make us get the cops involved," Jeremiah called out as she reached for the doorknob.

She didn't reply, didn't bother to defend herself or ask for mercy. She didn't point out that she'd given three years of her life to caring for their grandmother, driving her to doctors' appointments, preparing her meals, making sure she took her medicine, and keeping her company.

One false accusation and everything she'd done was washed away as if it had never happened.

She pushed the crumpled-up list Jeremiah had given her into the pocket of her coat. It was mid-February in Boston, which was pretty much synonymous for cold as fuck, though this winter seemed determined to go the extra mile. She bent her head against a gust of brutal wind as she walked to her piece-of-shit car. The air was so cold, her lungs stung. On the bright side, it was frigid enough that it froze her tears.

Climbing into the car, she started it, then slowly slid out onto the quiet street. Mrs. Maloney lived in an older section of the city, a sleepy, quaint suburb, away from the hustle and bustle of Boston's city center. The elderly woman lived on a street where all the neighbors knew each other by first name and said "hello" or "how are you doing?" in a genuinely kind way.

Hazel had always hated leaving at the end of the workday, forced to return to her own personal hell. For ten—sometimes twelve—hours a day, she could escape her real life and live here, where everything was quiet, where people were nice, where no one looked at her like she was white trash.

Hazel drove back to the shitty apartment she shared with her mother and, now, her asshole uncle. He'd been released from prison a few months earlier, banging on their door in the middle of the night, asking to crash on their couch. At the time, he'd assured them he would only be there a couple of weeks, that he would be moving on to bigger and better things.

Hazel soon learned that was Dennis's MO. He always claimed to have some big opportunity on the horizon, but it was just a bunch of bullshit words, spoken by a lazy, misogynistic thug. If there was a bright side to being fired—and she was being generous in referring to this as bright—at least now her uncle couldn't keep sponging off her.

At least not until she found another job…

Fuck.

She sucked in an unsteady breath as the severity of what had just happened continued to sink in. How the hell was she going to find another nursing job without a reference? There was no way the Maloneys would vouch for her abilities, no way they wouldn't warn off anyone who might consider hiring her.

Her resume was officially garbage.

Hazel pulled into the tiny parking lot behind her apartment building and rested her forehead against the steering wheel.

"Shit," she muttered. "Shit. Shit. Shit."

Lifting her head, she looked out the windshield and drew in a slow, deep breath, trying to calm down.

Then, she forced herself to play her "positive game." It was something she'd invented when she was eight and her life started to go to hell. That was the year her dad had been sentenced to life in jail. The year her mother lost one minimum-wage job after another, thanks to her bad temper and problem with authority figures.

It was the year her third grade teacher—wife of a cop—had stopped looking at Hazel as a bright, inquisitive student and had instead painted her with the Walsh brush, proclaiming to every adult in her elementary school that she was a troublemaker, a problem child. Those claims had followed Hazel all the way through middle and high school, even though she'd never broken a single rule or failed a test.

In order to survive all of that, Hazel had decided to find something good in every horrible thing, so as she looked at her run-down apartment building in the crappy part of town, she tried to find something positive about it.

"At least it has a parking lot," she whispered to herself.

She grabbed her bag from the passenger seat and dragged herself from the car, locking it. Trudging into the building and up the three flights of stairs—the elevator was broken, but the positive was, Hazel got in a cardio workout—she tried to figure out her next move.

She needed to find a new job, that went without saying, but she couldn't stop worrying that the Maloneys would carry through on their threat to call the cops. She anticipated spending a lot of time the next few days looking over her shoulder to see if the police arrived.

She could hear the TV blaring from inside her apartment when she was still half a flight of stairs down.

Wonderful. That sound meant Uncle Dennis was home. So much for opportunity knocking. The asshole had planted himself on her couch and was showing no signs of leaving anytime soon.

She opened the door, assaulted by the stench of cigarette smoke and stale beer. That was another thing she'd loved about Mrs. Maloney's house. It always smelled nice. Like lavender, which, yes, was sort of an old lady scent, but it beat the hell out of living in this stench.

Her mother had been a chain smoker since way before Hazel was born.

Thanks so much for spinning the roulette wheel on my health, Mom.

It was why Hazel always kept her closet and bedroom doors closed. It was the only way to keep the gross smell out of her clothing. It was also why she showered and shampooed every single morning, determined to wash the stench out of her hair.

The stale beer and old grease scents were new additions, brought into play by Uncle Dennis, who greeted her by belching loudly.

"What the fuck are you doing home?" he asked.

She sighed. Dennis was the last person she wanted to talk to right now. All she wanted to do was lock herself in her room and cry her eyes out. So she ignored his question and went to the kitchen to grab a bottle of water and a granola bar.

To her surprise, Dennis pulled himself off the couch and followed her. "Seriously. Why are you here? Thought you were working at the senile rich bitty's today."

Dennis had never met Mrs. Maloney, so his insults were based only on the fact Hazel told him she was working as a nurse for an elderly woman with dementia.

"I got fired."

Dennis scowled, and for a second, Hazel thought perhaps he was pissed off on her behalf.

"What the fuck is wrong with you? Why would you go and do that?"

She should have known better. She shook her head, then shoved by her uncle, ignoring his asshole questions. He didn't give a shit about her. Just his free ride.

Hazel had almost reached her bedroom when he grasped her upper arm, turning her around a little too roughly.

"What the hell?" She shook off his grip. Her uncle had never touched her, never even lost his temper with her—unlike her mother, who yelled at Hazel twenty-four seven.

"Why did they fire you?"

"They accused me of stealing, which I didn't do. Unfortunately, it was my word against theirs and they won."

Dennis ran his hand over his scarred cheek—the scar courtesy of some prison fight that had landed him in solitary confinement for two weeks. "Did they call the cops?"

Hazel shrugged. "They hadn't before I left."

"What's that mean? Are they calling them or not?"

"Why the hell do you care? The job is gone. They want their stuff back or yes, they *are* calling the cops. Since I don't have their stuff, I guess they're making the call. Now if you don't mind, I'm finished talking about this." She turned away from him and opened her bedroom door. This time, Dennis let her go.

She crossed the room to her bed, dropping down heavily. Alone at last, she gave in to the tears, crying like she'd never cried before as truth after truth crashed down on her.

She'd just lost the best job she'd ever had.

She'd never find another one in nursing.

The cops could be on the way right now.

And the one truth that had her curling in a ball, her stomach aching with pain—she'd never see Mrs. Maloney again.

"They didn't even let me say goodbye," she whispered to her empty room. That was the thing that hurt the worst.

She cried until she ran out of tears and steam. Then she fell into a deep, and mercifully, dreamless sleep.

/ Chapter Two

"I'm getting sick and tired of going to this shit stag with you," Kayden grumbled.

His best friend, Aldo Moretti, chuckled, but he didn't disagree.

They were the last two still sitting at their assigned table at the reception, the rest of their tablemates out on the dance floor, celebrating with the bride and groom.

To add insult to injury, they weren't just stag at a wedding, they were stag at a wedding on Valentine's Day.

"Not used to there being such slim pickings in the wedding party. Usually always a single bridesmaid or two for us to flirt with," Aldo said. "It figures Penny's bridesmaids would be Jess and that IT guy, Toby. Not much use for us there, considering Rhys and Tony haven't let their girlfriend out of their sight all damn night, and while Toby's a great guy, computer geeks aren't exactly our type."

Kayden rolled his eyes at Aldo's attempt at humor but didn't crack a smile, not willing to be joked out of his foul mood.

Aldo frowned. "Damn, man. You need to snap out of it. It's supposed to be a happy night."

Kayden sighed. "I know. And I *am* happy for Penny. It was a great wedding. I've never seen two people so freaking in love."

Which he meant. Kayden could admit he had a bit of a romantic streak running through him, so witnessing something like this wedding typically wouldn't send him down such a grumpy path. But it wasn't just the bride, Penny, and her new husband, Gage Russo, who were making lovey-dovey eyes at each other.

Nope.

Over half the guests here were partnered up, slow dancing, stealing kisses, and so lost in each other's eyes, it was like they weren't even on the same planet as the rest of them.

"It *was* a great wedding," Aldo agreed, even as he scowled. "Even if she did marry a Russo."

Kayden scoffed, not falling for Aldo's bullshit. "You like Gage, and you know it."

Aldo, like every true Moretti, refused to go down easy when it came to the Russo brothers. Probably because their families had been locked in some never-ending feud that had started four generations back and was showing no sign of ending with this current crop of offspring.

When Italians were slighted, they could hold a fucking grudge.

"Gage is alright," Aldo was forced to admit. "At least Penny picked the nicest of the Russos to fall in love with. I'm not so sure I could have stomached today if she'd walked down the aisle with Matt."

Kayden and Aldo had been best friends since elementary school, which meant Kayden understood there were levels of enemies when it came to the three Russo brothers. Gage was the least offensive, the one who hadn't done anything—yet—to prolong the feud, and had proven himself to be a fun-loving good guy, who loved their friend Penny almost to the exclusion of everything else. All points in his favor.

Conor, the youngest brother, was probably on the same tier as Gage, primarily because the man kept to himself and no one knew a damn thing about him.

And then, at the other end of that range, was Matt Russo, the oldest brother, and the one who had proven the fruit didn't fall far from the tree. Back in high school, Matt had lost the positions of quarterback and class president to Aldo's cousin, Tony. A sore loser, Matt had decided to seek his vengeance by seducing Tony's girlfriend and first love, then making sure Tony discovered the two of them together.

A dick move regardless of past family grievances, as far as Kayden was concerned, so he was in Aldo's camp when it came to Matt.

Aldo chuckled, drawing Kayden's attention, and he realized his friend wasn't laughing about their conversation but about something that was happening on the dance floor.

"Your sister, man," Aldo said, still grinning. "She's too much."

Kayden glanced toward the dance floor, and for the first time, managed to crack a legit smile. "Jesus."

His kid sister, Keeley, had recently fallen in love with not one but two of Kayden's close friends, Rafe and Gio. The three of them were in the center of a large circle on the floor, both men in an apparent dance-off to win Keeley's affections...like they didn't already have them.

His sister didn't have a shy bone in her body, so of course, she loved being the center of attention, really hamming it up, as if there was a decision to be made. There wasn't a person in the room who didn't know that choice had already *been* made.

If they could call it a choice, considering she'd fallen head over heels with both men. And they'd fallen right back.

As the song came to an end, Keeley crooked her finger at Gio, then at Rafe, the three forming a tight circle, proving it wasn't called dirty dancing for nothing.

Kayden looked away because one, she was still his sister and Gio was skirting a line with his touches; and two, she was living his dream. He was happy for her, truly, but witnessing that love only continued to drive home just how alone he was.

He sighed once more.

"And there you go again. Seriously, Kay. What the hell is wrong with you tonight? It's gotta be more than just us being here without a date...or dates," Aldo added somewhat begrudgingly, making it clear that he—like Kayden—would prefer it if they could attend these types of events with just one woman... their woman.

Kayden took a long swig of beer. "Look around us, Aldo. Look at all our friends, our family. Look at all the love in this room. Don't you get tired of the two of us always standing on the outside looking in?"

Aldo perused the room, taking in exactly what Kayden had just pointed out. When he looked back at Kayden, he nodded. "Yeah. I do. But, Kayden, we're going to get there. Just because we haven't found the one yet, doesn't mean we never will."

Kayden turned his attention back to the dance floor, where Jess was wrapped up in Rhys and Tony's arms, the three swaying together in a slow dance. "Tony and Rhys weren't even looking for Jess when they found her. And the idea of sharing a woman wasn't a blip on their radar. I think they're still trying to figure out how they got there."

The same didn't hold true for him and Aldo. They'd known for years what they wanted, and it was a relationship like the one Tony, Rhys, and Jess shared. Like Keeley had with Gio and Rafe.

Well, not exactly the same. Because while he and Aldo both hoped to find their Miss Right, they would do so with the knowledge they'd already found their *Mr.* Right.

"And I'm happy for Tony, Rhys, and Jess," Aldo said. "All their relationship shows me is that what we want isn't out of the realm of possibility. Not at all. Jesus, at this point, it feels more like committed threesomes are the norm in my family."

Aldo wasn't wrong. Because Tony and Gio weren't his only cousins in committed threesomes. Aldo also had two female cousins in Baltimore, Layla and Erin, who were both living with two men each. While Layla and Erin didn't come home to Philly often, they'd been back enough for Kayden to know—all the way to the depths of his soul—that he wanted what they had. He wanted his happily ever after to come with two people, not just one.

It was Layla's relationship that had opened his and Aldo's eyes and shown them a path they hadn't considered. It had been five years earlier, and Layla had come home for a Fourth of July picnic with her boyfriends, Miguel and Finn. Kayden hadn't spent more than ten minutes talking to the trio before he realized that Miguel and Finn weren't just with Layla; they were with each other too.

The foundation of their relationship had rocked Kayden to his core.

"We're thirty-five," Kayden pointed out. "And we've been looking for a long damn time."

"So what?" Aldo said. "That's it? You're giving up?"

Kayden shook his head. "You know I'm not. I'm just...fuck. Ignore me. I'm in a bad fucking mood."

Aldo placed his hand on Kayden's shoulder, and despite his depression, the touch—as always—turned something on inside. Aldo squeezed and Kayden shot him a look, one his best friend never failed to interpret correctly.

"It's been a while," Aldo said softly.

Kayden nodded, aware of what Aldo was referring to. The two of them had grown up together, but they'd never crossed that delicate line between friendship and something much, much more until their late twenties. Kayden had always felt an attraction to Aldo. Hell, he'd felt an attraction to more than a few men in his life, but he'd never acted on it because he'd always considered himself straight. He'd brushed off the guy crushes as him just being bi-curious.

Then Kayden's parents died in a plane crash. In one night, the future he'd always imagined for himself was erased, rewritten. He'd given up his room in the apartment he shared with Aldo, moving back into his parents' house, and taking over the raising of his little sister. Keeley, ten years younger, had only been fifteen at the time, and she'd needed him.

Fuck, he'd needed her too. They were the only family they had left and they'd clung to each other, even though they fought like cats and dogs. Keeley, the wild child, didn't exactly make things easy for him.

Of course, in hindsight, he could see he hadn't made things easy for her either. He'd stopped being the indulgent, fun-loving big brother and morphed into the overprotective, stressed-out-he-was-fucking-her-up mother/father figure.

He'd had one of his Keeley-is-out-of-control meltdowns over two years after his parents' deaths, toward the end of her senior year of high school. He and his sister had had a knock-down drag-out fight, something that had become too frequent as the eighteen-year-old girl continually insisted she was an adult and pushed every fucking button he had.

Aldo had intervened, suggesting the two of them take a break from each other. Keeley had gone out of town for the weekend with one of her girlfriends' families, skiing in the Poconos, and Aldo had shown up with a bottle of bourbon, claiming it the cure to all of Kayden's anxieties.

That hadn't been completely true. It wasn't the bourbon that had helped Kayden overcome his stress.

It was the kiss they'd shared.

To this day, neither of them could remember who made the first move. One minute, they were there on the couch, feet up on the coffee table, cussing out the ref after a shitty call in the hockey game they were watching.

The next minute, the two of them were in each other's arms, kissing like it was their last night on Earth. And a few minutes later, they were naked and in Kayden's bed, and that was when he realized he was less straight, and more bi, than he'd realized.

And the great thing was, Aldo felt the same way.

For the first few months, they'd come together like teenage boys who'd just discovered sex. They fucked like rabbits, stealing away for quickies every second they had the chance. They'd been obsessed with the sex because Jesus Christ...it felt so good.

After six months of nonstop horniness, they lay together one night, and for the first time, talked about what they'd been doing and what they were to each other.

And that was when they realized, they were definitely bi...not just gay. Aldo confessed to missing sex with women, and Kayden couldn't deny he felt the same.

That was when they agreed they'd always be best friends, but they couldn't be boyfriends. So Aldo had climbed out of Kayden's bed—Keeley had been at a sleepover—and the sex stopped.

Until two years later, when Layla came home with Finn and Miguel, and the light went on for him and Aldo.

They didn't have to choose any more than Layla did.

Everything had changed for them after that. They weren't denying a part of themselves, weren't forcing something to stop existing just because they knew they wanted to find a girl, get married, and make babies. Instead, they started searching for the one together, and the sex picked up again, though they managed a little more restraint than they had previously.

So far, they were failing miserably in their search because while they went out on dates—lots of them—they'd yet to find a woman they were both attracted to.

"Do you think you'd feel better if I went home with you tonight?" Aldo offered.

Kayden considered the request. He wasn't sure why they'd backed away from each other sexually, yet again, over the past year or so. It wasn't something they'd discussed and decided together. And it wasn't because the desire wasn't still there. Sometimes it burned so hot, Kayden thought it would render him to ash.

But the last time, it felt different. Felt like...not enough. They'd both sensed it, and by tacit agreement, they'd just stopped.

"Nothing's changed since the last time," Kayden said.

Aldo nodded, the ever-present twinkle in his cheerful friend's eye fading. "I know it hasn't."

Kayden hated that he'd ruined the night for Aldo. Hated that he'd brought his friend down to his same level of depression. "It's just..." He ran a hand through his hair, frustrated—sexually and emotionally.

"Have you changed your mind about us doing this together? Looking for a relationship like Layla has with Miguel and Finn?" Aldo glanced across the room to where Keeley, Gio, and Rafe now stood near the bar. "Like Rafe and Gio share with your sister?"

Kayden frowned, following the direction of Aldo's gaze. He'd had a sense lately, but...

"You think the status quo has changed between Rafe and Gio?" Kayden had been convinced when Keeley started dating Rafe and Gio, there was nothing going on between the two guys. Now...

Aldo shrugged. "Every time we're with them lately, I keep getting a feeling that their relationship is less like the one Tony and Rhys share with Jess," Tony and Rhys were the straightest straight guys in the world, "and more like Finn and Miguel's."

Kayden considered that, then nodded. "I think you might be right."

"So?" Aldo returned to his original question. "Have you changed your mind? Do you think we should give up and go it alone?"

Kayden didn't hesitate to reply. "No. I don't want to stop looking. Do you want to come home with me tonight?"

Aldo considered the invitation, then he nudged Kayden's knee with his under the table. "You know we could sleep together without sex. I know what a hopeless cuddler you are."

Kayden laughed, even as he rolled his eyes. "Says the king of spooning. I know what I want my future to hold, Aldo. And you're a part of that. You *have* to be a part of it. I'm not sure I could be happy without you."

Aldo grinned, and this time, the smile went all the way to his eyes. Kayden was the gloomier of the two of them overall, Aldo's quick-witted nature the perfect foil to keep him from going full-on Eeyore.

"Of course, you couldn't," Aldo joked. "But the rub is...I can't be happy without you either. So let's stay the course. There's a woman out there for us, Kay. I can feel it all the way to my bones. She's going to be pretty and sweet and smart, and she's going to knock our fucking socks off the second we see her. Then the three of us are going to get married and make beautiful babies together."

Kayden laughed, the melancholy of the last few hours lifting completely. "Okay. You've convinced me."

"Good. Because we've still got a lot of weekend yet to go. I vote we put a dent in that open bar, especially since it's on the Russos' dime. Then tomorrow after work, we can blow off some steam at the hockey game. Maybe if we're lucky, my baby bro will get in a fistfight we can live vicariously through. I love it when he gives us a show."

"Pretty sure Elio's fighting days on the ice are over." The two of them watched Elio lead his new ladylove, Gianna, back to the floor for a slow dance. Elio hadn't dropped just one bomb here tonight but two, revealing that in addition to retiring from hockey at the end of this season, he was completely in love with Gianna.

"Yeah. You're probably right. The fucker's too blissed out to throw a punch."

"Another one bites the dust," Kayden muttered, as he considered the ever-shrinking number of single members in their social circle.

Aldo knocked his knee against Kayden's under the table. "Twenty bucks says we're next."

"Feeling that confident, huh?"

Aldo gave him a huge shit-eating grin. "I've got a good feeling, man. All our dreams are right there, just on the horizon, ours for the taking. So is it a bet or not?"

Kayden held out his hand, hoping against hope that he lost the twenty bucks. "It's a bet."

Chapter Three

Hazel was groggy and confused when she woke up in the dark room. It took her a few seconds to remember where she was and why. Then the day's events crashed back over her, and she swallowed hard, determined she wasn't going to cry again.

The TV was still blaring in the living room, but it wasn't the usual shit her uncle watched. Right now, she could hear the canned laughter behind her mother's favorite sitcom. Which meant—miracle of miracles—Uncle Dennis had left the apartment. That was the only time she or her mother got control of the remote.

She considered staying in bed, but her growling stomach reminded her she hadn't eaten anything today, the granola bar she'd grabbed from the kitchen earlier still unopened on her nightstand.

Rising, she walked out of her bedroom toward the kitchen.

"You up, Hazel?" her mother called out from the living room.

Begrudgingly, she changed direction, peeking in the living room door. Her mom was in her tatty bathrobe, a cigarette hanging out of her mouth.

"Yeah."

"Dennis told me you lost your job. You think sleeping all day is a smart thing to do?"

Leave it to Mom to build her up after one of the worst days of her life.

"I'm making something to eat. Did you have dinner?"

Mom shook her head as she picked up the juice glass filled with cheap wine. "I'm drinking my dinner."

Typical.

"Great," Hazel said sarcastically, which was not the right way to end the conversation.

"You need a fucking job, Hazel. If you think you're going to lay around here all day, every day, you've got another thing coming."

Hazel laughed cruelly. "You're joking, right? I'm the only one around here who's held down a steady job for years. Who do you think pays the rent on this shithole? Who pays for the utilities and buys the damn food? Me. That's who. So if I took today—one fucking day—for myself because I was sad, then you're just going to have to deal."

Her mother wasn't one to let anyone have the last word, but Hazel wasn't sticking around to listen. Mom yelled, ranting and raving about how Hazel owed her—though she didn't have a clue what for—and how she should be more respectful, and blah blah blah.

It was the same shit Hazel had heard her entire life, so it was easy to tune it all out. She whipped up a peanut butter sandwich, using the last two pieces of bread—stale heels—and shoved a big bite into her mouth. There wasn't any jelly. Since Dennis moved in, it had been difficult to keep food in the house. Apparently, he worked up one hell of an appetite sitting on the couch day after day.

Hazel made a mental note to hit the store tomorrow, then she decided she'd sneak the food in and hide it in her room. The other two adults in the apartment could fend for themselves from now on.

She stood by the counter until she heard her mother stumble down the hallway, slamming her bedroom door behind her. Grateful for a few minutes alone, Hazel grabbed a glass of water, carrying it and her sandwich to the living room. She sank down on the couch and casually glanced around for the remote, even though she wasn't in the mood to watch anything.

Her gaze stopped when she spotted Dennis's duffel bag in the corner. It was unzipped, something shiny catching her eye. Rising, she crossed the room, kneeling to look inside.

"*Fuck.*" Her hands shook as she reached into the bag and pulled out the antique hand mirror Mrs. Maloney kept on her bathroom counter.

She'd told Hazel once, during the first year when her mind had still been sharp, that the mirror was a wedding gift from her great-grandfather to her great-grandmother. The frame was solid silver, and there was no doubt it was a very expensive heirloom.

Rifling through the bag, she found several more things from Mrs. Maloney's house...including the engagement ring Jeremiah had planned to propose with.

How the hell had her uncle gotten all this stuff?

She dug through, pulling out the stolen items, devastated to realize there were a lot of things still missing. Then she recalled her uncle coming home a few nights ago with a case of beer and a large pizza—that he'd eaten by himself without offering her or Mom a slice. She'd been so pissed off about that, it hadn't occurred to her to question where he got the money for the beer and pizza.

Now she knew.

She picked up the meager pile of stolen goods, wishing more of it was there, and placed it on the coffee table.

Then, she waited.

She hadn't been there an hour when the front door opened and a few seconds later, Dennis staggered into the living room. His initial reaction to seeing her there was surprise. She hadn't hung out in the living room since he'd moved in.

It quickly changed to annoyance. "You need to get out. I'm tired. Gonna go to—" He paused mid-sentence when he caught sight of Mrs. Maloney's things on the coffee table. "Did you go through my fucking shit?"

Hazel narrowed her eyes as she stood up. "Seriously? You're going to play high and mighty about that when you stole this stuff?"

"You had no right to go through my bag." He started toward the pile of stolen treasures, but Hazel stepped forward, blocking his path.

"How did you get it?" It was the question that had been burning in her brain since her discovery. The Maloneys suspected her because it was clear the house hadn't been broken into. Hazel had a key, but she kept her keys with her all the time.

Dennis, rather than looking guilty, gave her a grin that told her he was pleased with himself. "You left your keys on the kitchen counter one night a few weeks ago. I remembered you saying you had a key to the rich bitch's house, so I lifted it, took it to an all-night convenience store and had a copy made."

Shit.

Hazel felt physically ill. The robbery *had* been her fault. All because she hadn't been careful. With that one piece of the puzzle, the rest fell into place quickly, easily. Uncle Dennis's weird interest in what she was doing each day before she left for work. His questions were always posed in that shitty tone and laced with an insult, so it never occurred to her that he was digging for information about when she and Mrs. Maloney would be out of the house.

Just this morning, when he'd asked to borrow her car—which she'd thought was a strange request—she'd said he couldn't because she was taking Mrs. Maloney to get her hair done. No wonder he'd been pissed off when she came home early. He'd been planning a trip to the house to steal more stuff.

"Give me the key," she said, just in case Jeremiah's comment about changing the locks was an empty threat. She didn't want

Dennis to have a way into Mrs. Maloney's. She didn't want him anywhere near the beloved woman.

Dennis didn't move a muscle, just smirked at her. "No."

She lowered her hand, opting for bluff. "Doesn't matter if you have it." She pretended she wasn't concerned. "They changed the locks today anyway."

This time, she caught the slight narrowing of his eyes that told her he'd had every intention of returning to the house to finish the job.

"Fuckers," Dennis grumbled, as if them discovering his heist was an inconvenience to *him*. "There was still a lot of good shit there. We could have cleaned up."

"We?" she asked hotly. "We?! We weren't cleaning up anything. You stole from that poor old woman."

"She sure as shit ain't poor," Dennis interjected.

"You used me. And you cost me a job that I loved. Do you not understand how bad all of this is?" She gestured to the pile behind her. "Where's the rest of the stuff?"

Dennis lifted one shoulder, looking like he didn't have a concern in the world. "Hocked it."

"Where?"

"Why does it matter? The shit's gone."

"Give me the money you got for it." She held her palm up. She'd go buy the stuff back, return it all. She only prayed whoever he sold it to would let her buy it without some huge upcharge.

"I'm not giving you a fucking dime." Once again, Dennis tried to get to the remaining stuff on the coffee table.

She was closer, so she grabbed it all, clinging to it, holding it against her chest like it was a baby. "I'm taking this back."

Dennis had been an asshole up until that point, but he hadn't been angry.

That fact changed quickly, his face flushing a violent red.

"The fuck you are!" He pointed a threatening finger in her face. "You're not telling anyone about this."

She scoffed, laughing humorlessly. "That's where you're wrong. There's no way I'm going to let you get away with—"

Dennis grabbed her upper arm, his grip painfully tight as he shook her. "You're not going to rat me out, Hazel. Cops find out and that's it for me. Three strikes, I'm out."

In addition to the bank robbery, Dennis had a prior for holding up a liquor store.

She probably should have curbed her own anger, chosen her words with more care, but it had been one hell of a fucked-up day, so she wasn't thinking all that clearly. In truth, when he said "three strikes," the not-so-nice part of her immediately spied a way to get rid of Uncle Dennis once and for all.

So much for family love.

Hazel felt absolutely nothing for this man but disdain and disgust.

"Tough shit," she taunted. "You should have thought about that before you stole from the Maloneys."

His grip became punishingly painful, and she winced, struggling to break free.

"Let me go!" She tried to pull away with all her might, fighting him so hard, she almost fell when he—shockingly—released her.

"You're not going to return that shit. Not going to tell the family it was me. Not going to rat me out to the cops." His voice was eerily calm, given the fury he'd displayed a few seconds earlier.

"What would stop me? You?"

Dennis grinned at her, the look he gave her pure evil. She fought to school her features. If there was one thing she'd learned, growing up the way she had, it was to never let the bully see fear. Her mom had been a bully. Her dad. Her uncle. The people who were supposed to love her had never given her anything but threats and pain.

"You say one fucking word, and I'll tell everyone you were in on it from the start."

Hazel's blood turned to ice. "You wouldn't dare."

"I'm not going down alone for this, baby girl."

Bile rose to her throat as he used the despised nickname her father gave her. It had been used less as a term of endearment and more to remind her that she was low man on the totem pole in the family. It was typically preceded by, "Get Daddy a beer, baby girl," or "You're fucking annoying me, baby girl. Go away."

She fought for some argument, some way out of this, but she didn't doubt for a second that Dennis would do exactly what he'd threatened.

All those years of toeing the line, never straying the tiniest bit into any trouble, for fear she'd be painted with the same brush as her family, and it had all been for nothing.

If she turned Dennis in, he would lie, would accuse her as being his accomplice. It would be his word against hers, and she was pretty sure how that would go down. The same way it had this morning when she'd tried to convince the Maloneys she hadn't stolen from them.

She was a Walsh. And as far as the Boston Police Department was concerned, that name was synonymous with guilty.

Her biggest fear was coming true. She was going to jail.

"Dennis," she said, though the second she uttered his name, she knew whatever came next would be wasted breath.

"Give me that shit."

He thought he'd won. She could tell by his smug tone and the superior look on his face.

She shook her head. Her back was against the wall, but she would be damned if she'd give him the rest of this stuff.

"No." She clung to it even tighter. He would pry these things out of her cold, dead hands, and that was the truth. She'd lost everything today, and she needed a win.

"Goddammit, Hazel. I said give it to me!"

She never saw it coming as he backhanded her across the cheek, hard. Tears sprung to her eyes, but she didn't drop a single thing. He must have expected her to cower, so he wasn't expecting it when she moved toward him, shoving her body against his.

He'd been drinking, she could smell the cheap whiskey on his breath, and that fact worked in her favor.

He stumbled back against the coffee table. His arms waved around almost comically as he tried to stop himself from falling, but in the end, he lost.

He fell onto the coffee table, the cheap piece of shit collapsing beneath him, so he landed roughly on his ass, empty beer cans and the overflowing ashtray crashing around him. She didn't wait around for him to get up.

Instead, she turned and ran from the living room, his voice following her down the hall.

"I mean it, Hazel! You say a fucking word and you'll live to regret it!"

She slammed her bedroom door closed behind her, locking it, a huge sense of relief washing through her when it was obvious Dennis didn't intend to chase her.

Hazel walked to the bed and placed the stolen items on the mattress. Then she picked up her purse to pull out the list Jeremiah had given her. She had less than a third of the stuff they'd listed, which meant Dennis probably had a fat roll of bills hidden somewhere. That was assuming he hadn't already blown it all.

She sank down on the side of the bed, trying to figure out her next move. She wanted Mrs. Maloney to have her things back, wanted Jeremiah to be able to give this ring to Emily, who was a very sweet woman.

Hazel ran her fingers over her cheek. The skin was hot to the touch, though the sting had faded.

She wasn't sure how long she sat there, no answers coming, when she heard the door to the apartment open, then close. Her mom's room was beyond hers, away from the front of the apartment, so Hazel would have heard her walk down the hallway.

Which meant Dennis had left.

She glanced at the clock, slightly surprised to discover it was only eleven. It felt later. Of course, she'd screwed up her sleep schedule, napping all damn day. She was wide awake, wired, stressed out.

Opening her door, she peered down the hall. The TV was off, though every light was still on. Of course they were. It wasn't like Uncle Dennis paid the damn electric bill.

She slowly walked down the hall, just in case her uncle was trying to fool her. Once she determined he was indeed gone, she started to breathe a little bit easier.

She walked back to the living room, chuckling miserably when she realized Dennis's duffel bag was gone. Hazel didn't bother to hope he'd left for good. She knew better. More likely, he took it with him to keep her from snooping again. Which meant she must have missed something.

Dammit.

Sinking down on the couch, taking in the destruction of the coffee table, she tried to play the positive game, tried to find something in all this misery that wasn't horrible.

She couldn't come up with a damn thing.

And because misery loves company, she found her thoughts drifting down dark paths she usually left untrodden. Shitty memory after shitty memory pounded down on her as she stared at the black TV screen.

She recalled her first car, how she'd worked after school and weekends for three years saving up to buy it. It had been ancient, dented, and unreliable as hell, but it had been hers and she'd loved it. For four months. Then her mother got drunk one night, lifted her keys—which was why, except for that one stupid night she'd left them on the kitchen counter, she always kept them with her—and totaled it.

She considered the last phone call from her dad. How he'd raged at her for failing to send him enough cigarettes, calling her useless.

Ordinarily, she could find a way out of the heavy thoughts by finding something to be grateful for, but tonight, she just felt tired. Defeated.

Time for bed. Maybe—please, God—things would look better in the morning. She walked over to turn off the lights, glancing outside at the sound of car brakes squeaking.

Her heart began to race as a cop car parked by the curb in front of her building and two police officers got out.

Holy shit.

Had the Maloneys made good on their threat and called them?

Were they here to arrest her?

Hazel recalled the pile of stolen goods in her room and panicked.

Jesus. How could she proclaim her innocence when she was literally holding the evidence?

Then she remembered Dennis's missing duffel. Maybe he hadn't been trying to keep her out of it. What if he'd decided to make a preemptive move by calling the cops and pointing the finger at her? It would be just like him to call with an anonymous tip, and when the police showed up, she'd be left holding the bag while he was nowhere near.

She ran down the hallway, her hands trembling violently.

She couldn't go to jail. She *couldn't*.

She fought back the tears. Now wasn't the time for that. She needed to get out of here, needed to escape.

She grabbed a bag from the top shelf in her closet and hastily threw whatever clothes she could inside, then she walked to her desk—which also served as a makeup table—and swept the top clean, dumping everything on top of her clothing. The last items she added to the bag were Mrs. Maloney's things. She'd find some way to get her stuff back to her eventually.

Her backpack—with her laptop, planner, and a couple of books—was still packed up from this morning, when she'd driven to Mrs. Maloney's, blissfully unaware her life was going to take a sharp downhill turn.

Throwing the backpack over her shoulder, the other bag in

her hand, she grabbed her phone, keys, and purse, then slid open her bedroom window.

Stepping out onto the fire escape, she tried—and failed—to lower the metal ladder quietly. The thing was rusted as fuck and screeched so loud; she was surprised the neighbors weren't hanging out their windows to tell her to be quiet. She held her breath for a second, expecting the police to round the corner to find out what was going on.

When no one appeared, she slowly made her way down the ladder, her arms laden with all the bags. Once she hit the ground, she sucked in some much-needed air, her lungs seizing with fear and panic. Pulling her hoodie up to hide her flaming-red hair, she forced herself to walk casually—though quickly—to the parking lot. She didn't want to draw attention to herself by running, but she also wasn't willing to take her time and stroll.

Unlocking her car, she threw all her shit on the passenger seat, started the engine, and pulled out, driving down the back alley rather than turning onto the road where the police were parked.

Her gaze kept slipping to the rearview mirror, expecting to see the blue lights of the cop car coming up behind her. She was halfway through the city before she started to breathe somewhat easier. Mercifully, she'd filled her car up with gas the day before, so at least she had enough to get...somewhere.

Stopping by the bank, she pulled up to the ATM and cleaned out her bank account. Sadly, she only had a few hundred dollars, which wasn't going to get her very far.

She'd been able to save up a fair amount of money since the Maloneys had paid her well and she had zero social life, even considering she was basically supporting her mom and uncle. However, that nest egg had been depleted when her mom, while drunk, had assaulted another woman at a bar four months earlier. Hazel had used most of the money to bail Mom out, the rest to pay court fees and the fine, which had put her back at square one in terms of savings.

Once she had the cash in hand, she took the next exit, sliding onto the interstate, heading south, driving through the night.

She blinked wearily, grateful now for her long afternoon nap. It helped her stay awake as she increased the miles between herself and Boston.

Fuck that city. She was never going back. Nothing good had even happened in Boston.

Eventually, dawn turned the sky from coal black to slate gray.

A light on the dashboard captured her attention, and she let the gas tank decide her new home. She'd already refilled the tank once, and while she'd keep driving forever if she could, she didn't want to deplete her funds on more gas.

The next exit proclaimed she'd made it to Philadelphia.

Philadelphia.

That felt like a big enough place to get lost in.

Turning on her blinker, she left the interstate, grateful when the first thing she saw was the sign for a motel.

Crossings Motel was clearly not a five-star luxury hotel. In fact, it looked sketchy as fuck. Which meant it probably fit her budget just fine.

Pulling in, she grabbed all her bags—because it wasn't just the motel that looked sketchy but the neighborhood as well—and lumbered into the front office. A surly-looking man emerged from a back room, cigarette between his fingers.

"Well, hello there," he said in a gravelly voice that proved he smoked as much as Hazel's mom. She'd put him at a two-pack-a-day guy.

"I was wondering if you had any rooms available," she said.

"I sure do."

For the next few minutes, she made small talk with the man, who'd introduced himself as the owner of the motel, Rocco. He was gruff but nice enough. Because she needed to hoard as much cash as possible, she used her "just for emergencies" credit card for the first time ever. He handed her a key, proclaiming he was giving her the best room in the place with a friendly wink.

She smiled tiredly, then trudged up the stairs to the second floor. The motel didn't have interior halls, all the doors opening outside, overlooking the parking lot.

Hazel unlocked the door, dumped her stuff, quickly made use of the bathroom, then walked to the bed, falling down face-first, something she probably wouldn't have done if she hadn't been so tired. God only knew when this bedspread had last been washed.

That thought grossed her out enough that she found the energy to pull down the covers. She did little more than kick off her shoes as she climbed beneath, falling into a restless sleep.

Chapter Four

Aldo was just about the leave for the day when the scanner went off, the dispatcher reporting a fire. Ordinarily, he would have flipped his buddies the peace sign and headed out anyway. After all, his shift was over, and he wouldn't have even been here today, except he'd been covering for a buddy who needed a few hours off for his daughter's birthday party. Said buddy had just shown up for the remainder of the evening.

Aldo had big plans for his Sunday night, plans he'd been looking forward to for weeks. His brother, Elio, was playing in Philly tonight, and he'd managed to score awesome seats for Aldo, Kayden, and the rest of their gang. Considering this was going to be Elio's final season, Aldo suspected this might be the last time he'd ever get to see his brother play in person for the NHL.

After the game, they were all going to Rafe's restaurant, Divine, for a late-night dinner and drinks.

Aldo had just come off four twenty-four-hour days—not counting these extra six hours—and he was looking forward to some downtime.

Or at least he had been.

Until he heard the dispatcher mention Crossings Motel.

His dad and uncles all participated in the stereotypical old man monthly poker game, complete with bourbon and cigars. One of the regulars in their gang of old cronies was Rocco, who owned and operated Crossings. Aldo had known the guy most of his life.

He turned back, racing to his locker to grab his jacket, boots, and helmet.

Jeff, the guy he'd been covering for, gave him a funny look. "We got this, man. Go and enjoy the game with your family."

"It's Crossings Motel," Aldo said. "I know the guy who owns it."

Jeff nodded as the two of them ran for the truck. "Gotcha."

The tanker truck had already left. Jeff climbed behind the wheel of the engine truck, three other fellas grabbing the backseat, while Aldo took the passenger seat, quickly donning his gear and pulling his phone out as they fired up the lights and siren and left the station.

Kayden answered on the second ring. "Hey, man. I'm running a few minutes late. Logging out of my computer and heading home right now."

Kayden had also worked today. As a cop, his schedule was a bit more nine to five, while Aldo's job was a rotation deal. Four full days on—when he slept at the station—three off, then three on, and four off, and so on. Kayden swore that routine would drive him insane, but Aldo had been doing it for so many years, it didn't even faze him.

"Listen—" Aldo started, but Kayden cut him off.

"Is that the siren?"

"Yeah. We just got a call. Crossings Motel. Dispatcher called up three different stations, so it sounds pretty bad."

"Shit. I'll meet you there."

They didn't even say goodbye, just hung up.

Looked like they were going to be late for the game. Aldo fired off a text to his sister, Liza, to tell their friends not to wait for them. Even if the fire wasn't too bad, they were going to miss the initial puck drop.

Jeff roared around a corner, and that was when Aldo knew they weren't going to catch the game at all.

"Fuck," Jeff murmured. They'd both been professional firefighters for over a decade, so the fact they were slack-jawed proved how bad the fire was.

Aldo's eyes widened. "Jesus." Two-thirds of the building was already engulfed in flames, huge plumes of smoke blocking out most of the sky. Several police officers had arrived before them and were setting up a perimeter, keeping onlookers back at a safe distance.

They raced into the parking lot, braking roughly enough that Aldo flew forward in his seat. All of them disembarked and started unrolling the hoses, their fire chief calling out commands, organizing them in teams of three to attack the fire from different locations in front of the motel.

"Is everyone out?" Aldo asked his commander, perfectly aware that if anyone had still been on the second floor, there would be no saving them. The building had gone up in flames like a cardboard box and was already beginning to crash in on itself.

His commander threw his hands up. "We don't have that information yet. The manager was able to grab a list of guests staying here before leaving the building. We've handed it over to the police, who are doing a headcount, over there across the street."

Aldo sent up a prayer everyone had made it out, then he and Jeff manned the hoses, trying to beat down the flames. The fire had grown too large, sweat running down his back from the unbearable heat. He felt like he'd gotten one hell of a sunburn, his entire face stinging from standing too close to the fire. Two other fire departments showed up, setting up at the side and rear of the building.

After close to two hours, the fire was still burning though under control. Probably because it was running out of things to burn. There wasn't much of the building left that hadn't been touched by the fire. At least they'd managed to contain the flames to just the motel. The surrounding businesses would have smoke and heat damage, but they—mercifully—hadn't caught fire.

For which Aldo was grateful. There'd been more than a few minutes when it had been touch and go, and he'd feared the entire city block would be engulfed.

Kayden approached him. Aldo, his muscles exhausted from wielding the hose, handed it off to another firefighter, stepping back for a moment to catch his breath.

"I hope everyone was out."

Kayden nodded somberly. "According to Rocco, Sundays are his slowest night, so there weren't a lot of people in the building when it caught fire. We were able to account for all the guests except for one. A Hazel Walsh." Kayden glanced at the building. "Her room was on the second floor, very close to where the fire broke out."

"Shit." Neither he nor Kayden had to say it, but if Hazel had still been in her room and hadn't managed to make it out, there was no doubt she hadn't survived the fire. "Any guess on how it started?" Aldo asked.

"Apparently one of the guests was intoxicated. He passed out with a lit cigarette in his hand. When he came to, most of the room was engulfed in flames, and he says he barely got out of the room alive."

"The sprinkler system should have kicked in. Should have prevented this from getting so out of hand. I know Rocco. The place might be a dive, but he follows the city ordinances, keeps the place up to code."

"Yeah. Well, apparently there was a water main break a couple of streets over," Kayden said. "The city was fixing it all afternoon. They only managed to get the water turned back on a few minutes before you guys arrived."

"Shit. That was fucking unlucky for Rocco."

"Dispatch was working to call up tanker trucks in case the

hydrants were dry. Mercifully, it didn't come to that or this could have been a hell of a lot worse."

"Rocco okay?" Aldo hadn't seen the old guy yet, but he was worried about him. This motel, while a complete fleabag, had been Rocco's livelihood for his entire life, the property inherited from his father, who'd owned and operated it before him.

"I think he's shell-shocked at the moment. It hasn't sunk in yet."

Aldo studied the building, the flames dying down. It was a burned-out shell, a total loss. He was sure Rocco had insurance, but even so...this was going to be a big blow to him. He might bitch and complain about the guests or city permits or unreliable employees, but there was no mistaking Rocco's love for the motel.

"I'm sure it hasn't. You sticking around?" he asked, aware that, like him, Kayden was technically off duty.

"Yeah. For a little while at least. You want a ride home?"

Aldo nodded. "Yeah. I'll send my gear back with the guys."

"Okay. It might not be all that soon. Rocco's beside himself about the missing woman. I think I'm going to stick around until—"

"Hey, Kayden!"

Aldo and Kayden both turned around as Rocco approached them. He turned and pointed partway down the block. "That's her," Rocco said, clearly relieved. "Hazel. The pretty little redhead."

Aldo spotted the woman at the same time as Kayden. He knew that—because they both sucked in the same deep breath.

The woman's attention was focused solely on the motel, her mouth open slightly. She was dressed in ripped jeans and a green hoodie, old sneakers on her feet, her hair pinned up in a messy ponytail, with a backpack slung over one shoulder. She had flaming-red hair, the bright, rich color so vivid, Aldo couldn't stop staring at her.

He watched as she shivered slightly, and it occurred to him

that while he was so soaked with sweat someone could wring him out, the evening air was quite chilly.

"I'm going to go talk to her," Kayden said.

"Give me a second," Aldo said. "I'll come with you."

Kayden gave him a look that was halfway between confused and amused, but he didn't give him shit, waiting as Aldo walked back to the engine truck, stowing his jacket and hat. He pulled off his boots, grabbing his tennis shoes and slipping them back on. He reached for his winter coat, emblazoned with his fire station's logo on the breast. Not that anyone would have a doubt what his role here had been. Aldo didn't need a mirror to know his entire face was black with soot.

The two of them walked across the parking lot, until they stood on the opposite side of the street from Hazel.

Even from a distance, he could see that Hazel Walsh was fucking gorgeous.

As if she sensed their eyes on her, Hazel looked away from the motel and spotted them.

Aldo didn't know what to make of the brief, initial flash of panic in her eyes. Granted, he was covered with soot, but that was hardly something to fear. Then he realized it wasn't him she was looking at, but Kayden, who was still in his police uniform.

"Miss," Kayden called out as he stepped off the curb. Traffic had been diverted away from this street, keeping it clear for emergency vehicles, so they didn't bother to look both ways.

Hazel glanced around as if she wasn't sure Kayden was talking to her.

Then, she shocked them both by turning quickly, walking down the block, away from them.

Kayden shot him a "what the fuck" look, then continued toward her, picking up his pace.

"Miss," he called out again, louder.

Hazel didn't look back, just kept walking, moving even faster. At this rate, Aldo half expected her to break out in a run, which was weird as shit.

"Hazel," Kayden said. "Hazel Walsh."

This time his words permeated, and she stumbled for a moment before stopping. Aldo wasn't sure if he saw or imagined Hazel's shoulders slump, but it only lasted a second before she stiffened her spine and twisted around to face them.

Kayden cut the distance between himself and Hazel quickly, clearly worried she was going to take off again. "You're Hazel Walsh?"

Hazel hesitated, and while she'd turned, she didn't fully face them, her focus instead on the window of the convenience store they were standing in front of. "Did I do something wrong?"

Why the hell would she think that?

Kayden shook his head. "No. Of course not. I was charged with making certain everyone was out of the motel. You were the last person on my list not accounted for."

"Oh," she said, suddenly more at ease. She reached up, pulling her hoodie over her head, her hand remaining on the side to hold it up, though Aldo couldn't understand why. It wasn't like it was windy and she needed to hold the hood to keep it on.

Finally, she turned to face them more fully. "I...I had some errands to run."

"Guess you weren't expecting to come back to something like this." Aldo wondered if it was the fire that had freaked her out.

Hazel's attention turned to him, and Aldo was taken aback by her bright green eyes. Jesus Christ. Surely she was wearing contacts. No one's eyes could be that naturally green. She shook her head in response, her hand still lifted, blocking half of her face. "No. I wasn't."

"You *were* staying in the motel, right?" Kayden asked. "The owner, Rocco, gave us your name."

Hazel turned to take in what was left of Crossings Motel. "I was. I..." She tugged her hoodie farther over her face, and it occurred to Aldo, her initial shock was starting to wear off. "God. All of my things were in there."

"I'm sorry about that."

Hazel nodded her head just once, an acknowledgement of Kayden's kind words, but she didn't look at him.

"Is there...do you know if there's another motel nearby?" she asked Aldo.

"Walking distance?" Aldo considered her question. "No. We're on the outskirts of Philly, so most of the hotels and motels are closer to the actual city center. Do you have a car?"

She pointed across the street. "Somewhere behind all those fire trucks."

"Ahhh. I think the trucks are going to be there a few more hours but...well, if your car survived, we can move the truck so you can it get out." Aldo wasn't holding out much hope. Several of the cars closest to the building had been damaged by debris, water, and heat. A few had actually caught fire as well.

"That's okay," she said, closing her eyes wearily. "The keys were in my motel room."

"Shit. That sucks." Aldo was surprised when Hazel grinned.

"Yeah. I'm not having a great day. Probably shouldn't play the lottery."

"I'm Aldo Moretti," he said, introducing himself, holding his hand out intentionally, aware it would force Hazel to reach out with the hand still clinging to her hoodie. "And this big guy is Kayden Gallo."

"Nice to meet you." She looked at his hand for two heartbeats too long before politeness won out. She reached out to take it, and Aldo studied her face, fighting like the devil not to scowl.

Though she'd obviously attempted to cover them up with makeup, Hazel had a bruise on her cheek and the hint of a black eye.

She didn't offer her hand to Kayden. Instead, she simply said, "Officer Gallo," without looking him in the eye.

"Call me Kayden."

She peered up, though she kept her head down. "Um...okay. Well, as you know, I'm Hazel."

"Were you just passing through Philly, Hazel?" There was

something about her that sparked Aldo's interest. "Or are you here on vacation?"

"I was actually hoping to find a job and a place to rent. I'm planning to stay in Philadelphia for a while."

Aldo released the breath he'd been holding, her answer pleasing him more than it should considering they were complete strangers.

"Oh. So when you say you lost all of your stuff..." Kayden prodded.

Hazel looked down at her attire. "I would have dressed in something a lot nicer if I'd known this was going to be the sum total of my wardrobe for the foreseeable future."

Aldo wasn't sure what else to say because, damn... She had a backpack over her shoulder, but now that he was up close, it looked quite light, almost empty.

"Hazel," Aldo started, not sure how to comfort her, even though she didn't exactly look like she needed comfort. She certainly wasn't near tears or raging against the unfairness of it all. Instead, she looked...resigned.

Which bothered him. Because there was something about her that told him Hazel was no stranger to shitty days. Then he considered the bruises and who might have put them there. His protective instincts rose to the surface.

He exchanged a quick glance with Kayden, aware his best friend felt the same. It had always been that way between them. While they had very different personalities, at heart, they were kindred spirits. They'd recognized each other as warriors pretty much from the start, when the two of them had stepped forward on the playground, both in second grade, to stop Erick Menendez from bullying another kid in their class. Erick, a huge fourth grader, could have beaten their scrawny asses, but they'd stared him down until he slunk away.

No one in either of their families had been surprised by their chosen professions, by their desire to serve their community in ways that would protect and help others.

"It's cool," Hazel said, though he couldn't find a single thing cool about any of this. "This is my favorite hoodie, so it could have been worse. And I've got my phone and my money, and my car is a piece of shit anyway."

It felt as if Hazel was giving herself a pep talk.

Kayden rubbed his jaw. "That's a positive attitude."

Hazel nodded but didn't quite catch Kayden's eye. She was looking away again, though Aldo couldn't tell if it was the bruises she was trying to hide or if it was Kayden who was bothering her.

He glanced over at his friend, wondering if he was catching the same vibes. If he was, Kayden didn't let it get to him. There were some people who were intimidated by cops, even a bit afraid of them. Kayden had been on the force enough years that he'd developed a pretty good bedside manner, able to set people at ease.

Aldo could tell that was exactly what his friend was trying when he gave Hazel a kind smile.

"If you'd like, we can give you a ride to another hotel," Kayden offered in his slow, calming drawl. "My squad car is just over there." Kayden pointed down the street to one of the three police cruisers parked by the curb.

"Oh no." Hazel quickly dismissed the offer. "I can call for a Lyft or something."

Aldo was ready to put the kibosh on that idea, but Kayden beat him to it.

"It's no problem. Aldo and I are both off duty, so why don't you give me a few minutes to wrap up some stuff and we'll take you wherever you need to go."

Hazel looked ready to dig in her heels, but Aldo wasn't about to let her escape them. "This road is going to be closed for a while, so I'm not sure how easy it would be for a Lyft to get here."

It was a weak reason, but Hazel had her arms wrapped around her midsection, bouncing on her toes in a way that told him she really was cold.

"Come on." Aldo reached out, slipping the backpack off her

shoulder—intent on holding her bag hostage to gain her compliance. "I'll carry your stuff for you," he said with a friendly smile, gesturing toward the car, making it clear the discussion was over.

Hazel hesitated, but when she sighed softly, he knew they'd won the first battle.

She fell into step next to him, the two of them heading toward Kayden's car, while she muttered under her breath...something he thought sounded like "not sure an empty backpack counts as stuff."

"I'll meet you at the car in just a minute." Kayden crossed the street to say a few words to Rocco.

They walked in silence the rest of the way to the cruiser, as Aldo sought some way to set her mind at ease. He and Kayden were decent guys who only wanted to help, but the way Hazel's eyes shifted from left to right gave him the sense she was debating whether to turn tail and run.

"You've had a hell of a day," Aldo said, attempting to make small talk.

"Yeah. And yet strangely, it's still not one of my worst. Probably doesn't even rank in the top five." She laughed briefly, a soft, breathy sound that ended way too soon. Hazel blinked a couple times, and he could tell she hadn't meant to reveal so much.

"I'm joking," she said, though he knew with absolute certainty that was a lie.

Five minutes in Hazel's presence and Aldo would swear he'd already seen a half dozen different emotions flitter across her face. A couple were beautiful—like that brief smile—but most were concerning.

When they reached Kayden's car, he pulled open the back door. "It's getting chilly. You want to sit in the car and try to warm up while we wait for Kayden?"

Chapter Five

Hazel hesitated as she looked at the backseat of the cop car. What the fuck was she doing?

Part of her wondered if this was a trick. What if that cop, Kayden, knew who she was? What if this was his way of taking her into custody because the police in Boston were looking for her?

Of course, if that was true, wouldn't he just handcuff her and place her under arrest? It's not like he couldn't have chased her down if she'd run. And wouldn't he have to read Hazel her rights?

There's no way he would have walked away and left her alone with the firefighter.

Aldo winked at her. "Been in the back of a police car before?"

She hadn't. Yet. She'd spent her entire life making sure that was a ride she never took.

But she needed to stop giving off such skittish signals. Both men had spotted the bruise on her cheek. She'd tried to conceal it with cover-up earlier, but she hadn't managed to hide it completely. Plus, it had been a few hours since then, and she'd probably rubbed half the makeup off because she kept absent-mindedly touching the sore spot.

She took a deep breath and forced herself to match Aldo's teasing tone. "Have you?"

He laughed easily, and she liked the sound. She didn't spend much time with people who laughed. Which, when she considered it, was a pretty sad commentary for a life.

"I'll never tell. Come on." He stepped away, giving her space. "I can tell you're cold. Climb in."

She really was cold. She'd walked quite a distance today, and in her mad dash to pack her shit up last night, she'd failed to grab a heavy coat.

She glanced at the burned-out motel once more, aware that she was losing her will to fight. Replacing the key to her car would most likely cost more than the stupid piece of shit was worth. Not that it mattered anyway, because there was no way she could spend what was left of her money on a key. Of course, that was assuming the car hadn't burned with the building, which, given how close she'd parked, seemed highly unlikely.

So, now she had no vehicle.

Fucking lovely.

"Hazel," Aldo murmured. He had a nice voice, soothing almost.

It did the trick, prompting her to move. She climbed into the backseat, her chest growing tight, claustrophobia closing in on her. She almost immediately started to climb back out, but Aldo reached in and handed her the backpack.

Then he stood in the open doorway, leaning casually on it as if they were long-lost friends. She could tell he was attempting to block the chilly air while chatting with her, but the sensation of being caged in wouldn't fade.

"Where are you from, Hazel?"

She glanced toward the front of the cruiser while searching for an answer. She couldn't take her lie too far because her car had Massachusetts license plates. She wasn't sure how involved Kayden or Aldo might be in the cleanup, so she needed to keep her story close to the truth.

But there was no way in hell she was saying Boston.

"Um...Springfield," she said, not quite holding his eye. She hated lying. She didn't add Massachusetts because if he never saw the car, maybe he'd assume she was talking about Ohio or Oregon or fucking Simpson's Land.

She chanced a glance at him and noticed the slightest narrowing of his eyes.

God. Did he know she was lying?

If he knew that...

Did he know...

She swallowed heavily, looking around for the cop. Maybe she could still make a break for it. Of course, it would require shoving Aldo out of the way, and he didn't strike her as the type of man who would be easy to move. He was a couple inches shorter than Kayden, but he made up for that in width. His arm muscles were thicker than her thighs, no doubt a product of wielding the heavy fire equipment.

She could tell he was an attractive man, even with the layer of soot covering most of his face. Hazel did an internal eye roll. He wasn't just attractive; he was fucking hot. So was the cop. Which was a problem. Maybe if she didn't feel this instant attraction to them, her brain would kick in and she'd find some way to talk herself out of his car and away from them.

"Massachusetts, huh?"

She gave him a quick single bounce of the head in reply.

"Never been to Springfield before, but I've been to Boston once."

Hazel's chest constricted so tightly, she struggled to breathe. He was baiting her, playing a game with her. She was so fucking stupid for getting herself trapped in this car. After a lifetime of living with a bunch of thieves and assholes, she should have been better prepared to avoid danger.

It was just...

She was running out of answers, out of options. She'd run in the middle of the night with nothing more than a shadow of a plan, her only thought to put as much distance between her and Boston as she could.

Now she was in a strange city with less than four hundred bucks, no car, no job, no clothes, and no clue where to go from here. Somehow, she'd managed to drop from a stable job/roof-over-her-head lifestyle to rock fucking bottom in less than thirty-six hours. That had to be some kind of record.

What the hell was she supposed to do now?

She realized Aldo was looking at her like she was supposed to offer some sort of reply, so she weakly said, "I've never been to Boston." Part of her was certain this would be the part where he yelled, "Busted!" and the cop slapped on the cuffs.

"Oh, you should go sometime," he said easily. "It's a great city."

It took all she had not to scoff. Great wasn't the word she'd use.

Instead, she offered him another nod.

"I went there for a Boston Bruins game," Aldo continued as Hazel resisted the urge to look over her shoulder for Kayden.

Aldo seemed oblivious to her distress. "My brother, Elio, plays for the Baltimore Stingrays, and it was the Stanley Cup playoffs—first round. Kayden and I grabbed some nosebleed tickets and traveled up, since neither of us had ever been to Boston."

Hazel cleared her throat, grateful for the opportunity to keep him talking about himself, instead of him asking her a bunch of questions. Maybe all wasn't lost yet.

"Your brother plays professional hockey?" She had to admit she was somewhat impressed. She wasn't really a fan of the sport but playing for the pros like that was pretty cool, and she could see Aldo was proud of his brother.

"Yep. He sure does. Or, well, he will until the end of this season. Then he's retiring and moving back here to Philly. Got himself a new girlfriend."

Hazel tried for a smile but wasn't sure if she'd pulled it off. "Good for him."

"So, tell me," he started, about to hit her with another question.

She braced herself, but mercifully, Kayden returned before he could say anything more.

"Okay. All good here," Kayden said. "Rocco's going to spend the night at your uncle Frank's place, Aldo."

"Good. Uncle Frank will break out the whiskey and help Rocco figure out the next steps. I hate that the poor guy lost everything tonight. All of it gone...in the blink of an eye." Then Aldo looked at her as if remembering she was in the same boat. "Sorry."

She shrugged. The truth was the truth.

Her panic returned as Aldo closed the back door of the cruiser, effectively shutting Hazel in before she could come up with an excuse to climb out again.

She took a few deep breaths, then looked back toward the motel, spotting Rocco standing there, rubbing his hand over his balding head. His posture was stooped, and all she could think was...lost soul. She could relate.

She considered Aldo's comments about Rocco and felt bad for the man. They'd only had a brief conversation at the ass crack of dawn this morning when he'd checked her in, but he'd been kind, and her concerns about her safety in the sketchy motel were alleviated after just a few minutes of chatting with him. She got the sense he would keep an eye out for her.

Kayden crossed around the front of the car, claiming the driver's side, while Aldo took the passenger seat,

"Okay, so let's see. Hotels," Kayden mused aloud.

"Um..." Hazel struggled to find a way to bring up an uncomfortable subject. "I kind of need it to be...affordable."

She caught Kayden's slight wince through the rearview mirror, then he and Aldo exchanged a glance that proved they'd caught her drift. After all, she'd voluntarily chosen to stay at Crossings Motel.

"Gotcha," Kayden said.

Before anyone else could speak, Hazel's stomach growled loudly, and she felt the telltale heat in her cheeks that meant she was blushing.

Curse of a redhead. One embarrassing incident and she was fully capable of making her face match her hair color.

Aldo twisted slightly, looking back at her. "Have you had dinner yet?"

She shook her head. "No. I was, uh, going to order a pizza when I got back to the motel."

That was a lie. Her real plan had been to hit the vending machine for a pack of crackers.

There was that pregnant pause that made her feel as if Aldo had caught her in another lie, then he said, "Neither have we. What do you say we go grab dinner and while we eat, we can explore hotel options?" He waved his cell phone as he spoke. "Nothing like carrying around a computer in your pocket."

She considered her phone, recalling the battery was almost dead because she hadn't bothered to plug it in before falling asleep this morning.

Add her charger to the list of fire casualties.

She pulled it out of the front pocket of her hoodie and powered it off in order to conserve as much of the battery as she could.

"No thanks. I don't want to put you guys out for more than the ride. I'm sure you have better things to do tonight." Besides, she couldn't afford a Happy Meal right now, and she was pretty sure that wasn't the type of dinner Aldo was suggesting anyway.

Aldo ignored her. "Do me a favor, Kay. Swing by my place so I can take a quick shower. I can't go out like this." He pointed to his sooty face.

Kayden nodded. "Sounds good. We can switch cars too. I'll leave the cruiser at your place, and we can grab your truck."

"Um, seriously." Hadn't they heard her? "I think I'd just rather—"

"We gotta eat," Aldo interrupted her. "Might as well do it together."

"Yes, but—"

"I'm starving," Aldo spoke over her.

"Really, I—" She tried and failed again, as Aldo kept talking.

"Philly food is the greatest food. Wait until you try our cheesesteaks."

He spoke with a confidence that told her she could argue until the cows came home, and she still wouldn't get her way.

And then, as if Kayden could read her mind, he added, "Our treat."

She didn't reply to that, since her agreement didn't seem to matter. Instead, she leaned her head against the neck rest and closed her eyes, trying to play her game.

If there was a positive about all the shit that had gone down today, it was that at least Mrs. Maloney's things hadn't been lost in the fire.

Hazel had woken up early this afternoon, a bit bleary-eyed and panicky when she remembered where she was and why. After a quick Google search, she'd discovered there was a UPS Store a few miles from the motel. Unwilling to spend any more money on gas until she figured some things out, she'd decided to walk. She had intended to take a shower, but the water pressure had been wicked low, so she'd given up and simply thrown her hair in a ponytail. She'd tossed all of Mrs. Maloney's things in her backpack and—like an idiot—she had taken out her laptop and books, thinking to decrease the weight of her load.

If she'd lugged them along with her, she'd still have them. As it stood, the only thing in her backpack right now was Jeremiah's list of stolen goods.

The walk to UPS had been brisk without a jacket. At the store, she'd purchased a box and bubble wrap so she could make sure nothing was broken during delivery. She hadn't included a note or a return address, then she'd bitten the bullet, paying for the more expensive next-day delivery, hoping the quick recovery of some of the stolen items would encourage Annabel and Jeremiah to drop the charges against her if they had called the police.

The car stopped, forcing Hazel to open her eyes. They'd pulled up in front of a beautiful red brick building on a quiet street. The building was divided into four narrow condos, each with their own front door and stoop.

"It's not much, but it's home." Aldo took a set of keys out of his pocket, handing them to Kayden. "My truck is over there."

All the parking was on the street, but there were plenty of available spots. Kayden turned off the police car, then turned around to look at her.

She'd made a mistake, coming here with them. She was basically alone with two strangers, trapped in the back of a police car, on a narrow street without much traffic. There was no way in hell she was going inside Aldo's house. She might have been a fool up until this point, but as soon as they opened this back door, she was running.

She scanned the surrounding area, wondering how far she'd have to run to reach safety. This was a residential area, but it wasn't a run-down one like where she'd grown up. If she screamed for help, this felt like the kind of neighborhood where someone might respond. Of course, they'd also see the cop chasing her and assume she was the bad guy.

Kayden studied her face for a moment, without speaking. He was the quieter of the two men, but where Aldo steamrolled over her wishes with words, Kayden did the same with little more than a look. There was something in his face that had her calming down. Which was strange, considering what he did for a living.

She'd never felt at ease around the police. Not once in her life.

"We'll wait for you in the truck," Kayden said to Aldo, though he was looking at her. "Hazel's not comfortable going into a strange man's house because she's smart and understands how to keep herself safe."

Aldo glanced back at her quickly, then nodded, giving her an approving smile that told her she'd pleased him. And for some strange reason, it made her feel good.

"Sounds like a plan. Won't take me long at all," Aldo reassured her with a charming wink. He got out of the car and jogged up the five stairs to his front landing, disappearing inside.

Then Kayden got out, walking around the back to open her door.

Hazel stepped out and tasted freedom.

This was it. Her chance to run.

She looked both ways, trying to pick the best direction, but before she could take a single step away from the car, Kayden stopped her. Not with his hands but with his words.

"You don't have to run, Hazel."

She peered up at him—Kayden was at least half a foot taller than her—and for the first time, she allowed herself to look him right in the eye. Right into those dark chocolate-brown eyes.

He was as hot as Aldo, but in a different way.

Aldo had thick black hair that was a touch too long, which went well with his rugged face. He was also sporting a ten-o'clock shadow that made it feel like he was on the fence about whether he wanted to shave it off or just say fuck it and grow the beard.

Kayden, on the other hand, was clean-shaven, his light brown hair long on top, short on the sides. There was a slight bump in his nose indicative of a break at some point. His skin—like Aldo's —was a dark tan hue, nothing like her much-hated milk-white complexion.

"What?" she asked stupidly, even though she'd heard him.

He took a big step back, clearing a path for her. He held his hands out, palms toward her, proving he wasn't going to hold her back. "You're not a hostage. If you don't want to be here, just say so and walk away. I know Aldo can come on strong sometimes, but it's because he has the personality equivalent of a bull in a China closet. All his brothers and cousins are the same. It's in the Moretti genes. If they want something, they just keep chiseling away until they get it. Aldo wants you to go to dinner with us, so...here we are."

"Oh. Well, that's kind of sweet, actually."

While Aldo had been all quick grins and winks and deep, sexy chuckles, Kayden was a harder nut to crack, way more serious and slower to smile. In fact, while he was perfectly pleasant, he'd only smiled a couple times.

"You're fight-or-flight instincts are strong, and that's a good thing. You don't follow people meekly, don't put yourself in dangerous situations."

She wanted to argue that hopping into the back of his police car probably wasn't her brightest move, but he wasn't finished.

"I've been watching you. You don't act without thinking. But there's another instinct that can be just as powerful."

"What's that?" she asked quietly.

"Gut feeling. Do you think you're in danger with me and Aldo? What's your gut say?"

Hazel took a moment to consider because she spent her entire life honing the other instincts more. While she knew when to fight and when to run, she felt a little trigger-shy about judging people. The Maloneys had been kind to her, and then in the blink of an eye, she was public enemy number one. And while she could admit to herself their things had been stolen because of her stupidity, they'd cut her loose without any chance to explain or apologize or make it right.

Kayden waited patiently for her answer, not trying to plead his case or convince her that he was a nice guy. He studied her as closely as Aldo, the two men possessing an unnerving ability to make her think they saw more than she wanted them to.

"I don't think either of you will hurt me." The second she spoke the words, she realized they were true. And while that should feel like a good thing, it only drove home how out of her league she was right now. Because she'd lived her whole life in a house where she'd never felt entirely safe. She'd always been just that little bit on guard. So while she might believe herself safe, she couldn't stop herself from looking around, seeking an out if—when—this all went to shit.

Because everything always went to shit.

A wave of exhaustion washed over her, every crappy thing that had happened in the past two days crashing in on her. She was facing a mountain of problems, and she didn't have the answer to a single one of them. Her brain was shutting down. System overload.

Hazel's gaze fell away, and she sighed heavily, longing for some quiet corner where she could curl up in a ball and sleep for the next ten years.

She jerked slightly when she felt a gentle touch, Kayden's finger sliding slowly down her bruised cheek.

"Are you okay, Hazel?"

"I'm tired," she whispered, hoping he'd just think her sleepy.

"Tired of what?"

"Everything," she said, forgetting to shield her words.

Kayden nodded slowly, but he didn't reply right away. She didn't dare look at him. Instead, she pretended to be fascinated by the curb at their feet.

"Who hit you?"

She shook her head, lips tightly pressed closed, as she locked the vault on that.

Kayden didn't push her, though she could tell he wanted to. "Okay. Fine. You don't have to tell me. Yet." He added the last word after a pause, saying it softer. But it was still there, hovering in the air between them.

He was destined to be disappointed because she could never give him the answer to that question.

"One night," Kayden said.

Her gaze flew up, confused by his words, by the resolute look on his face.

"What?"

"You're going to take a break for one night."

"I can't. I have too many things to figure—"

"You don't know us well, but you said Aldo and I don't scare you. Did you mean that?"

This time, she didn't hesitate, didn't need to think it through. "Yes."

"Then we'll start from there. I get the feeling trust isn't something you give easily."

She snorted at that, proving he'd hit that nail on the head.

Kayden didn't acknowledge the sound. He just kept talking. "So instead, I'm asking for a leap of faith."

She frowned, confused.

"Hand us the reins tonight."

"What does that mean?"

"It means, we're going to call the shots for the next few hours. We're going to take you out for a nice meal, and then…" He paused, changing direction. "When did you eat last?"

She didn't want to say. Not because it would put more paint on the picture taking shape in his mind. No. It was because she knew—instinctually—that her reply would upset him.

"When, Hazel?"

There was something about his dark tone that had her replying before she could think it through. "I had a peanut butter sandwich yesterday."

His scowl was exactly what she'd expected. Kayden said Aldo pushed for what he wanted, but there was no denying what she was seeing right now on his face, in those damn expressions of his.

Determination and dominance.

And underlying that…concern.

It was the concern that had her swallowing the lump forming in her throat. Because she couldn't remember the last time anyone had looked at her like that. Suddenly, she wasn't thinking about finding a corner to sleep the next decade away.

Instead, she wanted to curl up in his arms or Aldo's—or better yet, with both of them—and just disappear. Forever.

She'd never been the hugging type. Probably because no one

ever offered, but Kayden looked like the kind of guy who could give a bear hug she'd feel all the way to the depths of her soul.

Tonight, she needed a hug.

Kayden reached his hand out, not taking hers. He was letting her make the decision. It wasn't a hard choice. She placed her hand in his, noticing how large, how strong, how warm it was compared to her icy one.

"So let us make all the decisions, solve all of the immediate problems for you. Dinner first," he said. "And then, we'll find you a safe place to stay tonight, a soft bed to lay your head down."

"It doesn't have to be soft," she murmured.

Kayden's only reply was to squeeze her hand gently, the gesture no doubt meant to be comforting, but she couldn't help imagining that hand squeezing...other parts of her as well. She felt herself blushing, her wayward thoughts going to places they really shouldn't go.

And, of course, the astute cop didn't miss her sudden discomfiture.

She needed to learn how to school her expressions because the second he mentioned that soft bed, she envisioned herself sleeping between him and Aldo.

God. She'd clearly gone round the bend. And she must have plastered that racy thought all over her face because she could swear Kayden's eyes darkened with...interest? With lust?

He ran his fingers along her bruise again, the touch so gentle and kind she had to fight back tears. No one had ever touched her with such care.

"What do you say, Hazel? Give yourself the night off. Let us take care of you."

"Leap of faith?" Her voice was suddenly too hungry, giving away her desperation. She couldn't recall a single day in her life when she'd simply stepped back and let someone else take over. It had always fallen to her to make the decisions, pay the bills, work the jobs, bail everyone out.

Handing all that over to someone else—even just for one night—was the most tempting offer of her life.

She might be a fool, and this might be the dumbest decision she'd ever make, but one fact kept screaming louder than all the rest.

She had nothing left to lose.

Chapter Six

Kayden held his breath as he watched Hazel wrestle with her decision. He knew the second he opened the back door of the cruiser she was searching for an escape, and it had taken every ounce of strength in his body to step away and give her that option. There was something wounded in this woman that had his protector instincts screaming.

Finally, she relented. "Okay."

Kayden felt the tension in his shoulders dissipate, all thanks to that one word, those two tiny syllables.

"Good," he said, holding his free hand out to gesture down the street to where Aldo's truck was parked, while he kept hold of the other. He liked the feeling of her hand in his. "It's cold out here. Let's sit in the truck."

Unfortunately, Hazel dropped his hand so she could reach into the cruiser for her backpack.

They fell into step together, and Kayden was tempted to place his arm around her back. One, because he was dying to touch her again, and two, because she kept shivering. Night had fallen and without the sun, the air had become downright frigid. She needed a coat, something warmer than the hoodie. He hit the unlock button on Aldo's fob, then opened the passenger door for her.

"I can sit in the back," she said. "Save the front seats for you and Aldo."

Kayden shook his head. "No. You sit in the front. It's closer to the heater, and you're cold. Your lips are turning blue."

"That's okay," she argued. "The cold hasn't killed me yet. You're too tall for the back and—"

"Hazel. Get in the car." Kayden was tall and commanding and —he could admit—a demanding son of a bitch when he wanted to be. As such, he wasn't used to too many people telling him no when he gave an order.

Hazel, however, was unfazed by his "cop voice," determined to argue. "Seriously. I don't mind and it doesn't make any sense for—"

"Hazel. Front seat. Now."

"But you'll be uncomfortable." Her look of surprise at his offer pissed him off. Had no one ever spared a thought for this woman? Because everything she did and said seemed to indicate that was the case.

He didn't reply to that, merely crossed his arms impatiently to show he was still waiting for her to do as he said.

"Are you sure?"

"Leap of faith, remember? Aldo and I are in charge tonight." He reminded her of their deal. "All you have to do is exactly what we say."

She crossed her arms. "I thought that only included decisions regarding dinner and a place to sleep."

The corner of his lips quirked up. The girl had claws, and he was fucking here for it.

"My exact words were, Aldo and I will call all the shots tonight."

"Yeah. I probably should have warned you," she said, with the faintest hint of a mischievous grin. "I'm shit at taking orders."

He didn't reply to that. Instead, he raised one eyebrow in a "we'll see about that way," then he gripped her tiny waist with his hands, half guiding, half lifting her into Aldo's Toyota Tacoma. Their sisters, Keeley and Liza, bitched nonstop about needing a stepladder to get into the damn thing.

He expected Hazel to tense up with his touch, so he was pleased when she went soft and followed his lead. Closing the door, he walked around the front of the car and climbed behind the steering wheel, starting the truck and cranking up the heat. "The front seats are the only ones that heat up," he said, turning on the seat warmers too.

"Oh, wow. Never been in a car with seat warmers. Those heat up fast. That feels nice or..." She paused.

"Or?"

"I kind of feel like I just peed my pants."

Kayden laughed.

They both turned at the sound of a tap on the driver's window, Aldo standing outside, his hair still wet from the shower.

Kayden thought he heard a slight intake of breath from Hazel, though it didn't surprise him. Aldo had been a good-looking bastard from the cradle, and now, with his face soot-free, that was shining through.

He opened the door and got out of the truck, grabbing Aldo's house key from him. He looked back at Hazel. "I keep a change of clothes here...for emergencies. Or unexpected dinners with beautiful women. I'm going to change out of this uniform and grab one of Aldo's coats for you. That hoodie isn't warm enough."

"That's okay," she said. Kayden suspected she wouldn't accept anything from them easily, no matter what she'd agreed to.

"Shit, I should have thought to get one for you," Aldo said to Hazel. "I was in too much of a hurry to get back down here. Didn't want to keep you waiting outside too long."

"I won't be a minute," Kayden said, as Aldo claimed the spot Kayden had just vacated.

Kayden took the steps to Aldo's front door two at a time, letting himself in. He and Aldo were both comfortable in each other's spaces. Kayden had a drawer full of clothes here, just like Aldo had one at his house. In addition to that, they both had toothbrushes and razors in each other's bathrooms, simply because it wasn't unusual for them to hang out to watch sports together, which, of course, meant bourbon or beer. They'd recently discussed Aldo getting out of his lease when it was up in the next month or two and moving in with Kayden, who had inherited his parents' house after they died.

It wasn't a new conversation—it came up every year just as the lease was set to expire—but they'd never pulled the trigger.

They both seemed to worry that by moving in together, they'd wind up crossing *that* line. The one where they stopped looking for what they truly wanted and settled for what they had. For right now, neither of them was willing to compromise, so they kept the status quo.

He loved Aldo with all his heart, but the two of them as a couple would never be enough. For one thing, they both liked women too much to give them up forever, and for another, they both resided firmly on the alpha side in their relationships with other people.

Kayden quickly tossed on a pair of jeans and threw a sweater over his head. He hung up his uniform and pitched his work shoes into the corner, pulling on a pair of warm boots. Traipsing back down the hall, he opened a closet, grabbing his coat and another of Aldo's for Hazel. Then he rummaged around in a basket Aldo kept beneath the coats for a winter hat for Hazel as well.

Hazel.

Damn if she hadn't captured his attention tonight and held on to it.

He hadn't intended to push the envelope about him and Aldo taking charge for the night, but the more he saw her shiver, saw her shut down when he asked about the bruise, saw those dark circles under her haunted eyes that told him her tiredness was bone *and* soul deep, the more he longed to take care of her and keep her safe. The fact that she was a virtual stranger didn't make a bit of difference.

He walked back out of Aldo's, locking the door behind him, as he tried to think of a place she could stay for the night. Money was obviously an issue, but he'd be damned if he would allow her to stay in another place like Crossings Motel on her own. Crossings was sketchy as hell, and he'd answered far too many calls from the motel while on duty. The place had seen its fair share of everything from drunk and disorderly to overdoses to even worse. The first time Kayden had met Jess Monroe, she'd been working there as a housekeeper and one of the guests had dragged her into his room and attacked her.

Kayden wasn't sure what would have happened to her if Tony and Rhys hadn't gotten there when they did. He'd come as soon as he got the call from dispatch, but by the time he'd arrived, Tony had subdued the fucker. Actually, he'd beat the shit out of him.

He and Tony had discussed the incident afterward, and given what Tony said about the man's hands around her throat, choking her, Kayden knew he would have arrived too late to save her.

Then he recalled the almost feral expression in Tony's eyes when Kayden had walked into that motel room. Kayden had tried to approach Jess, to check her injuries and question her about the attack, but Tony had moved to block him, to keep him from getting any closer.

He and Tony had been friends since high school, twenty years, their relationship evolving from high school football teammates to just-turned-twenty-one drinking buddies to practically brothers. They'd seen it all, done it all, but Kayden had never seen that kind of fierce protectiveness in his friend.

No. Protective wasn't the right word.

It had been outright possessiveness, which had shocked Kayden, because Tony hadn't known Jess more than a day or two at the time.

Yet...regardless of that, Tony had known, somehow, that Jess was his. To protect. To keep. To love.

Kayden wasn't sure how to explain it, but when he'd seen Hazel standing on that sidewalk, watching the fire with a look of utter desperation in her eyes and that bruise on her cheek, he'd known he would do anything, give anything to help her.

And for the first time, he truly understood Tony's feelings for Jess.

Walking down the steps, he grinned to himself as he looked through the windows of the truck. Aldo was talking a mile a minute, no doubt entertaining Hazel with some silly story, given the amusement on her face. She was grinning more than smiling, and Kayden wondered what it would take to erase all the darkness lingering in her eyes, to see her throw back her head and laugh for real.

He crossed around the truck, opening Hazel's door. She misinterpreted his actions, shifting as if she planned to move to the backseat.

He stopped her with a firm hand on her shoulder. "Where are you going?"

She glanced over her shoulder. "I'll move back there. I'm warm now."

He shook his head, handing her the coat and hat he'd pilfered from Aldo for her. "Nope. I'm sitting in the back. Here." He slapped the hat over her hair, thought it seemed a shame to hide that hair. "You can put the coat on when we get to the restaurant." Then he grabbed the seat belt, pulling it over her to snap it in place.

"I can do that." Hazel tried to take the buckle from him, but he didn't give way. Instead, he quietly murmured "leap of faith," until she sat still and let him finish the task.

Then Kayden climbed in the backseat, the space a little too tight for his long legs, not that he was about to complain.

Aldo twisted to look at him curiously. "Leap of faith? What's that mean?"

Kayden bent forward, leaning through the middle of the front seats. "Hazel has agreed to put herself in our very capable hands tonight. She's had a hell of a day, so we're giving her the night off from all her worries. We're going to feed her and find her a safe place to stay, and she doesn't have to think about a damn thing."

Aldo smiled widely. "Well, all right then. Sounds like a plan." He put the truck in drive and pulled onto the street. "Kayden and I were supposed to be at a hockey game tonight with our gang of friends and family, but we got called to the fire. Anyway, I texted my sister, Liza, right after I got out of the shower," Aldo said, more to Hazel than to Kayden. "They'd all just gotten to Divine, the restaurant a buddy of ours owns. When I told her we were joining them, she said they'd wait to order dinner until we got there."

"Oh. I don't want to impose if you already had plans," Hazel said.

"You're not imposing," Kayden said. "We want you to come with us."

"Yeah, but maybe it would be better if you just dropped me off at a mot—"

"Kayden," Aldo interrupted. "Does it sound to you like Hazel is thinking?"

Kayden chuckled. "It does."

"Already breaking the rules." Aldo shook his head, grinning.

Hazel narrowed her eyes, then glanced over her shoulder at Kayden. "Told you I'd be shit at it," she said, unapologetically.

Oh man...Kayden's fingers itched to take her over his lap and teach her a lesson or two. He shoved that thought deep down because, Jesus Christ, they'd just met the woman.

"What are we going to do about that?" Aldo's question was loaded as he looked at Kayden through the rearview mirror. His best friend knew him well enough to know exactly where his thoughts had drifted.

It was on the tip of Kayden's tongue to suggest they come up with consequences, but they were nowhere near that level with

Hazel. Hell, Kayden had to spend several minutes convincing the shivering woman to come sit in the heated truck.

There was no way they could barrel toward Hazel at a hundred miles an hour, revealing so much of themselves right out of the gate.

Time to put on the brakes and play this smarter.

The problem was, Kayden and Aldo had a one-track mind when it came to sex—they were both dominant, kinky fuckers who liked control. It was one of the reasons they'd known they wouldn't work as a couple. The two of them had gotten into too many pissing matches over who would be top. It was fine in the beginning because they'd been each other's first male lovers, so it had been a fuck-ton of exploration, both of them taking turns, trying each role. However, as the months wore on, it became evident neither of them would be happy as a full-time bottom, nor were they into being dominated.

They were both thirty-five, and while they'd dated countless women in the past, they had never managed to find the one woman who turned both their heads.

Hazel was clearly the first, because he saw the same desire emblazoned on Aldo's face that Kayden had felt the first second he'd laid eyes on her.

It was as if he'd been struck by lightning. Honest-to-God lightning. And it must have fried his brain because instead of thinking things through, like he normally did, he was acting on instinct.

Caveman-like instinct.

He wanted to dive into the deep end with Hazel, something that would freak the poor woman out. Especially considering they knew next to nothing about her.

"I don't know." Kayden tried to erase all the kinky ideas that kept popping into his head, but he couldn't do it. So he lobbed the ball into her court, curious to see how she would respond. "What do you think, Hazel? Should there be some repercussions, or are you going to behave?"

Hazel turned around, and Kayden's dick went from zero to sixty in an instant, his jeans suddenly painfully tight.

Because she didn't look confused, and she sure as shit didn't look afraid.

Nope, the look she flashed him was something much more dangerous.

She looked ready to play.

She bit her lower lip, looking so fucking submissive, he wanted to beat his chest like goddamn Tarzan and drag her to his lair. As she considered her answer, Kayden watched as her teeth cut into the plump, rosy flesh he wanted to suck into his mouth.

For a moment, he thought the minx might emerge, but Hazel regained control way too quick for his fucking sanity.

"I'll behave," she said softly.

Fuck. He thought he wanted the minx, but that answer was even better.

He and Aldo exchanged another glance in the rearview mirror, and Kayden spent the rest of the trip to the restaurant trying to will away the mother of all hard-ons.

It took them less than ten minutes to get to Divine. Kayden hopped out quickly after Aldo parked the truck in the lot, pulling the door open a second before Hazel could.

"I can do it." She tried to step down out of the tall cab on her own, ignoring his outstretched arms, but he wasn't having any of it.

"Nope. *I've* got *you*." He took the coat from her, then offered her a hand out of the truck. He grasped her waist again, steadying her as she stepped down. Twisting her to face away from him, he helped her put on the coat.

She took a quick look at the restaurant, then pulled the hat off, tossing it back into the cab of the truck, tucking the strand of hair that had come loose from her ponytail behind her ear.

"That coat swallows you." Aldo joined them, digging into the sleeve until he found her hand and clasping it.

Hazel looked down at their linked hands like a deer in the

headlights, like it had never occurred to her that hands could fit together like that. She'd done the same thing when Kayden had held her hand by the cruiser.

Kayden claimed her other side, placing his hand on the small of her back, under the jacket. She shivered, but this time, he didn't think it was because she was cold.

The three of them walked into the restaurant like that. Hazel's uneasiness returned when they entered and were greeted by a chorus of voices calling their names, waving them over.

"Kayden," his sister, Keeley, said, as Elio called out to Aldo.

"I don't think I'm dressed up enough for this place," she murmured.

She was looking for an excuse to leave.

"Of course you are," Aldo reassured her. "Our whole group of friends just came from a hockey game. Twenty bucks says every single one of them is in jeans too."

"Besides, we've got an in with the owner. He's dating my sister, so if he knows what's good for him, he won't kick you out." Kayden followed up that tough guy joke with a quick wink.

Hazel, unfortunately, didn't smile. Instead, she pulled her hand out of Aldo's grasp and stepped away from Kayden's arm. Kayden considered protesting, pushing her on her promise to behave, but he held his tongue.

Because, as he tried to remind himself again, he'd only just met the woman a couple hours ago. Of course, the sudden scowl on Aldo's face proved he was fighting the same internal battle.

Hazel asked if there was a restroom. He hated seeing her so nervous, so Kayden gave her the out, pointing toward the back left corner as she excused herself.

He and Aldo waited until she was out of earshot, remaining at the door.

"You feel it?" Aldo asked.

Kayden nodded. "Yeah."

"Fuck. It's all I can do to..." Aldo waved his hands around helplessly.

Kayden chuckled, equal parts amused and frustrated. "Yeah. Me too. We need to get a handle on ourselves though, or she's likely to crawl out the restroom window."

Aldo glanced the direction Hazel went, as if tempted to follow to make sure she wasn't shimmying her cute little ass over the ledge as they spoke.

"Come on." Kayden led the way to the table to greet their friends.

Elio stood up and gave Aldo a quick hug, slapping him on the back. "You missed my game, bro," he said, though it wasn't spoken in anger.

Aldo looked remorseful regardless. "Yeah, I know. Did Liza explain?"

Elio nodded. "We were just sitting here talking about it. How's Rocco holding up?"

Kayden lifted one shoulder. "I'm not sure it's sunk in yet."

"I bet." Elio reclaimed his seat next to Gianna, placing his arm around the back of her chair and tugging her close. Any closer and she'd be on his lap. Kayden wasn't sure he'd ever seen either of them look happier.

Last night, that made him grumpy.

Tonight? He glanced toward the women's room...well... tonight, he was feeling no pain.

"So who's the woman you came in with?" Liza asked.

Kayden took the seat next to her. "She was staying at Crossings Motel. Just got into town this morning. She intends to look for a job and settle down in Philly. Unfortunately, she lost all her possessions in the fire. As far as I can tell, all she has left is the clothes on her back."

"Oh my God," Keeley said. "That's awful. The poor thing."

Liza's response mirrored Keeley's, and within seconds, they were both discussing what they could do to help her.

They fell silent when Hazel emerged from the restroom. She really must have been worried about her appearance because he noticed she'd redone her ponytail, somehow replacing the messy waterfall with a more elegant-looking updo. Both styles were hot, but he couldn't help wishing she'd taken it down completely. He wondered if it was as long and curly as it looked.

She glanced across the restaurant at them, and Kayden could almost see her spine stiffening as she approached their table. Hazel was clearly nervous, but she had enough courage to stick around.

She was also harboring secrets. He was under no delusion about that, but he hoped a night with their friends and family would set her mind at ease about him and Aldo, prove to her that they weren't bad guys and she could trust them to help her.

She stopped a few steps short of the table, but Aldo, who hadn't claimed a seat yet, closed the distance and placed a friendly hand on her back, drawing her closer. She was still wearing the huge coat, so Aldo slipped it off her shoulders, hanging it on the back of the chair next to Elio and across from Kayden, before claiming the last seat at the head of the table between him and Hazel.

She tugged at her hoodie, her eyes darting around the table, checking out what the other women were wearing. Aldo hadn't lied. Everyone was dressed casually in jeans and sweaters or long-sleeved tees. Gianna was sporting an oversized Stingrays hockey jersey.

"Hey, everybody," Aldo said, taking up the introductions. "This is Hazel. Hazel, this is everybody."

Everyone laughed, while Hazel managed a weak smile. The table was packed, so Aldo had probably handled that the best possible way without overwhelming her.

She sat down, looking at Kayden as if seeking reassurance. She was out of her element. Which made him that much more determined to get to know her.

What the hell had happened to this woman? It was obvious she'd been hit, and the fact she'd carried all her belongings into the motel told him she didn't own much. All Rocco had said when they were making sure everyone had gotten out safely was the cute little redhead had checked in shortly after dawn, that it looked like she'd been driving all night, and he hadn't seen her again after he watched to make sure she got to her room okay.

Gianna leaned across Elio, reaching out her hand. "I'm Gianna, and this is my boyfriend, Elio." She flushed lightly; their relationship was very new. She grinned at Elio. "I'm still not used to calling you that."

Elio wrapped his arm around Gianna's shoulders. "Well, you better get used to it because I'm not going anywhere." He backed that pronouncement up with a kiss that turned into a nuzzle, until Gio called out from the end of the table.

"Get a room!"

Elio looked back at Hazel. "I'm Aldo's brother."

"Oh," she said. "The hockey player?"

"Aldo," Elio teased, "I'm telling you, man, you need to get a life so you can stop trying to pick up chicks by bragging about me." He looked back at Hazel. "Poor guy is dull as dirt. Wouldn't get a date at all if not for me."

Hazel giggled, though the sound was too soft and too short. Still...it was progress. "Riiiight," she drawled. "Because no woman in history has ever found a firefighter sexy."

Aldo cracked up at her sarcastic reply, reaching out and giving her hand a quick squeeze. "That's right, Hazel. Set the asshole straight."

"Got a girl fighting your battles for you, Aldo?" Elio tossed back.

Aldo grabbed a pretzel from the bowl in front of him and threw it at his brother, who dodged it deftly. "I finally found a woman who appreciates my worth."

Hazel shook her head at their antics, but she was obviously entertained, and Kayden knew in an instant, they'd made the right decision bringing her here. More of her natural personality was starting to come out.

"Ignore those two, Hazel." Keeley was the next to chime in. "Their one-upmanship games are so common, the rest of us don't even pay attention anymore." She pointed in Kayden's direction.

"I'm Keeley, Kayden's sister. He was just telling us about the fire. I'm so sorry to hear you lost all of your possessions."

Hazel shrugged, putting on a brave face. "To be honest, I didn't have that much to begin with. I'm bummed about losing my laptop and car keys, but the rest was crappy clothes. It'll be okay. I just need to find a new place to stay and maybe a Walmart to grab the essentials."

"Still, it's pretty awful considering you just got into town." Keeley looked over her shoulder at Gio and Rafe, her boyfriends, and Kayden knew that his second reason for bringing Hazel here was about to come to fruition.

The three of them exchanged a look. Kayden was impressed by how they could communicate without talking.

Decision made without a single word spoken, Gio took the lead. "I'm Gio Moretti," he said to Hazel. "Keeley's boyfriend."

Rafe cleared his throat, and Gio grinned, bumping shoulders with Rafe, who was sitting next to him. "And Rafe's boyfriend. Damn, man, you're such a jealous bastard." Gio gripped the back of Rafe's neck and pulled him close enough that he could plant a quick kiss on the other man's mouth.

And with that, Gio answered his and Aldo's suspicions about the change in status in his cousin's relationship with Rafe. Looked like the friends had become lovers.

Rafe rolled his eyes after the kiss, then looked at Hazel. "Gio, Keeley, and I are partners."

"Oh," she said.

Kayden studied her face as she took in that information because her response would impact his and Aldo's instant attraction if she was completely appalled by it. He could tell it took her aback at first, but the shock wore off fast, and he was relieved when she seemed to take it in stride.

"That's cool."

"We're also business partners," Gio explained, jerking his thumb in Elio's direction, "with the cocky hockey player."

Hazel giggled again, but this time she covered her mouth with her hand as if to dim the sound.

"And as luck would have it, we own an inn," Keeley added.

Hazel's smile faded just a bit. "That sounds...wonderful." Her eyes darted over to Kayden, and he got a sense of her growing discomfort. Obviously, she could figure out where this was going.

"If you'd like, you're welcome to stay there. It's not open at the moment, but Keeley, Rafe, and I still live there, so you wouldn't be alone. We've got a contract down on a house, but we don't close for another month. And Gianna is moving into the guesthouse behind the inn in a couple of weeks, so she's going to be there full-time soon. How would you like to be our very first guest?" Gio asked.

"I—" she started.

"Our grand opening is in three months," Gianna chimed in, cutting her off before she could refuse. "Rafe, Gio, and Elio have hired me to manage it. One of the rooms is made up, decorated, and ready to roll—we did that so we could take pictures for the website—so there's a place for you to sleep. Now, we just need to finish making up all the rest of the rooms since the construction phase is finished. Which means decorating—the fun part. We're also putting the finishing touches on the public spaces and doing the tech stuff, setting up cable and wireless internet, stuff like that."

"So what do you say, Hazel?" Gio pressed.

Hazel was shaking her head before Gio finished his question. "I couldn't ask you to do that. You're not even open. And I..." She was looking at him and Aldo for help, probably because an inn sounded a hell of a lot more expensive than a crappy motel.

Gio, a true Moretti, didn't take no for an answer any easier than Aldo, especially now that he'd heard about her shitty day. "We wouldn't even charge you, since there's no cable or Wi-Fi in the room yet."

"Oh, wow, um, I—" Hazel was about to say no, about to offer

up an excuse, but Kayden cut her off. She would be safe with Keeley, Rafe, and Gio.

"That's a really nice offer, Gio," Kayden said. "Hazel would love to stay there."

Hazel's eyes narrowed, and he caught his first glimpse of a temper from her. He wished it didn't turn him on so much.

"Kayden—" she started, but he cut her off at the pass. Because he knew exactly how to end the conversation.

Lowering his voice, he leaned forward, aware only Aldo and Hazel could hear him when he murmured, "Behave."

Chapter Seven

Hazel's mouth opened, then closed, then opened again. What the hell was she supposed to say to that? She had agreed to Kayden's leap of faith, grasping onto it like a life preserver as she watched her ship sink.

But even so.

Had he really just told her to behave?

She glanced in Aldo's direction, hoping for some support from him, but the serious look on his face told her he was solidly in Kayden's camp.

Keeley, who clearly shared her brother's stubbornness, ended the conversation once and for all. "Great. Then it's all settled. And until you replace your clothes, you can borrow some of mine. We look like we're about the same size, and Gio and Rafe are always telling me I have too many."

"You could open up three boutiques with all the shit in your closet," Gio grumbled to Keeley before looking back at Hazel. "That was the number one priority when we were house hunting. Walk-in closets...plural. And as it is, I'll still probably have to build her another one after we move in."

Keeley brushed off her boyfriend's complaint, though given

the way Gio looked at Keeley like she hung the moon, it didn't seem like he really cared about the abundance of clothes.

While Hazel had willingly given up control to Kayden and Aldo for the night, she hadn't expected them to take hold of it the way they had. She'd seen it as merely a nice gesture, offering her a meal before helping her find a motel she could afford. They were taking two relatively simple tasks off her overwhelming to-do list.

The opportunity to let someone else make a couple decisions for her had been too tempting to refuse. But now...it was starting to feel like something more.

And while she was the poster child for trust issues, she couldn't stop herself from responding to them in ways she didn't fully understand.

When they'd asked her to suggest consequences for failing to follow their lead, the first thing that popped into her mind was a spanking.

In what fucking world would she ask for that?

She was no trembling virgin, but she'd also never ventured into anything with her past lovers that could be called kink.

Refer back to the trust issues.

She'd had sex with four guys, two in high school, and two while she was in community college, taking classes to earn her LPN degree. Because she'd had to work three jobs while taking classes part-time, it had taken her longer to earn her nursing degree than her classmates.

The high school boyfriends had been nothing to write home about, neither relationship lasting more than six months.

Although, when she considered it, the guys after high school weren't that much more interesting either. There had been one guy in her class, Shawn—also going for a nursing degree—who'd been sweet and sexy. He'd been her most adventurous lover, but all that meant was they'd done it outside during a hike once, and in the shower a few times.

So she didn't know what to do with the fact that Aldo and Kayden had talked about consequences, and she'd immediately imagined herself draped over their laps—*both* of their laps—while they punished her for being bad.

Then she considered Gio introducing himself as Rafe and Keeley's boyfriend. She wondered if perhaps it was that information that had her thinking about both men in a sexual way, but she dismissed that excuse out of hand. Her thoughts about curling up with Kayden and Aldo had begun before they'd arrived at the restaurant.

Maybe they'd been giving off some sort of subliminal signals. Maybe threesomes were a thing for this group of friends. Although, Gianna and Elio didn't appear to have another girlfriend or boyfriend at the table.

"I have a ton of clothes too." The woman sitting next to Kayden reached across the table to shake her hand. "I'm Liza, Aldo's sister. How about you, me, and Keeley get together one night this week? I know between the two of us, we can build a fairly decent wardrobe of essentials, then you'll have more money to spend on signature pieces."

Signature pieces?

Hazel likened herself to Dorothy being dropped down in the middle of Oz. She'd felt it the second she'd walked into Divine. Her family wasn't the fancy restaurant type. The few times they'd gone out to eat—and Hazel could count those on one hand— they'd either hit some dark, smoky dive bar that served microwaved appetizers or a cheap all-you-can-eat buffet that always ended with her mom loading her purse with as much food as she could sneak out.

The one time she'd been in a more upscale restaurant—if she could call Outback upscale—she'd gone out with Shawn to celebrate earning their nursing degrees.

The waitress approached their table. "Hello. Can I grab you something to drink?" she asked her, Kayden, and Aldo as she handed each of them a menu.

Kayden and Aldo asked for some fancy IPA microbrew on tap.

"Water is fine," Hazel said.

"Do you like beer?" Aldo asked.

She shrugged. "Yeah. I guess. I don't drink much." Between her uncle's beer and her mom's wine, Hazel never wanted to blow any more of their grocery money on alcohol for herself.

"Why don't you try what we're having," Kayden suggested. "If you don't like it, one of us will finish it for you."

She nodded quickly because she felt the weight of the stares of the others at the table, and agreeing seemed like the quickest way to turn off the spotlight on her. "Okay. Thanks."

The waitress walked away, and Hazel opened the menu. She scanned until she spotted the beer listings, and then instantly felt guilty. The beer they'd ordered her was ten dollars.

Her gaze darted up, and she realized that while the rest of the people at the table were all engaged in quiet conversation, Aldo and Kayden were watching her.

"See anything that looks good?" Kayden asked softly.

She perused the menu, her attention focused solely on the prices. "I'm really not that hungry," she lied. "Maybe I'll just have a salad."

A side salad.

Kayden's eyes narrowed. "Do you eat meat?"

She nodded.

"Red meat? Burgers?"

Again, she nodded.

"And you like it?"

She hesitated a moment too long.

"Hazel," Aldo prompted.

"Yes. I like it."

"Perfect." Kayden plucked the menu out of her hand. "Then I know just what to order for you."

Okay. Enough was enough.

It was time to take Kayden down a notch. She'd obviously given him the impression she was a weak-willed woman with zero opinions. Which wasn't solely his fault. She'd been acting pretty meek since the moment they met, but that was because her mind had been reeling over losing everything in the fire. And before she could wrap her head around that, they'd immediately yanked her out of her comfort zone.

"Listen, Kayden—" She started to set him straight, but Aldo placed his hand on the back of her chair, leaned toward her, and cut her off.

"We just want to buy you a nice dinner."

"Why?" That was the question that kept ringing in her brain. In her experience, most people didn't go out of their way to help a stranger they'd just met. At least not without some ulterior motive. So what did they want from her? There had to be a catch.

"Because you look hungry," Aldo replied.

His response came too quickly, and he delivered it with that charming smile that was too sexy for her peace of mind.

She grinned, then huffed out a laugh. She was likely to give them whiplash if she didn't stop running so hot and cold. "Okay. I give up. Order me whatever. And...thank you. I *am* hungry."

"So you lied when you said you weren't." Kayden's voice had different levels of depth that seemed to express his emotions when his actual words didn't. There'd been no inflection of accusation. Just a deep rumbling tone that told her she was in trouble.

She was overwhelmed by the desire to apologize. Not because she was sorry for the lie, but because she felt as though she'd disappointed them somehow and that made her feel bad. Which made no sense at all. Hazel might toe the line when it came to doing the right thing, but she wouldn't call herself a people pleaser. Her actions had always been to protect herself, not make others happy.

So...what if she *did* tell a little white lie about not being hungry? It should have been no big deal, but there was something coursing between her and these two men that told her it was.

Mercifully, she was yanked off the hot seat by another guy at the table.

"Well, since no one else is going to do it, I guess I'll introduce myself."

Hazel, Kayden, and Aldo turned to look at the man sitting next to Liza, and Hazel did a double take, glancing farther down the table, then back again.

"I'm Luca," the man said. "And obviously, you've put together that Gio and I are identical twins. It's nice to meet you, Hazel."

She smiled. "You too."

The waitress returned with their drinks, then took everyone's orders. Hazel's mouth watered when Kayden ordered cheeseburgers with the works and fries for himself and for her. Aldo asked for the same, then added an order of onion rings for the three of them to split.

"I'm a little concerned," Luca said, picking up the conversation once the waitress left, "that no one felt it necessary to warn you about the inn."

"Warn me?" Hazel frowned, looking at Aldo and Kayden, who were shaking their heads.

"Seriously, Luca?" Aldo said.

"You were really going to throw her into one of those fancy rooms without giving her all the details?"

Hazel's concern was alleviated not by Luca's words but by the grins on everyone else's faces. "What's wrong with the inn?"

Keeley waved Luca's warning away. "Absolutely nothing. It's just...we have ghosts."

Hazel paused for a second, wondering if she'd heard Keeley correctly. She said "ghosts" the way someone might say mice or termites. Like it was just an inconvenience. "Ghosts?"

"Yes," Keeley replied, "but you don't have to worry about them. Because we know who they are and they're nice ghosts. Not a bit scary."

Hazel kept waiting for someone to yell "just kidding," but the sincerity in Keeley's expression made it apparent that she really did believe the inn was haunted.

"You're joking," Hazel finally said.

Gio shook his head. "We never joke about our ghosts."

She must have looked concerned because Rafe leaned forward. "You really don't have to worry. The ghosts are my grandparents —Albert and Marta—and they don't come around much unless they're up to some mischief or matchmaking."

Hazel didn't have a reply for that, but it didn't matter because the conversation suddenly became this odd, unchoreographed discussion between a group of people who were clearly very close. Every time someone started to tell one of the ghost stories, another person would finish it. A couple of times there were two or three people all speaking at once, yet Hazel was somehow able to follow them as they recited all the ways Albert and Marta had used their spiritual powers to bring people together.

Most of the stories revolved around Gio, Keeley, and Rafe, though Liza remarked that another couple who wasn't at the restaurant, Penny and Gage, had experienced a couple of encounters as well. Gianna wanted to gain the ghosts' approval of her relationship with Elio, so she was hoping for a sign.

Everyone also seemed convinced that the ghosts were going to be a huge selling factor when it came to booking the rooms in the inn.

The more they talked about it, the more Hazel sort of hoped for her own ghostly—only if friendly—encounter. How cool would that be?

Soon, the conversation turned to that night's hockey game, and there was a lot of good-natured trash talking about various plays as everyone filled in Aldo and Kayden on what they'd missed. Apparently, Aldo was pissed to have missed one of his brother's on-ice fights. According to Kayden, Elio was considered an enforcer on his team and no stranger to the five-for-fighting penalty.

Once the food arrived, Hazel expected the conversation to die down, but if anything, it got more animated and louder as everyone raved about their food. It probably helped that most of the people at the table were on their third round of drinks.

Hazel groaned after the first bite of her burger. If an orgasm from food was possible, this would be the meal to push her to climax. Kayden and Aldo looked up from their plates, and she felt herself blushing over the sound she'd made. Not that either of them seemed to mind.

"That good, huh?" Aldo gave her a sexy wink, his mind on the same track as hers. "I'm sort of jealous of that burger. Wondering if *I* could get you to make that sound."

She shook her head, tossing Kayden's word, "Behave," at Aldo in a voice that was too flirty to have come from her. Not that she cared because when both men laughed, she felt like a million bucks.

"What do you think of the beer?" Kayden asked when she took another drink.

When she'd seen the price, she'd intended to take a sip, then give it to one of the guys. But it was so good, she'd selfishly kept it.

"It's delicious. I've never tasted beer like this."

"Glad you like it. Want another one?" Aldo asked.

She quickly shook her head. "No. I don't think I should. This is stronger than I'm used to. It's already going to my head."

"So what do you do for a living?" Liza asked Hazel.

"Oh, I'm a nurse." Immediately, she silently kicked herself for revealing too much. She was letting herself get too comfortable with these people, and it was making her stupid.

"Good for you," Liza said. "I see one drop of blood and I'm passed out on the floor. Always amazed by people who can work around sickness."

Aldo brightened up. "I didn't know you were a nurse. No wonder I keep thinking you're a kindred spirit. I'm an EMT. In addition to fighting fires—which women find very sexy," he directed that comment at his brother, "I answer rescue calls as well. Did you work in a hospital in Springfield?"

She shook her head. "No, um, uh, a nursing home," she lied,

trying to mitigate the damage she'd done. Unable to look them in the eye, she glanced down at her plate, hoping that she'd gotten away with her fib.

She was going to have to break away from Kayden and Aldo soon or get a hell of a lot better at lying. Because when she finally looked up, she could see from the matching frowns on their faces that they didn't believe her.

"What do *you* do for a living?" she asked Liza, in an attempt to turn the attention away from her.

"I'm the Executive Director of the Philadelphia Initiative." Liza went on to describe her job, which sounded interesting, then she wound up launching into some story about a man from her work, Matt, who drove her crazy.

"Great job, Hazel," Aldo teased, tugging on her ponytail. "You managed to ring the bell on Liza's Matt Russo bitching."

She grinned because Liza was still going strong—she really didn't like Matt—flat-out ignoring her brother's joke.

"Um, sorry?" Hazel murmured, suddenly wishing Aldo would pull her hair for real.

What the hell was wrong with her tonight? It was as if she'd escaped Boston as one woman and arrived in Philadelphia as someone very different.

Or...more likely...it was Kayden and Aldo. They were unlike every other man she'd ever met. And there was something about them that had her wanting to throw caution completely to the wind.

Which she couldn't do.

The rest of the evening passed far too quickly, despite everyone ordering at least two more rounds as Hazel listened to them tell stories about their jobs, their more interesting relatives, and the fun times they'd shared. She'd never been around such a loud, close-knit group of people before. There didn't appear to be an asshole in the bunch. The dinner was a much-needed distraction from all the shit that had gone down the past couple of days.

However, now that it was winding down, and people were standing up, preparing to leave, her anxiety reappeared.

This time, it felt even worse. Because as she watched Liza and Luca say their goodbyes—Luca and Gio fist-bumping, Liza giving Elio, who was returning to Baltimore tomorrow, a big hug and kiss on the cheek—loneliness was now lingering with the stress as she longed for a group of friends like this. It was part of why it had been so easy for her to run from Boston. There'd been no one in that city to run *to*.

Keeley, Gio, and Rafe rose next.

"You want to ride with us, Hazel?" Keeley offered.

Since she had no car, she was about to accept the offer, but Kayden stepped next to her. "Aldo and I will drive her, help her get settled."

Hazel could see Keeley's confusion—especially since it would be out of their way—but she brushed it off, shrugged, put on her coat, then told Hazel she'd see her at the inn.

Elio and Gianna were the last to say goodbye, Gianna saying she'd see Hazel in the morning and promising to bring some clothes, as well as some of her extra makeup for her to use until she replaced her own. Hazel saw the woman's eyes drop briefly to her bruised cheek and she resisted the urge to raise her hand to cover it.

Flushing, Hazel thanked her, and then it was just the three of them.

Aldo helped her back into his oversized coat, then slung his arm around her shoulders. "We really threw you into the fire with that dinner, didn't we? I didn't really think about it because Kayden and I are used to the craziness attached to our group of friends. We should have warned you."

"They're amazing, and everyone is so nice. I had a good time," she reassured him. "It's just..."

"Just?" Kayden prodded.

"I feel bad about staying at the inn. It's not even open yet, and it wouldn't be right for me not to pay."

Kayden tilted his head. "The inn is the only place I'd be comfortable letting you stay on your own." He didn't add "with your lack of funds," but she could hear it just the same, and she started to suspect setting her up at the inn was one of their reasons for dragging her along to dinner.

Aldo guided her toward the exit, his arm still wrapped securely around her. She wasn't used to being touched so much. And while their touches were innocent—hand-holding, a gentle hand on her back, playfully tugging her hair—they still managed to pack a punch, lighting up her libido like fireworks on the Fourth of July.

Aldo stopped when they reached the truck. "They wouldn't have offered if it was a problem, and when you see the size of their haunted mansion, you'll understand. You could walk around that place for days without ever running into another person."

He unlocked the truck with his fob, walking to the driver's side, while Kayden opened the passenger door for her.

"I'll sit in the back this time," she said.

Now, as before, her offer was wasted breath.

"Nope. I want you to have the heated seat." Kayden already had her lifted into the cab by the time he finished talking. Once again, he pulled the seat belt over her, latching it, and this time she let him without resistance.

"Thank you," she said, when he pulled away.

Kayden grinned, then gave her a quick, platonic kiss on the cheek. "Progress."

She narrowed her eyes, and he laughed. Then he bopped her on the nose with the tip of his finger playfully.

The ride to the inn was a quiet one, though the silence wasn't awkward. Aldo found a classic rock station and was humming along to "Stairway to Heaven."

As they pulled up to the inn, Hazel's eyes widened. "Holy shit. One person lived here? Alone?"

Keeley had explained during dinner that Rafe inherited the mansion from his grandpa Albert, who had lived alone in the place for decades after his beloved wife, Marta, passed away. And while they'd constantly referred to the home as a haunted mansion, it still hadn't prepared Hazel for the sheer size of the place.

"See why they're turning it into an inn instead of living here?" Kayden asked. "It's too big for three people."

The building was an absolutely beautiful, huge, three-story Colonial-style mansion with a wraparound porch, giant pillars, and large windows.

"I've never seen anything like it."

Aldo parked right in front of the inn, which had a circular driveway, before turning the truck off.

"You guys don't have to come in," she said as she opened her door. For a big guy, Kayden moved fast. The second she turned to climb down, he was there, ready to help. She liked the feeling of his hands on her waist. And his strength.

She liked it a little too much.

A girl could get used to this.

Stop, Hazel.

She needed to get her head in the game. In the course of one dinner, she'd come to realize Kayden and Aldo—like their friends—were genuinely nice people. They'd seen her as the epitome of a damsel in distress, and they'd stepped forward to help.

That was all this was.

Because she didn't belong in the world of people like the Morettis and the Gallos.

They were good-hearted, kind, and she... Well, she was the daughter of a bank robber, a cop killer—and she was possibly wanted by the Boston police for robbery. She was on the run, for God's sake, so flirting with a cop would make her literally the dumbest person on the planet.

She needed to distance herself from the whole group because nothing good could come of being here. At some point, she'd fuck up, say the wrong thing, and that would be it. She'd be back out on her ass again. Or even worse, in a jail cell.

"We're coming in." Aldo reached for her hand.

She hesitated, something he noticed, given his frown, and that strange feeling of wanting to please him had her reaching out to take his hand before she could reconsider. She did a mental head-shake at how she kept doing the exact opposite of what was smart.

They walked up the front steps as Keeley opened the huge door, smiling widely.

"Come on in." She stepped aside so the three of them could walk in. The front foyer was wide and impressive, the first indication—since there was no sign outside yet—that this wasn't a house but an inn. They'd put in a long counter that would serve as their front desk, though it looked more like the kind of bar you'd find in a pub rather than the utilitarian-style found in hotels. It was dark oak and ornate rather than pressed wood and laminate.

"What do you think?" Keeley asked.

"It's incredible," Hazel said. "I'm blown away."

Keeley gave an excited squeal, then linked her arm through Hazel's like they were new best friends, guiding her around the main floor, while Aldo and Kayden followed. She showed Hazel the kitchen—blowing her mind when Keeley told her to help herself to anything—the dining room, the main living room space that was serving now as a social area for guests, and the "business center," which Keeley confided used to be Rafe's office.

Then they all headed up the wide staircase, stopping at the first landing.

Keeley pointed down one long hallway. "Gio, Rafe, and I live in the left wing on the second floor, and your room is in the right wing. It's perfect because you'll have your privacy, but you won't be too far away if you need to find us for something."

"This is all too kind." Hazel was overwhelmed by the sheer generosity of what Keeley was offering. "You really do need to let me...pay you."

Hazel had a credit card. She'd only used it once at Crossings. She'd applied for it as an emergency backup plan because there had been a few times in the past when she'd worried about being able to keep the heat on in their apartment. She'd bitten the bullet and gotten the card to use as a last resort.

If Keeley agreed to take her money, Hazel would use it to pay her. It was the only way she could afford to. Then she'd have to figure out how to pay that bill later. She was suddenly becoming an expert at robbing Peter to pay Paul, making all of today's problems tomorrow's issue.

"You're not giving me a penny. I'm glad to have you here. I'm always outnumbered in this house, but with you staying here, and Gianna working during the day, the guys are now the minority."

"Shit."

Hazel turned around, realizing Gio and Rafe, who were just joining them, had overheard.

"We didn't consider that, did we, Gio?" Rafe asked.

Gio grinned. "That's okay. Just means Aldo and Kayden need to start spending more time here. To shift the tide back in our direction."

"Sounds like a plan," Aldo said.

"Okay," Keeley said, as she started toward her own bedroom. "Aldo, Kay, you guys have gotten the grand tour of this place enough to know the lay of the land. Take Hazel to room three, while I pop over to my room to grab her a pair of pajamas. Rafe, do you mind running back down and grabbing one of those complimentary toothbrush/toothpaste bags we put together for guests who forget theirs? I neglected to get it while we were down there."

"No problem." Rafe headed down the stairs, Gio following him, to grab some bottled water for her as well.

Kayden gestured down the hall, opposite from the direction Keeley went. "Come on. We'll show you the room."

The door to room three was unlocked, so Aldo opened it, the three of them stepping inside.

Hazel stood speechless for a few minutes, trying to take it all in.

Kayden talked as he guided her through the small sitting area to the larger bedroom with en suite bathroom. "They combined several of the bedrooms on this floor to create a bank of luxury suites. The third floor has the more traditional hotel rooms—just a bedroom and bathroom."

They'd given her a suite. God, she could fit most of her apartment back home in this room.

"It's too much," she said again, mostly to herself.

"You keep saying that," Aldo countered. "It's just a room in a house that's not currently being used. Keeley, Gio, and Rafe are happy to let you stay here."

"It's just...no one has ever..." Hazel shut up fast. She was saying too much, revealing too much. Between driving through the night, the fire, the beer, and the honest-to-God feeling of being overly full—something she wasn't used to—she was forgetting to shield her words.

Keeley returned before Aldo and Kayden could question her, handing her the pajamas as well as the toothbrush and toothpaste. "There's soap, shampoo, conditioner, and all that jazz in the bathroom if you want to take a shower. I think I'm going to call it a night, unless you need anything else, Hazel."

She shook her head. "I don't. This is all perfect. I can't thank you enough, Keeley."

Keeley waved her thanks away as if it was unnecessary, then she lifted on tiptoe to kiss Kayden on the cheek. "Good night. Gio and Rafe—the night owls—are downstairs, watching TV. They'll lock up after you guys leave."

"Night, sis."

Keeley left, and once again she was alone with Kayden and Aldo. It occurred to her belatedly that the three of them were standing in a bedroom.

"You sure you're okay?" Aldo asked.

She nodded. "I'm good. Really good. I...thank you. For dinner and this." She lifted her arms. "For everything."

"We'll come back tomorrow and check on you," Kayden said.

As nice as that sounded, Hazel knew it was time to end things before she said or did something stupid. "No. That's okay. I can figure things out from here."

Kayden didn't accept that response. "I'm sure you can, but that's not why we're coming back."

"Then why?"

"Because we want to see you again," Kayden replied.

"Why?" she repeated.

Aldo laughed. "You ask more questions than a toddler."

She waited for him to elaborate, or to at least answer her, but he didn't.

Before she could push the issue, Kayden stepped closer, leaned forward, and gave her a soft kiss, right on the lips. She might have been able to convince herself it was just a friendly buss if he hadn't lingered a few seconds too long.

And she didn't have a chance to recover after he pulled away because Aldo was there, giving her the same gentle, too-long-for-friends kiss.

"Good night, Hazel," Aldo said when they parted.

"Good night," she echoed, her head spinning.

"We'll see you tomorrow." Kayden made it clear the subject was not open for discussion, in that voice that was to blame for the reason she'd spent the entire evening sitting in damp panties.

"Sweet dreams," Aldo said, as the two of them left, shutting the door behind them.

Yeah. There wasn't going to be a damn thing sweet about her dirty, dirty dreams.

She couldn't wait to fall asleep.

Chapter Eight

Aldo was whistling as he walked up the sidewalk to Kayden's front door.

Freaking whistling.

He'd woken up with a huge smile on his face. And a huge something else, which he'd taken care of in the shower, the image of Hazel's flushed cheeks as he and Kayden kissed her good night, helping to bring him to completion in record time.

Kayden must have seen him coming because he was standing in the open doorway, rolling his eyes as he spotted Aldo's shit-eating grin.

Not that Kayden had a leg to stand on. The guy looked almost giddy, which was a far cry from his typical too-serious expression.

Aldo walked right up to him, cupped his face in his hands, and gave him a big kiss on the mouth. He'd intended for it to be a quick one, more hello and happiness than sexual, but when Kayden gripped his hips and smashed their crotches together, it took on a life of its own for a minute or two.

"Sleep well?" Kayden asked when they separated, stepping aside as Aldo walked into the house, the two making their way to the kitchen and the coffeepot. Aldo had spent as much time in

Kayden's house as he had in his apartment over the past decade. Aldo had a key, clothes in the closet, beer in the fridge, and toiletries in the bathroom.

"Like a baby." Aldo grabbed a mug from the cabinet. Kayden already had a cup poured, so he took a seat at the small kitchen table. Aldo added some cream to his coffee, then joined him.

"What's today's plan?" Kayden asked, as Aldo sat down, kicking back in the chair, his legs stretched out in front of him, crossed at the ankles.

They both had the day off. Thank God. Because there was no way in hell Aldo would have been able to concentrate on his job today. He was too anxious to get back to Hazel.

"Thought we were heading over to the inn to check on our girl."

Kayden shook his head. "Our girl, huh? You think she would agree with that assessment?"

Aldo took a sip of his coffee. "Probably not, but that doesn't change the facts. Regardless, we should come up with a game plan."

Kayden ran a hand through his hair, a sign he had something heavy on his mind.

Aldo wasn't surprised by Kayden's hesitance. His best friend was the kind of guy who thought before he acted. And then he thought twelve times more.

"So we're going straight to game plan? Doesn't this feel like something we should have a conversation about?"

Aldo leaned forward, placing his elbows on the table. "We've spent years looking for what we want, Kay. We've discussed our hopes and dreams for the future a thousand times, and we know we both want the same damn thing. We've put the effort into making those dreams come true by doing a fuck-ton of dating and fuck-ton of fucking. I know the type of woman you're attracted to as well as I know my own. Do you really think we need to discuss whether or not Hazel is someone we want to pursue?"

Kayden sighed, then shook his head. "No. We don't need to

talk about that part. Because you're right. We know what we want. But that's not what I'm concerned about."

Aldo frowned, confused. "What then?"

"We've been two sides of this triangle, looking for the third for more years than I can count. We've seen relationships like the one we want up close and personal, by watching my sister with her guys, Layla with hers. None of this feels strange to us. In fact, we view it as pretty normal."

Aldo understood that, but he didn't see it as some major roadblock because he'd been watching Hazel closely last night, when Keeley, Gio, and Rafe introduced themselves as partners.

"I don't think that will be a problem for her," Aldo said. "Last night, when she forgot to keep her guard up, she let herself flirt... with *both* of us. And she liked those good-night kisses. The problem is..."

"She rarely lets her guard down," Kayden finished.

"Yeah. There is that little issue," he said sarcastically, because there was nothing little about it.

Kayden scowled. "Someone hit her."

"I know." Aldo toyed with the rim of his mug. Kayden had run more than his fair share of domestic calls over the years, and the ones where he'd discovered serious abuse had always hit him hardest. "And hopefully, in time, she'll trust us enough to talk about that."

"Trust." Kayden's mutter made it clear that wouldn't be an easy thing to gain from her.

But Aldo refused to be dissuaded. "This is *right*, man. I feel it all the way to my bones. There's just something about her."

"I'm not denying that, but I think until she gets to know us better, we can't go in there guns blazing, tossing her over our shoulder, carrying her off to our lair, and then asking her to offload all her problems on us. You only have to look at the woman to know she's got serious trust issues."

Aldo glanced out the kitchen window, considering that. "You think she'll reject us?"

"I don't know *how* she'll react. She's obviously been through some shit."

Sometimes Aldo appreciated Kayden's ability to be the voice of reason. But today, he was pissing on Aldo's parade. "So we show her she can trust us, that we can help her. She agreed to put herself in our hands last night, to let us make the decisions."

Kayden hmphed. "Because she was fucking overwhelmed. God. I've never seen anyone so lost. It just about killed me. She'd lost all her shit in that fire. She had nowhere to go. She looked completely defeated. Like she was ready—"

"To pack it all in," Aldo interjected. "I saw the same thing."

"I'm pretty sure it was shock that prompted her agreement on letting us call the shots last night."

Aldo chuckled. "You think that's all it was? You forget how well I know you. I might not have been there when you got her to agree, but I suspect your alpha male reared his head, refusing to take no for an answer."

Kayden didn't bother to deny it. He could be an overbearing bastard when it came to protecting people he cared about. Aldo couldn't count the number of epic battles waged between Kayden and Keeley after their parents died. Kayden took "overprotective brother" to new heights. Aldo should invest in the *Find My Friends* app because Kayden was probably single-handedly keeping it afloat.

Now it appeared his best friend was ready to give Hazel that same level of protection—God help the woman.

"Yeah, well, however I talked her into it, the timeline ended at the end of the evening. Now she's had a good night's sleep and time on her own to think things through. I don't think we're going to find her as amenable to handing her problems over to us. She was beaten last night and almost out, but something tells me Hazel doesn't stay down for long."

Aldo ran a hand through his hair. "I get that. It's just...I'm pretty sure she's all alone, man. I watched her last night at dinner, the way she took all of it in. It was almost like she'd never experienced something as normal as a night out with friends."

"Money is obviously an issue too."

Aldo could see the wheels turning in his cop friend's mind. Could see Kayden putting all the clues together, trying to form a picture.

Kayden rubbed his jaw. "Whoever hit her did it recently. That's a new bruise on her cheek. So maybe that could be what prompted the move. She packed her stuff and drove through the night to Philly. Or maybe she's running from something else. When she first saw me…"

"She walked away, fast," Aldo said. "Some people are afraid of the police, you know that. You've experienced it firsthand. Besides, that fear subsided pretty quick."

"True. What do you think? Boyfriend?"

Aldo resisted the urge to growl. He didn't want to think of Hazel with *any* man, but definitely not with some abusive bastard. "She wasn't wearing a wedding ring, so that seems like a logical answer. Dammit."

"So the game plan is *no* game plan, Al. Today, we're going to go over there, offer to help her again, and get to know her. That's it."

Aldo scowled. "You really know how to bring the room down."

Kayden laughed, slapping him on the shoulder. "Slow and steady wins the race." Then Kayden's smile faded. "Do you think I came on too strong last night?"

Aldo chuckled. "Hell yeah."

His words were a joke because he didn't realize just how worried Kayden was. "Shit. You think I scared her?"

Aldo backtracked, shaking his head quickly and leaning forward, his kiss hitting Kayden's clean-shaven jaw. "Hell no. The truth is, I'm pretty sure Hazel found it hot. Even if she didn't want to."

Kayden grinned. "A man could get used to those pretty blushes of hers."

Aldo took a last long swig of his coffee, then stood up. "Come on. Let's go see *our* girl."

Kayden rolled his eyes, but he didn't deny it.

Progress.

Half an hour later, they were walking into the haunted mansion. Gianna was tapping away on the computer at the front counter.

"Hey, Gee," Aldo said as they stepped into the foyer. It didn't matter how many times he visited here, he never managed to get used to the sheer size of the mansion.

"Hello." Gianna waved. "You guys are up and out early."

Aldo hadn't considered that. It was only a little after nine, and they'd stayed out until nearly midnight. There was a chance Hazel wasn't even awake yet. Aldo wouldn't blame her for sleeping the entire morning away after the day she'd had.

He leaned on the check-in counter. "We've both got a rare day off together. Thought we'd stop by and see how Hazel is doing."

Gianna smiled. "She got an even earlier start than you two."

What the hell did that mean? Images of Hazel escaping in the wee hours of morning, disappearing forever, had Aldo on the verge of panicking.

"What do you mean?" Kayden asked.

"She was already awake and dressed when I got here this morning. It's my first day on the job, so I came in early. I might be a little excited. I'm hoping to make a good impression, which I'll admit is kind of silly, considering Keeley is one of my best friends," Gianna confessed.

"Did Hazel leave?" Aldo tried to keep Gianna on topic.

"What? Oh. No. She's still here."

Aldo started to breathe easier.

Then Gianna launched into a complete rundown of the morning. "Apparently, Gio left for a worksite at dawn. I swear I could never keep his early morning hours. When I got here,

Keeley and Rafe had just come downstairs. They got me set up before they left for work. They've moved most of the Baros Corporation business out of the mansion and over to their offices at Eclectic. Anyway, Hazel was waiting for *all* of us. She asked if there was a way to earn her keep, then she offered to put the rest of the inn's rooms together. Keeley told her she didn't have to, but Hazel insisted. Anyway, she's spent the last hour hanging shower curtains and making beds. It's a huge help. She is *so* freaking sweet."

Aldo wasn't surprised to discover Hazel working. She'd been uncomfortable accepting dinner from them last night, and she'd asked more than a few times if she could pay Keeley for the room, despite the fact he and Kayden were fairly sure she didn't have much money.

"That's nice of her," Kayden said. "Since she doesn't have a car at the moment, we were going to see if she wanted us to drive her around town to grab some clothes, makeup, stuff like that."

"I bet she'd like that." Gianna pointed above her head. "She's up on the third floor."

He and Kayden nodded their thanks, then started up the stairs. When they reached the third floor, it was easy to find Hazel. All they had to do was follow the humming.

Peering through an open door, Aldo caught sight of Hazel facing away from them, bent at the waist, tugging a fitted sheet onto the queen-sized mattress. She was wearing the same jeans as last night, but he wasn't complaining because the denim hugged her ass in all the best ways.

He let loose with a wolf whistle that had Hazel straightening and spinning toward the door.

She grinned when she saw them, then narrowed her eyes, pretending to be mad. "How long have you been ogling my ass?"

"Not long enough." Kayden elbowed him. "This jackass gave us away too quick."

She giggled, and like last night, the sound was too brief. It seemed like every time she caught herself laughing or smiling, she autocorrected, resuming her more serious demeanor. Aldo longed to make her really laugh. A loud, long belly laugh.

"What are you guys doing here?"

Kayden frowned. "We told you last night we'd be back."

"Yeah, but...I mean...I said you didn't have to." Hazel seemed to think she'd let them off some imaginary hook.

"Since you're sans car," Aldo explained, "we thought we'd drive you around the city, give you a tour, take you out for lunch. And then you can grab some new clothes, stuff like that. If you want, we can swing by the motel and check on your car. See if it survived."

Kayden had been right. Today's Hazel was a hell of a lot feistier than last night's version, more than prepared to dig her heels in on all their offers. "You guys don't have to drive me all over the place. I hopped on Gianna's computer for a few minutes this morning and there's a bus stop a few streets over. I can run all the errands on my own."

"You can," Kayden all but growled. "But you're not going to."

Hazel's eyes narrowed again, but this time, she wasn't amused. "I think I might have given you the wrong impression of me last night, Officer Gallo."

Aldo stepped forward, placing himself between the two. "Hazel, we'd really like to take you out today. Show off our city to you. Kayden and I are both Philadelphia born and raised. We enjoyed spending time with you last night, and we want to get to know you better."

Aldo preferred to catch his flies with honey.

Hazel stared at him for a moment, pointedly ignoring Kayden —who wasn't going to take that well.

"Please?" he added. "If you say no, I'm going to have to spend my day off with," he jerked his thumb toward Kayden, "this grumpy ass."

Her shoulders relaxed, then she looked around the room. "I told Keeley and Gianna I'd help them put the bedrooms together."

"The inn doesn't open for a few more months. There's no rush," Kayden said. "No one expects you to work here, Hazel."

"I know, but..." She sighed. "I really do need some clothes. I borrowed this shirt from your sister, but the pants she loaned me didn't quite fit. Too long."

Keeley probably had a good three or four inches on Hazel, who resided in the petite range.

Aldo stepped closer, slipping his arm around her shoulder, trying to guide her toward the door. "Keeley's got the Gallo height genes. Why don't we go down and grab that coat I loaned you, and we'll head out?"

Hazel glanced around the room again, no doubt looking for another excuse not to go with them. He was relieved when she came up empty and let him lead her into the hallway.

"Okay. I need a phone charger too," she said, as if she was making a mental list. "My phone is dead."

"We'll be sure to pick one up." Kayden fell into step behind them as they walked down the stairs.

"If the car is still there and functioning...how much do you think the replacement key will cost?" she asked. "Because that might have to wait until after I find a job."

"I don't think it will cost much." Aldo didn't have a clue if that was true or not. He considered offering to loan her the money, but he had a pretty good feeling Hazel would turn him down flat.

They stopped outside the room Keeley had given Hazel last night, he and Kayden waiting in the hallway while she grabbed her coat and wallet.

Aldo helped her slip it on. They walked down the final flight of stairs, said goodbye to Gianna, then climbed into his truck.

"Where to first?" Aldo asked as he started the vehicle. He didn't put it in drive, waiting for her reply. "Tour then shopping, or shopping then tour?"

Hazel grinned. "Surprise me.

"Tour it is." Aldo started to put the car in drive, but Kayden's next question had him pausing.

"So what made you choose Philadelphia?" he asked as he leaned forward.

Hazel had admitted last night at dinner that she'd never been to Philadelphia before.

"Well, I, um..." She glanced out the side window, and Aldo knew before she spoke, whatever she said next would be a lie. She never looked them in the eye when she told a lie.

Kayden seemed to recognize that as well, because he spoke before she could. "Don't lie, Hazel. You're shit at it."

She turned her head, glaring at him over her shoulder. The confidence that had been on shaky ground last night had rallied today. "Excuse me?"

Aldo jumped in because Kayden had all the grace of a caveman around this woman, which was telling, considering his best friend was usually mild-mannered. "We said we wanted to get to know you better. You're new in town and on your own. We figured you might like to make some friends to help ease your way."

Hazel blinked a couple of times. "Oh. Um...that would...be nice. But..."

But?

How the hell could she say no to that offer? He recalled her reaction to all of them last night at dinner, and once again, he was struck by the feeling Hazel didn't have a lot of friends.

"But you're not comfortable sharing yourself with people you've just met," Kayden answered for her.

Thank God Mr. Mild-Mannered decided to make an appearance.

Hazel nodded. "I...I've been burned in the past...by people I trusted."

While still vague, Aldo considered the response progress, and he was about to let her off the hook.

However, Kayden got there first with a much better proposition. "So, we'll give you a choice. Every time we ask you something about yourself, you can either answer or—"

"Or I can just get better at lying," she interrupted. The spitfire looked more than ready to make the effort. Quiet, sweet Hazel last night had turned his head, but this feisty smart-ass got his motor running.

Kayden shook his head. "No lying. If you don't answer, you pay a penalty."

Aldo closed his eyes, certain Kayden had overstepped and Hazel would get out of the truck. When he didn't hear the slamming of the door, he chanced a glance at her, his cock growing thick at what he saw.

Hazel wasn't scared. She was intrigued.

"Penalty?"

Kayden leaned back, resting his arm along the seat, looking way too at ease. "For every time you fail to answer, you have to give whichever one of us asked the question a kiss."

Hazel shook her head, but it wasn't a refusal. It was amusement. The twinkle in her eyes told him just how much she liked this game. "Are you that hard up for kisses, Officer Gallo?"

He chuckled at her taunt but didn't take the bait. "Is it a deal?"

Hazel studied his face a few moments longer before turning to Aldo. "What do you think?"

Aldo grinned. "I think I'm composing a list of questions to ask. I've got about fifty lined up and ready to roll."

Hazel giggled, covering her mouth with her hand as if to block the sound.

Kayden, still relaxed, chimed in from the back. "Just go ahead and agree to the terms, Miss Walsh, since we know you're going to say yes. Then we can start our tour."

She tapped her chin playfully, but Aldo could see Kayden was right. Hazel was in.

"Fine. I agree."

Kayden nodded his head toward Aldo, just once. "I'll concede my first kiss to Al, since he's sitting next to you."

"What first kiss?" Hazel asked.

Kayden never missed a beat. "I asked why you moved to Philly. You didn't answer."

She looked like she wanted to argue the point, simply because Aldo got the feeling Hazel wasn't the type to give in easily. However, her libido caught up quickly because the look she gave him was pure sin. "Okay."

She leaned toward him, and Aldo, anxious to claim his treat, closed the distance.

At the last second, Hazel gave him a quick peck on the cheek, looking too pleased at having bested them.

Aldo shook his head and wrapped one hand around the back of her neck. "Do it right or answer the question."

Then he realized Kayden wasn't the only caveman in the truck when he didn't wait for her to move, just shifted to claim. Last night's kiss had been a gentle, impromptu one. This time, he knew exactly what he wanted. He pressed his lips more firmly against hers, loving the way she kissed him back, her hand resting on his shoulder. She wasn't resisting, wasn't fighting.

When her mouth opened, her tongue slipping out to stroke his lower lip, he knew he'd died and gone to heaven. He repeated her touch, taking a quick taste of her before pulling away.

Hazel's eyelids rose slowly as she blinked, trying to refocus.

"Now that's more like it, Fireball," Aldo whispered.

The second her wits returned, she slid away, her back leaning against the door as she looked from Aldo to Kayden.

"Doing okay?" Kayden asked with a shit-eating grin.

She nodded, her eyes narrowed. Then she turned back toward the front and fastened her seat belt.

Aldo heard her mutter, "I'm going to have to get better at lying," aware she'd purposely spoken too softly for Kayden to hear. Which told Aldo she'd assigned them good cop, bad cop roles. He felt the need to disabuse her of that misinformation right now. Kayden might come on stronger, but if this thing between the three of them ended where he hoped, she needed to understand she would be dealing with two demanding males.

He reached over, grasped her hand, and kissed her knuckles. "You can try to get better at it, Hazel, but you won't like the consequences if you do."

A quick glance in the rearview mirror proved him right. Kayden hadn't heard. Though from his smirk, Aldo had given enough context clues for his best friend to figure it out.

Hazel Walsh might be locked up tighter than a bank vault, but she was starting to thaw, starting to show them shades of an amazing woman.

Besides, he loved a challenge, loved that she was going to make them work to earn her trust and her secrets.

Nothing worth having comes easy.

Nonno had said those words to him a million times when he was growing up, and something told him Hazel was going to be worth *all* the work.

Aldo took them to the city center, lucking into a parking spot on the street. They walked around for nearly three hours, showing Hazel the historic downtown, touring Independence Hall, and snapping photos in front of the Liberty Bell and the Rocky Statue. She fell into her role of tourist with great enthusiasm, genuinely enjoying the sights and asking a ton of questions. Aldo, who'd done it all before, had expected to be bored, but seeing it all through Hazel's eyes made him appreciate things he'd taken for granted for years.

It was nearly one in the afternoon when Aldo suggested they hit Terminal Market for lunch. There were countless stalls, serving everything from seafood to donuts. He figured they could pick whatever they wanted, then eat together at the tables set up near the back.

Hazel roamed up and down every aisle twice, unable to decide. "I want it all."

"So let's get it all," Aldo suggested. "We can get one of everything that looks good and split it three ways."

They hit six different stands, ordering DiNic's famous roast pork sandwich, a roast duck platter, a whoopie pie, a soft pretzel, a sweet potato pie, and a huge slice of pepperoni pizza.

Hazel shook her head as they carried their feast to an empty table. "You guys are insane. This is too much food."

After so much walking, it felt good to simply sit and relax as they sampled everything. Hazel treated them to at least four of those sexy food moans that sent Aldo's mind straight to the gutter. The woman was clueless about how hot she was. The more time they'd spent together, the more at ease Hazel had become. She was an avid listener, genuinely interested in learning more about them. She asked questions about their families, their jobs, and how they'd become friends. They'd both answered her without hesitation, telling her whatever she wanted to know. Aldo was sort of hoping she would follow their lead, but no luck so far.

And while Aldo still hadn't gotten that big belly laugh from her yet, he'd managed to pry at least a dozen giggles out of her.

She was very animated as she talked about her favorite parts of the tour, which prompted Aldo and Kayden to begin sharing stories about the countless field trips they'd taken when they were in school, proclaiming they'd probably seen the Liberty Bell no less than two hundred times in their lives.

"You ever go on any field trips?" Kayden asked.

"Oh, hell yeah. And believe me, the Liberty Bell is a heck of a lot better than traipsing around—" Hazel stopped short, blinking a couple times. "Uh, a bunch of boring museums."

Aldo and Kayden exchanged a quick glance, aware that wasn't what she'd intended to say, especially when she looked away. Aldo caught the quickest glimpse of a wince...like she'd stopped herself from saying something she didn't want to reveal.

And just like that, an invisible wall popped up, Hazel's guard firmly back in place.

Two steps forward, ten steps back.

Chapter Nine

"Hazel." Kayden was ready to call her on her lie.

"Are you guys finished?" She stood up to clear their empty paper plates and trash. "If so, I'll go pitch all of this."

He had to hand it to her. She was a master when it came to distraction.

"Here," Aldo said, rising as well. "I'll help."

The two of them cleaned off the table while Kayden tried to beat back his frustration.

Rome wasn't built in a day.

Then he gave himself a mental kick in the ass because it hadn't even *been* a day.

"Should we hit a couple of clothing stores?" Aldo asked, as the two of them returned to the table.

Kayden helped Hazel put Aldo's oversized coat back on as they left the market. While it was a chilly day, it wasn't the typical frigid coldness that usually lingered in February.

"Sure." The smile Hazel had worn throughout lunch was gone now. "I still need to get a phone charger and some toiletries too. But I vote we skip checking on the car. I'll do that another day on my own. I'd like to head back to the inn. I'm kind of tired, so I might rest for a little while before tackling a few more rooms."

Hazel had admitted while they were standing in front of the Rocky statue that she was going to start the job hunt tomorrow so that she could stop "imposing" on Keeley, Gio, and Rafe. Kayden had tried to convince her she could remain at the inn for as long as she needed, but Hazel insisted she wouldn't stay beyond a week, less if possible. He suspected if she had the money, she would leave now. By offering to work around the inn, she'd managed to assuage her guilt enough to stay a few days longer.

Kayden reached for her hand. "So I assume you'll be looking for nursing jobs? There are several hospitals in the city, and it seems like there's always a nursing shortage."

"I was actually thinking I might look for a waitressing job," she confessed.

"Waitressing?" Aldo said, surprised.

Hazel flushed, a sure sign this was yet another topic she wasn't comfortable with. However, this time, instead of avoiding the subject, she explained her reasoning. "I can make money faster in a restaurant. Tips are instant. Paychecks take time." Though she was looking away as she responded, Kayden knew this was the truth. Finally.

And it proved she was just as broke as he and Aldo had suspected. He hated to think about how she'd been staying at Crossings Motel with so little money. The idea of her struggling to make ends meet all on her own didn't sit easy with him.

Kayden didn't fool himself into thinking there weren't countless women like Hazel all over the city. Rhys and Tony's girlfriend, Jess, had been in the same dire straits when they'd met her, the single mom sleeping in her car in the dead of winter. He wondered if Hazel would have had to resort to the same if the money had run out before she was able to find a job.

While he hated her reasons for the career change, he couldn't help smiling because at least she'd given them some morsel of truth. When Kayden looked back on the morning, he realized exactly how little she'd shared about herself.

Actually, little was too big a descriptor. She'd shared nothing, except the museum field trip lie and now the waitressing job hunt. They'd hoped to spend the day getting to know Hazel, and while her personality had shone through, they hadn't managed to learn anything about her past.

He hadn't thought to be annoyed about that until now because they'd initiated the kissing game. Kayden had considered it a stroke of genius when he'd suggested it because it was a playful way to explore the attraction the three of them shared. If Hazel had balked at the idea, he would have backed off, but she'd given them too many signals that they weren't the only ones feeling this pull.

He'd suggested to Aldo that they go slow and steady in their attempts to encourage Hazel to open up to them. But that patient approach was nowhere to be seen when it came to their flirting. He and Aldo had each claimed a dozen lingering kisses—that'd gotten hotter each time—for unanswered questions, with Hazel initiating the last few...always with a seductive smile.

In addition to the kisses, they'd taken turns holding her hand or wrapping their arms around her shoulders or placing their hand on the small of her back. Twice, Kayden had wrapped her up in his arms under the guise of warming her up when she'd complained about the cold, and he loved the way she sank into the embrace liked she'd never been hugged before. Aldo tickled her every time she made a smart-ass comment—the woman had a serious cutting wit—and they'd both run their hands through her vibrant red hair countless times, pushing it back whenever the wind blew it in her face.

He'd spent the better part of the morning trying to ward off a hard-on, and the best part was, as the day continued, the physical distance between them had all but vanished.

Unfortunately, there was still that Grand Canyon-sized chasm between them on a personal level. Now he felt like a jackass for the kiss option because she'd held him to it. It had been a miscalculation on his part, one he needed to find a way out of. Because while he loved kissing her, drawing each embrace out longer and longer, he'd trade them completely for a few damn answers.

He wanted to know more about Hazel.

Fuck that.

He wanted to know *everything* about her. Where she came from, who her family was, why she was moving to Philadelphia on her own...and who the hell had put that bruise on her cheek.

They browsed their way through a couple of clothing shops, but so far, Hazel hadn't found anything she liked. Or so she said. Of course, she checked the price tags every time she thought they weren't looking.

Something had to give.

"These are nice," Aldo said, pulling a pair of black pants off the rack. "Aren't they your size?"

She nodded but didn't reach out to take them to try on, instead glancing toward the front of the store, as if ready to leave. "I, um, I'm not really a fan of—"

Kayden cut her off. "What did I say about lying, Hazel?"

Pride be damned. She needed clothes.

Hazel took exception to Kayden's tone because her gaze found his and held. "I'm not lying."

Kayden studied her face, then ran the back of his finger along her cheek—the unbruised one. "Let's stop skirting around the issue. You don't have money to blow on a bunch of new clothes. I know you don't want to admit that, so we won't make you. But the fact remains, you can't wear that same pair of jeans every day. So try on the damn pants. If they fit, I'm buying them for you."

Hazel shook her head, forcing Kayden to add, "And you can pay me back later." He didn't want to be paid back, but he suspected that was the only way to convince Hazel to buy anything.

"I..." She hesitated, rubbing her forehead.

Kayden had been patient all day, handling her with kid gloves, toning down his natural instincts around her, as well as his desire to lighten that heavy load she carried on her slim shoulders twenty-four seven.

Then he recalled last night how exhausted she'd been, how overwhelmed. She might not be as tired today, but that didn't mean she wasn't still stretched so thin she was in danger of tearing in half. Her problems hadn't vanished overnight.

She had responded to their control, and Kayden had gotten the sense she was grateful for it, for the opportunity to let someone else call the shots for a few hours.

He glanced in Aldo's direction, aware his best friend would read him the riot act if he overplayed his hand and drove her away, but he felt like he had to try.

Hazel needed help and Kayden intended to give it to her.

"Fireball, you can go try the pants on in the dressing room by yourself, or I'd be happy to give you a hand. Either way, we're not leaving the store without clothes."

Hazel blinked several times, and while she was stronger today, she still responded to *that* tone in a way that sent too much blood to Kayden's dick.

"You wouldn't dare," she whispered, though she clearly wasn't sure.

Kayden bent until his face was just an inch or two from Hazel's. "Try me and find out."

Hazel's cheeks flushed a brighter red, and for a split second, he could see her considering her options.

Jesus. She wanted to test him, and he found himself hoping she would.

Sadly, common sense won the day as she thrust her hand out to Aldo. "Give me the pants."

He handed them to her, and she started to walk away, but Aldo captured her hand, holding her still. "Hang on. If we get to buy you clothes, I want you to try these on too." Aldo grabbed a pretty green blouse from the rack that would match her eyes perfectly, and a pair of skintight jeans Kayden couldn't wait to see her in.

"That wasn't…" She sighed, but Kayden noticed her shoulders seemed less tense, her posture less stiff. It was working. "I give up."

But then, because she would never go down without a fight, she pointed her finger at both of them. "I am paying you back for these."

Kayden crossed his arms but didn't agree. He noticed Aldo didn't either.

She made her way to the dressing room.

Once she was out of earshot, Aldo turned to him, and he knew what was coming. "Don't say it," Kayden warned.

"Dude, you're gonna have to dial back that alpha shit. It's starting to work on *me*."

That wasn't what Kayden had expected, mainly because Aldo was as dominant as he was, though he muted his baser instincts with humor.

Kayden laughed loudly, Aldo joining in, and the sound prompted Hazel to peek her head out the dressing room door.

"Everything okay?" she asked, clearly amused by them.

Kayden walked back to the dressing room. "How do the clothes look?"

Hazel's body was shielded behind the door. "The pants are okay, but the shirt…it doesn't look good. I'm just going to—" She started to close the door, but Kayden threw his hand out, holding it open.

"Let us see."

Kayden already knew what her problem was with the shirt, and it had nothing to do with looking bad. He'd been tempted to kiss Aldo when he pulled it off the rack. The blouse was silky and soft and low-cut.

"No. I—"

"Hazel." Kayden said nothing more. Just her name.

She blinked a couple of times, her brow furrowed. Then she stopped trying to close the door, allowing him to swing it open.

"Jesus." Aldo stepped next to him. "I'm buying you that shirt."

Hazel was tugging at the neckline uncomfortably. "Are you sure it's decent?"

Kayden reached for her hand, pulling her out of the dressing room so they could get a better look, swatting her other hand away from the neck. "Stop messing with it."

"I don't usually...I mean, in my last job, I dressed a lot more conservatively."

Another tidbit, but Hazel was self-conscious enough she didn't realize what she'd said. Kayden was curious about the comment because he would have expected a nurse in a nursing home to wear scrubs. He didn't question her though, because that was a surefire way to get her to shut up again.

"It looks great," Aldo reassured her.

"Oh." She looked down at herself. "Okay then."

"Which places your count at three," Kayden said.

Hazel tilted her head, confused. "Count?"

Kayden looked at Aldo. "Three lies so far, right? Last night at dinner, she said she wasn't hungry when she was. Today at lunch, she lied about her field trips. And just now, when you said that blouse didn't look good on you. Because you look fucking *awesome*."

Aldo nodded, crossing his arms. "To be fair, Kay, those are the only three we've *caught* her in."

Hazel looked back and forth between them, and he saw that same interest from last night and this morning in the car when he proposed the kissing game.

The problem was, she had issues with trust, which meant she'd most likely never explored the submissive side she kept giving them peeks of. "Is there a reason you're keeping count?"

"We never established consequences last night," Kayden pointed out. Now, like then, Hazel flushed, her eyelids heavier, and it was obvious that word provoked a definite picture in her mind. A sexy one.

"Damn. There's that look again," Aldo murmured.

Hazel tilted her head. "What look?"

Kayden leaned closer, lowered his voice. "Tell us the first thing that comes to your mind when we talk about consequences."

He expected her to balk at his request, so he was blown away when she didn't hesitate.

"A spanking." Then her eyes widened for a second as if appalled by her unshielded honesty, and she shook her head. "I'm mean...that's not...I shouldn't have said..."

Kayden raised his hand. "Stop."

She fell silent.

"Have you ever been spanked before?"

She nodded.

"Sexually?" he clarified.

Hazel shook her head, frowning. "I don't understand what's going on here. Why I respond to the two of you like this. We just met, for God's sake. None of this is *me*. I'm not this woman."

"Maybe you are." Aldo reached out, taking her hand in his. "Maybe this is exactly who you're meant to be."

"Maybe," Kayden added, "you haven't felt comfortable enough or trusted anyone enough to let *this* Hazel out."

She fell silent, and Kayden could see she was taking their words to heart.

"I've never felt safe," she whispered.

Kayden's heart cracked in the face of her admission, wishing he could wipe away the desolation that crept into her eyes forever. "What do you hope to find in Philadelphia, Hazel?"

She shook her head. "Not find. *Lose*. Me. I need to escape all of—" She stopped, and her eyes, which had been distant and distracted, focused on them. Kayden knew in an instant she'd slammed the vault door closed again.

"I'm going to change back into my clothes." She was trying to dismiss them, but Kayden wasn't letting her off the hook that easily.

"That's one non-answer and three lies," he said.

She stared at him, waiting for him to elaborate. Finally, she said, "I don't know what that means."

"It means we're going to finish shopping for everything you need, then we're going to drop you off at the inn. You can take tonight to think about something."

"What?"

"Us." He nodded. "The three of us are going out to dinner tomorrow tonight."

"I don't think—"

"We're going to dinner," he said, speaking over her refusal. "And then Aldo and I are going to help you escape."

Chapter Ten

Help you escape.

Those three words had replayed over and over so much, Hazel thought they must be tattooed on her brain by now.

Aldo and Kayden were going to help her escape.

How?

She might be relatively inexperienced, but she wasn't naïve. She had a pretty damn good idea of what they were thinking.

Because...consequences.

That was the other word that wouldn't leave her alone.

Consequences—a spanking.

Had she really said that out loud to them? She'd never had a conversation like that with anyone. Never even considered spankings or threesomes. Probably because both required a fuck-ton of trust and that wasn't something she had to give.

So...a threesome. That was what they were offering. There was no question that tonight was a date with two men. Two men who were more than willing to help her escape and who were keeping track of her lies and non-answers because...consequences.

Boston Hazel would have already run for the hills because what the actual fuck?

But Philadelphia Hazel? That bitch wasn't blinking an eye. Not only did it feel normal to her, it felt *right*.

So here she sat, on the edge of her bed, looking at the dress boots Liza had brought by on her lunch break, playing the words escape and consequences over and over and fucking over until her nipples were tight, her panties damp, and her pussy clenching.

Guess that technically meant she'd done what Kayden said and thought about it.

Keeley hadn't gone to the office today. Instead, she and Gianna had spent all morning working in Gianna's brand-new office on a marketing plan for the inn, while Hazel had worked on setting up a few more rooms.

After that, she'd spent the better part of an hour using one of the computers in the inn's business center, perusing the help wanted ads. She'd made a list of several restaurants hiring waitresses—Gianna and Keeley both offering suggestions on which ones would probably earn her better tips—and tomorrow's plan was to apply at all of them. With any luck, she'd have a job by the end of the week.

Hazel had tried to hide in her room last night after Aldo and Kayden dropped her off, her mind whirling over everything they'd said and done. The kissing game, the tour, the shopping, the way she couldn't stop responding to what would feel like over-the-top macho bullshit from any other man.

That wasn't what it felt like with them though. She was her own woman, independent as the day was long, yet she was overwhelmed by the desire to hand herself—her whole self—over to them, lock, stock, and barrel. Because she wasn't just tired, as she'd told Kayden; she was exhausted and shattered. Just fucking done.

They'd given her one night off from stressing out, buying her dinner and finding her a place to stay, and it had felt like freedom.

She wanted more.

Unfortunately, Keeley was as tenacious as her brother, so hiding in her room hadn't been an option last night. Keeley had come upstairs, inviting Hazel to join her, Gianna, Rafe, and Gio for dinner, and she hadn't taken no for an answer. Gianna had stuck around because she was missing Elio, who had returned to Baltimore to finish his final season, and she hated cooking for one.

They'd asked Hazel about her day, so she'd told them about the sightseeing and purchases and then—overcome with nerves and two glasses deep on wine—she mentioned the dinner date, asking them for advice on how to get out of it.

It wasn't that she didn't want to go. It was more that she knew she *shouldn't* go.

She'd done so well yesterday morning, managing to avoid answering any personal questions by evoking the kissing payment option.

God...that had been no hardship at all.

In the end, she kept wishing they'd ask her more personal questions because Aldo and Kayden's kisses knocked her socks off. By the time they'd arrived at Terminal Market, she was giving new meaning to the words hot and bothered.

Her vibrator—sadly—was still in her nightstand drawer back in Boston. It didn't typically see a lot of action, due to her working long hours, as she almost always chose sleep over self-care. But damn if she didn't wish she had it now.

She'd been nailing it on playing it cool as far as she was concerned. Right up until lunch. When she stumbled. It had been on the tip of her tongue to complain about her countless field trips around the Freedom Trail, which would have revealed her lie about never being to Boston before.

It had been a close call, so she'd attempted to shut down completely again, tried to give herself that same stupid pep talk about getting out while the getting was good.

It hadn't worked.

Because her attraction to them was off the charts. Aldo and Kayden were obviously interested in her, and the incredible part was that there was absolutely no competition between them.

They worked as a team, which was probably why this didn't feel the slightest bit strange to her.

She'd been determined to break the date until Keeley and Gianna got involved. She couldn't tell them the real reason she was trying to back out, and she couldn't claim she was uninterested because one, she was apparently a shit liar, and two, she couldn't say it would feel weird to date two guys—it wouldn't—because Keeley had been sitting right there with Rafe and Gio, and there was no way Hazel would insult their lifestyle choice after they'd been so kind.

So, she'd taken the old "I don't have a thing to wear" route, which had backfired spectacularly.

Gianna had made a call that resulted in today's lunch break powwow. Aldo's sister, Liza, and another woman Hazel hadn't met, Jess, had arrived shortly after one, armed with clothes, shoes, and makeup.

Any hope of getting out of the date was shot to hell as the four women excitedly rallied around her, encouraging her to try on clothes and shoes, the five of them launching into discussions on fashion, hairstyles, and shoe addictions.

Well, it was probably more accurate to say four women were discussing those things as Hazel sat on the sidelines, listening, half shell-shocked, half amazed. Hazel had girlfriends in school, but those friendships had never ventured out into the real world because she'd been working two part-time jobs from the time she was fourteen.

She'd actually started her *first* job when she was just twelve, which was illegal as hell, not that her mother cared. That was the year Mom decided Hazel needed to pull her weight.

Now, it was just after three in the afternoon, and she had a few more hours to kill before Aldo and Kayden arrived to pick her up. Liza had left ten minutes ago to return to work, Keeley and Gianna doing the same. Hazel assumed Jess left as well, until there was a soft knock at the door.

Walking out of the bedroom to the small sitting area, she said,

"Come in." She smiled when she saw Jess. "I thought you'd gone home."

Jess shook her head. "Nope. I took the rest of the afternoon off. Benefit of sleeping with your boss," she joked. "So..." Jess lifted a bottle of Chardonnay and two glasses. "I thought we could do a bit of day drinking. Just a glass or two. I figured it might take the edge off."

Hazel smiled because a glass of wine would go a long way toward calming the frogs currently jumping in her stomach. She hadn't had time to feel nervous when surrounded by all the women, but the second they'd left, the anxiety reappeared, and it had doubled down.

"Wine would be amazing."

Jess poured a glass, handing it to her before pouring one for herself.

"It's overwhelming, isn't it?" Jess asked.

"What is?"

She gestured toward the open door, where they could hear Keeley and Gianna laughing downstairs. "The Morettis, the Gallos, etcetera."

"It is. But not in a bad way," Hazel hastened to add, not wanting to insult Jess's friends.

"Not in a bad way." Jess claimed the overstuffed chair near the door as Hazel perched on the couch.

"I hope I'm not stepping over a line, but I feel like you and I have a lot in common."

"How so?" Hazel asked.

"I told you that I'm dating Aldo's cousin, Tony, and his roommate, Rhys."

Jess had dropped that bomb about five minutes after introductions.

"I'll admit, I've never met anyone living in a committed threesome, and now, in the course of a few days, I've met two coup... er...I'm sorry. I don't know what word to use."

Jess laughed. "Oh, you'd be surprised how many options there are. I've heard us described as a threesome, a triad, a throuple. Someone even called us a trinity once, although that sounds totally cloak and dagger/secret society to me."

Hazel grinned. Jess had also revealed that she was working for Moretti Brothers Restorations, the business Tony ran with his brothers, hence the sleeping-with-her-boss comment.

"I assume all of your families are okay with your relationship?" Hazel was curious what the older generation of Morettis thought of Gio and Tony's threesomes.

She couldn't begin to imagine what her mother would say if she found out Hazel was dating two men at the same time. Actually, she could. It would be a litany of words like slut, whore, tramp.

Funny. Because as Hazel looked at Jess and Keeley, the only word that sprang to her mind was lucky, and it was accompanied by honest-to-God jealousy.

"The families are fine. Of course, Tony's family had a head start. His sister, Layla, was the first Moretti to find not one but two partners. Then his cousin, Erin, followed suit."

"Wow."

"Right? Rhys's sister Penny was on board from the beginning, but it took his parents a bit of time to wrap their heads around it. Don't get me wrong. They're lovely and supportive, but it was still an adjustment for them."

"And your family?" Hazel asked.

"My mother and I are estranged. I never met my dad. The only family I have who matters is my son, Jasper, and he thinks Tony and Rhys hung the moon."

Jess had been correct in her assessment. It appeared they did have a lot in common, and she found herself offering a tiny nugget because she genuinely liked the woman. "I'm estranged from my parents too."

"I thought you might be. I traveled to Philadelphia with a girlfriend right after high school graduation. We were both on the run from shitty family situations. I sort of got the feeling..." Jess's eyes drifted to the bruise on Hazel's cheek, though she knew Jess couldn't see it.

Gianna had done her makeup after Hazel tried on a mountain of clothes, and while no one had mentioned it—or the smidgeon of a black eye—Hazel knew they'd all noticed.

"I came to Philadelphia looking for a fresh start too." It was as much as Hazel dared to say, so she took a sip of wine.

"Like I said, I know the Morettis and Gallos can be a lot to take, primarily because there are so many of them, but I want you to know that they're genuinely good people. You're safe here with them. It took me some time—too much time—to feel like I wasn't imposing, but the truth is, now that I know them, they really mean it when they say they want to help."

Hazel valued Jess's words. They helped alleviate some—but not all—of the guilt she felt over staying here for free.

Kayden had talked to her about gut feelings, and Hazel's gut was telling her this was a good place, that she could trust these people.

That didn't mean there still wasn't a little voice in her head warning her to get the hell out.

Of course, that wasn't because of them but because of *her*. Who she was. What she was running from.

"I appreciate you saying that," Hazel said.

Jess smiled. "I wish someone had said it to me. Because I wasted a lot of time trying to reject Tony and Rhys's help, certain I had to do everything on my own. My stubbornness and my pride put my son in some bad, even dangerous situations."

"I might know a thing or two about pride," Hazel admitted.

Jess gave her an understanding smile. "I know you're nervous about tonight's date."

"It's a date with two men." Though as she said it, she knew that wasn't really what was causing her anxiety.

"Don't knock it 'til you've tried it," Jess joked, and they both laughed. "Seriously, though, Kayden and Aldo are two of the good ones. They won't hurt you, Hazel."

Jess's gaze slid to her cheek again, only for a second, but long enough for Hazel to understand what she meant.

Hazel didn't reply. She couldn't.

Jess topped up her own glass, then held out the bottle to Hazel. "Bit more? I don't want to get you drunk, but you've still got a few hours to go until the guys get here, and wine and girl talk is as good a distraction as anything."

Hazel nodded, rising to offer her glass, grateful for Jess's company. "Sounds like exactly what I need."

"Great." Jess stood as well. "Now...where do you stand on being a bad influence?"

"What did you have in mind?"

"Let's go downstairs and see if we can convince Gianna and Keeley to play hooky with us as well."

Hazel took another sip of wine. "I may not know them well, but I have a feeling we won't have to do more than show them the bottle."

Jess laughed, the two of them walking toward the door. "One day in and you've already got our number. I think you're going to fit in just fine."

Fit in.

Hazel wasn't sure she'd ever heard two more wonderful words.

Actually, that wasn't true. She knew two better ones.

Escape.

Consequences.

* * *

Hazel paced the floor of her bedroom suite, wishing she'd consumed the rest of Jess's wine. She'd hung out with the women for an hour or so, none of them drinking more than a glass.

Actually, Gianna hadn't had any at all, proclaiming it was too early in her employment to start drinking on the job. Keely had told her it was fine, but Gianna held resolute.

The impromptu happy hour lasted until Keeley and Gianna insisted they had to get back to work. Jess had headed home, and Hazel had come back to her room to freshen up her makeup and get dressed for her date.

She glanced at the clock. They would be here in half an hour, and she'd worked herself up into one hell of a state.

She had no business staying here, but leaving—given her lack of funds, car, and job—wasn't really an option. Or at least not a smart one. She suspected there were plenty of cheap motels she could stay in, but without a job, she couldn't afford more than a few nights at best.

Then she forced herself to admit the real reason she was staying. After just two nights in this inn, sleeping in a soft bed, in a safe place, she was reluctant to return to the real world.

Because in her real world, she didn't get to just "help herself" to someone else's food, she wasn't given a shit-ton of clothes from virtual strangers, she didn't have two sexy men ask her out on dates, and she never—ever—felt totally safe.

Hazel jumped slightly when her phone rang. She'd gotten a charger yesterday while she was out with the guys, but she hadn't remembered to plug the phone in until just before the women had converged.

Glancing at the screen, she groaned when she saw it was her mom.

Aaaaaaand there was the real world, calling at the worst possible time. Because of course it was. This was why Hazel couldn't have nice things.

Picking up the cell, she answered, "Hello."

"Where the fuck are you, Hazel?"

Hazel *shouldn't* have answered. Because as much as she hated it, this was how every conversation went between her and Mom. Mom would snap at her for something, Hazel would push her buttons, and within minutes, it would devolve into her mother cussing her out, calling her every name in the book.

Unfortunately, she'd been stressed out about the police parked in front of their building since the night she left Boston and her curiosity had gotten the better of her. The problem was, she wasn't sure if it was better to *wonder* if they'd been there to arrest her, or to know for sure.

"I'm looking for a job." Hazel didn't bother to add that she wasn't looking for that job in Boston.

"It's about time. I'm out of cigarettes, and there's no fucking food in this house. Bring some home with you."

Hazel frowned. "I'm not coming home." She'd been gone three nights. Had her mom not even noticed?

"What's that supposed to mean? I need cigarettes, Hazel. And wine. Stop fucking around and get your ass home!"

"I'm not in Boston, Mom. I haven't been there since Saturday night."

"You haven't? Are you with Dennis?"

That question took her aback. "No. Of course not. Is he gone too?"

"Haven't seen him in days."

So she realized Dennis was gone but not her daughter. Lovely. The maternal instincts ran strong in her mom.

"Where are you?" Mom asked.

"Pennsylvania." It was a big state. Hazel decided that answer was enough information for her mom, considering she didn't even care enough to know she hadn't been home the last three nights.

"Jesus Christ. What is this? Some kind of temper tantrum because I yelled at you the other day? You're too old for that shit."

"It's not a tantrum. I'm just not coming home." The idea of returning to that apartment with or without the police looking for her was too depressing to consider. Especially as she looked around this gorgeous room that didn't stink of cigarette smoke, stale beer, and body odor.

"So that's it? You're just abandoning me? How the fuck am I supposed to pay the rent?"

It was on the tip of her tongue to tell her mom to get a job and hang on to it, but she didn't have the energy for the fight that would start. "If I get a job soon, I'll try to send you some money." Hazel wasn't sure that would be feasible. She needed to save enough money for a security deposit and first month's rent.

Then there was the issue of Mrs. Maloney's things. In addition to looking for a job online this morning, Hazel had looked up all the pawnshops within walking distance of her family's apartment, certain Dennis wouldn't do any more than the bare minimum in regard to hocking his stolen wares. She still had the list of missing items, and she was hoping—though it was a long-shot—that she could locate more of what had been stolen, buy it back, and have it delivered to the Maloneys anonymously. She owed it to them to try to recover whatever she could since it was her fault it was stolen in the first place.

"Mom, have the cops been by there?"

"Cops? No. Why? Jesus. What did you do?" Mom asked, her tone more resigned than pissed all of a sudden.

Hazel hadn't been in trouble a day in her life, but that meant nothing to Mom. Funny how she was pissed off about Hazel not coming home until she mentioned the police. Obviously, Mom figured it was just a matter of time before Hazel lived up to the Walsh name.

"No cops have come by the apartment?" Hazel repeated, wondering if her mother had been too drunk to hear them knocking on the door Saturday night. But even if she had been, wouldn't they have come back?

"I already said no, Hazel. What's this about?"

"Nothing." Hazel released an unsteady breath. She'd been looking over her shoulder for three days now. The idea that the police might not be looking for her...

Had she jumped the gun when she ran Saturday night? After all, cops in her neighborhood were not a rare occurrence. In truth, they were always freaking there.

"So you're sending money?"

Naturally, that was all her mother cared about. Hazel rubbed her forehead, the pressure that constantly pushed down on her chest growing even heavier. "I'll do my best."

"Do it soon," Mom demanded. Because why on earth would Hazel expect her to say thank you.

There was a knock at the door. "I have to go, Mom."

She didn't bother to wait for her mom to say goodbye. Mainly because she didn't. She was still demanding money when Hazel disconnected the call.

Hazel crossed the room and opened the door, surprised to see Rafe standing there. He was the one Hazel had spoken to the least, but she chalked that up to Keeley and Gio's huge personalities. It didn't seem like the man had much of an opportunity to get a word in edgewise.

"Sorry to bother you," Rafe began. "I know you're getting ready for your date with Kayden and Aldo."

"No bother at all. I've pretty much been ready for hours, thanks to Keeley and her friends."

Rafe grinned. "You made the rookie mistake of giving them a mission. There's nothing they love more than a project. And now that Penny's wedding is over, they've been floundering for something to do. Cleaning out their closets so they could replenish yours was the answer to a prayer."

She'd learned Sunday night at Divine that another of the girl-friends, Penny, had gotten married this past weekend. It sounded like a fairy-tale wedding, and Hazel would have loved to have been a fly on the wall, to see all the decorations, eat the incredible food, hear the music.

"I was grateful for their help. And the clothes." She'd borrowed a short black skirt from Jess that she paired with the green blouse Aldo had bought for her yesterday, and Liza's knee-high boots. She couldn't recall the last time she'd dressed up, and while she was nervous as hell, the outfit was helping boost her confidence a bit. At least she didn't look like her usual raggedy self in ancient, ripped jeans, a hoodie, and tennis shoes.

"You look very nice. You're going to turn Kayden and Aldo's heads for sure. Actually, scratch that. You already have."

She laughed softly.

Rafe leaned against the doorframe. "I was hoping I could discuss something with you for a moment."

Hazel's heart sank to her feet. He wanted her out. They'd offered her a room for a night, and like an asshole, she'd overstayed her welcome. "Of course. If it's about me staying here, Rafe, I can leave—"

Rafe raised his hand, cutting her off. "It has nothing to do with that. As we said, you're welcome to stay. We're months away from opening the inn, and Keeley and Gianna love having you here. Gianna says you've put her at least a week ahead of schedule in terms of setting up the rooms. Which you really didn't have to do."

"I was happy to," she reassured him. Because she really was.

"Well, we appreciate it. Keeley just told me that you're looking for a waitressing job."

She nodded.

"Not nursing?"

"No. I...well...I need a more immediate income. Tips seem like the best way to achieve that."

"They do. So how would you feel about waiting tables at Divine? You were there the other night, so you're familiar with the restaurant."

Hazel started to shake her head, thinking the offer was more charity. He, Gio, and Keeley had already been far too generous. "You don't have to—"

"I'm in a bind," he said, before she could refuse.

"What do you mean?"

"One of my waitresses is on maternity leave. She's not slated to come back for three more weeks. We've been making it work with the other waitstaff picking up extra hours. This afternoon, one of the waiters gave his notice. Friday will be his last day.

Covering one person was doable, covering two is out of the question."

So he wasn't offering just to be nice but because he genuinely needed a waitress. "Oh my God. I would be more than happy to help out. Let's face it, I owe you. I can work as long as you need me to."

Rafe smiled. "What do you say we do a trial run for a couple of weeks, and if it works out, the job is yours. It's fourteen dollars an hour, plus tips."

Hazel took her first easy breath since answering her mother's call. "That would be great."

"Think you could start Thursday? I know it's just two days away, but that would give you a chance to shadow the waiter you'd be replacing for a couple nights to get the hang of it."

"My schedule, as you know, is wide open. Thursday is great."

"I can't thank you enough. We're slammed on weekends and hiring someone on such short notice was going to be impossible."

"I should be thanking you, Rafe. For everything."

"You just took a load off my plate. And as far as the room goes... Hazel, seriously, no one plans to kick you out anytime soon. Take the time you need to save up for a deposit on a safe apartment to rent."

"Not sure safe is in the budget, but I'll take livable," she joked.

"Have you shared that plan with Kayden and Aldo?"

Hazel frowned, confused, until Rafe waved the comment off, though he murmured something that sounded like, "Good luck with that."

Before she could question him, they heard the front door open, and Kayden calling out "hello" to Keeley and Gianna, who were at the front desk.

"Sounds like your dates are here. Have a good time tonight."

"Thanks again, Rafe."

"I'll go let the guys know you'll be down in a minute." He gave her a friendly wink, then headed for the stairs.

Hazel walked back into her room to grab the clutch Keeley

loaned her, and her phone. She turned it off, in case her mother tried to call back again.

She wasn't about to let Mom ruin this night for her.

She walked to the mirror to take one last look at herself, struggling to recognize the woman staring back. Gianna was an artist when it came to makeup. Hazel couldn't see the bruise on her cheek or the black eye anymore, but the makeup was light enough that it felt natural. Except around her eyes. Because Gianna had lined her eyelids and used mascara in such a way that Hazel's eyes had never looked brighter or bigger.

She'd opted for leaving her hair down because four straight days of ponytails had left her with a sore scalp. Her hair was curly, so she'd basically washed and conditioned it, then let it dry naturally. Liza had oohed and ahhed over her ringlets so much that Hazel found herself feeling lucky about the curls for the first time in her life.

The dark circles beneath her eyes were also gone. It was amazing what sleeping in a comfortable bed in a quiet, safe house could do for a person.

But it was more than just the physical things that had Hazel looking harder at the reflection. She felt like she was looking at an entirely different person from the one who'd crashed in that run-down motel Sunday afternoon. She was more relaxed, more at ease.

It helped knowing that the police hadn't come by the apartment for her the previous night. Perhaps the Maloneys had been bluffing about calling them. Or maybe they'd been waiting, and now that they'd gotten some of their stuff back, they'd changed their minds.

Regardless, she didn't regret leaving Boston, even if she hadn't needed to. She didn't leave a damn thing back there that she would miss.

It was amazing the difference two days could make. And it had everything to do with Kayden and Aldo and their family and friends. She was suddenly surrounded by positive, kind people who weren't seeking to use her, but instead to help her.

So tonight, she was going to turn a corner, start over. She was going to leave the pathetic, lonely woman from Boston behind and embrace this new Hazel. The one with a job, the potential for real friends, a beautiful, safe room to sleep in, a date with two incredible men and—God willing—sex.

She smiled at her reflection as Philadelphia Hazel kicked Boston Hazel to the curb once and for all.

Chapter Eleven

Aldo's eyes widened when Hazel walked down the stairs, and Kayden's sudden intake of breath told him he wasn't the only one taken aback by how pretty she was. This was the first time they'd seen her with her hair down, and while it was as long as he'd guessed, it was still the color that blew his mind. Deep fiery-red curls flowed over her slim shoulders, and all he could think about was running his fingers through them.

"You look beautiful," he said the second Hazel joined them.

She blushed, smiling shyly. "Thank you."

Keeley stepped next to Hazel. "Doesn't she? That blouse is the bomb. I swear it matches your eyes perfectly."

Hazel, uncomfortable with—or perhaps unused to—praise, turned the spotlight away from herself. "You guys look great too."

They'd both eschewed their usual well-worn jeans and long-sleeved tees, opting instead for dress slacks and button-down shirts. Aldo's pants were navy, his shirt light blue. Kayden had gone a bit darker, with black slacks and a charcoal-gray shirt.

"Are you ready to go?" Kayden offered his hand.

Hazel nodded.

"Don't wait up, sis," he called out to Keeley.

"I expect you to be perfect gentlemen," she retorted. "No

shenanigans. And don't drink too much and don't stay out too late." She had her hands on her hips, rattling off her list for them with a shit-eating grin. "Behave yourselves, and remember, nothing good happens after midnight."

Aldo had witnessed many—MANY—years of Kayden standing at the door, telling his little sister the exact same things before she went out for the evening.

"We'll take good care of Hazel." Aldo wrapped his arm around her waist. "But I make no promises when it comes to behaving."

"Oh wait! I almost forgot." Keeley crossed the foyer to a coatrack and retrieved a black peacoat for Hazel. "It's freezing out there."

Aldo helped her slip it on as Hazel thanked Keeley, and then they walked out into the chilly February air to his truck. It was a clear, cloudless night, the full moon bright.

Kayden helped Hazel into the passenger seat, though she insisted again—to no avail—that it made more sense for her to sit in the back.

Once they were on their way, Aldo glanced over at her. "Hope you're hungry. We made reservations at Alpen Rose."

"Reservations?" she asked. "Sounds fancy."

"It *is* a little fancy," Kayden said, "but that's not why we picked it."

"Oh?" she asked, curious.

"You'll understand why when we get there," Kayden replied mysteriously.

She gave him a suspicious glance over her shoulder but let the subject drop.

"I was going to wait until the end of the date to tell you this, because I didn't want to ruin the night, but I think you should know," Aldo started.

"What is it?" she asked, alarmed.

"I drove by the motel this afternoon. There was only one car with a Massachusetts license plate. Yours, right?"

She nodded.

"It was one of the ones that caught fire. It's...well..."

"A complete loss," she finished for him.

Aldo grimaced. "I'm afraid so."

He'd anticipated her being upset, so he was surprised when she shrugged the news off. "I sort of figured it was gone. I mean, I couldn't see behind the fire trucks, but I knew where I parked it. It would have been a miracle if it had survived."

"Do you have insurance?" Kayden asked. "Maybe you'll get enough money back to replace it."

She shook her head. "My policy wasn't comprehensive. Basically, it was just a liability one that only covered me if I hurt someone else in an accident."

"Shit," he muttered.

"It's okay. Luckily, I moved to a city with great public transportation. Plus, now I don't have to worry about paying for gas or parking."

Aldo chuckled. "You're very good at finding silver linings."

"It's a game I started playing when I was little. When things started going bad, I tried to find something good amongst all the shit. It keeps things from getting too overwhelming."

Kayden reached forward and placed his hand on her shoulder. "I like that. Like your positivity. That's a rare ability these days, with so many people focusing just on the bad stuff."

She smiled at him.

"Common sense is another thing that's dying off." Aldo launched into a funny story about one of the younger firefighters, who used the oven like a grill, putting his burger on the metal rack without a baking sheet. "The idiot almost set the firehouse on fire."

Kayden was howling with laughter, while Hazel—sadly—didn't give him more than a giggle. What did he have to do to get a genuine laugh out of her?

"How about some music?" Aldo messed around with the radio until he found a good station, playing "Bang on the Drum

All Day," by Todd Rundgren, the three of them singing along, amused by the silly lyrics. Hazel seemed more relaxed tonight, her smiles coming easily.

Once they arrived at the restaurant, Aldo parked, then climbed out of the truck, joining her and Kayden. He wrapped his arm around her waist at the same time Kayden did.

Aldo playfully shoved Kayden's arm away, laughing. "My spot."

Hazel shook her head, amused. "Play nice, boys."

Kayden leaned toward her, his lips next to her ear as he said loud enough for Aldo to hear, "Being bad is a hell of a lot more fun."

When they entered the restaurant, Hazel stumbled a step or two before stopping completely.

"Hazel?" Aldo asked.

"This place is..."

She didn't finish her comment, but she didn't have to. Aldo and Kayden had chosen the place on purpose because ambiance was exactly what they were looking for. The intimate restaurant only seated forty people, and the dining room was enveloped in dark wood. The ornate chandeliers provided dim mood lighting, and as the maître d' guided them to their table, a circular booth tucked in the corner, it was easy for them to pretend they were the only three people in the place.

Hazel slid into the booth as Aldo and Kayden both claimed a side of her, the three of them forming a cozy half circle around the table.

The waiter was there in an instant, offering menus and pouring them each a glass of water before promising to return in a few minutes to take their drink orders.

Hazel had been laid-back in the truck, but the second they'd stepped inside the restaurant, her confidence seemed to wane, and she was uncomfortable again.

Kayden stopped her before she could open the menu.

"Do you not like the restaurant?" He'd obviously noticed the same reticence Aldo had.

"No. It's fine. It's not that. It's just...how expensive is this going to be?" she whispered.

Kayden sighed. "We wouldn't be here if we couldn't afford it. We wanted to take you out somewhere special for our first date."

"And I appreciate that, but honestly, you don't have to spend so much money. I'm just as happy with a pizza place, or maybe we could go for one of those cheesesteaks you keep raving about."

Aldo wrapped his arm around her shoulders. "Tell you what, why don't we hold those plans in reserve for dates two and three."

She rolled her eyes, and he felt the tension in her shoulders subside a little. "Dates two and three? Don't you want to wait to see how tonight goes?"

Aldo shook his head. "No need."

Before they could say more, the waiter returned. Kayden ordered a bottle of red wine for the table, and the man went to get it from the bar.

Hazel opened the menu and Aldo waited for her to launch into the next round of protests, especially when he heard her gasp.

Kayden didn't bother to open his menu. Instead, he watched Hazel. "Are you scanning it for the cheapest thing, like the other night at Divine?"

Hazel didn't respond, but the two spots of pink on her cheeks told Aldo that was exactly her plan.

"Okay." Kayden took the menu from her. "Where do you stand on seafood?"

Hazel pursed her lips and for a second, Aldo wasn't sure she'd reply.

"What kind of seafood?" she finally asked.

Kayden rattled off a list. "Shrimp? Crab? Lobster?"

"I've never had lobster. I'm not a fan of shrimp, but I've only had it deep-fried from a fast-food place, so that probably doesn't count. I'm not sure about crab." She paused, as if waging some sort of internal debate. "I guess you can tell I grew up poor, so I'm afraid I don't know how to answer your question."

Kayden accepted that answer. "Do you consider yourself a picky eater?"

Hazel shook her head. "Not at all."

"Can I order for you?" he asked.

She tilted her head, considering his request. "You wouldn't mind?"

Kayden smiled and gave her words back to her. "Not at all."

Aldo handed his menu over to Kayden without opening it. "Why don't you order for all of us? Pick out three different things and we can switch plates around if Hazel decides she doesn't like seafood."

"Is this going to become a habit?" Her smile was back in place. "Sharing meals?"

Kayden nodded. "Yeah. I think it is. I like sharing...with you."

Aldo noticed the slight pause and realized it wasn't intentional. Most likely, his best friend had nearly misspoken, had almost forgotten the word *with*.

The waiter returned with the wine, pouring them each a glass, then Kayden gave the man their orders.

Hazel picked up her wine and took a quick sniff.

"Not a wine drinker?" Aldo asked.

She shook her head. "I've never really liked it, but today, Jess and I had some Chardonnay and I loved it. Of course, the shit my mother drinks is like four dollars a bottle so...I...um..."

Aldo hated it when Hazel cut her stories off mid-stream.

"Try it," Kayden prodded, letting her off the hook. "See what you think."

Hazel took a sip, her eyes widening. "Oh wow. That's delicious." She took another drink, then looked at Kayden. "Do I want to know how much that bottle cost?"

Aldo tugged her closer, placing a soft kiss on the side of her head. "Stop worrying about money. Kayden and I are single guys with good-paying jobs. Let us spoil you for one night."

"Spoil," Hazel said to herself, her brow furrowed. Aldo got the feeling she was trying the word on for size. Like it was something new. "I do appreciate you bringing me here. You're going to have to let me return the favor and take you guys out one night soon. Now that I have a job, I can—"

"You have a job?" Aldo interjected.

"I forgot to tell you. Rafe hired me this afternoon to wait tables at Divine. He's two servers down, so he's giving me a shot."

Kayden lifted his glass, tapping it against hers. "Congratulations."

Now Aldo understood why Hazel seemed so much happier. He suspected having a job was a load off her mind.

"Thanks. I didn't expect to find something so quickly, and with the fire and no car...well, it will help having an income. Your sister and her guys are the absolute best, Kayden." Hazel was probably unaware that she'd just said the most perfect thing ever to the man. He adored his sister.

"They really are," Kayden agreed.

"And you were worried you were going to screw her up," Aldo teased.

"Screw her up?" Hazel asked.

"Kayden's parents were killed in a plane crash when he was twenty-six," Aldo explained.

Hazel reached out and took Kayden's hand in hers. "I'm so sorry. That's awful."

"Yeah. It is. Nothing really prepares you for something like that." Kayden kept hold on Hazel's hand, stroking his thumb over her palm. "Keeley was sixteen, so I moved back into my parents' house to take care of her. It was a rocky time for both of us because Keeley was a bit of a wild child."

"Was?" Aldo interjected.

He chuckled. "*Is* a wild child."

"Meanwhile..." Aldo jerked a thumb toward Kayden. "Kay, here, was the world's most overprotective parent. The battles the two of them waged were epic."

"It couldn't have been easy for you," Hazel said. "And Aldo's right. You didn't screw her up at all. She's lovely."

Kayden picked her hand up and pulled it to his lips, giving her knuckles a kiss. "So are you."

Hazel's smile was sweet at first, but it morphed into something much hotter, and more seductive, when Kayden added another kiss to her palm, stroking it with his tongue.

Aldo's arm had been resting along the back of the booth behind her, but he decided to get into the game as well. Dropping that hand to her knee, he drew up the hem of her shirt, just a few inches, so he could caress the inside of her thigh.

Hazel's gaze darted to his, then around the restaurant.

"No one can see us." Aldo was aware the long tablecloth, combined with the fact they were tucked into a cozy, private corner, ensured they could ramp up the play without fear of discovery. They'd specifically requested this table for that very reason. They weren't sure how Hazel would feel about being alone with them somewhere private yet, so they'd created a work-around.

Hazel studied his face for a moment...then parted her legs farther, an obvious invitation. "You said you'd help me escape."

Aldo remembered. God, it was all he'd been able to think about since Kayden offered it.

"You understand how we would do that?" Kayden asked.

Hazel tilted her head, taking a moment before replying. "Sex?"

Kayden's eyes darkened with lust. "We're attracted to you, Fireball. I think we've made that pretty obvious."

"You have," she said. "I'm attracted to you too. Both of you. I've never felt anything like this...this pull. I keep thinking I should resist it, but I can't."

Aldo gripped her knee, squeezing it. "We feel it too."

"I've never given up control of *anything* before that night with you. Never let someone else take charge. It was...I mean... I know this isn't exactly the same thing, but I still..."

"Want it," Kayden finished for her. "Are you willing to give yourself to us again? No thinking. No worrying. Just doing. And feeling."

She studied their faces for a long moment, and Aldo knew his friend was pushing her too fast, so he quickly spoke up before she could reject the idea. "We're going to do some exploring. Just a little bit tonight. Dip our toe in the water. That's all."

"That's all?" she clarified, proving to Aldo that while she wanted them, the cautious side of her was still firmly in control and making all the decisions.

Aldo nodded.

"Tell us, Hazel...are you ready to escape?" Kayden murmured in her ear, his eyes dark with desire. Aldo recognized the look because he'd been on the receiving end of it many times. Damn if he hadn't missed it this past year.

No matter what happened here, Aldo decided he wasn't holding back his need for Kayden any longer. A year was too fucking long.

Hazel's eyes drifted closed when Aldo's fingers slowly slid along her inner thigh, up and down, up and down, getting close to her panties but not touching more than her leg.

"So ready," she said, low enough that Aldo barely heard her.

Aldo pulled his hand away from her leg, loving her sudden scowl of disappointment. "Go to the ladies' room, Hazel, and take off your panties. Bring them back to us."

It only took her a second to process his request. "Okay."

Aldo slid out of the booth, helping her out. He pointed toward the corner. "It's over there."

She nodded and walked away, treating them both to the sexy swish of her ass.

Aldo dropped onto the seat beside Kayden. They hadn't discussed what happened next. They knew they both wanted her, but even without talking, they also understood they would need to take this slow. Especially until they learned more about Hazel's past. She'd clearly been hurt, physically as well as emotionally.

He glanced at Kayden, neither of them speaking. Aldo wasn't sure he could even find the words. He and Kayden had been best friends—closer than brothers—for most of their lives. Then they'd become lovers.

But what they hadn't done—ever—was share a woman.

Now that they were here, now that they'd found the woman they both wanted, it was overwhelming.

"Kayden," Aldo started.

"She's incredible."

Aldo grinned, gripping the back of Kayden's neck to pull him close. He stole a hard, hungry kiss. "She is."

Kayden pressed his forehead against Aldo's. "I didn't expect... didn't let myself hope that she would respond to us the way she has. Not so quickly."

Aldo felt the same way. Hazel was a puzzle; one he was desperate to solve. She clearly had a kind heart, a good soul, and it almost felt as if her inability to trust people was at odds with her true nature. The two of them smiled, then moved apart.

Kayden's gaze shifted from Aldo to something over his shoulder. Aldo glanced back and saw Hazel emerge from the restroom, returning to the table. He rose, noticing the way one fist was clutched around something, the other clinging to the hem of her skirt to hold it down. It was perfectly long enough, but shyness had her overcompensating.

Both things also proved she'd done exactly as they asked.

Once they were both seated again, Kayden reached for the clenched hand, prying it open to retrieve his keepsake. He slipped her panties into the front pocket of his pants.

"I'm going to need those back," she said. "I only own three pairs."

Aldo chuckled. "Or maybe we'll just steal the other two so there's never anything between us and you."

The waiter returned with their salads, so they separated slightly, their conversation returning to less risqué topics as they ate. Since Kayden had talked about his family, Aldo decided to tell Hazel more about his, hoping perhaps she'd decide to reciprocate.

She had already met his brother Elio, and his sister Liza, so he talked about his oldest brother, Bruno, his wife, Vivian, and their three crazy kids. It was never a hardship for him to talk about his niece and nephews because he loved being an uncle and couldn't wait to be a father someday as well.

"I can't believe how big your family is," she remarked. "I don't know how you keep everyone straight."

"Do you have any siblings?" Kayden slid the question in so innocuously that she replied without thinking.

"No. I'm an only child. My parents didn't want any kids, but..." She stopped midsentence again.

Aldo pretended not to notice, finishing her sentence for her. "But then they got lucky and had you."

Hazel gave them what he was sure she hoped would pass for a grin. Unfortunately for her, it was a grimace. "I'm not sure lucky is the word they'd use."

"Not close to your family?" Kayden asked.

She shook her head but didn't offer any more details.

Aldo still considered it a win. "My family is definitely huge, and it gets bigger with every passing year as my siblings and cousins fall in love, get married, make babies."

"And take in strays," Kayden added. "The Morettis basically adopted me and Keeley after we lost our parents, welcoming us into the fold, inviting us to do all the holidays with them, treating us like family."

"I think that's wonderful." She took another sip of wine. Aldo reached for the bottle, topping up each of their glasses as they finished their salads.

The waiter came to clear the plates, promising their meals would be out soon.

Once they were alone again, Aldo closed the distance between him and Hazel. "Now, where were we?" He placed his hand on her knee again, under the hem of her skirt.

Kayden wrapped his arm around her shoulders, nuzzling closer, placing a soft kiss on her cheek, his lips at the shell of her ear.

"Before we leave this restaurant tonight, you're going to come on Aldo's fingers."

Hazel's eyes widened. "No. I can't do that."

Kayden nipped her earlobe, applying enough pressure that Hazel gasped. "I don't remember phrasing that as a question."

"We're in public," she whispered.

"No one will hear or see anything." Aldo proved his point when he drew his hand higher on her leg, not stopping until he reached the apex.

"Do you like his fingers on you?" Kayden murmured.

Hazel's eyes darted from Kayden to Aldo, watching as he lifted his wineglass with his free hand, taking a sip, as his fingers stroked her slit. Her hot, *wet* slit.

"Aldo." She gripped his wrist with her hand, and he expected her to try to pull him away. Perhaps that *had* been her intent. Until he dipped one finger inside her.

"Let go of him, Hazel." Kayden's voice was suddenly stern. "Put both your hands on the table where we can see them."

Hazel responded, doing exactly as Kayden said. Aldo didn't miss the confused look that told him she wasn't quite sure why she kept obeying without question. She'd admitted this was new to her, but there was no denying that just like kindness was part of her DNA, so was submissiveness.

He and Kayden exchanged a glance—his best friend, his lover, giving him the slightest nod.

"Spread your legs farther apart," Kayden said.

Hazel looked around the restaurant again, nervously.

"Look at me," Kayden demanded.

Hazel turned to him.

"It's our job to protect you, and we're going to do it. All you have to do is come for us. Do you understand?"

"Yes."

"Keep your eyes on us, or there will be consequences."

Aldo's finger was still tucked inside her, stroking in and out. Not deeply. Not yet. The moment Kayden said consequences, Hazel's pussy constricted.

Fuck. She liked the idea of punishment.

Aldo's dick had been rock-hard since Hazel had returned to the table without her panties on. It thickened even more, and the slacks that had felt loose enough when he left home were now uncomfortably tight.

"Maybe you should spell out what the consequences will be, Kay." Aldo added another finger to her pussy, taking another sip of wine. "While I stretch out this tight little hole."

"How wet is she?" Kayden asked him.

Aldo grinned at his best friend. "Soaking."

Kayden muttered a curse under his breath, and Hazel's pussy clenched again.

"Let's see. Consequences." Kayden acted as if he hadn't created a list in his head the second Hazel said she wanted to be spanked. "If you keep questioning us, second-guessing whether or not to obey us, we'll be forced to tie you to our bed and withhold your orgasms until you promise to do better."

Aldo swore her pussy got even wetter. "You like that idea."

She opened her mouth to reply, but the only thing that came out was a low moan. It was quiet enough no one else in the restaurant heard, but Hazel still reacted as if they had. She slammed one hand over her mouth.

"Where are your hands supposed to be, Hazel?" Kayden reminded her.

Hazel uncovered her mouth, her shaky hand returning to the table. She pressed the palms down flat and attempted to take slower breaths.

It didn't work. Because he wouldn't let it.

Adding a third finger to her pussy, he applied pressure to her clit with his palm, loving the way Hazel's hips tilted, seeking more.

"God," she murmured, so low he almost couldn't hear her. "Too much."

"How many fingers?" Kayden asked her, still whispering in her ear.

"Three." The word ending on a gasp when he pushed in deep. "I can't..."

"You can." Kayden bit her earlobe. "You will."

He and Kayden shared a glance, and Aldo nodded. Hazel was close. He couldn't believe she was there already, but obviously some part of this—or perhaps all of it—was a kink for her. The fear of being caught, the public setting, having to be quiet, Kayden's commands, Aldo stretching her beyond her comfort level. Whatever it was...it was working.

He increased the speed, added more pressure to her clit with the heel of his hand. Hazel squirmed under his touch, not to escape, but to ensure he hit all the right spots. She was responsive as fuck, so goddamn sexy.

"Hazel, look at me." Kayden placed one finger on her chin, drawing her face to him. "Come."

Hazel went off like a sprinter to the starter gun. Her body trembled and her moans would have been loud enough to at least draw the attention of the most immediate surrounding tables, but Kayden muted them, claiming her lips in a hard, hungry kiss.

Hazel's pussy throbbed as Aldo sought to draw out her orgasm. He wasn't moving as quickly, but he was still thrusting his fingers in deep, relentless, wringing out every drop of pleasure he could steal.

Hazel was the first to break the kiss, falling back against the seat, her breathing staggered, rough, her chest rising and falling, drawing his attention to those gorgeous tits of hers.

Her hands remained on the table, and Aldo wondered if she realized she was still obeying them.

Aldo slowly slid his fingers free, lifting the hand to his mouth. Hazel watched as he licked his finger.

"Give me a taste." Kayden didn't wait for Aldo to offer but

instead grabbed his wrist and pulled it across Hazel, sucking all three of Aldo's fingers into his mouth.

Hazel's eyes widened for a split second, but then her eyelids were heavy, her cheeks pink, though not from embarrassment this time. Her arousal lingered. Hell, for all they knew, they'd only whet her whistle for more.

"I can't believe…" she started, clearing her throat, which had grown husky. "I've never come that quick."

Kayden released Aldo's hand, then gave her a quick kiss on the cheek. "Aldo's got magic fingers."

She gave them a breathy laugh. "He really does. Plus…well… it's been a long time."

Another opening. Aldo didn't intend to waste it. "How long?"

"I…um…maybe a couple of years."

"You haven't been with a man in two years?" Kayden asked.

Suddenly his and Kayden's assumption that she'd been hit by a boyfriend seemed less plausible.

"That wasn't even with a man. It was with a vibrator," she confessed softly.

She was being forthright, honest. It appeared the orgasm had loosened her tongue or left her too lethargic to remain on guard.

"When was the last time you slept with someone?" Aldo asked.

Hazel shrugged. "My last boyfriend and I broke up just over three years ago."

Aldo wasn't sure what to make of that information, and it appeared Kayden was in the same boat. So it hadn't been a boyfriend who'd hit her.

Then who?

Before they could continue the conversation, the waiter arrived with their meals. Aldo was certain no one in the restaurant —the waiter included—had a clue what they'd just done, but Hazel still couldn't manage to look the man in the eye, her face blood-red.

Once he'd served the food and left, Kayden tipped Hazel's face up, giving her a quick kiss. "Okay?"

She nodded quickly. "So okay. I like escaping with you guys."

Aldo chuckled. "Eat your dinner, Fireball. You ain't seen nothin' yet."

Chapter Twelve

Kayden kicked back on the couch, his legs stretched out in front of him, crossed at the ankles. He took a long swig of beer and sighed.

It had been nearly a week and a half since their date with Hazel. Nine long-ass days. While they'd texted with her every single day, the three of them hadn't managed to find a single hour in their schedules when they could all be together...until tonight.

Hazel had taken the job at Divine, and after two days of training—though Rafe said she hadn't needed more than an hour—she'd worked nonstop, taking every double shift she could. She was still helping around the inn as well, doing odd jobs for Gianna, who was knee-deep in interviews for all the positions she needed to fill.

Hazel's schedule had been challenging enough, but when they threw in Aldo's fucked-up full days and nights at the fire station, finding time for those second and third dates had been impossible.

Aldo's work schedule, though weird, had never really bothered Kayden until now. Primarily because, after dropping Hazel off following their dinner date, they'd agreed they would only see her together until they established themselves more firmly in her mind as a matched set. They'd known after that one date that they wanted to pursue something more with her, and they wanted her to fully understand they both wanted her...together, not separately.

They'd pushed her hard that night, maybe too hard, yet neither of them had been willing to put on the brakes. It helped that Hazel seemed to be as eager as they were. At least as far as sex was concerned. Unfortunately, she was still holding other, big parts of herself back.

The three of them getting together tonight hadn't been intended—because if Kayden had known Rafe would send Hazel home early due to a slow night at the restaurant, he and Aldo wouldn't have made plans to spend the evening watching a hockey game with the entire gang. Hazel had, of course, offered to be the last cut, but Rafe insisted she'd been working too hard and deserved a night off. Then he'd threated to sic Keeley on her if she didn't go home and join them for the hockey watch party.

Keeley seemed as taken by Hazel as he and Aldo, the two women becoming fast friends.

Now, Kayden curled his arm around her shoulders, trying to draw her closer—again. Three times, she'd resisted, pulling away, and it was starting to bother him.

"Hazel," he murmured in her ear.

Aldo was sitting on her other side. Turning his head, he watched them.

"Your sister is sitting right behind us," she whispered.

No one in the room—with the exception of Aldo—could hear her. They were all too engrossed in the game. Elio's career in the NHL was winding down, so they'd begun to organize more hockey nights, trying to catch as many as they could together.

Part of the renovations for the inn included changing the large family room into a small theater. Gianna planned to offer movie nights, Sunday football, and other fun events to the guests once the place opened. Her ideas for the inn were innovative, creative, and fun, and Kayden understood why she'd been hired. While it was technically an inn, she was including a lot of touches that made it similar to a B&B.

He, Hazel, and Aldo had claimed the second row of recliners. Luca and Gianna, as well as Penny and Gage—who were just home from their honeymoon—were in the front row, Gianna wanting the best viewing spot to watch her boyfriend on the ice.

Liza had called earlier and said she'd be late because she wanted to check on Nonno and Nonna before heading over to watch the game.

That left Keeley, Gio, and Rafe, who were directly behind them in the back row. Kayden didn't have to turn around to know the three of them were probably fooling around like *he* wanted to. If Hazel would stop pulling away.

Kayden tightened his grip on her shoulder. "Stop resisting, or we'll drag you out of here, find a private corner, and spank that cute little ass of yours."

Hazel stilled, and Kayden cursed under his breath. The pure, unadulterated lust in her eyes had his cock going rock-hard in a second.

"Keep fighting, Hazel." Aldo leaned closer. "Because you don't know what I'd give to watch him follow through on that punishment."

The way Aldo said punishment made it sound less like correction and more like foreplay.

Hazel tossed Aldo a smile over her shoulder. "Dare me?"

"Hey, Hazel." Rafe leaned forward, unaware of how big a cock block he was being at the moment. "I just got a text from Mitchell, asking for Sunday off. We're already fully booked for brunch. How would you feel about filling in as bartender? All you have to make is mimosas and Bloody Marys."

Hazel turned around. "I could do that. No problem."

"I feel bad asking," Rafe admitted, "because I swear you've been at Divine almost around the clock since I hired you."

She grinned. "That's an exaggeration. Besides, you're really doing *me* a favor."

"That's nice of you to say, but you're still going to have to take the compliment. You've been a damn lifesaver. Hardest worker I've got."

Gio leaned forward as well. "Rafe was just saying yesterday if he could clone you, his employee issues would be obsolete."

Hazel smiled but didn't reply, still uncomfortable with praise, and the guys leaned back to continue watching the game.

Kayden ran his finger under her eye, gently touching the dark circles that had already returned. "You've been working a lot of hours."

"I need the money," she said quietly. "Besides, I've always worked a lot. It's no big deal."

"Always?" Aldo reached for her hand. He didn't give her a choice, just gripped it and held on. Hazel let him have the win. Not to be outdone, Kayden wrapped his arm around her shoulders again, moving closer. Their asses might be sitting on three different recliners, but the top halves of their bodies were sharing Hazel's, the three of them tucked tightly together.

"Yeah. Got my first job when I was twelve—uh, I mean... um..." She was about to correct her truth with a lie.

"We're still keeping track of lies, so why don't you let that comment stand without adding to the tally," Kayden murmured in his ear.

Hazel looked like she might still go for broke, but in the end, she simply closed her mouth.

"Twelve is very young," he observed, hoping for more, but it was obvious Hazel had retreated behind the wall again.

"You happy waiting tables?" Aldo asked.

"Um...sure."

He and Aldo exchanged a look. Hazel had a tell. Her lies were typically accompanied with a slow start and the word "um."

"Try again." Warning infused Kayden's tone.

"How do you know that was a lie?" she challenged.

"It was, wasn't it?" Aldo asked.

Hazel sighed, which was all the answer they needed.

Kayden gave her a cocky grin. "I've told you, you're shitty at lying. So answer the question. Are you happy at Divine?"

Hazel narrowed her eyes, but there was no true annoyance in her expression. "It's fine. It's just...well, the truth is, I miss nursing. I liked working with...the elderly."

Kayden wasn't sure if he heard or imagined the pause, and for a second, he got the impression she'd nearly let something else slip.

"You could always go back to it," Aldo said. "Start applying for jobs at nursing homes here."

Hazel nodded, but it was very noncommittal, and something about her demeanor told Kayden she wasn't going to start applying.

Yet another facet to the mystery surrounding Hazel Walsh.

"Hey. What's the score?" Liza asked as she arrived late to the party. She walked into the theater room with her arms laden down with beers.

Penny and Gage stood up to help her put them in the large chest filled with ice, as Luca said, "Glad to see you got my text. I almost had to stand up and walk to the kitchen for the next round."

"Lazy fucker," Liza muttered good-naturedly.

"The Rays are getting their asses handed to them," Gio grumbled. "Elio's taken a couple shots, but nothing's hitting the back of the net. He needs to get his head in the game. He's distracted or something."

"It's my fault," Gianna said. "We were texting right before he had to leave for the stadium."

Luca growled. "Dammit, Gee! We've been over this. No sexting on game days."

Gianna giggled but didn't offer an apology. "I regret nothing."

Kayden could relate to her lack of regrets. Because while he, Hazel, and Aldo hadn't managed to spend any actual time together, they'd burned up the Wi-Fi, texting nonstop. They'd started a three-way group text the morning after their dinner date, and they hadn't stopped talking since.

Hazel was still resistant to share personal information about her past, but she'd become an open book about her daily life now. She was funny and energetic, showing them shades of that positivity game she played every day. She'd confessed a couple of days earlier that moving to Philadelphia was the best thing she'd ever done.

Hearing that had warmed Kayden, but it had also created more questions for him about her past. Hazel was a beautiful, smart, compassionate woman. What—or who—had made her life so unhappy?

And why the hell was she working at twelve years old?

Penny and Gage started handing out the next round of beers.

"Hey, Liza, how's Nonno?" Aldo asked his sister, the entire gang aware Nonno Moretti had a doctor's appointment today. He'd been feeling light-headed the past few days, something he hadn't mentioned to anyone until this morning—when he'd collapsed on the kitchen floor. The episode had been brief and had passed by the time the rescue squad arrived. Nonno—being Nonno—had refused to go to the hospital, claiming he'd merely stood up too quickly and gotten dizzy. The compromise Nonna demanded from him for his refusal was that he make a doctor's appointment immediately, and his regular doctor had insisted he come in right away rather than wait for the next available appointment.

Aldo's Nonno had suffered two mild heart attacks over the past couple of decades, something that worried Nonna to no end.

Liza glanced at Gio, who muted the TV, something in her face clueing them in that the news wasn't good. They all stood from their seats, crowding around Liza.

"The doctor insisted that he go straight to the hospital. They admitted him a couple hours ago. I was on my way to their house when Nonna called to tell me to come there instead. He's set up in a room, but he needs surgery," Liza said.

"What kind of surgery?" Aldo pressed.

Liza cracked open a beer and took a sip. "He has a full blockage, and apparently it's in the largest artery or something. That's what's been causing the light-headedness, which he confessed hadn't just started a few days ago, but has been coming and going for a few *weeks*."

"Shit." Aldo ran a hand through his hair, something he did a lot when he was frustrated or upset. Kayden put a hand on his shoulder, and Aldo shot him a grateful look.

Unfortunately, Nonno Moretti was the strong, silent type, and Kayden suspected what the man was calling a few weeks was actually more like a few months.

Hazel placed her hand on Aldo's forearm, offering her own support. "Are they talking about doing bypass surgery?"

Liza nodded. "Yeah. It's scheduled for the day after tomorrow. They think he'll be in the hospital another five days after that."

"It's a serious surgery, but it's actually relatively safe and the outcomes are positive. Continuing to deal with the light-headedness is not a good idea," Hazel explained.

"Why not?" Luca asked.

Hazel sighed. "They actually call that type of blockage a widowmaker. I suspect that's why they admitted him immediately. So they can keep him under observation. It's good that he went to the doctor."

Luca cursed, while Liza took another drink of her beer. Kayden could see her hands shaking slightly.

Nonno and Nonna were the nucleus of the Moretti family. Kayden couldn't imagine not having Nonno there, offering hugs, smiles, advice, and holding onto the TV remote with a firm, unyielding grip, insisting his house, his choice. Which was a source of amusement and annoyance considering he was typically asleep, head tilted back, mouth wide open, as he snored through "his choice."

Kayden could see Aldo's worry as he explained his concerns to

Hazel. "The thing is, Nonno's not exactly young. And he's had heart attacks before."

"Fucking Russos," Luca muttered angrily. "Sorry, Gage."

The Gage apology had become a standard, as Gage—the lone Russo ever welcomed into their ranks—was no stranger to their anger toward his ancestors.

Gage sighed, though affable as always, the sound was clearly amused. "We almost made it through one night."

Penny leaned toward her husband, wrapping her arm around his waist to give him a squeeze. "Sorry."

Gage reached down, patting Penny's ass suggestively. "You can make it up to me later."

She laughed. "*I'm* not the one bitching about your family."

"I don't understand what the Russos have to do with your grandfather's heart issues," Hazel said.

"And there goes the bell for round two," Kayden joked. "You're already a master when it comes to instigating the Russo bashing, Hazel."

She grinned, clearly recalling that she'd set Liza off the first night they'd met about Matt Russo.

"Nonno used to own a construction business."

"Moretti Brothers Restorations?" Hazel asked Gio, aware he was in business with his brothers, Tony, Luca, and—when he wasn't filming his TV show, *ManPower*—Joey.

Gio shook his head. "No. My dad and Uncle Renzo started Moretti Brothers. Nonno's business was different, Moretti Construction. He was about the same age as Gage's grandfather, Riccardo, and the two of them grew up together here in Philly. There had been some bad blood between their fathers, and apparently it trickled down to Nonno and Riccardo, especially when they both fell for the same woman."

"Our Nonna," Liza chimed in, taking up the tale. "Nonna chose Nonno, and Riccardo didn't take it well."

Hazel glanced toward Gage, who caught her looking him. He lifted one shoulder casually. "I knew my nonno was in love with a woman named Domenica, but according to my grandfather, Giovanni stole *her* from *him*."

"That's not how it happened," Luca insisted.

"History is subjective," Gage argued. "It depends on the storyteller. But go ahead and finish because, unfortunately, I know how the rest of this story goes, and as much as it pains me to say it, that's the part that's definitely true."

Luca considered that, and he gave Gage a sympathetic look before saying, "Riccardo was well-connected in Philadelphia."

"Well-connected?" Hazel asked.

"He was a wealthy businessman, and there wasn't a crooked city official or politician he didn't have in his pocket." Luca paused, clearly waiting for Gage to object, but he didn't.

"Are you talking about the Mafia?" Hazel looked at Gage, rather than Luca.

"I will not confirm that," Gage said with a grin, "even though you have to admit it makes my family sound totally badass."

Penny elbowed her husband. "Remind me to define morally gray to you."

Gage winked. "That's why I married you, my cute conscience. To keep me on the side of right. All I'm willing to say is, my nonno tried to beat one thing into my head from the moment I was born—money equates power. That might as well be the damn Russo family motto."

Aldo finished the story. "Riccardo was angry when Nonna married Nonno. So he destroyed him financially through his connections with local policy makers and county administrators. For decades, Nonno dealt with countless inspections, audits, and fines for trumped-up violations, all in his attempt to keep the business going. But Riccardo was relentless, and the man held a fucking grudge.

"In the end, Nonno's health suffered from the stress, and he had a heart attack. He recovered from that one and went back to work, but a few years later, he had the second. That was when Nonna put her foot down and demanded he retire. She said he could choose pride, or he could choose love, but he couldn't have both. Then she made sure he understood that choosing wrong meant no more eggplant parmesan," Aldo added. "Believe me, Nonno chose right because that threat..."

Aldo and Gio shuddered as if the idea of losing their grandmother's eggplant parmesan was a fate worse than death. Luca went so far as to make the sign of the cross.

Of course, Kayden had eaten it at countless family gatherings, and he had to admit...they weren't wrong. Still, he rolled his eyes, amused, as Hazel giggled.

"That's quite a story," she said. "But I still think he'll be okay. This surgery will help. Honestly."

Liza nodded, grateful for Hazel's reassurance. "The doctor said the same thing. But Aldo's concern about his age is valid."

"How old is he?" Hazel asked.

"Eighty-five," Liza replied. "But he swears that's just on paper. That inside, he's no more than sixty."

Hazel smiled. "He sounds like a character."

"He's going to love you." Aldo wrapped his arm around her waist. "He's got a thing for redheads."

"The problem isn't just the surgery," Liza continued. "There's a long recovery time involved, which means he's going to need care once he's released from the hospital."

"Nonna won't let him out of her sight," Gio said.

"She also has shitty knees," Liza reminded her cousin. "She needs double knee replacement, but the stubborn woman insists she's leaving this world with all her original working—or not working—parts. There's no way she can provide much in the way of physical support. She hobbles enough on her own."

"That's true, but you know Aunt Berta would stay with them, help out," Luca suggested.

Liza shook her head. "Think about what you just said. Nonna has been freaking out ever since the doctor said 'surgery.' You know how she worries about Nonno. She's a rock when it comes to everything else in her world, but when faced with Nonno's health, she works herself up into a state. And while Aunt Berta is wonderful, she would only compound Nonna's fears because of—"

"Uncle Renzo," Aldo finished.

Liza nodded, then looked at Hazel. "Our aunt Berta's husband, Uncle Renzo, died of a massive heart attack when he was in his late fifties. Putting her and Nonna together wouldn't be a great combination because they'd both fuss and worry and stress out, and they'd transfer all of those feelings over to Nonno, who would go insane dealing with all their overbearing care, no matter how well-meaning."

Luca sighed. "Yeah. We can't do that to Nonno. You know how he hates when Nonna makes a fuss over him. The problem is, everyone else still works."

"He's looking at six to eight weeks of recovery time. The breastbone and chest muscles need to heal."

Aldo winced...then Kayden saw Liza's gaze settle on Hazel.

"You're a nurse," Liza said simply, drawing her attention.

"Well...yeah, I am."

"And you're still looking for a place to live, right?"

Hazel nodded. Kayden knew she hadn't had much luck in that regard, simply because she hadn't had time to launch a real search, working long hours every day. And it wasn't like Rafe and Keeley had been after her to do so, since she'd been doing such great work at Divine.

"Shit," Rafe muttered. "I'm going to lose my best waitress, aren't I?"

Hazel looked over at him, alarmed, but Rafe was grinning, making it clear he was joking.

"I'm kidding, Hazel. Lindsey comes back from maternity leave next week." He looked over at Liza. "And consider me her reference. I've never met anyone who works as hard as she does. Reliable, responsible, and great with people."

Hazel looked shocked, and Kayden saw tears welling in her

eyes. "Rafe," she said, her voice slightly choked up. "That's so nice of you, but I promised—"

"Seriously, Hazel. Divine will be fine. And if you'd like, once Nonno Moretti is all healed up, you can come back if you want. Though I think it would be a shame to waste your degree if nursing really is your calling."

Aldo turned to look at her, taking both her hands in his. "Hazel, if you're hesitating because of money, we'd pay you well."

"And it would give you a free place to stay for the next two months. Nonno and Nonna still live in the house where they raised their four kids. They've got three guest rooms. You could take your pick," Liza said.

Luca added, "And there are enough of us in the family that we can make sure you aren't working twenty-four seven. We could come up with a schedule, so you'd have time off every day."

"It would be a huge help for Nonna too. She puts on a brave face, but I know it really hurts her to walk too much," Gio added.

Hazel looked from Moretti to Moretti to Moretti, quietly listening as they each added their arguments in hopes of convincing her.

"You just said you missed nursing and working with the elderly," Aldo reminded her. "This gives you a chance to get back to what you love. I swear you're going to love my grandparents, and they're going to love you."

Kayden recognized the second Hazel gave in. Her smile was so wide, Kayden couldn't help grinning as well.

"You're all way too good to be true," Hazel said. "How can I say no when you've been so kind? I would love to be your nonno's nurse."

Aldo hooted, then gave her a long, hard kiss on the lips that made it obvious—though Kayden didn't think anyone in the room wasn't already aware—that Aldo was smitten.

Not to be left out, Kayden wrapped his arms around her waist when Aldo released her, pulling her back to his chest and placing a kiss on her cheek. "*You're* too good to be true too."

Liza pulled her cell phone out of her purse. "Let me call Nonna and tell her the good news. Then I'll call Aunt Berta, so she can start the phone chain."

Hazel looked at Aldo. "Phone chain?"

Aldo chuckled. "Berta will call my mom and the other aunts to let them know what's happening. By this time tomorrow, everyone will know about you taking the job, will have been assigned their duties for the next eight weeks, and the aunts will have started cooking. I wouldn't plan on being hungry anytime soon, because I can't even begin to imagine how many lasagnas and casseroles are going to start rolling in."

"They understand he can't eat all that after surgery, right?" she asked.

"The food will be for the rest of the family, because they'll be stopping in regularly to check on the old guy," Aldo explained.

"Good thing Nonna has two kitchens and three refrigerators," Luca joked.

"Is he being serious?" Hazel quietly asked Kayden, who was still holding her against him. "Two kitchens? In one house?"

Kayden laughed. "You're in for some culture shock, but don't worry. You're going to love living at the Morettis' house."

"Okay," Liza said, putting her phone away. "I talked to Nonna and Berta and they're both thrilled you've agreed to be Nonno's nurse. Apparently Aldo's already talked you up, so she was dying to meet you anyway."

Hazel glanced at Aldo, who shrugged. "Told her I'd met a girl," he said without a bit of embarrassment. "Nonna and I have no secrets."

Liza snorted. "She'd like to meet you before—"

"I'm off tomorrow," Aldo interjected. "I'll take Hazel by the hospital to meet Nonno before the surgery. Maybe she can talk to the doctor too."

"I have the lunch shift at Divine," Hazel said.

"Not anymore." Rafe already had his phone in his hand,

texting. "Mitchell owes you for covering for him on Sunday. Gonna make it a swap."

"Perfect. I would have done it, but I have a meeting at ten with," Liza glanced over at Gage, "he who shall not be named, and God only knows how long *that* will last."

Gage winked at Liza. "Thanks for giving me a heads-up. I'll be sure to avoid Matt tomorrow, since meetings with you ensure he's a bear for the rest of the fucking day."

Liza smirked. "I do what I can."

After the business about Nonno's surgery was settled, they resumed their seats and watched the last period of the hockey game. The Rays lost, but at least Elio scored a goal, which got Gianna out of the doghouse with Luca.

About an hour later, Gianna, who'd apparently given up alcohol for Lent, offered rides to drive Luca and Liza, who'd had a few too many rounds, and Penny, who'd only had one glass of wine, left with Gage, the newlyweds obviously still in honeymoon-mode.

Keeley offered rooms to Kayden and Aldo, even though both of them were far from drunk. She said they could use the suites on either side of Hazel's, then gave him a knowing look. Apparently, it wasn't just the ghosts who liked to play matchmaker. Not that Kayden was complaining.

Gio, Rafe, and Keeley said good night, while he, Aldo, and Hazel hung back, under the guise of tidying up.

Once they were alone, Kayden reached for Hazel, tugging her into his arms. "Alone at last."

Hazel lifted her face to his, clearly anticipating a kiss. So she frowned when he leaned back and narrowed his eyes.

"Kayden," she started, but falling silent when he shook his head.

"No kisses. Not yet. I think we need to pick up our conversation where it left off."

Her cute little nose crinkled when she was confused. "Conversation?"

Kayden looked over at Aldo, who'd stepped next to him, the three of them invading each other's personal space.

"I think it had something to do with a dare," Aldo reminded her.

Hazel's expression cleared, a small, sexy smile tilting up the edges of her lips. "Oh yeah," she all but purred.

Kayden's dick thickened in an instant, and the way Aldo shifted his jeans proved he was in the same boat.

"We're returning to our previous arrangement," Kayden said.

"Which one is that?" Hazel asked coyly.

Aldo leaned close, nuzzling her cheek with his nose. "The one where we call the shots."

"Thought that was just during the date?" she asked.

"You know what? Let's just say that agreement stands until further notice." Kayden gripped her hips, pulling her body against his, letting her feel the effect she was having on him.

"Feels like I'm giving you a lot of power," she said, though Kayden could practically hear the desire in her voice. She might be playing hard to get, but that didn't mean she didn't want them to catch her.

"You're working too hard," he said.

"I'm working the same amount I always do," she replied, the flirtiness replaced with a core of strength that told them her submissiveness had limits. "I'm not giving you control over that. I know how to take care of myself."

Kayden didn't like that response, but he couldn't exactly argue with her. This thing between them was still brand-spanking-new.

"Fine. We'll restrict the control," Aldo said too quickly, as aware as Kayden that they were losing ground.

"To?" she prompted.

"Our relationship," Aldo said. "Our *physical* relationship."

Kayden didn't think Aldo meant to say the last part, but neither of them had missed the brief flash of panic on her face when he referred to this as a relationship.

Hazel might not be resisting the attraction between the three of them, but she was going to fight tooth and nail before agreeing to anything deeper.

Only one other woman in his life had ever tested his patience to this extent, and that was his sister.

"Do you agree?" Kayden pressed her for an answer, deciding that giving her too long to think about it wouldn't work in their favor.

She made them wait, and it took everything he had to keep quiet. She was clearly thinking, which Kayden had to respect. While Aldo was more impulsive, Kayden—like Hazel—needed time to study all angles.

"Okay. I agree," she said at last.

Kayden pressed his cheek against hers, his voice quiet. "You pulled away earlier when I put my arm around you."

"But your sister and—"

"My sister—hell, everyone who was here tonight—knows Aldo and I are interested in you, and they're fine with it. So don't do that again," he warned. "Unless you didn't want us to touch you."

Her immediate response soothed the edges that were still sharp from her resistance. "It's not that. I swear. I want you to touch me," she hastily reassured him. "Both of you."

Kayden rewarded that reply with a slow kiss.

When they parted, she shifted back just a little bit so Kayden could see the pure mischief that had snuck into her eyes. "But, just for argument's sake, what happens if I don't do what you tell me to?"

He enjoyed this side of her too fucking much, his dick rock-hard. "You sure you want to know?"

"I do. I *really* do."

And just like that...it was game fucking on.

Chapter Thirteen

Hazel didn't have a clue where this flirty woman was coming from, but she wasn't about to take it back. She'd spent the majority of the night in damp panties, thanks to Aldo and Kayden's constant touches, murmured sweet nothings, and outright sexual innuendoes.

She'd tried to put some distance between them, using their family and friends as an excuse, when in truth, it was taking all she had not to drag them up to her bedroom and beg them to have their wicked way with her. Which she couldn't do. She'd known these guys two weeks, and they hadn't even seen each other the last nine days.

Not that it felt that way. They'd texted so much during the last week and a half, Hazel had gotten cramps in her thumbs.

"Fuuuuuck," Aldo murmured. "We better set some ground rules right now before I lose all ability to speak reasonably. There's not a lot of blood pumping through my brain right now. It's all traveling south."

Hazel laughed, aware she'd never felt this happy in her life, and damn if it didn't feel good. "South, you say?" She went for broke as she ran her hand over Aldo's cock, which was pitching quite the denim tent in his jeans.

Then she gave Kayden a similar stroke, loving the way he groaned just a split second before he gripped her wrist, holding her hand against him, but still. "We definitely need rules and a conversation."

Hazel tried to pull her hand away, but Kayden held tight, lifting it to his lips to kiss her palm.

"Talking kind of takes all the mystery out of it." She didn't even bother to hide her pout, hoping it would work. Talking tended to get her into trouble. The more time she spent with these men, the less able she was to keep control of her wayward tongue. She longed for the closeness they offered. She'd spent a lifetime being lonely, but with them, that feeling went away. She found herself being wrapped tighter and tighter into their web, and she liked it.

Aldo lifted her hand when she started to touch him again, kissing her knuckles. "Behave, Fireball."

Every time they used that nickname for her, her insides turned to mush.

While Aldo came off as the milder of the two men, there had been a few times when he'd given her a look or used a tone that convinced her both men possessed more than their fair share of the alpha gene. She had always thought her uncle and dad classified as alpha males, but now she'd decided they were really just misogynistic assholes. Kayden and Aldo were alpha in a much different, much sexier way, and it was ridiculously hot.

"Fine," she grumbled.

Kayden led them back to the row of seats—large, soft recliners —they'd just vacated, sitting back down in his own. She was about to reclaim her spot when she stumbled, pitching forward, right into Kayden's lap.

"You read my mind." He wrapped his arms around her waist to keep her there.

"I tripped. Or..." That wasn't exactly right. She glanced up at Aldo. "Did you push me?"

He held his hands up innocently. "I didn't touch you." Then

a wide grin crossed his face. "Looks like Albert and Marta approve."

Hazel frowned, taking a minute to try to remember who Albert and Marta were. When she recalled, she tilted her head. "The ghosts?"

"Did you trip, or did it feel like you were pushed?" Kayden looked as pleased as Aldo.

It had honestly felt like she'd been shoved, but, while the idea of ghosts was kinda cool, she didn't really believe the stories. "I must've tripped." She looked down at the floor, but there wasn't a damn thing there she could blame.

Kayden chuckled. "If it makes you feel better to believe that, fine. But just in case..." He looked out into the room. "Thanks, Albert. I owe you one."

She rolled her eyes. "You're ridiculous."

"And *you* are right where I want you." Kayden tightened his grip when she twisted around, determined to shift back to her seat from earlier.

She stopped trying once Aldo claimed it, reaching for her feet, and drawing her legs over the low arms of between the recliners.

"We've done a lot of texting since our date," Kayden began.

"We have." Hazel had never sat on a man's lap before—or at least not that she could remember. Her dad hadn't exactly been father of the year. Though she didn't have very many memories of the time when he was there. He'd been arrested when she was eight, so most of her recollections of her dad involved him sitting behind a glass window, the two of them talking on a phone once a year at the prison. Mom wasn't wife of the year either, bitching that it was too much hassle to get to the penitentiary, which was two hours away, and that it cost too much in gas money. Hazel had gone by herself the last few years because Mom couldn't be bothered.

Kayden's lap was surprisingly comfortable. She could feel his hardness pressing against her ass, and it was doing precious little to help her regain control of her own arousal. When Aldo slipped off her shoes and started rubbing her feet, all chance of that faded into the mist.

Kayden ran his fingers through her hair. "I know you like to play your cards close to your chest and there are some things you're not comfortable talking to us about."

Hazel's heart sank, a tiny tremor of panic reappearing for the first time in over a week. As more time passed, she looked over her shoulder less and even managed to go hours at a time without worrying that there was a warrant out for her arrest.

Her mom had called three more times, but Hazel had sent it to voicemail every time. She refused to let her old life creep into this one, though she had sent her mom most of her tips from her first weekend working at Divine. Two hundred bucks. It was all she'd felt comfortable parting with because she needed to save every penny for a security deposit and building what she was calling her Maloney nest egg, the funds she would use if she managed to track down some of the stolen items.

She held no illusions that Boston Hazel wasn't going to have to pay the piper eventually, that this dream world she'd drifted into would vanish once Kayden and Aldo learned who she really was.

A stronger woman would move on before that happened, before it all came crashing down, but she couldn't. She'd spent a lifetime hungry, lonely, cold, scared, and tired.

Why shouldn't she grab as much of this—friends, good food, a soft bed, and the attention of two of the sexiest men she'd ever met—for as long as she could?

Shit. She'd never sounded more like a Walsh in her life.

Take the money and run.

But in her case, it was happiness she was trying to abscond with.

"I'm, um, just a private person." She couldn't quite manage to look either man in the eye.

Kayden sighed. "We get that. But there are some things we

need to know before this thing between the three of us can continue."

"What things?" She was perfectly aware that question could very well spell the end of all of this.

"You told us you haven't had sex in three years," Aldo said.

She nodded.

"There's been no one since then?" Hazel didn't miss the tone of surprise in Kayden's voice, though she couldn't understand it.

"No one."

Aldo applied more pressure on the heel of one foot. It felt like bliss. "The last guy was a boyfriend?"

"Yes."

Kayden growled. "This is going to take a long time if we have to play twenty questions all night, Hazel. In case you couldn't tell, this is the sharing-past-relationships part of our dating routine. I know you're relatively inexperienced, but we'd like to know more."

The pressure on Hazel's chest lifted. Because that was something she could share. She had admitted to her inexperience one night when they were texting about turn-ons. It had been their most risqué text thread, and she'd devoured every word of it.

Kayden had serious kinks when it came to bondage and spankings, while Aldo admitted to enjoying voyeurism and, God help her, anal.

"Oh," she said, lifting her arm from her lap and wrapping it around Kayden's neck. "Trust me. My sex stories won't take long at all. I lost my virginity my junior year of high school to a guy in my English class. He had long hair, played the guitar, and got high. A lot."

Aldo chuckled. "Sounds like a great guy."

She rolled her eyes. "He was a bit of a goofball, but he was nice to me, always trying to make me laugh. He started giving me a ride home after school. He owned a van."

"Of course he did." Kayden's grumpy sarcasm gave Hazel a

pretty good idea of what Keeley had dealt with when she was in high school.

"Anyway, after a couple months of rides, he asked if I was his girlfriend. That hadn't even occurred to me, but I figured why not. So I said yes. That day, he kissed me goodbye when he dropped me off. Things sort of progressed from there, getting a little hotter and heavier until..." She waved her hands around. "You know."

Kayden scowled, and Hazel let herself pretend the look was driven by jealousy because...wouldn't that be awesome. "We know," he grumbled.

"Summer break started a few weeks after that, so we didn't see each other for a couple of months—I was working and he was stoned, both were full-time jobs. By the time we came back for senior year, he had a new girlfriend."

Aldo scowled. "What an asshole."

Hazel frowned. "What do you mean?"

Aldo tilted his head. "Wasn't he your first love? Didn't it hurt when he broke things off?"

Hazel snorted. "Jesus. Not at all. I didn't love him."

"What about the next guy?" Kayden asked.

Hazel realized maybe she shouldn't have been so quick to dismiss this as an easy conversation. She wasn't coming out of it sounding too good. "I worked at a fast-food place my senior year. Hooked up with a guy who worked with me. I thought we were exclusive until I caught him doing it with another girl in the manager's office one night after closing."

"Broken heart?" Aldo asked, and she realized he seemed hung up on the feelings part of her stories.

"I didn't love him either. I thought you were asking about my sexual history," she pointed out.

Aldo drove his thumbs into the base of her foot, and she moaned. Kayden hadn't lied about Aldo's magic fingers.

"We *are* asking about that," Kayden said. "But usually..."

There had been several times since she'd landed herself a place in the "Moretti and Friends" gang when Hazel felt like she'd dropped down on an alien planet. She'd felt uneasy at Divine and Aspen Rose because she'd never eaten at such fancy places. She'd never had a girlfriend loan her clothes—mainly because the girls she'd grown up with had been as poor as her and none of them had clothes to spare. Or maybe it was that they didn't have any clothes worth sharing.

Love had never been a part of sex for her. Ever. But it was clear the guys thought maybe it should have been.

"I wasn't in love with any of my past boyfriends," she forced herself to say. "The last guy I dated, Shawn, was in nursing classes with me at the community college. I really liked him. But... nothing more than that."

What she didn't admit was Shawn felt more for her than she had for him. He'd envisioned them as a couple, saw a future for them. Something that had shocked the hell out of Hazel, when he'd dropped those three little words on her at Outback after graduation. She'd felt horrible breaking things off, but she couldn't say them back, couldn't even hide the horror she felt when he'd said them to her.

She'd worried for months afterward that maybe something inside her was broken. After all, her parents hadn't exactly been the model couple, and her mother had said on more than one occasion the worst thing she'd ever done was get knocked up and marry Danny Walsh. That comment usually came after a bottle or two of wine, and followed up with what Mom considered stellar advice, telling Hazel to do what she hadn't if she ever got pregnant.

Abort.

So...yeah. No wonder Hazel was fucked up.

Her concerns had been alleviated by Mrs. Maloney, who—when still lucid—had asked her about her last boyfriend. She'd described the conversation at Outback and when Hazel suggested that perhaps she couldn't fall in love, Mrs. Maloney had waved her concerns away and told her all it meant was she couldn't fall in love with Shawn.

Since then, Hazel had hung on to the hope that someday she would meet the one. A man she could not only fall in love with, but also trust not to leave her, not to hurt her.

As the years passed, that began to feel like a pretty tall order, but now with Kayden and Aldo...

Hazel shut that line of thought down in an instant.

Hope was a killer.

Time to get herself off the hot seat. "Enough about me. How about you guys?"

"Ashley Baxter was my first love," Aldo said. "Broke my heart, and I swore I'd never love another woman after her."

"Oh my God," Hazel said. "That sounds awful."

Aldo gave her a crooked grin. "It was, but it only lasted until I got to third grade. Then I fell head over heels for Jenny Cross, who left me crushed, devastated beyond all repair. Until fourth grade when I met Lizzy Russell."

Hazel glanced at Kayden. "I think I'm starting to sense a theme here."

Kayden chuckled. "Aldo was an early bloomer."

"Maybe so, but all those broken hearts just made me stronger," Aldo interjected.

"Why don't we skip ahead a few years, Aldo? Or do I dare to ask how many women you've fallen in love with since puberty?" Hazel asked.

Aldo placed a soft kiss on the sole of her foot that tickled, and she giggled. "I had a serious girlfriend my sophomore and junior years of high school. She was my first everything. It fell apart when she went off to college. I've seriously dated probably half a dozen women since hitting my twenties and thirties, but nothing that lasted more than a year, and most a lot less than that."

"And you?" she said to Kayden.

"My story is about the same, except the first girl to break my heart was named CeCe, and she and I lost our virginity to each other our freshman year in high school."

"And you call me the early bloomer." Aldo punched Kayden on the arm playfully.

"And lately?" Hazel asked. "Because it sounds like I'm not the only one who's been suffering a dry spell."

Kayden and Aldo exchanged a glance, one she couldn't quite decipher, though she had a suspicion. She waited for them to say something, but in the end, Aldo simply agreed with her. "Yeah. I guess you're right."

She studied his face, and while he was looking her straight in the eye, his words spoken without hesitance, he was holding something back. Which was interesting. Because she was a hundred percent certain he hadn't held a damn thing back before now.

Looked like she wasn't the only one with secrets to keep.

It also looked like she could take a lesson or two from Aldo, because he was much more accomplished when it came to playing his cards close to his chest.

"Is that all we needed to talk about?" She nuzzled closer to Kayden, drawing her lips along the side of his face. She'd spent every single night since that orgasm in the restaurant fantasizing about their next encounter.

"Not exactly." Kayden's fingers drifted beneath her shirt, stroking up and down her sides. "Do you understand what we mean when we say we're in control?"

Ahhhh. And now they were getting down to it.

"I realize I'm probably lacking experience in the type of sex you're talking about, but I'm not new on the planet," she joked. "I read dirty books, watch porn. My fantasies have always run a little darker than the realities of my sex life."

"You liked what we did in the restaurant." Aldo hadn't posed it as a question, but she answered anyway.

"So much. I've never come that hard before."

"What part turned you on the most?" Aldo asked. "The

public aspect, the way you had to be quiet, the way we were in charge and told you exactly what to do, the actual act?"

Hazel took a moment to consider his question because she hadn't broken the feelings down that way. She had looked at the entire encounter as one thing, one mind-blowing thing that she wanted to do over and over again.

"I liked it all," she admitted, "but if I had to pick the part that turned me on the most, it was the way I gave up all control. I didn't have to think about anything. Just feel. I never have the chance to just...shut everything down. Ever."

"I'm glad you like that." Kayden placed a kiss on the side of her head, his fingers running through her curls, then fisting around them at the base of her neck. He wasn't exactly pulling her hair, but there was a slight tension in her scalp. A tension that sent electrical pulses straight to her pussy. "Because we like being in charge."

Hazel twisted slightly, facing away from Kayden so that she could push her ass back against his erection.

"But, Hazel, before this goes any further, we need to establish some things."

"What kinds of things?" She wasn't overly concerned with the answer. Not when Aldo abandoned her feet, running his hands along the underside of her legs, up to her knees, his touch firm enough that she could feel it through her jeans.

She reached out to him, unbuttoning the top two buttons on Aldo's shirt. She was dying to see their chests, to explore the ink she'd caught glimpses of during their tour of the city and on their first date. She'd spent too much time this past week imagining what they looked like naked.

Kayden reached for her hands, stopping her before she could make any more progress on getting Aldo out of his shirt. "We established control when it came to ordering food and finding you a safe place to stay, but this is different, more like what we did the other night at Aspen Rose. We need to spell out a few things because what we want to do with you, Hazel—"

"*To* you," Aldo added, cutting Kayden off.

To her?

Kayden continued. "We don't just want to have sex with you. We want to own you, your body, your moans, your orgasms. All of it. We want to tie you up, spank you, take you in ways you've never been taken before, in *places* you've never been taken before."

She swallowed heavily. Because she knew he wasn't talking about Paris or a swimming pool. She'd never given a blow job—never wanted to. Just like none of her past lovers had gone down on her. That seemed to bring a level of intimacy to relationships that were way too wham bam, thank you ma'am. Rushed encounters for the sole purpose of coming. Missionary, doggie, in and out, one and done. Nothing she'd ever done had been more than that. Which was why she knew Kayden was talking about her virgin places, her ass and her mouth.

"You understand what I'm saying?" Kayden asked.

She nodded.

"All of that...it requires trust."

Both men stilled, their touches remaining—Kayden holding her wrists, Aldo's hands loose beneath her knees—but they didn't stroke, didn't move. It was clear this was important to them.

So she took the time to consider what Kayden was asking for.

Apart from their one date, this was the first time the three of them had been alone together. Which was somewhat shocking to her. Probably because they only stopped talking when they were asleep, the texts between them constantly flying. She felt like she knew them—really knew them—despite that lack of time together.

But trust came hard for her. As she looked back, she couldn't think of a single person in her life that she'd trusted completely.

God. Maybe she really was broken. No love. No trust.

Her parents and uncle were the last people she'd ever trust, and while the Maloneys had been kind, she'd never really felt comfortable with them, never not been reminded that at the end of the day, she was still just the hired help.

The closest she'd come to trust had been during that first year with Mrs. Maloney, when her mind was still good, but even that wavered, not because of anything the elderly woman did but because of her disease. She couldn't trust from day to day that Mrs. Maloney would even know who she was.

"We like you, Hazel," Aldo murmured. "A lot."

Hazel blinked a few times, fighting to believe that was true. Good things didn't happen to her. They just didn't.

She was twenty-five years old, and she could count on one hand—with fingers left over—the good things she'd gotten in her life. Her first car, her first nursing job with the Maloneys, and her degree all came to mind—and even those were things she'd had to work for, struggle for, save for. They sure as hell hadn't just been handed to her on a silver platter.

To make things worse, they'd all been yanked from her. Her mom totaling her first car, the Maloneys firing her. She hadn't dared to dream she could ever work as a nurse again until tonight, resigned to waiting tables.

That little voice she hated reared its head, warning her to proceed with caution. She'd tossed it to the wind since the night of their date, but it was back now, reappearing with a vengeance, causing her to doubt, to lose faith. She swallowed heavily, finding it hard to draw a deep breath.

Kayden ran the back of his knuckles along her cheek, drawing her out of her dark thoughts.

"Tell us what you're thinking."

She wouldn't. Couldn't.

"I hate wherever it is you've just gone," Kayden said softly.

"Stay here with us," Aldo said. "Put the bad thoughts away and just be here. With us."

"I want to do that. It's just...I can't...I don't..." She stopped talking.

"You don't trust us. And you shouldn't. We're at the beginning stages of this and trust takes time. All we're asking you to do is give us a chance to prove we're worthy of it," Kayden said. "Maybe someday you'll trust us enough to tell us your story."

"So, no fucking. Not tonight," Aldo said. "Tonight, we keep getting to know each other."

She wanted to protest because her girl parts were hungry, but she knew they were making the right decision. Kayden and Aldo were assuming control for more than just the physical aspects of their time together. They also were taking control of the things she couldn't—her ability to walk away from them, to hold herself apart as much as she could.

She was spiraling out of control. Longing for things she couldn't have. And they were saving her from herself. Even if they didn't realize it.

She'd only known them two weeks. And Kayden was a cop, for God's sake. While the police hadn't come for her yet, that didn't mean she was in the clear. The Maloneys could decide to press charges at any time because she hadn't sent back nearly enough of their things. All she'd done was put a Band-Aid on a gaping wound.

She should never have gotten inside that police cruiser outside the motel. She should have turned and walked away because now...

Now, she was playing with fire. Letting herself get swept up in their world.

She glanced toward the door, overwhelmed by that smothering exhaustion that never truly left her and the desire to run away. From them, from this house, from...everything.

She must have given herself away somehow because Kayden's hold tightened as he kissed her forehead. "Hazel. Shhhh. Let it all go for now."

Aldo moved his hands once more, using them to shift her legs apart. She still wore her jeans, so it was ridiculous to feel exposed, but she did.

He ran his fingers along the inside of her thighs, all the way to the button and zipper. "We're going to escape for a little while, Fireball. The three of us."

"But you said—"

"Not sex," Aldo clarified. "Just exploring. We're going to help you forget all the shit that's rambling around in your head."

"I want that," she whispered. "So much."

Her words loosened whatever had been holding them back, as Aldo unfastened her pants, tugging them off her before she had time to feel shy or uneasy. Her panties went next.

Her gaze flew to the doorway of the theater room again...for a different reason this time.

"They won't come back down," Kayden assured her.

"Here." Aldo reached out. "Give her to me."

Kayden lifted her easily, shifting her from his lap to Aldo's. They were both incredibly strong men, something that Boston Hazel would have seen as dangerous, threatening.

But not Philadelphia Hazel.

She fucking loved it.

She started to curl up in Aldo's lap the same way she had Kayden's, but he had other plans. He drew her back to his chest, facing away from him, her ass snug against the crotch of his jeans —and his oh-so-evident erection.

"Open your legs, Hazel," Aldo directed. "Hook your feet around my calves."

She hesitated, aware she'd be able to hide nothing if she did that.

"Do it, Hazel. Now. Thinking isn't part of this, remember?" Kayden's voice was dark and gruff, and it spoke to that newly discovered part of her that wanted to please him, to please *them*.

She stretched her legs apart to do as Aldo had instructed. She didn't have to look down to know the tops of her inner thighs were glistening with arousal.

Aldo's hand wrapped around her body, his fingers sliding along her slit, the touch prompting a curse.

"Fuck, Kay," he hissed. "She's drenched."

Then Aldo went the extra mile, drawing his legs apart, taking advantage of the wide seat of the recliner. Her legs went along for the ride, spreading her apart even more.

Kayden was in motion in an instant, leaving his seat until he stood directly in front of them. He only remained there for a second before he dropped down to kneel between her open legs.

Hazel's eyes widened in amazement. "Oh my God," she whispered.

Kayden gave her a ghost of a smile before his finger followed the same path Aldo's had just taken. "So fucking wet," he murmured. "I'm going to have to be careful not to drown in there."

The meaning of his words didn't fully register until he bent his head, his breath hot on her pussy. She jerked, trying to close her legs. It was too much. He could see...everything.

Kayden and Aldo were prepared. Aldo's hands gripped her thighs, his voice sharp in her ear. "Back in position."

His words weren't necessary because Kayden's wide shoulders ensured she couldn't close her legs if she wanted to.

She struggled to hook her feet back around Aldo's calves, not due to discomfort or embarrassment, but because Kayden hadn't been dissuaded from his goal. He shifted even closer, then his gaze lifted to hers, his mouth less than an inch from her pussy.

She knew instinctively what he was waiting for, and it wasn't permission.

No. What he wanted was for her to ask for it.

"Please," she whispered.

His eyes darkened with lust as he finished the journey.

Hazel gasped at the first touch of his mouth, her hips lifting of their own accord, seeking out more, her body accepting what he was doing light years before her brain could catch up.

Aldo's grip on her inner thighs relaxed, then shifted. He gripped the hem of her shirt, pulling it over her head as efficiently as he'd managed to rid her of her jeans and panties. Her bra went next, until she was sandwiched between them, completely naked while they were both fully dressed.

"We're going to make up for lost time," Aldo murmured in her ear. "Three years is a long time to take care of yourself, Hazel."

Kayden's lips found her clit and he sucked it into his mouth.

"Holy shit." Bright lights flashed behind her closed eyes. This was unbelievable.

Kayden licked, sucked, and nipped at her clit, at her pussy like it was his job. She gasped when he drove his tongue inside her, writhing beneath him as much as she could. Which wasn't a lot because Aldo's arms were wrapped around her midsection, holding her steady.

Kayden alone was enough to make her lose her mind, but Aldo wasn't content to simply observe.

His lips brushed her earlobe as he whispered dirty, hot things to her.

"You were too quiet in the restaurant," he said. "We didn't get to hear your moans, so you're going to give them to us now, aren't you?"

Hazel hadn't even been aware that she'd been attempting to muffle her cries, her sounds, but that was probably because sex had always been a quiet affair for her. The walls in her apartment were paper thin, so she tried very hard not to make any noise when she masturbated, for fear her mother would hear.

Even with her past boyfriends, she'd been sneaking the act in at a parent's house or the backseats of cars. She'd never been free to let it all out.

Kayden replaced his tongue with two fingers, driving them deep and hard, her cry coming out louder this time, though still tempered.

"That's not good enough, Fireball. Stop holding back," Aldo chastised.

"I...God...I..."

Kayden increased the speed, his fingers going faster, taking her to another level.

"Say his name," Aldo demanded. "He likes to hear it."

"Kayden," she said. "God, Kayden."

Aldo kissed the shell of her ear, grasping her breasts in his hands, squeezing them with a force that took her by surprise.

She whimpered not so much from pain but because they were suddenly so sensitive...too sensitive. Aldo pinched her nipples at the same time Kayden bit her clit, and her back arched in response.

"Fuck." Her breath was coming out in harsh pants. She was so close but she couldn't quite get there, and she didn't understand why.

"You want to come, don't you?" Aldo asked.

She nodded, a bead of sweat running along the side of her face.

She didn't understand Aldo's dark chuckle...at first...

"But we haven't given you permission, have we?"

She frowned. Surely that couldn't be the reason. They hadn't made that demand, hadn't told her she had to wait.

But when she thought about that night in the restaurant, she recalled Kayden's voice, the way she hadn't managed to reach the pinnacle until he told her to come.

"You want to please to us," Aldo whispered. "Submit to us. Want to do only as we say. Because you want to give yourself to us, be ours. Only ours."

"Please." Hazel was unashamed at the outright begging tone because she couldn't deny the truth of his words. Didn't *want* to deny them. "Aldo, please. Let me."

Kayden never lifted his head, never missed a beat, though she knew he was listening. His fingers drove in harder as he sucked her clit roughly into his mouth.

"You want it?" Aldo asked.

She snarled, aware he was teasing her, forcing her to hold back.

Stars flashed behind her eyelids, and it felt as if she'd lost all control of her body. She wiggled like a worm on a hook as she fought to get herself there.

Goddammit. She *was* there.

So why couldn't...

"Please," she said again.

"Come for us," Aldo whispered in her ear and Hazel detonated, exploded with enough force she was shocked the mansion was still standing. Every nerve ending burst into flames, and she cried out—God, *screamed* out—a string of curses, and then their names.

"Fuck. *Shit*. Kayden. Aldo!"

Aldo held her steady as Kayden's fingers slowed, still thrusting as he drew out her climax, made it last so long it became almost painful.

She gripped his wrist, her hold weak and completely ineffectual. "Can't take any more."

Kayden curled his fingers, gave that special spot one more brush that had her jerking in Aldo's arms again, then he took mercy on her, withdrawing completely.

"Jesus Christ," Aldo said softly. "A man could get addicted to your orgasms. I've never seen anything more beautiful."

She remained on his lap, in the same position he'd put her, every bone in her body soft as warm butter.

Kayden still knelt between her legs, grinning cockily, not that she would call him to task for it. He deserved to take a damn victory lap for that.

He leaned toward her, and she thought perhaps he was going to offer her a kiss, so she was surprised when he lifted his hand, pushing his fingers—wet from her arousal—into Aldo's mouth. They'd done the same thing in the restaurant, their lack of boundaries confirming a suspicion that continually hovered in the background of her mind.

Moaning, Aldo sucked the juices off as Hazel watched, spellbound, her mind whirling over what she was seeing.

When his hand was clean, Kayden resumed his seat and

reached over to pluck her back into his lap, cuddling her as he had earlier.

The three of them remained there, simply staring into each other's eyes, smiling, sometimes sharing a breathy laugh but not saying a single word.

Yet, Hazel felt as if they'd spoken volumes. The cracks that had started appearing in her wall gave way, and a huge chunk fell.

She was in deep shit now.

Chapter Fourteen

Aldo took Hazel's hand as they walked into the hospital. He could tell she was nervous despite the fact he'd assured her this meeting wasn't a job interview...just an introduction.

"They're going to love you," he said, though this wasn't the first time. Hell, it wasn't even the fifth time.

Last night, after Hazel had come apart in his arms, the three of them cuddled for another hour in the recliner. Hazel had tried to initiate more, insisting it wasn't fair that she was the only one who'd come the last two times they'd been together.

He and Kayden had refused, determined to take things slow. The more time he spent with her, the more convinced he was that they'd found the one. So they were taking their time, doing this right.

He'd hated seeing the shadows in her eyes when they'd talked to her about trust and opening up about her past, wishing she felt comfortable sharing with them. Whatever she was running from was bad enough that she'd completely uprooted her life to get away from it.

So they'd made out on the recliners until nearly midnight,

then they'd helped her get dressed, tucked her into bed—alone—and headed home. To their own homes, which had bothered Aldo more than he might have expected.

He and Kayden had banked the fire between them for too fucking long, but these interludes with Hazel had stoked the flames into a goddamn bonfire. Aldo was burning for both of them, certain the first time the three of them truly came together, he would spontaneously combust, reduced to ash.

"Here we go," Aldo said, as they approached Nonno's room. "You ready?"

Hazel nodded, but the way she tightened her grip, pulling him away from the door, told another story. "You said you told your grandmother about me?"

"Yeah. She and I talk on the phone a couple times a week. She called a few days after the fire to ask about it and to see how Rocco was doing. I mentioned meeting you, how you'd lost your things, and that you were staying at the inn. She asked if there was anything you needed, ready to run to the store to get it for you."

Hazel smiled. "So you got your generosity from her."

"And Nonno. I reassured her the girls had taken care of you as far as getting a wardrobe together. The next time I called her, she asked about you. It was the day after our date, and, well, Nonna has a sixth sense when it comes to romance. I thought I was playing it cool, but she called me on it. Said she was thrilled I finally met a girl I liked."

He expected that fact to amuse her, so he couldn't understand her sudden frown. "Does she know...I mean...well, Kayden..." Whenever she was uncomfortable discussing a subject, Hazel began speaking in disjointed words.

He chuckled, wrapping his arm around her waist. "Is that what you're worried about?"

"Would it upset her?"

Aldo gave her a quick kiss on the cheek. "Have you forgotten about Gio? And I know you haven't met my cousins Erin or Layla, but they're both in threesome relationships too."

"And your Nonna is okay with that?"

"She is. I'm not going to say it didn't take the family by surprise when Layla showed up with Miguel and Finn in tow, but we Morettis tend to roll with things."

"Unless it's the Russos," she pointed out, clever little smart-ass.

He laughed. "Unless it's those assholes."

"So she knows Kayden was on the date with us?"

"She does. She loves Kayden like he's one of her own. She wants him to be happy too." He could see Hazel was still struggling. "And you, Fireball, make both of us very happy."

Finally, at last, he managed to get a smile out of her.

"Okay now?" he asked.

"Yes."

This time, she allowed him to open the door.

"Everybody decent in here?" Aldo joked as he peered into the room.

Nonna rose from her chair beside Nonno, gesturing for them to come in. "Of course," she said. At the same time, Nonno grumbled, "No one can be decent in these damn hospital gowns. My ass hangs out every time I go to the bathroom."

"Vanni," Nonna admonished, using her nickname for Nonno, whose given name was Giovanni. Gio was named after him. "Aldo's brought Hazel."

Hazel stepped into the room, clearly amused. "It's okay, Mrs. Moretti. Hospital gowns are the worst."

"Now, now. I will not be called Mrs. Moretti." Nonna reached for Hazel's hands. "You're going to be living in our house and helping me take care of my Vanni. Call me Nonna."

Before Hazel could reply, Nonna pulled her into her arms and gave her a big hug. Nonna was the queen of hugs, and she gave them out freely—to family members and strangers.

Hazel's shocked expression quickly morphed into one of happiness, and Aldo couldn't help but smile.

"Nonna," Hazel said softly when they parted, as if she was trying it on for size.

"And the guy in the bed," Aldo pointed to his grandfather, "is Nonno. The Mr. Moretti thing won't work for him either."

Nonno tried to sit upright in the bed, Nonna quickly crossing to fluff a pillow behind his back. Obviously the fussing had already begun, as Nonno shook his head, waving his wife away.

"Domenica, I'm fine. Leave it be," Nonno insisted. "It's nice to meet you, my dear." Then he looked over at Aldo and gave him a wink. "Hard for a man to complain about having surgery when he has two such pretty nurses ready to take care of him."

Nonna lightly slapped Nonno in the shoulder. "You old charmer." Then she looked at Hazel. "He's a shameless flirt, Hazel. Consider yourself warned."

Nonna directed Aldo and Hazel to the couch by the window, reclaiming her chair, and the four of them spent the next hour talking about the surgery, the aftercare, and the living situation. Nonna promised to have the biggest bedroom ready for Hazel to move into, even though Hazel told her she didn't need to make a fuss, that her time was better spent with Nonno.

The time passed quickly and pleasantly and only ended when an orderly came in, announcing it was time to take Nonno for some tests the doctor ordered.

Nonna hugged them both goodbye and thanked Hazel for the hundredth time for agreeing to help them.

Hazel was still smiling when they left the room.

"Well?" Aldo asked.

"They're incredible," she gushed. "I absolutely love them. Your Nonna is so sweet, and I was right, your grandfather *is* a character."

"They liked you too. I could tell."

"It sounds like they won't need me for another week, which is perfect because I can keep working at Divine until Rafe's waitress gets back from maternity leave. That way I'm not leaving him in the lurch."

Aldo was tempted to suggest she take the week to move her things and get settled in at his grandparents' house, but given the little comments she'd dropped here and there, he got the sense Hazel had never taken a vacation in her life, working since she was twelve.

Twelve!

Who the hell even hired a twelve-year-old? He was pretty damn sure that was illegal.

They'd just gotten into Aldo's truck when both of their phones beeped at the same time. Looking down, he saw they'd gotten the same text from Kayden in their group.

I'm off in an hour. Dinner at my place?

Aldo looked at Hazel. "What do you think?"

"I think it sounds great."

Aldo replied for the two of them.

We're both in. Just finished up at the hospital. Need us to run to the store for anything?

Kayden texted back a list of a few items, thanking them as it meant he would get home sooner.

He and Hazel headed to the grocery store, taking their time, perusing the aisles, discussing what wine to buy for dinner. Hazel, unsurprisingly, was a budget shopper, comparing costs to ensure they got more for their money. He didn't tell her he was a speed shopper, meaning his goal when at the store was to grab what he needed and get the hell out, prices be damned.

As they put their items on the conveyor belt to check out, she read the funny headlines on the tabloid magazines to him. It was a simple thing. Shopping together, but the domesticity of it had Aldo dreaming of the future.

At thirty-five, he'd had plenty of time to decide what he wanted his life to hold. In addition to Kayden and a wife, he longed for a home and children, a lifetime of doing stuff like this

—walking around a grocery store, doing laundry and lawn work, fighting over the remote—with the people he loved.

"Okay. There we go." Aldo loaded the bags into the backseat of his truck. "Kayden's probably getting out of work right about now. Let's head over there and unpack these things. Then the three of us can get to work on dinner." Kayden's meal plan was lasagna, garlic bread, and salad, and Aldo liked the idea of the three of them cooking together.

He was right. Kayden was just getting out of his cruiser as Aldo pulled his truck next to it in the driveway. He and Kayden grabbed the bags of groceries, while Hazel carried the bottle of wine.

Kayden lived on a quiet suburban street, the home inherited after his parents were killed. And when Aldo envisioned his future home, it was always this two-story house. It had three bedrooms, a family room, a decent-sized kitchen, and an old wooden swing set in the backyard, remnants from Kayden and Keeley's childhood.

There were flowerpots on the front porch that had belonged to Kayden's mom, but Kayden only remembered to fill them with flowers every third year or so. And then he'd bitch himself out for wasting the money because he never remembered to water the damn things.

As they reached the porch, Aldo saw Hazel taking in everything, the flowerpots, the porch swing, the wrought-iron rocking chair.

"Your house is beautiful," she mused aloud.

Kayden unlocked the door, ushering them inside. "Let's put the food away and I'll give you a tour."

Aldo found himself curious about where she'd grown up. She'd been quite at ease today, so he decided to push his luck.

"Did you grow up in a house like this?" Aldo asked.

Hazel shook her head, her response coming after enough of a pause that he knew she was about to offer them a careful answer. "No. I grew up in an apartment. Nowhere near as nice as this. I love the big windows, the rich colors."

"My mom hated white walls," Kayden explained. "Said it was the most boring, least imaginative decorating choice in the world."

"I'd never considered that, but I think she was right. Oh, green is my favorite color," she announced when they walked into the dining room. Kayden's mom had painted the walls a dark green, the old-fashioned white chair rail around the middle of the room breaking up the color. There were a bunch of framed black and white photographs on the wall, old family portraits that Kayden explained, pointing out his grandmother and a great-grandfather he'd never known.

"I haven't done much in the way of redecorating," Kayden confessed. "Right after our parents died, I tried to keep everything the same for Keeley. I figured she'd had enough upheaval."

"So had you." Hazel rested her hand on Kayden's forearm.

"Of course, I've had plenty of chances to change things since my sister moved out. I just haven't made the time. I'm shit at picking out stuff like paint and new carpet, so I put it off. Which means the whole place is in need of some freshening up."

Aldo heard the words Kayden wasn't saying. His friend hadn't redecorated because, like Aldo, he was waiting for the next chapter to start, waiting for him and their future partner to move in, so they could make the place their home as well.

He hadn't considered the fact the two of them had been treading water the last few years, so tied to their hopes for the future that they hadn't bothered to fuck around too much with the present. Aldo hadn't thought about it that way until now, when he realized just how many years they'd let slip them by, everything operating by rote.

"How do you feel about home improvement stores?" Kayden took Hazel's hand and led her down the hallway to continue the tour.

"Why?"

"I'm hoping I can talk you into going with me one day to pick out some new paint colors."

Hazel lit up like a Christmas tree. "Really? Are you sure you wouldn't want to take Keeley? I'm sure if you told her you wanted to redecorate, she'd help."

"She's spent the last six months knee-deep in decorating an inn, and they're about to close on a house where she'll have to start all over again. Trust me. She'd thank you for taking one for the team."

"I'd love to go one day. Maybe after Nonno is better and—" Hazel stopped mid-sentence, and Aldo had a sinking suspicion why.

"Keep going," he prodded.

She blushed and shook her head. "Got a little carried away, didn't I? Making plans for two months in the future when..."

Kayden pushed Hazel's face up with a finger under her chin. "Hazel. Keep making plans. We like it."

She gave them a smile, though it felt forced, and there was no missing those same damn shadows that reappeared whenever she let herself get too happy. Hazel lived her life like a person waiting for the other shoe to drop.

Kayden pointed to the stairs. "Come on. We'll finish the tour and then start dinner."

* * *

Hazel pushed away from the table, crying uncle first. "I can't eat another bite, but damn if I don't wish I could. Kayden, that was the best lasagna I've ever eaten in my life."

Kayden wiped his mouth, tossing his napkin to the table. "Wait until you taste Aldo's mom's lasagna. It's her recipe, and while I've tried to replicate it no less than fifty times, I still can't quite master it."

"There's no way you can top this." Hazel gestured to the remaining lasagna and glanced at Aldo, as if expecting him to join the conversation.

"And there's no way *I'm* stepping into that minefield. Call me Switzerland. The most I'm willing to say is my mom and my best friend both make really awesome lasagna."

"How about you?" Hazel asked. "How's your lasagna?"

"Inedible," he and Kayden said in unison, both of them laughing.

"Curse of growing up around a family full of great cooks," Aldo explained. "It meant I never needed to learn. In my family, food is love. And the Moretti women love us guys a whole fucking lot."

"And you, Hazel? You know your way around a kitchen?" Kayden asked.

Hazel shrugged. "I can heat up canned ravioli, but I can't make the real thing. I can microwave soup, but I wouldn't have a clue how to make it homemade. I can open a package of cookies, but I've never baked them from scratch. So...does that count?"

Aldo nodded, while Kayden scrunched up his nose and said, "Absolutely not."

"Not to worry." Aldo rose from the table. "You say all that to Nonna, and I suspect she'll start your cooking classes that day."

He wasn't sure what response he expected from Hazel, but it wasn't the sheer look of joy.

"You really think she'll teach me?"

"Not a doubt in my mind," he assured her.

Kayden stood as well, picking up his plate and the leftover lasagna, taking it to the kitchen.

Hazel and Aldo followed with the rest of the dishes. He rinsed them, handing them to Hazel, who loaded the dishwasher. Meanwhile, Kayden wrapped up all the leftovers and put them in the fridge.

This activity was just as ordinary as grocery shopping had been and yet, Aldo couldn't get over the feeling he'd spent the day at a carnival. Everything with these two—even the boring-as-shit stuff—was fun.

Kayden topped up their wineglasses and the three of them walked to the living room. Hazel started to claim a cushioned chair, but Kayden cut her off at the pass, grasping her hand and tugging her down next to him on the large sectional.

Aldo plopped down on her other side, and since the couch was ridiculously big, the three of them filled only half of one side.

Hazel gave them knowing, amused looks, pointing to the unused half of the sectional. "Lots of room over there."

Kayden ignored her comment, taking her wineglass and putting it next to his on the end table. Aldo leaned forward to set his on the coffee table.

"So...where did we leave off?" Aldo wrapped his arm around her shoulders, kissing her on the cheek.

Hazel laughed softly. "Leave off?"

"Last night," he explained, even though he knew exactly how their night had ended. He hadn't made out like that since he'd been a teenager, and he wondered where along the line he'd lost the desire to just hold someone and kiss them, without any expectation for more.

Kayden was already skimming the side of her neck with his lips, his hand inching up her jeans-covered thigh.

"God," she sighed. "This is all so good. I keep waiting to feel overwhelmed, so why don't I? I mean...there are two of you and one of me."

Kayden lifted his head. "You're doing the math wrong. There are three of us. Period."

"I like that, but to be honest, so far, this has been a pretty lopsided affair. I mean, if we work the equation another way, I'm two orgasms to your zero. I..." She paused, and Aldo's cock thickened at the sight of her pretty blush. "I want to even that up tonight. Somehow," she added, waving her hands around.

"Are you talking blow jobs?" Kayden asked with a grin.

She nodded, just once.

Aldo cupped her cheek, turning her face to his for a kiss. "We said we'd take this slow. Go at your pace. If you want to up the ante, I'm pretty sure you won't hear me and Kay complaining."

"Good. Though I should tell you, I'm counting on you two to guide me through how this works with three people since you've done it before."

Aldo stiffened slightly, and Kayden lifted his lips from her neck.

Hazel frowned. "You guys *have* had a threesome before?"

Kayden shook his head. "No, we haven't."

"We never said that," Aldo added.

Hazel's eyes widened. "That's not possible."

"Why not?" Aldo asked.

"It's just...you're so at ease with each other. *Too* at ease. There's no way I'm the first woman you've done all this with, together. That just doesn't make sense."

Aldo and Kayden shared a look. If they were going to come clean about their previous affair, and the truth behind their relationship, this was a good time. But they'd already discussed that and had decided to move this relationship with Hazel forward by inches rather than miles.

She was still skittish about being with them—sexually and emotionally. And until she settled into that, they'd decided to wait to tell her exactly why it wasn't two of them and one of her.

But now...remaining quiet no longer felt right. Hazel had enough secrets of her own. Throwing one of theirs into the mix seemed wrong.

Before Aldo could say anything, Kayden replied for them. "We've never met a woman we wanted to share before you, Hazel."

Which was one hundred percent the truth.

"I'm really your first?" There was no mistaking her shock.

"You are," Aldo said, thinking she'd let it go.

Hazel was too clever for that. She was obviously seeing what they weren't saying, even without them saying the words.

"But this all feels so natural between you," she pointed out. "Like you've been down this road a few times."

Kayden's arm slid around her middle, holding her tightly. "We've been best friends forever. And while we've never been in a relationship like this, we've seen it up close and personal. Watched my sister and Aldo's cousins with their special people."

"We've known for years," Aldo added, his hand resting on her thigh, "that we want what Keeley, Gio, and Rafe have. The problem was, we never found a woman we were both attracted to, or one who might accept what we want."

He hadn't come right out and said the words, but Aldo hoped by claiming they wanted what Gio, Rafe, and Keeley had, Hazel would understand. Because she'd been staying with the trio, and she'd obviously seen that Rafe and Gio kissed each other as much as they kissed Keeley.

"What they have is amazing," Hazel whispered, giving Aldo no clue if she'd made the leap or not. "I...I have something I need to tell you."

Aldo froze, wondering—hoping, praying—that Hazel was ready to open up to them about her past.

"You can tell us anything," Kayden reassured her.

"I've never..." This time her face bypassed the cute pink-cheeks blush and went straight to the blood-red flush.

"Never..." Aldo prodded.

She pursed her lips, her gaze dropping to his crotch. "You know. Never, um..."

"Given a guy a blow job?" Kayden asked.

She closed her eyes and blew out a long sigh. "I never liked a guy enough to, well, you know."

"But you like us well enough?" Aldo felt as if she'd just given him a million dollars.

She nodded.

"Say the words, Hazel," Kayden demanded. "Tell us you want to give us blow jobs."

She grunted. "Kayden," she started.

He tilted her chin toward him, his forefinger and thumb holding her there so she couldn't look away. "All you have to do is say it."

"I want to give you blow jobs." Hazel never failed to respond to Kayden's commands, but sometimes Aldo wasn't sure if that was based on submissiveness or stubbornness. She had ample amounts of both.

Then he decided he didn't give a shit either way. Both those attributes turned him on.

Kayden gave her a hard kiss, a reward for her obedience, then he shifted away, grabbing a throw pillow from the couch.

He tossed it to the floor at their feet. "Kneel there."

Aldo went light-headed, a serious lack of blood to the brain, when Hazel moved without a second's hesitation.

"Jesus." Aldo was suddenly terrified of embarrassing himself, coming way too fucking fast. Especially when she bit her lower lip, looking so fucking innocent and sexy.

She and Aldo both frowned when Kayden grabbed another pillow and tossed it to the floor next to hers, kneeling beside her.

"I'm going to teach you," Kayden said.

Aldo was fucked. Big-time. Maybe he could have saved face with just Hazel, but if Kayden put his lips anywhere near his dick, he'd blow like Old Faithful.

"Stand up, Aldo. And take off your pants." If his friend had used the dark, rumbly Dom voice he used with Hazel, Aldo probably would have refused, despite wanting what they offered. Because Hazel wasn't the only one with more than their fair share of stubbornness.

But Kayden wasn't giving a command. He was moving them on to the good stuff.

Aldo stood, toeing off his shoes and socks, then drawing his jeans and boxers off as well. It occurred to him the second he heard Hazel gasp that this was her first time seeing his dick. If he'd remembered that, maybe he wouldn't have stripped down like his pants were on fire.

"Aldo's got a nice cock," Kayden murmured in her ear. "Doesn't he?"

Hazel nodded, her gaze locked on Aldo's dick.

He expected Kayden to ease Hazel into things, to offer her instructions. After a lifetime of being best friends with the guy, he should have known better.

Kayden lifted Hazel's hand, drawing it to Aldo's cock. "Wrap your hand around the base. Feel how thick he is." Rather than leave her to her own devices, Kayden kept his hand on hers, so that when her fingers closed around him, Kayden's were there too.

"Fuck me." Aldo closed his eyes, hoping that by blocking out how fucking hot they looked on their knees, he would be able to combat blowing his load too fast.

"Now we're going to stroke it, imitate the sensation of how Aldo's dick is going to feel when it's inside you."

Hazel started to move her hand, slowly—too slowly—and gently—too fucking gently—until Kayden tightened his grip.

"Like this," he said. "I said to make it like your pussy. Nice and tight."

Aldo was wrong. Closing his eyes didn't help a goddamn bit. If anything, it only served to heighten his other senses. Gazing down at them, he watched as Hazel and Kayden drew their hands up and down his dick. They kept the pace steady, but Kayden wasn't letting up, gripping him with the perfect amount of force.

"Kayden." Aldo cleared his throat when it came out too rough. "If this is going to last—"

Kayden, the bastard, ignored him. "You want a taste?"

She nodded.

"Go on then. Use your tongue to lick up that precum. Like this."

Kayden was there before Aldo could gird his loins, giving the tip of his dick a quick swipe of the tongue. Hazel's gasp was one of surprise. Kayden's intimate touch shocking her, but damn if she didn't recover quick. A second later, she mimicked Kayden's lick. Aldo hissed, and Hazel's gaze flew up to his face, concerned.

"Does that hurt?" she asked him.

Kayden responded for him. "Remember how it felt when I pushed my tongue inside you last night."

"God, yes."

Aldo caught sight of her nipples, pushing their way through the soft cotton of her long-sleeved tee.

"Did *that* hurt?" Kayden asked.

She shook her head. "No. It felt...too good."

"It's the same for Aldo. Give him another lick. Then take the head of his cock in your mouth. Just this far to start."

Once again, Kayden led by example, showing her exactly what he wanted her to do. Hazel's gaze flew up to Aldo's face, and though she said nothing, he knew she'd snapped the final piece into place.

Hazel was suddenly doing the math the right way, and when she gave him a knowing, sexy-as-fuck smile, he lost all hope of holding on.

Let the cards fall where they may. He'd have to find a way to prove to her later that he was capable of not coming at the speed of light.

Any concerns Hazel might have had about him being in pain were washed away when her attention returned to his cock. She ran her tongue along the head before sucking him inside her mouth. Aldo reached out, wrapping her hair around his fist, struggling to keep his grip loose.

"Oh yeah. He likes that," Kayden said. "You can take him deeper now."

Hazel did as Kayden said, following every command to the tee. She was a fucking natural.

Soon, she was taking him deeper on each return, her hand and Kayden's still gripping the base of his cock, stroking in time with the motion of her mouth.

"One of these nights, we're going to fuck your mouth," Kayden promised.

Hazel's brows furrowed, but she was unable to question how that was different from this, her mouth too full of him.

"You're in control during this blow job," Kayden explained. "When we fuck your mouth, *we* are. We decide how fast, how deep. You'll take us all the way down your throat."

Hazel whimpered—the sound one of need, not fear—and it added to the incredible sensations of her swishing tongue and the firm grip of their hands.

Time and place faded away as the edges of Aldo's vision went gray. He was vaguely aware he was gripping her hair too tightly, tugging it, using it to increase her pace, but Hazel didn't pull away. Instead, she responded to it, moaning louder around his hard flesh.

"Fuck," Aldo said with a gasp. "I'm there. I'm gonna—" He loosened his grip, his eyes wide open as he sought Kayden's help.

Kayden was whispering something in Hazel's ear, but Aldo couldn't hear it over the thudding of his heartbeat. All he felt was the subtle nod of her head, even as she continued driving him out of his fucking mind.

If she was going to pull away, the time was...

"Hazel."

She held him tighter, worked him faster, and Aldo was lost, come bursting from the tip of his cock, exploding inside her mouth.

His body jerked, then trembled as his balls clenched. Hazel didn't push away, didn't let go of him. Instead, she released her grip on his dick, her hands flying to his ass as if to hold him in place.

Jesus. Fucking. Christ.

When he finally came down, he saw Kayden drawing Hazel back, until Aldo's dick popped out of her mouth. Then, holy shit, her eyes lifted to his and...she swallowed.

Aldo's legs gave out. He sat back down on the couch heavily.

He remained there, probably resembling a zombie, watching as Kayden and Hazel kissed, shared his taste.

And in that moment, he knew. Knew with such conviction, such certainty, that this was it.

He'd found it.

His family. His future.

Forever.

Chapter Fifteen

"**I**'ll have the special," Kayden said, the last to place his order.

Their waitress, Debbie, nodded and smiled. "Sure thing."

Kayden took a drink of water and leaned back in his chair, grinning at the guys around him. Every Wednesday, he and a bunch of his buddies had a standing lunch date at Paulie's Diner. Some weeks, only a couple guys might make it or some weeks—like this one—almost the entire gang was there. He was sitting between Aldo and Tony, while Luca, Gio, Rafe, and Rhys took up the rest of the seats. The only guys missing were Joey and Elio, who were both out of town, Joey filming *ManPower*, Elio finishing up his season with the NHL.

"Guess in a few weeks, Elio will start being a regular for lunch," Tony mused.

"Twenty-eight days," Gio replied, quickly enough that everyone stared at him. He sighed. "Gianna has a countdown going on a big whiteboard at the inn office. Makes a big deal of marking off a day every single morning. It's not a bit annoying," he said sarcastically.

"Those two are so sticky-sweet in love I get a toothache every time I'm around them," Luca groused.

Tony slapped Luca on the shoulder. "I'm going to remember you said that when you find your girl because I know you, brother. When you go down, it's gonna be a hard fall."

Luca snorted. "I'm not going to be a sap about it like you two," he said to Tony and Rhys, before jerking a thumb toward Gio and Rafe. "Or these two." Then his gaze landed on him and Aldo, and he added, "Or *those* two."

Tony and Rhys were both happily shacked up with Jess, and now the proud fathers of her young son, Jasper. As such, they didn't hang out with the gang as much as they used to.

"The nurse?" Tony looked toward him and Aldo. "Jess mentioned you'd asked her out on a date a few weeks ago. I take it that went well."

Aldo answered for them. "Very well. Hazel is..." He didn't finish the sentence. Probably because he couldn't land on a word big enough. Of course, he didn't need to finish. His huge, shit-eating grin pretty much said it all.

Tony chuckled. "Like that, is it? Good for you. I only met her once, when I stopped by to check on how Nonno was doing after the surgery. We talked for a minute or so, but it's not hard to see she's good at her job. Nonna was fretting, like she does, over his lack of appetite. Hazel very calmly explained that it was normal, answered all her questions, reassured her he was fine. Never seen anyone able to talk Nonna down off the ledge like that, especially when it comes to Nonno's health."

"She's a very good nurse." While Kayden was impressed by her work ethic, he was also—selfishly—annoyed by it. Because Hazel was taking her job very seriously. So seriously, she hadn't left the Morettis' house since Nonno came home from the hospital nine days earlier.

He and Aldo had gone over a few times, hoping to lure her out for a quick dinner date. Liza hadn't lied about the family schedule.

Someone in the family had come by every evening to help with dinner and Nonno's care, so Hazel could take a break. Aldo had told her numerous times that no one expected her to work round the clock twenty-four seven, but Hazel refused to leave her patient.

Or more accurately, patients. Because Hazel was taking care of Nonna as well. Keeley had mentioned the family's concerns that Nonna would work herself to exhaustion looking after Nonno, but none of that had come to fruition with Hazel in the house. What's more, Aldo had been shocked when Nonna mentioned she was actually considering knee replacement surgery—something she desperately needed—thanks to Hazel's influence.

"I know I told Hazel I'd hold the waitressing job for her, but I'd hate for her to go back to waiting tables when it's clear she was born to be a nurse." Rafe slathered butter on one of the hot rolls the waitress had just delivered to their table.

"Nonno's crazy about her," Aldo said. "And the feeling seems to be mutual. The two of them took to each other right away."

"She appreciates his sense of humor," Kayden added.

"Get this," Aldo started, and Kayden knew by his best friend's grin exactly what story he was about to tell. "We picked Nonno up at the hospital, brought him home, helped get him settled. Hazel is there and she's reading a list of do's and don'ts from the doctor. Tells him he can't lift anything over ten pounds. And Nonno, the old scamp, looks at her with a straight face and asks, "Then how am I supposed to pee?"

The table exploded with laughter, their reactions the same as Hazel's. Kayden could still see how it took a split second for the joke to land before Hazel erupted in a full-fledged belly laugh, complete with wiping tears from her eyes. It lasted long enough that he and Aldo had exchanged a glance, both thrilled to see such unabashed joy on her face. They'd grown too accustomed to her soft giggles and too-short laughs that she always hid behind her hand.

Kayden vowed to himself that he'd try to find a way to provoke that laugh from her every single day. Because it was obvious there'd been too little genuine happiness in her life. And damn if it didn't look good on her.

"So Nonno's doing okay?" Gio asked.

Kayden knew from Keeley that Gio was feeling guilty for not getting over to see his grandfather yet, but between finishing the inn, Moretti Brothers Restoration projects, and closing on their new house, he was burning the candle at both ends, working from sunup to sundown.

"He's doing well," Kayden reassured his—hopefully—soon-to-be brother-in-law.

"They kept him at the hospital an extra day than previously planned," Aldo explained explain.

"Which is not at all uncommon, given his age," Rhys hastened to include. "I suspect they were erring on the side of caution, rather than from any real concerns."

The men continued to discuss the surgery and the healing process, asking Rhys questions. Kayden could hear the concern in their tones, and he was grateful to Rhys—Dr. Beaumont—for taking the time to explain things and reassure them, much like Hazel had done for Nonna.

Kayden had never been close to his maternal grandparents simply because they'd lived on the West Coast, both of them dying a few years before the plane crash that killed his parents. His father's parents had divorced, badly, with Dad the weapon they'd used to hurt each other until he put his foot down and cut off all ties with both of them, moving in with a distant cousin his last two years of high school.

So when Kayden lost his parents, he'd been struck by the fact that Keeley was the only family he had left in the world. It was one of the reasons he'd lost his mind a bit, smothering her, because of the bone-deep fear that if he lost her too, he'd be utterly alone.

That fear faded within a year because the Morettis had stepped in, and not just Aldo, Tony, Gio, and the other guys, but Nonno and Nonna, and the aunts and uncles as well.

They'd rallied around him and Keeley and taken them in as their own.

Nonno had been the one to sit Kayden down and tell him that while he understood his need to keep his sister close, and therefore safe, what he was really doing was pushing her away, forcing her to do somewhat dangerous things in order to buy herself some freedom. The old man had seen Kayden's fear, recognized it for what it was, and helped Kayden find ways to overcome it.

In the past decade, he'd decided there was the family he was born with, but there was also the family he'd chosen—and who'd chosen him. Thanks to the Morettis, he and Keeley would never be alone.

"Anyone talked to Rocco lately?" Aldo changed the subject once Rhys had addressed all their concerns about Nonno.

Tony nodded. "Yeah, he went to the old geezer's poker game Monday night. It was at Dad's." Tony's father and Aldo's took turns hosting a poker game once a month with a bunch of their buddies. Rocco had never missed, though there'd been some concern he wouldn't come to this one.

"How's he doing?" Aldo was clearly worried about the man. Crossings Motel had been Rocco's entire life.

Tony murmured "thanks" when the waitress refilled his water glass, then replied, "Dad said he was doing good, apart from dealing with the insurance company, and trying to figure out how to clean up the mess. Had to run some guy off the property the other day who was poking around the debris, messing around with the burned-out cars and shit, despite the caution tape and no-trespassing signs. Dad said Rocco planned to stop by and say hello to Nonno yesterday. Not sure if he did or not."

"Oh," Aldo said. "I'll have to ask him tonight when we stop by. Hope he did. Nonno loves him, and, despite all his own health issues, he's been worried about Rocco since the fire."

"Is he planning to rebuild?" Kayden asked.

Tony shook his head. "Nope. Dad said he's taking the insurance money, adding it to the nest egg he'd built up over the years, and retiring. He's trying to talk my dad and yours into joining him on a hunting trip out west in the fall. Been looking at cabins to rent in Wyoming."

"Good for him," Luca said, as the waitress returned with their food.

Conversation slowed as they began to eat, Kayden's thoughts wandering to the coming evening. He and Aldo planned to have dinner with Hazel...and Nonno and Nonna...again. They'd seen her three times since the night Kayden taught her how to give a blow job, but since Hazel wouldn't leave Nonno, they hadn't had much opportunity to expand on that lesson or anything else.

Instead, they'd all five sat in the living room, watching *Wheel of Fortune* and *Jeopardy*. When the shows were over, Nonno and Nonna always retired to their room, just down the hall—leaving the three of them quietly necking on the couch like a bunch of teenagers.

It was silly and fun and such a fucking turn-on that Kayden felt like he was living with a perpetual case of blue balls that no amount of jacking off could cure.

"So you're heading to Nonno's tonight?" Luca asked. "Because it's my night to help with dinner and hang out, according to the schedule the aunts came up with."

"Hazel refuses to leave them alone. If we want to see her, we have to go there," Aldo replied.

"Maybe between the three of us, we can convince her to go out for a few hours," Luca offered.

"Maybe we can." Kayden wasn't holding out much hope.

After lunch, he returned to work, clocking out at five, anxious to pick up Aldo and head over to the Morettis'.

Aldo must have been just as anxious, because he answered the door the second Kayden knocked, his coat already on. The second he stepped out onto the stoop, he gripped Kayden's shoulders, giving him a hard, hungry kiss. Aldo was obviously in the same horny-as-fuck state.

"Something's gotta give," Aldo murmured against his lips.

"Agree. Tonight." Kayden said it with more confidence than he felt. Though in truth, if Hazel turned them down again, Kayden was pretty sure nothing would stop him from tossing her over his shoulder and dragging her out. So maybe tonight wasn't out of the realm of possibility.

Kayden left his cruiser at Aldo's, the two of them taking Aldo's truck instead. If they did manage to convince Hazel to go out, they thought it better to have the truck. Hazel seemed very uneasy in the cruiser, even when Aldo jokingly offered to sit in the back and look like the criminal.

Luca was already there when they arrived, he and Nonna in the kitchen fixing dinner.

"Smells good." Aldo gave his grandmother a kiss on the cheek. "What are you cooking?"

"Chicken and rice with steamed vegetables," Nonna replied. "And I'm going to need you boys to talk it up, make it sound like the most delicious thing you've ever eaten because Vanni is grumpy without his cheesy lasagna and eggplant parmesan."

"Actually, we were hoping to convince Hazel to go out to dinner with us. Just for something quick like cheesesteaks," Aldo hastened to add when a brief flash of panic crossed Nonna's face.

It looked like Nonno wasn't the only person in the house who'd grown dependent on Hazel's presence.

"Hazel hasn't had a break since Nonno came home," Luca gently reminded his grandmother.

"Oh no. That's true, isn't it? That's no good. Poor girl," Nonna said, Luca's words hitting home. "A few hours won't hurt and Luca is here. You boys have a good time."

"A good time where?" Hazel walked into the room, about to reach for an apron to help with dinner. Aldo's prediction that Nonna would teach Hazel how to cook had come to fruition, and now their pretty nurse was obsessed with learning everything she could.

Kayden watched Luca's eyes widen as Aldo walked over and

gave her a big, lingering kiss hello—with tongue. Most of the family was unaware of just how far things had progressed between the three of them.

Nonna, however, never blinked an eye at Aldo's show of affection. "The boys are taking you out for cheesesteaks."

Hazel started shaking her head the second Nonna said *taking you out*. "Oh no, I couldn't possibly leave you and Nonno alone."

Nonna may have had her reservations, but she wasn't letting them show. She walked over and placed her wrinkled hand on Hazel's forearm. "We're not going to be alone. Luca will be here. You haven't left the house since you moved in, Hazel. Go take a break for a few hours, enjoy some alone time with your boyfriends."

Hazel glanced at them nervously, obviously to gauge their response to Nonna's label of "boyfriends."

"Yeah," Luca piled on. "Your *boyfriends* miss you. And Aldo said you've yet to have a cheesesteak from Pat's, which is a crime."

"She hasn't had one from Geno's either," Kayden chimed in. "Which might be even worse."

Luca rolled his eyes. Kayden was used to going to war with the Moretti boys over the best cheesesteak in Philly.

Hazel looked ready to dig in her heels, but Kayden wasn't having it. Wrapping his arm around her waist, he turned her toward the kitchen door. "Three hours, Fireball. That's all we're asking for."

Hazel looked over her shoulder hesitantly. "If you're sure," she said to Nonna, who shooed her on.

"Go have some fun, Hazel. You've earned it."

They walked to the front door, Aldo retrieving Hazel's winter coat and slipping it on before stealing another quick kiss.

"Not sure how you could miss me. We just saw each other four days ago," Hazel pointed out once they were all settled in the truck, referring to the last time they'd spent the evening necking on the Morettis' couch.

Neither he nor Aldo took that bait. Nor did they correct what Luca had said because they *had* missed her.

Kayden had claimed his usual spot in the back, giving her the heated passenger seat. Resting his arm along the back, he relaxed for the first time in four days. It wasn't that he was uptight or stressed out or anything like that. It was more like the world didn't feel right when they weren't together. When it was just the three of them, he could kick back and be himself, confident that two people he cared about were where he could keep an eye on them.

It had been the same way with Keeley after their parents died. The nights he slept best were the ones when she was in her bedroom across the hall, safely within his reach. He'd hated the years she'd been away at college because he never knew where she was or who she was with. God help him—and his children—when he became a real father.

None of them spoke, yet there was comfort in the silence. In the way Aldo hummed along with the radio and Hazel watched the world fly by from the window.

"So which cheesesteak place are we going to?" she asked after a few minutes.

"Both," he and Aldo said in unison. "They're right across from each other. Figure we'll get a large with the works from each of them. You can have some of Aldo's and some of mine, then set our boy straight on which one is the best."

Hazel shook her head. "Not sure it would be smart to step into the middle of that argument. I get a feeling it's been going on for a while."

"Epic battle," Kayden joked. "Lots of bloodshed on both sides."

"Yeah, I'm just gonna go ahead and peace out on that now." Her bright green eyes twinkled. God, she was gorgeous. And feisty. And funny. And fun.

And he had it bad for her. Tony claimed Luca would fall hard, and it occurred to Kayden, he'd gone down twice. First for Aldo, and now Hazel.

"How have things been going back at the house?" Aldo asked Hazel.

"It's wonderful. I've never stayed in a house that feels like a real home. You know what I mean?"

Kayden didn't, actually, but Hazel didn't stop talking to wait for a reply.

"All the furniture is plush and clean, and the bed I'm sleeping in is so cushy and comfy and huge, and your Nonna actually *made* the quilt on it. It's so beautiful, I can't believe she uses it. Something that special feels like it should be tucked away. And the house always smells like fresh-baked bread. It's like the smell is soaked into everything and it's just...God, it's just Heaven on earth."

Kayden grinned, happy that *she* was so happy, but curious once more about where she came from. She'd never been in a house that felt like a home? That might be the saddest thing he'd ever heard in his life.

"Nonno doing okay?" Aldo asked.

She nodded. "He's doing great. We take little walks every day. He's eating well, taking his medicine, the healing is going slower than he'd like, but that's because of his age. Liza wasn't kidding about him thinking he's only sixty. He seriously believes he should be able to just hop out of bed and carry on as normal. And I've never met such a sharp guy. His mind is like a steel trap. You've seen him playing *Jeopardy*. The man is a walking encyclopedia. He knows so much about so many fascinating subjects, and his stories! Oh my God, he's so funny. I could listen to him talk all day."

Hazel stopped, looking at both of them. "Sorry. Got on a bit of a roll there, didn't I?"

Aldo reached over and grasped her hand. "You never have to apologize for liking my nonno. Just proves you have great taste in people. He's a hell of a guy."

"He really is," Kayden chimed in from the back.

"And your nonna is so sweet," Hazel said, smiling. "She's been so patient while she tries to teach me how to cook. Tomorrow, she's promised to teach me how to make pasta from scratch, which I have to admit, I didn't even know was a thing. I swear she makes the best food I've ever tasted."

"Wait until you taste Aunt Berta's cooking. She might be the only woman on the planet who can give Nonna a run for her money in the kitchen. Uncle Renzo swore that's why he grabbed hold of her and married her so quick. They only dated two months, going out to restaurants until Aunt Berta invited him over for a home-cooked meal one night. Uncle Renzo said after the first bite, he knew she was the woman for him and by the third bite, he was planning his proposal. Aunt Berta always used to give him shit when he told that story. Kept at him until he'd relent and say he married her for love. Of course, the second she looked away, he'd wink at us."

"Sounds like he got Nonno's sense of humor," Hazel observed. "The Moretti men do like to tease."

Aldo chuckled. "That we do."

"This is the best job I've ever had, Aldo. I can't thank you and your family enough for giving me a chance."

He shook his head. "We're the ones who should be thanking *you*."

Hazel didn't look like she agreed, but she didn't argue the point. Just smiled at Aldo like he hung the sun.

Aldo parked near the two restaurants, and the three of them placed their order at Pat's, then headed over to Geno's. It was too cold to eat them outside in the park, so they returned to the truck, the savory smell of cheese and onions filling the cab.

"Oh my God." Hazel treated them to her food moans after trying both. "So good."

Kayden's cock twitched at the sound of her moan, and he made a mental note to do whatever it took to hear it again at least three more times tonight. He was riding the razor's edge here, aware he'd never wanted a woman as much as he wanted Hazel. If they got her alone tonight, all bets were off.

"So you guys used to be roommates?" Hazel picked up a new conversation, deftly avoiding telling them which cheesesteak she preferred.

Kayden nodded. "Yeah. Until my parents died, and then I moved back home."

Hazel considered that. "You never considered living together again after Keeley moved out?"

"We have," Aldo replied. "Conversation comes up every year when my lease renews. We've just never pulled the trigger."

"Seems wasteful to pay rent when Kayden has such a nice, big house," she mused.

"You're right," Aldo agreed. "My lease is up at the end of next month," he said to Kayden. "Maybe this year..."

Kayden knew what Aldo was thinking—or maybe *hoping* was a better word. They were both falling for Hazel Walsh, and while they'd only known her a month, they were showing shades of Aldo's uncle Renzo, ready to make huge leaps to claim her, keep her.

"We should talk about it again," Kayden said. "Take it a bit more seriously this year."

Aldo's face broke into a big grin. "We should."

Hazel polished off the last of her cheesesteaks, wiping her hands and mouth.

"Okay. So we're going to need an answer. Which one is better?" Aldo asked.

She narrowed her eyes. "They're both equally great," she replied diplomatically.

"Chicken shit." Aldo chuckled, collecting their trash and hopping out of the truck to toss it. "Do me a favor," he said when he got back in, "don't tell Nonno we had cheesesteaks, or we'll catch holy hell for not bringing him one back."

"He can't eat that," Hazel said.

"I know, but that doesn't mean he won't still be pissed. The man loves his cheesesteaks." Aldo started the car. "Where to next?"

Hazel glanced at the truck clock. "I really should—"

"We've only been gone an hour. Which means you're ours for at least two more," Kayden interjected. "Luca's there and not going anywhere until we get back. If they need you, they'll call."

"Fine. You win." Hazel peered at him over her shoulder, then gave him the sexiest grin he'd ever seen. "Sooo," she drawled, "whose place is closer? Yours or Aldo's?"

Aldo put the car in drive. "We can be at my apartment in ten minutes."

Hazel laughed when he hit the gas hard, pulling back out onto the street quickly.

"Don't make me write a speeding ticket from the backseat," Kayden joked.

Aldo ignored him and, thanks to some traffic light luck, they made it to his apartment in eight minutes.

The three of them walked in together, and the second the door closed behind them, Kayden pushed Hazel against it, his lips slamming down on hers.

Aldo's hand landed on his shoulder. "Take it easy on our girl, Kay."

Kayden considered the request, but before he could act on it, *their* girl nipped his lower lip, hard, adding her own sense of urgency to the kiss.

He pulled his face away, just barely. "You want to play rough?"

His question had Aldo shifting, coming to stand where he could see both of them. "Rough?"

"*Our girl,*" Kayden said, repeating Aldo's words, stressing them, "has teeth."

Kayden could taste the slightly salty tang that told him she drew blood. Aldo's gaze landed on his lips, his eyes darkening with lust.

"That she does." Aldo reached out to grip Hazel's hip.

"What are you going to do about it?" Hazel was purposely provoking them, which meant she knew exactly what she wanted.

Kayden rested his forehead against hers. "Playing the brat?"

She grinned shamelessly. "Who says I'm playing?"

"Need your ass spanked, Hazel?" Kayden kept his tone deliberately light, almost playful. "You know you don't have to misbehave. Just ask for it. Like a good girl."

He saw her quick intake of breath, knew his words had packed a punch, so he added more fuel to the fire.

"You want to be good for us, don't you? You want to behave, but you also want me to put you over my lap and spank that cute little ass. Spankings aren't just for bad girls."

Hazel licked her lips, her eyes growing heavy with lust.

"Ask him," Aldo murmured in her ear. "Ask him to spank you."

Hazel's lashes fluttered as she struggled to keep her eyes open. Her body soft in his arms as her arousal took over. "Spank me," she whispered.

Kayden shook his head. "Ask nicer."

Her gaze lifted to his, her cheeks flushed the prettiest pink. He was going to make sure her ass matched her face in a few minutes.

She drew in a deep breath. "Please spank me, Kayden. Please," she added a second time.

He pulled away from her, taking her hand in his as he led her to the bedroom. They'd spent too much time on couches these past few weeks, and he was done with that. Their make-out sessions at the Morettis' had done little more than leave them all sexually frustrated, as they'd limited their play to kisses and touching—with clothes on. Nothing more serious than dry humping, which—to Hazel's credit—was still pretty fucking hot.

No. Tonight, it was time for a bed.

Hazel stumbled just a step as they crossed the threshold to Aldo's bedroom. His best friend wasn't exactly a neat freak, but he typically kept his mess contained to a pile of dirty clothes in one corner, his bed made—not necessarily with hospital corners but with the cover pulled up at least.

Aldo was right behind her, so he wrapped his arms around her waist. "All you have to say is stop, and we will." His words reminded Kayden why they hadn't ventured into their kinks, his comments about trust still true.

Hazel stared at Aldo for a moment, then looked back at Kayden. "I know you won't hurt me. I know you'll stop if I ask."

Her words struck him like lightning, and while he wasn't sure Hazel realized exactly what she'd given them, *he* did.

She'd just proved that she trusted them.

Aldo grinned at him, then kissed her on the cheek. "Good. Now take off your pants. It's your first spanking and I want you to feel every single bit of it."

Kayden might have expected some level of shyness, considering how inexperienced she was, but Hazel revealed nothing more than outright enthusiasm. She quickly unfastened her jeans, bending at the waist to tug off her shoes and socks. Aldo, still behind her, took advantage, looking at her ass then wiggling his eyebrows at Kayden.

Kayden rolled his eyes, fighting the urge to laugh.

Once she'd shed her jeans, Kayden grasped her hand, leading her to the bed. Sitting on the edge, he lost no time tugging her over his lap. Hazel put up no resistance, but he suspected that wouldn't always be the case. She wanted this experience, so for tonight, she was all-in.

However, she was a headstrong woman who took far too much onto her shoulders. At some point in the future, she was going to balk when he told her to slow down, was going to push the dominant man inside him too far, and that was when he was going to show her how spankings weren't just for pleasure or punishment, but for those times when she needed to escape as well.

He ran his hand over her bottom, the skin soft, smooth. She was pale, a blank canvas that he couldn't wait to add color to.

Aldo approached, kneeling down in front of him. Their eyes met, for just a moment, before Kayden lifted his hand and brought it down. He didn't hold back. Hazel jerked in his lap, her hands pressing against his thigh as if she might try to stand up and run away. He was prepared to keep her in place, but he didn't have to because she didn't move.

Instead, she sighed. A contented sigh that sounded at peace. And it told Kayden that she was truly made for him. For them.

Aldo ran his hand over Hazel's long red curls, brushing them out of her face. She turned to look at him, the two staring at each other as Kayden added another smack, then another, and another. She held still through it all, though her breathing grew more rapid. She didn't look away from Aldo, who was now cupping her face, telling her how beautiful she was, how brave, how incredible.

Kayden ran his fingers along her slit, the tips slipping through her arousal. She was soaking wet. Hazel's legs parted, offering him better access, and he took advantage of it, pushing two fingers inside her.

Her ass rose and when she started to move, it wasn't to pull away, but to thrust back on his fingers, driving him deeper. He let her. Gave her free rein to take what she wanted, what she needed from this.

He wouldn't always do that. In fact, most times, he wouldn't. He hadn't lied about his need for complete control. It was why he was so fond of bondage, of tying his lovers up so they had no choice but to cede all the power to him.

Hazel whimpered when he curled his fingers inside her, added a third, added more force.

"God, yes. Please."

Aldo shifted closer, placing kiss after kiss on her flushed cheek, whispering sweet nothings and dirty, dirty descriptions of what they would do to her. Her pussy clenched tight around his fingers, and she cried out when he removed them.

"No!" Her complaints died on her lips when he struck her ass again, a half dozen more hard slaps that had her writhing on his lap.

"Hold still," Kayden demanded.

She tried. He could tell she did, but when he continued the spanking, Kayden realized she was too far gone, too deep in subspace to be cognizant of her surroundings.

He caught Aldo's eyes, tilted his head, telling him with expressions rather than words what to do. It spoke to their long friendship that Aldo knew exactly what Kayden wanted.

Aldo moved slightly, Hazel completely unaware, her ass rising and falling, her pussy searching, seeking for more.

She was right there at the brink, so when he and Aldo both thrust in with a finger each, she flew apart at the seams, yelling their names, gasping for breath, trembling between them.

It was the most beautiful thing Kayden had ever seen.

Aldo's eyes met his, and they were filled with the same wonder Kayden felt. The two of them leaned forward, reaching over Hazel's body until their lips met. Her orgasm still twitched around their fingers as they kissed.

It was a hard, passionate kiss, one of promise and relief and joy. Because they'd found it.

True love. With each other. And with Hazel.

Now all they had to do was tell her.

And pray she didn't run away.

Chapter Sixteen

"I'll get it," Hazel called out when there was a knock at the door. Nonno was in the bedroom, reading a book, while Nonna was in the kitchen starting dinner. She hesitated when her hand reached the knob, pulling away briefly.

She hadn't said anything to anyone, but for the past few days, she hadn't been able to shake the feeling of being watched. She'd suffered the same thing when she first arrived in Philadelphia, constantly looking over her shoulder, expecting the police to show up and arrest her. But it had faded after talking to her mom and learning the police hadn't come by the apartment.

She wasn't stupid enough to believe she was out of the doghouse, because Hazel couldn't recall a single time in her life when the rug hadn't been ripped out from under her feet. So the return of this feeling was unnerving, giving her the sense that things were about to go horribly, horribly wrong.

"Stop it," she muttered to herself. While she knew she was in a safe place, Boston Hazel still rose to the surface, prompting her to walk over to the front window and peer out to see who was there.

She was relieved when she spotted Jess and several others standing on the porch.

"Hey!" Hazel opened the door and stepped aside as Tony, Jess, and Aunt Berta filed in. She smiled at the little boy holding Tony's hand.

"You must be Jasper," she said, reaching out to shake his hand.

The boy, who was the spit of his mother, gave her a wide, missing-several-teeth grin, as he took her hand and shook it. "And you're Nurse Hazel," he replied. "Mommy said you're taking care of Nonno."

"I am."

"Mommy says I'm not allowed to jump on him or hug him too hard," Jasper went on to say.

"Your mommy is right," a man Hazel didn't know said, stepping forward. "Hi, Hazel. I'm Rhys Beaumont."

"Nice to meet you." Hazel shook Rhys's hand, recalling Jess telling her that her second boyfriend was a doctor. Hazel had met most of the Morettis by now, and there was no denying they had a very, *very* good gene pool. The entire family was unbelievably attractive, every single guy drop-dead gorgeous. The same held true for their friends as well, because Rafe, Kayden, and Rhys were equally handsome.

"If I promise to be gentle, can I go see Nonno?" Jasper asked.

Hazel nodded. "I think he'd love to see you. He's in his bedroom."

Jasper started down the hall at a sprint until Tony called out, "That's not a gentle walk."

The boy stopped in his tracks, then sighed heavily before moving at a slower pace.

Hazel couldn't help but laugh as she looked at Jess. "He's the cutest little boy I've ever seen."

Jess smiled and hugged her. "Okay, we're here now, so you're relieved of duty."

"What?"

Before Jess could reply, the front door opened again, Kayden and Aldo walking in.

"What are you guys doing here?" Hazel felt a slight heat that told her she was probably blushing. It had been four nights since she'd seen them, since they'd whisked her out for cheesesteaks, then rocked her world with that spanking. Hazel's libido had been on a slow, constant simmer since then, her body refusing to settle down. One look at them, and it was as if all her fun girlie bits came to life, ready to strike the bell for the next round.

"We're picking you up for our date." Aldo pulled a bouquet of flowers out from behind his back.

Hazel's eyes widened as she took the flowers, catching the sweet scent of the roses. "These are for me?"

No one had ever given her flowers in her life. If she was being honest, she'd always thought men only did that in the movies, like it was just fiction and something that never happened in real life.

"Of course, they are." Kayden leaned down to give her a too-chaste kiss on the cheek.

"But...did we plan a date for tonight? Because I'm working. And, um..."

She looked down at herself. She was in her ratty pair of jeans, the only pants she owned that had survived the midnight run and then the fire, and an old sweater of Keeley's. Her hair was pinned up on her head in a messy ponytail. "Well, I look like shit."

Jess, Tony, and Rhys laughed easily, while Aldo and Kayden both frowned. "What are you talking about?" Kayden asked. "You look gorgeous."

"Kayden," she said. "I can't go out looking like this. Actually, I can't go out at all. I'm working."

"Which is why we're here," Tony said. "We're relieving you of duty for the night."

Hazel shook her head.

"We're also not taking no for an answer, Hazel," Rhys said kindly. "We're here for dinner, and then we've planned to play cards and watch a movie. After that, Aunt Berta is going to stay the entire night. If there are any issues with Nonno, Aunt Berta is calling me."

"But—" she started.

"No buts," Kayden, Tony, and Aldo all said in unison.

"Wow. I'm clearly outnumbered." She glanced down at her outfit again, trying to gauge how long she needed to mitigate the damage.

"We're eating at my house," Kayden said. "Not a restaurant, so honestly, you look fine the way you are. But if you want to change, it's no problem. We can wait."

"I'll just dash upstairs to change my clothes," she said over her shoulder as she walked away. "And fix my hair." When she reached the first step, she turned to face them. "And put on makeup."

Aldo and Kayden laughed, waving her on, and she darted up the stairs, trying to contain her excitement. When she stepped into her bedroom, her eyes landed on the Maloney list. She'd managed to track down Mrs. Maloney's missing silverware at one of the pawnshops near her old apartment in Boston. She'd sent most—too much—of the money she'd made so far to the shop to purchase it, asking that it be delivered to the Maloneys anonymously.

She'd begun drawing lines through the things she'd managed to return. Sadly, there were still too many items missing.

She folded the paper and shoved it in the desk drawer, putting all thoughts of the past away.

Time to focus on the future. Or better yet, the present.

Dinner at Kayden's. And the whole night off.

Now, as always, she hoped that if this was all a dream, she never, ever woke up.

* * *

Hazel carried her empty plate to the kitchen, walking behind Aldo. Kayden had made a pot of homemade vegetable beef soup as well as home-baked bread because he remembered her saying how much she loved the smell of it.

It was a wonderful dinner, but as it crept ever closer to the end, Hazel found her thoughts drifting to what came next.

Once the kitchen was cleaned up, Hazel started toward the living room. Kayden halted her, his large hand circling her upper arm.

"You're going the wrong way," he said.

"I am?" She tried to be coy but ruined it by grinning.

Aldo chuckled. "Come on, Fireball. We have another surprise for you."

She'd been in the house before, gotten the grand tour, so she knew where they were going. She let Aldo lead her down the hallway to Kayden's bedroom.

Hazel gasped when she stepped inside, and this time, she knew—once and for all—she was dreaming. Because there was no way this was real.

The room was lit by at least a dozen candles, and scattered on the bed were rose petals.

"You did this for me?" she whispered.

"We want tonight to be special." Aldo looped his arm around her waist.

Hazel had to blink rapidly to beat back the tears. "It is. It's just...no one has ever done anything like this for me."

Aldo nuzzled close to her, his nose tickling her cheek. "You deserve to have someone do this for you every night. We care about you, Hazel, and we wanted to show you how much. Wanted to pull out all the stops in hopes that you might agree to a relationship with us."

"A relationship?" Hazel wasn't sure how one word could produce equal amounts of joy and panic at the same time. Joy because she wanted what they were offering. Panic because she knew this was all going to fall apart eventually. She was going to hurt them.

God, she really didn't want to hurt them.

And to add insult to injury, she knew all the way to the depths of her soul that losing them would destroy *her*. Destroy her in a way that she wouldn't be able to pick up the pieces again.

Kayden studied her face, and she knew he was seeing more

than she wanted to show him. "I realize this is going fast, but yeah, a relationship is what we're hoping for with you. You okay with that?"

"I..." She wanted it so bad she could taste it, but that little voice—the one that never let her be completely happy—was talking too loud in her head. "Um...are you sure?"

It was the wrong question to ask. She could see it the second it crossed her lips.

"Goddammit, Hazel." Kayden scowled. "When you ask things like that, it makes me want to find every person who's ever hurt you and beat the shit out of them."

She cleared the lump blocking her throat. "That might be the hottest thing anyone has ever said to me."

Aldo shook his head, chuckling and defusing the situation, something he was very good at. "Come on." He reached for her hand. "Let's move this to the bed. This erection is getting painful."

Hazel could relate to that. "You guys have lit a fire in me, and I'm having a hard time putting it out. Of course, it doesn't help that I'm living in your grandparents' house, the two of them sleeping directly below me on the first floor. Or that I haven't managed to replace the toys I left behind in B—Springfield."

Hazel froze in place, too afraid to look Aldo or Kayden in the eye, in case they caught her near slip of the tongue.

Kayden cupped her cheek, forcing her gaze up to his. "It's okay."

She had no idea what he meant by that. Did he know she was lying, and he was telling her he was okay with it? Or was he mistaking her sudden panic as nerves?

They were both curious about her past, she knew that. But since the day they'd toured Philadelphia, neither of them had asked her questions about it or pushed her for details about her family, her upbringing, her reasons for moving to Philadelphia, or that damn bruise on her cheek, that had faded away completely.

They'd let it go. So she would too.

"Okay," she repeated, giving him the simplest response she could muster.

Kayden stroked her cheek with his thumb, giving her a wicked smile. "And in the interest of full disclosure, I feel compelled to warn you that I'm a dominant, possessive, overprotective bastard, and as my girlfriend, you're going to feel the full extent of that."

"Jesus Christ, Kay," Aldo muttered. "You're going to scare her away before she even agrees to be ours. He *is* all those things, Fireball, but don't worry. That's why I'm here. To keep him in line."

Kayden rolled his eyes comically, but Hazel didn't laugh.

"I'm not afraid of any of those things," she confessed. "I'd like to know what it feels like to have someone care about me that much."

Kayden clenched his fist, and the idea of him facing down her parents and her uncle in her defense, slipped between the cracks in her wall, widening the gaps until it was left in ruins.

How did they always know how to help her? How could they look at her and see the bad stuff rumbling around inside her and find the right words to calm her down? No one else had ever done that for her.

Of course, no one else had ever cared about her the way Kayden and Aldo did.

She'd been in Philadelphia one month. Just one. And yet, she felt closer to these two men than she ever had to her own family.

Boston Hazel was screaming that this was a mistake, but Philadelphia Hazel shut the bitch down, gagging her once and for all. Maybe this *was* a mistake, but she didn't care. And with the decision made...the weight on her chest lightened and it became easier to breathe.

The first night they'd met, Kayden had asked her to take a leap of faith, and she had.

It had been the best thing she'd ever done.

So she'd do it again tonight. And if she needed to, tomorrow, and the next day and the next day. She'd take that leap every damn day if it meant she could stay here with these two incredible men and be their girlfriend for as long as it lasted.

"Take off your clothes," Kayden demanded.

Wow. So that was what zero to sixty felt like.

Neither man moved, and Kayden didn't repeat his words. They simply stood there, waiting.

The ball was in her court. She trusted them.

God.

She. Trusted. Them.

So that wasn't going to be her issue in this. Her problem would be giving up complete control. She had less experience with that than she did sex, captain of her own ship for pretty much her entire life. Hell, she'd been the captain of her mom's and her uncle's ships as well.

"Stop thinking, Fireball." Aldo stepped next to Kayden, looking completely relaxed, though she suspected—no, she *knew* —that was a false face, probably meant to set her at ease.

Because she could see the crouching tiger inside, which should make her want to run.

It should not make her...

Her hands dropped to the hem of the sweater, and in one quick tug, she'd pulled it over her head and off, tossing it to the floor.

One corner of her mouth lifted, a grin fighting to get out, as their gazes dropped lower, shamelessly taking in what she'd revealed. They'd seen her before, but it didn't matter. Every time she bared herself to them, they looked at her with such appreciation, it soaked deep inside, warming all the cold places.

She reached behind her, her gaze locked on their faces as she unhooked her bra and added it to her sweater.

Aldo blew out a long, breathy word. Just one. "Jeeeesus."

That word was exactly the encouragement she needed to keep going. She unbuttoned her jeans, then drew down the zipper.

She glanced at Kayden, his attention focused on her hands as she pushed her jeans and panties down together. She didn't have it in her to draw this out, and it wasn't because of nerves but because of need.

Hazel had never considered herself much of a sexual person before. Never felt like sex was something she needed all that often. Aldo and Kayden had proven that to be the biggest of all her lies. And they'd been drawing more and more of her sensuality out of her with their sexy talk, their heated looks, their continual touches.

Bending down, she shed the rest of her clothing until, at last, she stood completely naked.

Instinct had her lifting her hands to cover herself, but Kayden gave her a single shake of his head and she lowered them instantly.

Aldo moved first, crossing to her, running the backs of his fingers over her bare arm. "Beautiful," he whispered. "Fuck me, Kay." He was looking at her but talking to Kayden. "We're the luckiest sons of bitches on the planet."

Hazel shook her head, but he wouldn't let her deflect his compliment.

Leaning closer, he placed his lips against her cheek, reinforcing it. "The. Luckiest." Aldo cupped her jaw, kissing her.

Kissing wasn't something she'd had a lot of practice with. Her past boyfriends had been less love affair, more friends with benefits. Kissing was just part of the foreplay and it never lasted long, never did much in terms of turning her on.

This.

Kiss.

It changed everything for her. Hazel could stand here all night, doing nothing more than kissing Aldo, and it would be enough.

He was a master in the way he held her face—cradled it— between his large, rough hands, his lips worshiping hers, his tongue drinking in her taste, his deep, guttural moans so fucking sexy.

She had no idea how long the kiss lasted, neither of them giving any sign of coming up for air, until she jerked slightly, the touch of Kayden's hand gripping her ass, taking her by surprise.

Aldo opened his eyes, gazing over her shoulder at Kayden, giving his best friend a shit-eating grin.

"You're hogging her," Kayden chastised.

"If you're looking for an apology, you'll have to keep looking. Because I'm not a damn bit sorry."

Hazel glanced downward, toward where Kayden's hand was still on her ass. "Take off your shirt." She didn't realize her words had come out more demand than request until the slight narrowing of Kayden's eyes, which told her she'd poked the bear.

He'd called himself a dominant bastard, and while she'd seen shades of his dominance, this was the first time he'd truly laid that man bare for her to see.

He shook his head. "No."

Hazel twisted until she faced him. "No?"

Kayden stared her down, and she suddenly felt her nudity acutely. Rather than argue with him, she reached for the top button of his shirt, intent on undressing him herself.

Kayden grasped her hands before she could pop a single button.

"Bad girl." His voice was low, gravelly.

Kayden cast Aldo a look, communicating without words because before she knew it, Aldo was reaching around her, taking both her wrists in his hands and pulling them behind her back. The position ensured her breasts were thrust out, which had clearly been Kayden's intent.

He stepped over to her bed, sitting down on the edge of the mattress. Aldo used his grip to propel her forward, the two of them following in Kayden's wake until she was standing directly in front of him, her breasts mere inches from his face.

She expected Kayden to take her to task for trying to assume control, maybe even—please God—spank her again.

But he didn't say a word. Instead, he reached out and took her nipple between his finger and thumb, applying pressure until she gasped at the pain. She tried to twist her body, tried to push back, but Aldo held her too tightly for her to move.

"Kayden," she said.

He released her nipple, and she fell silent. Until he treated the other nipple to the same painful pinch. This time, he tugged as well, pulling her breast away from her body. It hurt…but it didn't.

She tried to resist again, failing a second time. For her efforts, Kayden decided to use two hands, applying the rough treatment to both nipples at the same time.

"Stop fighting him," Aldo murmured in her ear. "Stop fighting *us*."

Hazel struggled to obey, but her mind and body weren't exactly in synch. Because the pain no longer felt all that bad. She squeezed her legs together, aware that she was far too aroused, too wet.

Kayden shifted his legs, one foot tapping against her inner ankle, forcing her to move it. Then he repeated the same unspoken demand, and she shifted the other foot as well.

The new position left her open, with no way to tamp down the sensations coursing through her. She tried to close her legs but Kayden was there, shoving his knees between, holding her thighs apart.

"God," she gasped.

Aldo moved her forward slightly, those few inches assuring she was straddling Kayden's muscular thighs.

Of course, it meant Aldo and Kayden were closer as well.

They were both still dressed, dammit. If he would have let her strip him out of his shirt and jeans, it would have taken little effort on her part to close the distance between them completely. She longed to push herself down on his hard cock. She could see the outline of his erection beneath the denim, and she was dying to know if his dick was as thick as it appeared.

She'd seen Aldo's, thanks to the blow job lesson, but she'd yet to see Kayden's.

"One night, I'm going to put nipple clamps on you," Kayden

promised, just before he released her nipples. His pinch had been tight enough and long enough that blood rushed back in, causing them to sting. He replaced his fingers with his lips, his tongue stroking them in a gentle caress that was in direct counterpoint to what he'd just done. The burning morphed to tingles and her pussy clenched once more, too empty, too needy.

"Please," she begged. "Please."

Kayden looked up at her, and she realized it was the first time he'd looked away from her breasts since they'd started this game.

She thought he wanted to say something, but he remained silent, and she realized it was a test. He was waiting to see if she planned to make another plea.

Hazel pressed her lips together tightly, and Kayden smiled, then offered a reprieve.

He started to rise, Aldo pulling her away to give Kayden space, and once again, she was amazed by the fact they'd never had a threesome before. They were so aware of each other, of their actions, their moves, their desires.

Finally, Kayden began unbuttoning his shirt.

Aldo released her wrists so he could do the same. She turned sideways between them, not wanting to miss either striptease.

When Kayden pushed his shirt off his shoulders, she was treated to a kaleidoscope of colors, his chest and arms covered with tattoos.

A quick glance toward Aldo proved he had the same.

"I've never seen either of you without your shirts," she admitted.

Kayden looked surprised, like he was just realizing that. They'd done so much, and yet so little, when she considered their make-out sessions on the couch and in the theater room, the blow job lesson, and spanking.

"So many tattoos," she mused.

"Got our first ones together during senior year. After that, we were hooked, and we've added more ink every year. Although we're running out of canvas above the waist," Aldo joked.

She drew her fingertips along the lines of the tattoo on his pec. "I love them."

"You ever think of getting a tattoo?" Aldo asked.

"I'd love to, but we never had the money to blow on something like that." Hazel could never afford such an extravagance. She worked too hard just to make enough money to pay the bills and put food on the table.

Aldo stood still as she explored his tattoos, slowly gliding around him, touching here or there, before stepping over and giving the same long look to Kayden.

"You're both so fucking sexy." Hazel reached out, running her fingers over Kayden's rock-hard pecs, tracing the lines. At some point, she'd ask them what each tattoo signified, what they represented, and why they'd gotten them, but not now.

Now, she needed to see more.

Aldo brushed her hair over her shoulder, baring one side of her neck so that he could kiss it. She bent her head, giving him easier access, Aldo the first to discover that spot just behind her ear was a major erogenous zone for her.

"That feels so good," she whispered.

He stroked the same place with his tongue.

"Please." She closed her lips quickly after that, too afraid she'd slip up and demand they take off the damn jeans so they could get down to the good stuff.

Unfortunately, the moment that thought crossed her mind, she realized what the good stuff entailed.

Two men. Two cocks. Two *large* cocks, if the bulge in Kayden's jeans was to be believed. She already knew Aldo was well-endowed.

How did this work? Did they take turns or...

"I've never done anal." She winced the second the words crossed her lips, closing her eyes, too mortified to see what they might think of the outburst.

Hazel felt a finger under her chin.

"Open your eyes," Kayden demanded.

She did so, aware she was blushing.

"That was never on the table for tonight, Hazel. It's our first night, our first time together, just the three of us. Despite our kinkier interests, we thought we might go a little more vanilla." Kayden's charming grin was too sexy for her own good.

"We'd intended to take turns, Fireball," Aldo added. "But if that's too much, it can just be one of us tonight."

She shook her head rapidly. While she appreciated the compassion behind the offer, she sure as hell didn't want that. How could she choose?

"No, I just...I don't know why I said...God...I want to be with both of you. I'm just..." Wow. Hello, Queen of Incomplete Thoughts.

Kayden cupped her cheek, pressing his forehead against hers. "I know that trust is hard for you. I also know we're moving at the speed of light, which isn't helping. We don't have to take this to the next level if you're not ready. We would be just as cool going back to the living room and making out like teenagers on the couch if you want."

"Kayden's right. We're typically patient guys." Aldo ran his hand through his hair. "But when it comes to you, we're failing miserably on going slow."

"I don't mind how fast this is going. It feels right to me. *Honestly*," she stressed, hating that she'd spoken up at all.

"So we're forging on?" Kayden asked.

She nodded. "Hell yes."

Chapter Seventeen

Aldo had never heard two sweeter words. He grasped Hazel's hand, pulling her to the bed. He drew the duvet down with a flourish, creating a rainfall of rose petals. Then he pushed her down to sit on the edge.

She remained perched there as he and Kayden faced her, standing side by side.

"Good. Because we're about to get serious," Kayden warned her.

Aldo hadn't lied about his lack of patience. He had his pants unfastened and around his ankles in record time, provoking two very different responses from his lovers.

Hazel gasped.

Kayden chuckled. "Jesus, man. It's not a race."

Aldo realized Kayden hadn't even unzipped his jeans yet. He also noticed his best friend's gaze was locked on his cock, and he felt it twitch under Kayden's scrutiny. It had been too fucking long. When he looked back now, he couldn't recall why they'd thought abstinence was a good idea.

Hazel hadn't noticed where Kayden's attention lay, her hungry eyes glued to his dick as well. Aldo figured he was in the upper average range as far as size went, but damn if her expression didn't feed his ego just the same.

"You ready for this, Fireball?" Aldo asked.

"God, yes."

He was moved by her steady tone, enthralled by her bravery. Hazel Walsh had clearly been through some shit, abused by God only knew who, and knocked down enough times that her ability to trust others stood on shaky ground.

Yet here she sat. With the two of them. Putting herself in their hands.

"Kayden," Aldo said, not looking away from Hazel. "Hurry up, man, or I'm starting without you."

He scoffed. "You might try."

They were empty words because Aldo could see from the corner of his eye that his threat worked. Kayden was moving, making haste.

Aldo stepped forward, urging Hazel to shift more fully onto the bed. Once she was in the middle, he claimed his side.

He and Kayden had discussed how tonight would go, had agreed that if she was willing to take things to the next level, then this first time would be all about her. God willing, there would be plenty more nights after this one. Ones where they could expand on the play between the three of them, he and Kayden taking each other as well as her.

But not this time.

Kayden crossed around the foot of the bed, the mattress dipping as he climbed in as well.

"This only goes as far as you want it to." Aldo felt the need to offer her that reassurance once more. "We might be in control, but you hold all the power. You say stop, we stop. It's as simple as that."

"I don't want to stop," she said hastily.

That wasn't what he said, and he needed to make sure she understood the difference. He tapped one knuckle under her chin. "You say stop, and we do," he repeated. "Okay?"

She smiled. "Okay."

Kayden took her face in his hands, drawing her into a kiss, and Aldo realized his friend hadn't grabbed his yet because, as he'd said earlier, Aldo had been "hogging her."

Aldo had kissed countless women in his life, but there was something about Hazel's unguarded responses, the way she took her cues from him and let him guide her through the kiss that was so heady, it was hard to pull away, to share.

Now, as he watched his best friend kiss her, he realized this impacted him just as powerfully. Aldo had always been a voyeur. He loved watching others in the heat of the moment. He'd viewed more than his fair share of porn, and he'd gone to a couple sex clubs, finding as much pleasure from watching as he did from participating.

But nothing he'd ever witnessed before held a candle to watching Kayden, his best friend, his lover, kiss their girl.

Nothing.

They still had miles to go as they tried to take what they had here—three independent souls—and meld them into one being, one perfect triad. But for the first time since he and Kayden had decided what they wanted for their future, he felt real hope that they were on the precipice of achieving it.

Aldo watched them for a few moments, and he realized Kayden was struggling with the sharing part as well. They were in uncharted waters here. Hazel had been shocked to learn they'd never shared a woman before, and while they wanted to make this good for her, there were bound to be a few missteps as he and Kayden figured shit out.

Kayden deepened the kiss, pushing Hazel to the bed, on her back. He followed her down, reclining next to her. Once settled, he broke the kiss and looked up at Aldo.

"You planning to hop in at some point?" Kayden taunted.

"I was waiting for you two to come up for air." Aldo lay down next to Hazel, drawing his hand down the center of her chest, through the valley of her gorgeous breasts. Her nipples were tightly pebbled, thanks to Kayden's rough treatment before. Not that she'd complained.

He'd seen the brief wince of pain and he'd started to step in, to demand Kayden take it easy. But that flash of hurt had passed quickly, replaced by something so hot and hungry, Aldo had been forced to count to ten and then to twenty in his head to stop himself from stripping off his clothes, pushing her down on the bed, and taking her hard and fast.

Kayden gave Hazel another kiss, their tongues touching, but this one didn't last. Aldo bent his head to hers when they split apart, stealing another kiss.

Kayden was right there, their faces only a few inches apart, and Aldo was tempted to give him the same hot, wet kiss, but they'd vowed to make tonight just about Hazel.

Kayden must have recognized the desire because he increased the distance between them, even though his eyes lingered on Aldo's lips long enough to let him know he was thinking the same thing. "Soon," he mouthed.

Hazel didn't notice their shared look, but that was because her eyes had drifted shut, her body trembling as Aldo continued stroking up and down the middle of her body, his fingers starting at the base of her throat, traveling between her tits, not stopping until he brushed over her stomach. She was slightly ticklish, giving him a breathy laugh and a wiggle whenever he hit a sensitive place.

He always stopped just below her belly button before making the journey back north. He was on his fourth trip down, amused by Hazel's less than subtle attempts to keep him heading in a southerly direction. When he caressed between her breasts, she twisted slightly to one side, trying to toss her tit in his path. He kept going, grinning when she tilted her hips as his fingers brushed over her belly button.

He didn't give her what she wanted. Not yet. Because he wanted to hear Hazel scream his name and Kayden's before the night was over.

"Aldo. Touch me." Her tone was somewhere between a whine and a demand. "Now."

Obviously, she hadn't learned her lesson.

Kayden gripped Aldo's wrist, stopping his touches. It took a second or two for Hazel's brain to catch up, to realize he wasn't stroking her anymore.

Her eyelids fluttered open, her gaze landing on Kayden's stern face.

"Please," she added belatedly, as if that was all it would take to make things right.

"Roll over, Hazel." Kayden rose to his knees beside her.

A crease formed between her brows, but not because of confusion. No. It was more like she was trying to decide whether to obey.

Fortunately for her, she did as Kayden asked without too much delay. Aldo suspected her actions were driven more by horniness and the fact they'd already determined how much she liked spankings than by true submission.

Once she'd flipped over, treating them to a bird's-eye view of her tight, round ass, she rose up on her hands and knees, looking over her shoulder at Kayden.

He shook his head, pressing her down until she lay flat, her right cheek resting on the pillow.

Kayden ran his hand over her body, from the nape of her neck to the small of her back, repeating the same slow stroke Aldo had been doing to her front. Hazel let him make the journey twice, before—once again—she wiggled her ass, trying to entice him to get started.

The second she moved, Kayden raised his hand and slapped her. Hard. The slap rang out in the room, and Aldo could tell by the way she jerked that this spanking was harder than the first.

Hazel sputtered. "K-Kayd—"

Kayden spanked her again, six times in rapid succession.

Apart from her initial outburst, Hazel remained silent though not still. She shifted her hips from side to side, prompting Aldo to place a firm hand on her lower back, hindering her movement.

Kayden stopped for a moment, studying Hazel's face.

Aldo couldn't see her as clearly as he'd like, given she was facing away from him. One look at Kayden, who shot Aldo a cat-who-ate-the-canary grin, told him all he needed to know.

Kayden added a few more slaps on her ass, varying his placement. They both knew, regardless of Hazel's reassurance that she wanted this, they needed to take things slowly.

They'd only known her a month, for God's sake. A fact that seemed impossible to Aldo.

He and Kayden had sprinted out of the gate the second they'd laid eyes on her, and since then, they'd come on hot and heavy.

Aldo stroked her ass after Kayden's spanking ceased. Her skin was pink and warm to the touch. Unable to resist, he bent down and placed a soft kiss on one of her ass cheeks.

Hazel laughed, one of the signature quiet ones that ended too quickly.

Lifting his hand, Kayden began to stroke her back again, up and down, never crossing the boundaries Hazel wanted him to cross.

However, rather than make more demands, she gave herself up to the touch, relaxing, sinking deeper into the mattress.

Kayden lay back down next to her, giving her a soft kiss on the forehead. "We're going to give you what you want. Everything you want. But *we're* going to decide how we get there."

Aldo saw her nod as he resumed his place as well, propping himself up on his elbow. "Roll back over, Fireball."

Hazel twisted to her back, sighing contentedly when Aldo cupped her cheek and placed his forehead against hers.

"I'm not sure spanking will ever work as a punishment," she murmured. "I like it way too much."

He and Kayden both chuckled. Hazel might have laughed too, but Aldo's patience was in tatters. Reaching down, he ran his finger along her slit—her soaking-wet slit—loving the way she moaned in pleasure.

"You weren't kidding about liking it." Aldo placed a kiss on her bare shoulder. His comment captured Kayden's attention and he touched her as well, determined to see for himself.

"Jesus, Hazel," Kayden whispered. "Baby."

Neither he nor Kayden removed their fingers, working in tandem to push her closer to her first orgasm of the night.

Aldo found her clit, alternating between lightly pinching the tight nub and rubbing it.

Kayden slipped a finger inside her, then another, as Aldo watched him stretch her pussy.

Hazel's hips seemed to move of their own accord, rising and falling in time with Kayden's thrusts and strokes.

"God," she breathed. "Please!"

"You want to come, Hazel?" Kayden asked.

She nodded, her eyelids heavy, her focus wavering. "Yes."

"Wait for permission," he demanded.

Aldo applied more pressure to her clit, determined to test her.

Kayden must have had the same plan because he added a third finger.

Hazel whimpered, but her hips didn't stop moving, didn't stop seeking, even if Kayden was stretching her beyond what was comfortable.

"Kayden." Her hands fisted the sheets beside her. "Aldo."

They exchanged a glance, then pushed harder.

Hazel had submissive tendencies—they were easy to see—but she'd had no opportunity to explore that side of herself.

"I...I..." Her eyes were closed tightly, her body stiff as she fought to hold back. She wanted to obey them, and it was the most beautiful fucking thing Aldo had ever seen.

Kayden watched her, just as spellbound, then they exchanged a look.

Aldo nodded, so Kayden lowered his face next to hers. "Come for us, Hazel."

She exploded before he'd finished saying her name, her back arching, crying out with her pleasure.

Kayden's fingers slipped free—only for a second—as he grasped Aldo's hand, pulling it from her clit to her pussy. "Together."

As they'd done the other night, they each slipped a finger inside her, triggering another orgasm—or prolonging the first.

Hazel's mouth fell open, but this time no sound emerged.

Her pussy clenched, squeezing their fingers tightly. So fucking tightly.

Again, Aldo was overcome by the desire to kiss Kayden.

The two of them had shared pretty much everything over the years—clothes, shoes, homework, their bodies, an apartment, and a dream.

This dream.

It was coming true, and he'd never felt closer to his best friend in his life.

"Kay," Aldo whispered.

Kayden looked at him, gave him a grin, and he knew they were on the same page. Fuck, they were on the same sentence, the same word.

Kayden leaned forward, the two of them kissing. A slow, sexy kiss driven not only by their desire for each other but by the last vestiges of Hazel's orgasm, still fluttering around their fingers.

The kiss ended just as Hazel's climax faded.

She'd missed it, her eyes still closed, her breathing heavy, hard.

Kayden's finger slid free first, and as Hazel slowly began to come back to them, he rose from the bed.

"Don't leave." Hazel reached out to him.

"I'm not going anywhere," he reassured her. "Aldo and I need condoms."

Kayden pulled two foil packets from his discarded jeans, tossing one to him. They were rock-hard, their erections brushing against their stomachs, ready for action.

"You go first." Aldo reached down to grip his cock in his

hand, running his fist along his flesh. "I want to watch. Plus, I've already had her mouth."

Aldo had only managed one stroke before Hazel's hand found his, shoving it aside so she could take over. He gritted his teeth, biting back his own groan of pleasure.

The sound of foil tearing drew both their attention, as Kayden slid the condom over his thick dick. Aldo knew firsthand how full that cock would make Hazel feel. Because he'd been filled with it before, stretched tight around it.

Hazel's legs parted, but she still retained her grip on Aldo's cock, though her strokes grew less practiced as Kayden knelt and guided himself to her opening. He slid in slowly, see-sawing in and out, giving her body time to adjust to his girth.

Hazel's hand started to fall away from him, so Aldo covered it with his own, using his grip to move her the way he wanted.

Kayden paused once he was fully seated, looking over at Aldo and Hazel's combined hand job, then he pulled out again, until only the head remained.

When he thrust back in, it was faster, harder.

Hazel lifted her legs around Kayden's waist, hooking her ankles behind his back. The position tilted her ass up so Kayden could slide in deeper.

Aldo was riveted, his gaze locked on the spot where his two lovers were connected. God, it was almost too much.

He wanted Hazel more than he wanted his next birthday, but he was perilously close to coming, simply from watching Kayden fuck her.

They were beautiful together, perfect, a work of goddamn art. And, by God, they were *his*.

For Aldo, there was no other option.

He'd watched his brother Elio and his cousins, Gio and Tony, fall hard. He'd been jealous, and even slightly concerned that perhaps there was something wrong with him. Something inside that was holding him back from finding the same happiness.

Now, he could see he simply hadn't found it.

He'd gotten halfway there with Kayden, and in this moment, the circle was complete.

Kayden's skin grew slick with perspiration, Hazel's voice hoarse from her cries. They rocked together harder and harder.

Aldo released her hand because, dammit, he was too close.

He and Kayden had tried to keep their distance from each other, determined to make this night all about Hazel. To show her, to convince her that they would take care of her...but with their kiss, that plan had gone out the window.

Unable to resist, Aldo reached out, his fingers finding the place where they were joined.

Kayden's eyes flew up with the first touch of his fingers, sliding around Kayden's cock before stroking Hazel's clit.

She gasped, then said his name, and Aldo was sure he'd never heard anything sweeter. "Aldo. Yes! So good."

Kayden's forehead creased, a quiet growl escaping.

It was his tell. One Aldo recognized well. One he'd missed.

Kayden was there.

"Aldo," he said through gritted teeth.

He understood the plea, increasing the pressure on Hazel's clit.

Kayden didn't want to come until she did, but Aldo's fingers were clearly the equivalent to throwing gasoline on a fire. He'd been able to hold back until that.

"Come, Hazel," Kayden demanded.

Hazel's head flew back, her orgasm striking mere seconds before Kayden's.

Their bodies jerked in a dance as old as time, and Aldo couldn't take his eyes off them.

It was several minutes before the two of them recovered enough to move, Kayden dropping down beside Hazel, placing kiss after kiss on her shoulder and neck, murmuring a litany of sweet nothings.

Aldo remained where he was, kneeling on Hazel's opposite side, his knees pressed against her hip.

"Hazel."

She was new to this—hell, so were they—so they needed to take care.

"Come inside me, Aldo." She lifted her arms to him.

He hesitated. "If you're too tired, or sore, or—"

"Please," she whispered.

It was an offer he couldn't refuse. Slipping on the condom, he knelt between her legs. He considered pushing her to her hands and knees, a different position from the one she and Kayden had shared, but he wanted to see her face, needed to be able to read her expression, to kiss those soft lips, to look deep into those bright green eyes, when he slid inside her for the very first time.

Hazel wrapped her hands around his neck, pulling him down to her, as if she needed the very same thing.

They kissed as he slowly pushed inside her tight, hot pussy.

He entered with one firm slide, not stopping until he was buried deep.

"Perfect," he whispered to her.

She blinked a couple of times, and he saw the sheen of tears in her eyes. "No one has ever..." Her throat seemed to clog on the words, but it was fine. He didn't want to hear them. Didn't want to think of her spending her life with people who couldn't see her for the incredible woman she was.

"You're perfect," he repeated, determined to say the words a thousand times a day until they sank in.

She gave him a watery smile, then a kiss, then a low groan that told him he'd found the right spot. He lifted his hips, then pushed them back down, making sure to hit that same place over and over.

And when he was there, ready to fall over the cliff, he pressed his lips to the shell of her ear.

"Together."

Hazel's body responded immediately, her orgasm shoving him off the precipice, the two of them falling, falling, falling...

Perfect.

Chapter Eighteen

Kayden smiled when he heard the front door open.

"Kay. We're here," he heard Aldo call out.

"I'm in the kitchen," he replied. "Make yourselves comfortable in the living room. I'll be right there."

Kayden finished putting the wings on a plate, then popped the top on three beers. Aldo had gone to pick up Hazel while he got the food ready. The three of them had opted to do their own private hockey viewing party tonight versus joining the whole gang.

Their jobs were seriously interfering with the amount of time they got to spend together, which meant it had been a week since they'd seen each other. Seven whole days since they'd spent that incredible night in his bed.

Sex with Aldo and Hazel had been a life-altering event for him, and Kayden had spent every day since then replaying it in his mind, while fantasizing about all the other things he wanted to do with them.

Aldo was coming off a four-day work stint, and since taking that previous night off, Hazel had doubled down on remaining close to Nonno, even though he was doing great. At his last checkup, the doctor had been shocked by how quickly he was recovering. The Morettis were crediting Hazel with that, everyone impressed by not only her work ethic but the genuine care she was giving Nonno. He was a stubborn guy, so the fact Hazel was able to get him to eat the proper diet—without cheating—exercise when he didn't want to, and rest upon her command was nothing short of a Festivus miracle.

Kayden picked up the plate with one hand, juggling the three bottles of beer in the other, and joined Hazel and Aldo in the living room. Setting everything on the coffee table, he bent over to give her a quick kiss hello.

At least, quick had been his intention, but she tasted so good, he decided to linger.

Aldo stopped fiddling with the remote to watch them. Kayden was accustomed to Aldo's penchant for playing voyeur, making little secret over the years that he liked to watch.

Hazel smiled when he broke the kiss.

"Hello to you too," she joked.

Kayden plopped down on the couch next to her, the three of them picking up their beers before leaning back against the cushions, settling in to watch the game.

"Looks like the puck doesn't drop for another few minutes." Aldo twisted to face the two of them. "Goddamn, I missed you two this week. We're going to have to figure something out with our schedules because I'm not going another seven days cold turkey again."

Kayden agreed wholeheartedly. "This wouldn't be a problem if we all lived together." He hadn't meant to throw that out there, and definitely not as casually as he did, but it was the one thing that kept coming up this week as he crawled into bed alone. He wanted them with him. Every night.

"Damn, man. Why don't you just put it out there?" Aldo attempted to make light of his slip of the tongue.

Hazel, thank God, just laughed. "I'm not a bit surprised by that leap. Let's face it. We've approached this relationship like we're living in dog years. Hot and heavy and so damn fast, I can't believe we don't all have whiplash."

Kayden leaned toward her, grateful she'd taken his comment in stride. "I wasn't suggesting we start packing up yours and Aldo's stuff tonight."

Hazel gave him a wry grin. "I could pack up my entire life in ten minutes and fit it all in one suitcase."

And while Kayden gave her the response she was going for, chuckling, he couldn't help thinking how sad that truth was. It was another reason he wanted her here, in this house. It was clear Hazel had never really lived in a home, and he wanted to give her that. Wanted to give her a closet full of clothes—one to rival Keeley's—wanted pictures of their lives together hanging on every wall, and he wanted her girlie shit junking up the bathroom counter.

He wanted to give her a place to put down serious roots.

"Not me," Aldo chimed in. "I have way too much shit in my place, and I can tell you right now, when I finally do move out, half of it isn't coming with me."

"You planning to move out?" Hazel asked.

Kayden expected Aldo to backtrack out of the conversation, but instead he said, "Sleeping alone sucks."

He nodded. "Tell me about it."

"You know, my lease is up soon," Aldo reminded him. "If you're really serious about us—"

"I am," Kayden interjected without hesitation. "Tell your landlord you're moving out. I think it's way past time we did this."

Aldo tapped his bottle against Kayden's. "I agree. Now then, all we have to do is convince this one." Aldo turned his attention to Hazel.

Hazel shook her head. "I've committed to staying with the Morettis for at least another five weeks. Then, after that, I'm finding my own place to rent."

"Or..." Kayden pressed. "You move in here."

Hazel threw her hands up. "I can't move in with you guys after a month of dating."

"Why not?" Aldo asked. "It's not like there are hard-and-fast rules about cohabitation. Think about it, Hazel. The house is paid for, so no mortgage, which means the three of us would only have to split utilities and food."

Hazel flipped her hair over her shoulder, and it was obvious she wouldn't be swayed tonight. Which was fine. Because Kayden truly hadn't intended to speak those thoughts aloud.

"I'm tabling this discussion until such time as you two come to your senses. Right now," Hazel pointed at their crotches, "you're thinking with your dicks."

Kayden laughed. "Let me reassure you that I'm thinking with both heads, but I'm cool with putting off making any decisions about this...for another five weeks."

Hazel snorted—an actual, adorable snort. "You're so kind."

Aldo ruffled her hair as she swatted his hand away. Kayden decided to hop in, tickling her sides as she began to wrestle in earnest, attempting to get away, laughing hysterically.

"No fair," she complained. "You're ganging up on me."

"That's because you won't just give us what we want and agree to move in." Aldo grasped her wrists, making it easier for Kayden to continue tickling her.

"You're both crazy," she cried, still laughing.

Kayden relented, gripping her waist to hold her steady while he gave her a kiss on the cheek. "Crazy for *you*."

Hazel's laughter faded, morphing into that same amazement she flashed whenever they told her how they felt. Kayden had witnessed the same look when they told her they wanted a relationship with her.

"I'm crazy for you too," she admitted softly. "Both of you. I've never—" She stopped short, still not able to make the final leap.

It didn't matter. Kayden, all on his own, was relentless when it came to getting what he wanted. Add Aldo's Moretti stubbornness to the mix, and their lovely girl didn't stand a chance.

"Can I ask you guys a question?" Hazel tugged down her T-shirt, which had ridden up during her struggles. Kayden was tempted to strip it off her completely, but there was something in her tone that told him she was moving on to a more serious topic.

"Of course," Kayden replied.

"When did you guys first start hooking up?"

Aldo chuckled, but Kayden didn't, trying to determine if she was okay or appalled.

"Guess we haven't done a very good job of hiding it," Aldo replied. "I'm mean, Kayden was pretty hands-on during the blow job lesson."

She frowned. "Were you *trying* to hide it?"

Aldo shook his head. "No. We weren't. Not really."

Kayden sighed. "Hazel, we were already asking you to take a pretty big leap by going out with two men at the same time. We thought we'd give you time to adjust to that before we added another layer."

She tilted her head. "When were you going to tell me?"

"Honestly?" Kayden said. "Tonight."

Hazel raised one eyebrow, but Aldo quickly held his hand up Boy Scout style. "We swear."

"And to answer your question, we first hooked up seven years ago," Kayden added.

"Really? But you've been friends forever. Why did you wait so long?" she asked.

"I always thought of myself as a straight guy who was just bi-curious, and it was the same for Aldo. One night, we fell into a bottle of bourbon, and the next thing we knew, we were exploring that curiosity together. It was..."

"Amazing," Aldo finished. "Incredible. We fucked like rabbits for months, obsessed with the sex and each other."

Hazel frowned. "That feels very past tense."

"We realized what we had—even as good as it was—wasn't going to be enough for either of us. We like sex with women...a lot. Plus, we both lean toward the dominant side, and while we don't have issues switching from top to bottom, there was still a bit of power play happening in the bedroom. We need someone to—"

"Boss around?" Hazel interrupted before Kayden could finish. Then she gave them a true smart-ass smirk.

Aldo laughed, but Kayden shook his head.

"We need someone to even us out. To allow us to let our inner alphas out. If Aldo and I had become a couple, we would have been forced to put that part of ourselves away too often for it to feel comfortable."

"So you just stopped?"

Kayden nodded. "For a couple years."

Aldo took a swig of his beer before elaborating. "Then we realized we were thinking inside the box. Something we didn't understand until my cousin Layla came home with her new partners, Miguel and Finn. We took one look at what the three of them had and a light went on. That's when we knew we were two parts of a three-piece orchestra."

"So you've been together since then?"

Kayden shook his head. "Not completely. Not in the way we want to be. After the last time we were together in bed...we knew there was something missing, so the sex stopped again."

"For how long?" she asked.

"A year," Kayden replied.

"A *long* fucking year," Aldo added with a groan. "We've spent a long time looking for..." Aldo reached out, running his hand through her hair. "You."

"Me," she whispered to herself, that same tone of disbelief in her voice.

Kayden gave her a soft kiss, cupping her cheeks in his hands. "You." He was determined to make their feelings for her sink in.

Aldo took another drink of beer, then put the bottle down. "Game's about to start." It was clear from his tone and the way he didn't pick the remote back up that he could care less if they saw it.

"You're running out of chances to watch your brother play," Hazel said, even as she shifted closer to Aldo, stroking his thigh.

Kayden loved the moments when Hazel let loose enough to flirt with them.

"Can I ask you guys something else?"

Aldo nodded, his gaze locked on her hand, which had drifted closer and closer to his cock.

"Can I watch you together?" she whispered.

Aldo's eyelids grew heavy, his eyes going dark. She was speaking to his best friend's voyeuristic heart.

Kayden didn't wait for Aldo's answer. Instead, he stood up, reaching his hand down to her. "Come on."

Hazel took his hand instantly, Aldo rising to follow. None of them said another word as they walked to Kayden's bedroom. He'd cleaned it today, vacuumed, dusted, changed the sheets. He'd known the second they made plans for the evening this was where they'd end up.

Kayden crossed the room to the bed, drawing down the duvet. "Take off your clothes, Hazel."

She frowned. "But I want—"

"You want to do what I say," Kayden interjected.

Hazel responded to the tone now as she always did. With obedience.

Kayden wasn't even sure if she realized it, but her hands went to the hem of her shirt, and she pulled it over her head. The rest of her clothing followed.

Once she was naked, he gestured to the bed. "Crawl into the middle. Sit with your back against the headboard."

Again, she did exactly as he asked, looking at him expectantly, waiting for his next demand.

"You want a show?" Kayden murmured.

She nodded.

"Then you'll get a show."

Aldo cursed under his breath, the long, slow "fuuuuuck"

telling Kayden just how turned on his best friend, his boyfriend, his lover was.

Kayden stepped to the end of the bed, crooking a finger to Aldo. "Our girl wants to see us."

Aldo approached, the two of them turning to face each other.

They closed the distance and their lips met. Unlike the softer, gentler kisses they shared with Hazel, this one was brutal, hard, hungry. Like soldiers returning home after years at war, they came together in a flurry of fierce passion. Kayden bit Aldo's lower lip, and he tasted the tang of blood. Then he fisted a handful of Aldo's hair, pulling it roughly.

Aldo gripped Kayden's hips, dragging him forward until their erections brushed against each other.

The kiss grew hotter, lingered, as Kayden began to unbutton Aldo's shirt. He stripped it off his shoulders, tossing it to the floor, before gripping Aldo's upper arms, deepening the kiss even more.

Aldo wasn't idle, wasn't passive. His fingers worked Kayden free of his jeans, pushing them to his ankles before he shoved a hand inside his boxers to grip his dick.

Kayden hissed at the firm, strong touch, then nipped at Aldo's bare shoulder. They'd let a whole fucking year go by without this. No sexual innuendoes, no flirting, no flat-out come-ons. He took Aldo's lips once more.

Through it all, Kayden felt her eyes on them, saw from the corner of his eye how much their kisses, their touches were impacting her. She shifted, squeezing her legs together.

Kayden broke the kiss, took two steps back, forcing Aldo to release his cock. He got rid of his shirt, and Aldo followed his lead, patience something neither of them seemed to possess.

Once they were naked, Kayden turned to look at Hazel. She'd pulled her knees up to her chest, looped her arms around her legs. Her face was flushed, her eyes cloudy with arousal.

"You can watch," Kayden said. "But so are we."

She gave him a confused look.

"Open your legs, Hazel. Show us how wet that pretty pussy is."

She bit her lower lip, but Kayden didn't mistake the look for nervousness. Hazel was one of the most sensual women he'd ever met, though he was certain if he told her that, she'd argue he was wrong.

She parted her legs, then her eyes lifted to his again.

Waiting.

Waiting for him to tell her what to do next. There was nothing more addictive, headier, than the submission of an independent, powerful, brave woman. Hazel was all three.

"Touch yourself. Rub your clit, finger yourself. Get yourself close, but don't come. Not without us."

Hazel licked her lips, nodded, her fingers slipping over her stomach, lower, lower.

He heard Aldo's deep intake of breath.

They watched her fingers slide through her slippery folds, then Kayden moved to the nightstand, grabbing what they'd need for the next part.

Lube and condom secured, he returned to the foot of the bed, he and Aldo exchanging a look.

Words weren't necessary because they understood each other.

Aldo nodded just once, then shifted, bending over the mattress, his hands flat on the bed, his ass high, Kayden's for the taking. He stepped behind him, running his hands over Aldo's bare ass. Where Hazel's was smooth, Aldo's was rougher, hairier.

Hazel's eyes were glued to them, her fingers still stroking, though Kayden wasn't sure she was feeling much. She was too focused on the two of them, failing to pay attention to her own pleasure.

Kayden uncapped the lube, squeezing some on his fingers, on Aldo's ass.

They knew each other's bodies intimately, so he knew all the places to stroke to drive Aldo out of his mind.

Aldo's fingers white-knuckled the bed covers when Kayden pushed in, starting with two fingers.

"Goddammit," he cursed through gritted teeth.

Kayden knew it would be a pinch, a sting, but he also understood that was what Aldo craved. He worked his ass, stretching him slowly, adding more lube. Aldo began anticipating Kayden's thrusts, driving backward to meet him. Two fingers became three.

A rustling from the bed captured Kayden's attention and he looked up at Hazel, who'd abandoned her own masturbating, shifting to steal a better view.

Kayden narrowed his eyes. "What are you supposed to be doing?"

She remained in place just long enough that he thought she might refuse.

"Hazel," he prodded.

She moved back to her spot, spreading her legs, stroking her clit.

"I can't see," she muttered.

Kayden chuckled, and he suspected Aldo would have too, if he weren't so fucking turned on and ready for more.

"Next time." Aldo's breath was ragged.

Hazel nodded, pushing two fingers inside her pussy.

Kayden prided himself on his self-control, but all bets were off tonight. If all went as he hoped, the three of them would have a lifetime to learn restraint. And from the looks of things, it might take at least that long.

He ripped open the condom and drew it on, covering it with a thick layer of lube. While he and Aldo had fucked no less than a hundred times in the past, it had been a very long year without.

Guiding the head of his dick to Aldo's ass, he slowly started to glide in. He closed his eyes, his jaw locked tight as he realized just how screwed he was. "Fuck me," Kayden breathed. "Aldo."

Aldo's arms gave way and he dropped from his hands to his elbows, his ass the only part still raised. Aldo looked over his shoulder. "Fuck *me*," he said, though those two words held a different meaning for him.

Kayden glanced at Hazel, still spellbound. "Use three fingers, Hazel. And stop screwing around. Fuck yourself like you mean it because if you aren't coming at the same time as Aldo, I'm going to flip you face down on this bed when I'm done and spank your ass until you can't sit for a week."

Hazel's eyes widened, but there wasn't a trace of fear there. More like, she was debating whether to let the bad girl out.

Kayden almost hoped she would.

Instead, she added another finger to the two pulsing in and out of her pussy, moving faster and deeper.

It was on the tip of his tongue to say "good girl," but Aldo stole his ability to speak, taking matters into his own hands when Kayden failed to move.

Aldo pulled forward a few inches, slamming back a second later.

"Goddammit!" Kayden's jaw locked, bright lights flashing behind his eyes.

Aldo managed two more of those thrusts before Kayden recovered his wits enough to take over. He tightened his grip on Aldo's hips and began to pound inside, taking Aldo forcefully, driving him to the peak quickly. Ordinarily, Kayden took his time, teased as he slowly drove Aldo out of his mind.

That wasn't possible this time.

This...this was primal, animalistic, almost brutal.

Aldo grunted, jerking himself off with his own hand. The way he was always there, meeting Kayden blow for blow, kept him going.

Hazel fucked herself faster, adding a fourth finger, her hips rising and falling, her own breath rapid.

Kayden was on the edge, hovering right there.

"Fuuuuuck!" Aldo cried, coming hard, Hazel a split second behind him, her sweet "uh, uh, uh" music to Kayden's ears.

Kayden's balls grew tight, and he gave himself up to the

moment, his own climax so powerful, he swore he felt his bones rattle.

"Jesus! Aldo. Hazel…"

The only sound in the now steamy room was their labored breathing. Kayden withdrew slowly, stroking Aldo's ass with a touch that was half comfort, half apology. He'd taken him too roughly, too fucking hard.

Aldo stood as Kayden walked to the bathroom to pitch the condom and wash his hands. He was surprised when Aldo followed him in.

"Listen," Kayden began.

Aldo hip-checked him, pushing him over so he could wash his hands too, grinning widely at Kayden through their reflections in the mirror.

"Fucking amazing." Aldo dried his hands before reaching to cup Kayden's face and kiss him. This kiss wasn't as hungry as before. It wasn't hungry at all. It was affection, pure and simple, and Kayden felt his heart swell.

"No fair." Hazel's voice came from the doorway. "You're leaving me out."

Kayden laughed and reached for her hand. She glanced at the sink, and he knew she'd probably planned to wash her hands as well. He lifted the fingers she'd used to bring herself off, sucking the juices.

His cock, which he would have thought out of commission for a few hours, rebounded in record time, something Aldo and Hazel both noticed.

"Sex in the shower?" Aldo suggested.

He and Hazel nodded, and Aldo went to turn on the water.

"Just think…" Aldo had a teasing glint in his eye. "If you moved in here with us, we could do this every night."

Hazel laughed. "We'd be dead within a week."

"But what a way to go," he joked.

What a way indeed.

Chapter Nineteen

"I'll be back as soon as I can." Hazel grabbed her purse and Nonna's car keys.

"Take your time, dear. Vanni's going to help me whip up a batch of chocolate chip cookies, since it's Bruno's night to visit."

Bruno, Aldo's older brother, was married with three kids, all of whom he'd warned he was bringing by tonight because they wanted to see their nonno. What Bruno actually said was that he would be traveling with "the demon seed" and they should all take cover.

Bruno was a big, burly guy with a thick, bushy mountain-man beard and a huge, booming voice and laugh. Like Aldo, he had a great sense of humor, and she'd enjoyed the nights when he'd come over to visit.

She'd been a part of the Moretti household for five weeks, the time flying by too quickly for her. She'd signed on to serve as Nonno's nurse for the entire six-to-eight weeks of his recovery. And while she wanted Nonno better, there was no denying his recovery was closer to the six weeks than the eight. She wasn't sure what she was going to do once the Morettis no longer needed her.

The weeks had passed in the blink of an eye, and she wished she could freeze time or at least slow it down.

Because this time was hands-down the best of her life, and she knew—even though she tried hard to keep playing the positive game—that shit was bound to hit the fan soon. It was simply the way her world worked.

So if she was smart, she'd start thinking about a practical future, instead of letting Kayden and Aldo pull her into their beautiful dreams.

It had been two weeks since Kayden had suggested they all live together. At first, she'd thought he was joking, but when he and Aldo persisted, she let herself imagine what that would be like.

Philadelphia Hazel had been so tempted to say yes, right then and there, but Boston Hazel refused to play along, refused to let her get swept away by things she couldn't have. So she needed to be realistic and come up with a genuine plan. One that didn't involve a dominant cop and a sexy firefighter.

The Morettis paid her well, and while she'd saved as much as she could, she'd also spent a fair amount attempting to buy back Mrs. Maloney's things. She'd tracked down three more items, asking the guy at the pawnshop to hold them for her while she raised the money.

She stepped out onto the front porch, zipping up her light-weight jacket—a loan from Penny—and headed for the car. Nonno had a prescription ready to pick up and Hazel had offered to run to the drugstore for Nonna. This was the first time she'd driven since her car had burned up in the fire at Crossings Motel.

Then it occurred to her this was actually the first time she'd been out of the house by herself since taking the job with the Morettis. The only time she'd left Nonno had been when Aldo and Kayden had taken her out on dates. If she could call them dates, she thought with a wicked grin. Dates for the three of them basically meant stealing a few hours at Kayden's house, wrapped around each other like pretzels, before they brought her back here and gave her the steamiest good-night kisses in history on the front porch. God only knew what the neighbors thought.

As far as she was concerned, their dates were perfect.

The hair on the back of her neck stood up as the now familiar feeling of being watched hit Hazel again. For weeks now, she'd been unable to kick the feeling, but she hadn't told anyone. Most likely, it was remnants of her run from Boston.

She scanned the neighborhood, searching to see if someone was looking in her direction. The street was—as always—sleepy. The old guy across the street in his front yard was trimming his shrubs and weeding the flower bed. A runner jogged by, giving her a friendly wave as she passed. A new mother, whom she'd stopped to chat with for a few minutes last week, was out for a walk, pushing the baby down the sidewalk in a stroller. They smiled and said "good morning" to each other.

Hazel chastised herself for being paranoid and climbed into the car. It was only a ten-minute drive to the drugstore. Parking the car on the street, she fed the meter, then walked inside. She paid for the prescription, then meandered down the makeup aisle, looking at mascara. She'd been replacing her makeup here and there because makeup was expensive and she couldn't justify dropping a hundred bucks on mascara, eyeliner, foundation, and all the rest.

The store was empty of other customers...so when she caught a familiar scent, her stomach twisted into knots.

No, she thought. Just fucking no.

"Found you, baby girl."

She resisted the urge to keep walking and pretend she hadn't heard him. Instead, she forced herself to turn and face her uncle.

"What are you doing here, Dennis?"

"Is that any way to greet your favorite uncle?" Dennis smelled like beer, cigarette smoke, and stale sweat. He was at least a week overdue for a shower.

"You're my only uncle. Listen, I'd love to stay and catch up," she said sarcastically, "but I need to run."

"Guess you do. Wouldn't want that old Italian couple to up and croak on you, would you now?"

Hazel managed to school her features, but just barely. "I don't know what you're talking about."

"Of course you do. Took me a few weeks to track you down, but once I found you, I kept watch."

"Why the hell were you tracking me down?" She and Dennis had zero love for each other. And while she'd threatened to call the cops on him for robbing Mrs. Maloney, he had to know she wouldn't do that after he swore to take her down with him.

"Your mom's getting fucking evicted. Can't hold down a job because she's a drunk piece of shit. Said the measly couple hundred bucks you sent her wasn't enough. Just so you know, she's fucking pissed at you for leaving."

Hazel couldn't give two shits about that. She'd remained at home, in that shitty apartment, for way too long. The only reason she'd stayed was because for the past three years, she'd spent the majority of her days at Mrs. Maloney's, only using the apartment as a place to sleep and store her clothes.

She crossed her arms, wishing she could find a way out of this conversation. "None of that answers my question."

"You sent her money. Figured that meant you'd found a job."

She scowled. "So what?"

"So...a credit card bill showed up around the same time as the money you sent. Your mom flipped her shit when she saw you were staying in some motel in Philadelphia. There wasn't nothing keeping me in Boston, so I thought I'd give Philly a try."

Hazel knew her uncle well enough to read between the lines. "Why are the cops looking for you?"

Dennis gave her a dirty look but didn't even bother try to lie. "Got into a little fight with some asshole bouncer at a bar. Fucker came at me first, but I finished it." Dennis cracked his bruised knuckles. "Prick called the cops, pressed charges. Figured it was a good time to lay low, and since your useless mom is going to be on the streets soon, I borrowed a car from a friend and headed this way."

"Borrowed or stole?"

Dennis just grinned, which answered that. Given the wrinkled state of his clothing, she'd guess he was sleeping in the stolen car.

Philadelphia was a big place, so how in the hell had he tracked her down?

"I went to the motel from the credit card to look for you. Fucking place was burned to the ground. Started to leave until I saw what was left of your car. Tried to take a closer look at it and the guy who owned the motel chased me off. I stuck around, decided to wait until the fucker left to take another look. Imagine my surprise when some cop stopped by and struck up a conversation with the old guy. He asked how you were doing, if you were still waiting tables at some place called Divine. How about that?"

Shit. She recalled Kayden mentioning that he'd stopped at the motel one afternoon when he was on patrol and saw Rocco's car in the parking lot. He'd even mentioned that Rocco had asked about her.

It figured that conversation would happen while Dennis was within earshot. Because that was exactly how luck worked for her.

It didn't.

"Couldn't hear the cop's answer, so I looked up the restaurant."

Knowing Dennis, he cased the place for a few days, waiting for her.

"When you never showed up, I caught up with the busboy in the back alley, taking out the trash one night."

Hazel's heart sank as she saw the busboy Todd's face in her mind. He was only twenty and special needs. Sweetest kid on the planet. "What did you do to him?"

Dennis smirked. "Not a fucking thing. That kid was all too happy to tell me about your new nursing job."

Todd had been sad when she'd said she was leaving to take the nursing job, until she told him who she was working for. Apparently, Todd's family had lived down the street from the Morettis when he was growing up, and Nonno had taught him how to throw a football. On her last day, he'd told her to take good care of Mr. Moretti.

"Told him you were my niece and that I was in town to surprise you. Stupid kid bought the story, told me exactly where you were working. Didn't even have to threaten him. Couldn't fucking believe it."

Hazel was sure he couldn't. The people who ran in their usual circle were suspicious of everyone—paranoid to the nth degree, but Todd was the opposite. He'd never met a stranger and didn't know the meaning of the word danger. No doubt, he took Dennis at his word, thrilled to be a part of what he assumed would be a happy surprise for her.

"Yeah, well, good for you. You found me. You win," she said, without a drop of sincerity, as she turned to walk away. Fuck this. She didn't have to talk to him.

Dennis gripped her arm tightly, pulling her toward him. "Not so fast, Hazel. You and me got business to discuss."

She tried to jerk her arm free, but prison had made him strong. "Let go," she said in a low voice, "or I'll scream."

Dennis leaned closer, and she gagged at the smell of his foul breath. "You're not gonna scream because if you do, I'll ruin you. You know you're wanted by the cops in Boston, right?"

Hazel shook her head. Mom said the police hadn't been by the apartment. Of course, she hadn't talked to her mom since that first phone call over a month ago. She'd decided to cut the cord for good after sending Mom money to help her get by until she found a job. Clearly, despite Hazel telling her that was the end of the free money, Mom hadn't believed her.

"They came by the place with a search warrant right before I left for Philadelphia." Dennis looked way too happy to tell this story. "Imagine everyone's surprise when they found some of the old bitch's jewelry under your mattress."

Hazel felt like she'd been punched in the stomach. He'd fucking set her up.

Dennis chuckled. "So go ahead and scream, Hazel. Let's see who they arrest first. The man trying to convince his niece to turn herself in or the wanted thief."

She swallowed thickly, bile clogging her throat. She'd let this time in Philadelphia blind her to reality because no matter how many times she told herself this couldn't last, there was that stupid, hopeful part of her that believed she'd escaped her past for good.

"What do you want?" she asked, her tone dead even to her own ears.

"I'm short on funds. Been sleeping in the car the past couple weeks or so. Fucking uncomfortable."

Hazel hesitated too long.

"Surely you've got a few bucks to spare. Or maybe we could go back to that nice fancy house you're staying in and ask that feeble old couple."

Hazel shook her head vehemently. "You're not going anywhere near them."

Dennis just gave her an evil grin. "No? Don't want to ask them? Then how about that cop and his boyfriend?" Dennis's grip on her arm was painful enough that he had to be leaving bruises. "I always pegged you for a fucking prude. Thought your legs were locked together at the knees. Never knew you were such a slut. Fucking two guys at the same time. Wonder what those old assholes would think if they knew their nurse was a whore."

Obviously, Dennis hadn't been watching closely enough if he failed to realize the Morettis knew about her relationship with Aldo and Kayden.

"Fucking a cop." Dennis shook his head, grimacing in genuine disgust. In his fucked-up mind, her sleeping with a police officer was clearly more revolting than sleeping with two men. "You think that prick is gonna save you from the Boston police? Is that why you're spreading your legs? If so, you're as stupid as that busboy. Cops stick together. Once he hears about who your dad is, what he did, he'll cut you loose so quick it'll make your head spin."

Hazel tried hard not to let those words penetrate, but she couldn't deny the part of her that feared Dennis was right. She'd learned that lesson in third grade when the teacher she'd adored turned on her, declaring an eight-year-old a bad seed, based solely on the sins of her father.

"So here's how this is gonna play out." Dennis gave her arm a vicious shake. His grip hurt like hell, but she'd be damned if she'd let him see how much. No crying. No wincing. She just swallowed the pain down, along with the bad emotions. It was how she'd survived most of her life.

"You're gonna open up that purse of yours and give me all the money you have on you."

Hazel wanted to believe that was it. That she'd give him some money and he'd go away forever, but she knew better. Her family only had two gestures, the middle finger and upturned palm.

She slipped her hand in her purse awkwardly. Dennis wasn't giving up his vise grip, probably afraid she'd run the second he released her. Opening her wallet, she slipped out the cash she had on her, which mercifully wasn't all her money. In the past, Hazel never would have left cash in the apartment, always keeping her money either on her person or in the bank. But she'd become complacent with the Morettis, confident they wouldn't steal from her. So she'd started stashing her funds in an envelope she kept in her nightstand drawer.

She handed him several bills...a few twenties, two tens, three ones.

"That's it?" Dennis asked in disbelief. He knew Boston Hazel, so he probably expected her to hand him a month's worth of salary.

"That's it."

He grabbed her purse and finally released her arm. She reached up to rub it, partly to soothe it and partly to keep it covered so he couldn't grab her there again. Rifling through her purse, he shoved it back at her, cursing.

"Where's the rest of your money?"

"In the bank," she lied. There was no way in hell she was telling him anything that might draw him to Nonno and Nonna's house.

"How much is there?"

She shrugged. "Not much. I sent some to Mom. Used the rest to buy back Mrs. Maloney's things from the pawnshops where you hocked everything."

Dennis scowled. "What the fuck is wrong with you?"

"If I had to pick the main thing, I'd say my family." Hazel was accomplished at hiding her fear behind sarcasm.

Dennis didn't appreciate her smart-ass response. "I'm sure you're making plenty of money off those Italian bastards. Nice house. Nice setup. Bet the place is packed with expensive shit they'll never miss."

Her hands started to shake, so she closed them into fists, desperate to hide the reaction. "I'm not stealing for you."

"No? Too good for that? You're a fucking Walsh, Hazel. You might as well face it. You're no better than the rest of us."

"I'm not stealing from them," she repeated again.

"You're going to give me money, or I'm talking to that cop. Bet he'd love to know how you ripped off the last old lady you took care of. Or maybe I'll talk to the other one. He's the Italians' grandson, right? Twenty bucks says that family kicks your ass out as quick as those rich pricks in Boston. Because *they'll* see what you refuse to believe—you're nothing but poor white trash, the daughter of a cop killer."

His words cut deep, opening wounds she'd thought had healed. Now she could see they'd *never* truly heal. Instead, she would spend the rest of her life living with big, ugly scabs that could be ripped off with just a few hateful reminders from Dennis.

Hazel held her breath, fighting hard no to cry, not to show her uncle an ounce of weakness.

"No smart-ass comeback, baby girl?" Dennis taunted.

She didn't answer. Couldn't. She wasn't sure she could keep the quiver out of her voice.

"You and me are a good team. We'll drain these Italians dry, then move on to the next city. The perfect partnership."

She wanted to shake her head but doing so would only prolong this conversation and she needed to get the fuck out of here.

"There's a bar in Fishtown. Happy Tap. Meet me there in three days. Come with cash or shit that's worth something. You don't show up and I'm talking to the cop. And if you run again, know right now that I'll fucking find you no matter where you go, and when I do, I'm gonna make it hurt."

Hazel didn't reply. Instead, she turned around and walked away, Dennis calling out behind her.

"I mean it, Hazel."

She knew he did. Knew he meant every word.

But he was wrong about one thing. One very big thing.

He was never going to find her again.

Chapter Twenty

"**A**ldo?"

"Hey, Nonna. Everything okay?" Aldo asked after answering the phone. He was doing some general upkeep on the fire equipment, counting down the hours until he was finally off-shift. He and Kayden had a date with Hazel tonight, and they were determined that this time, they'd take their girl out on the town.

The three of them had very little—okay, no—self-control whenever they got together. It was always the same thing. The clothes fell off, they fell into bed, and they fucked like they hadn't seen each other in decades.

"Is it Nonno?" His grandmother didn't typically call him when he was at work, so Aldo was a bit concerned.

"He's fine, *patatino*."

Aldo grinned. Nonna had been calling him, his brothers, and male cousins little potatoes for as long as they'd been alive.

"I was just wondering if Hazel had stopped by there."

Aldo frowned. Why would Hazel come by the fire station? "No. I haven't seen her today. Should I have?"

"Oh dear, I was afraid of that," Nonna murmured, more to herself than Aldo.

"Nonna, what's wrong? Where's Hazel?"

Nonna's voice when she replied was shaky and he could tell she was upset. "First thing this morning, she came into the kitchen where Vanni and I were having breakfast. Said she'd gotten a call from home and that there'd been an emergency."

Aldo's heart started to race. As far as he knew, Hazel hadn't been in touch with anyone in her family since arriving in Philadelphia. She'd given them the impression she was estranged from her parents, and she'd admitted to being an only child. So what could the emergency be?

His mind drifted back to that bruise on her cheek when she first arrived, and his blood turned cold.

"Did she say what the emergency was?" he asked.

"No. Just that she needed to leave immediately. She'd already called Berta and asked her if she could stay here the next few weeks, so we wouldn't be left shorthanded. You know Berta. She was here an hour after Hazel asked."

Aldo couldn't believe Hazel would leave Nonno. It went against everything she'd done the past five weeks. He'd never seen a more devoted caregiver.

"Vanni is doing fine," Nonna reassured him. "The doctor said it would be a six-to-eight-week recovery and at the last appointment, he said Vanni was definitely falling closer to the six-week end. I told her we'd be fine because I could see how upset she was about having to leave."

"Did she say how long she'd be gone?" Aldo tried to wrap his head around this information. None of it made any sense. Although, when he considered it, Hazel had been somewhat quiet last night on their texting thread, claiming she had a headache and was going to bed early. Kayden had teased her about living with eighty-year-olds for too long. Told her if she wasn't careful, she'd be eating dinner at four p.m. soon.

"No. She didn't say. I asked her if she'd told you and Kayden, and she said she was stopping by to explain why she was leaving and say goodbye to you on her way out of town."

That made Aldo feel a little bit better. Maybe she'd started with Kayden. If she had, Aldo had a pretty good feeling their partner was doing his damnedest to get all the details, and there was no way Kayden would let her leave town without them.

"Okay. Maybe she's still with Kayden," he said aloud. "How long ago did she leave?"

Nonna sighed heavily. "Four hours ago."

Aldo shook his head, hope fading. There's no way Kayden wouldn't have called him by now if she'd gone to say goodbye. Then something else occurred to him. "Why are you just calling me *now*, Nonna, instead of earlier?"

"Because I believed her when she said she'd go see you. It's just...well...I went into Hazel's room to tidy up a few minutes ago. The bed was covered with piles of folded clothes."

"What clothes?"

"All the clothes the girls gave her. She had a pile for each, with a little piece of paper on top, claiming who it belonged to. She left all of it here with a note asking if I could return the clothes to them. That didn't feel right to me. The girls gave her those clothes to keep."

"They did."

"And there was money on the nightstand. We'd paid her through the week, but she gave it back, claimed she couldn't take money she hadn't earned."

That sounded very much like Hazel. She had a hard time accepting help, the stubborn woman determined to make her own way through life. Even so, that didn't explain why Nonna was calling him now.

"Was that all she left behind?"

"That seems to be all she left behind on purpose," Nonna replied. "When I was leaving the room, I saw a piece of paper on the floor near the bedroom door. I assumed Hazel had dropped it without realizing."

"What was on the paper?"

Aldo heard paper rustling. Clearly, Nonna had it and was planning to read it to him. "It's a list of items, stuff like silverware, jewelry, an antique mirror, and a bunch of other stuff. Some of the items have lines drawn through them, some don't."

It was a curious list, but not exactly concerning. "Okay."

"The thing is, Aldo," Nonna said, "at the top of the page, it says, 'Stolen items.'"

Aldo had no idea what to make of that. "Did Hazel say anything else, Nonna? Did she tell you specifically where she was going?"

"No. And I'm wishing I'd asked her, but she was sort of frazzled and in such a hurry to go, I didn't want to add stress by asking her a lot of questions. She'd only taken a backpack, so I took that as a good sign that she was coming back. Until I found the clothing on the bed."

Aldo rubbed the back of his neck, tension setting in. "Thanks for calling, Nonna. I'll get in touch with Kayden and we'll see if we can track her down."

"You think she's in trouble?" The true fear in his grandmother's voice told him he'd said exactly the wrong thing.

"No, no," he hastily lied. "We just want to help her and her family if we can. If you hear from her, will you let me know?"

"Of course."

"And you and Nonno are good for now?" he checked.

"Right as rain. Berta's staying here this week, and tonight is Tony, Rhys, and Jess's night to join us for dinner and visit. I'll ask Rhys to make sure Berta and I are doing everything right with the medications, though I don't see how we can mess it up. Hazel left me a two-page list of instructions for everything."

Ordinarily, information like that would have made Aldo smile, but he was on the border of freaking out right now. He said goodbye to his grandmother, hung up, then clicked on Hazel's cell number. The call went straight to voicemail, which—sadly—didn't surprise him.

His next call was to Kayden, who was working at his desk at the precinct today.

"Hey, Aldo. What's up? Thought you'd still be at work."

They were both off duty at five. They had intended to shower, change, then pick up Hazel at six, but it looked like that was off.

"Hazel left," he said.

"Left where?" Kayden asked, perplexed. Those two words confirmed Aldo's suspicions that Hazel had lied to Nonna. She hadn't intended to say goodbye to either of them.

Aldo took a few minutes, filling Kayden in on everything Nonna had told him, including the list of stolen items. Kayden didn't know what to make of that any more than Aldo did.

"Give me a few minutes to make some calls," Kayden said. "I'll call you back if I find something out."

Clearly, Officer Gallo was about to launch an investigation.

Aldo hung up, any hope of finishing his work to-do list dashed. He paced for close to twenty minutes before Kayden called back.

"Well?" Aldo said.

"Hazel bought a one-way ticket and got on a bus headed for Chicago two hours ago."

"Chicago?" Aldo wasn't sure what to make of that. "She said she was from Springfield."

"She said a lot of things," Kayden said with a heavy sigh.

"She also left a fuck-ton of shit *unsaid*." Aldo raked his hand through his hair. "Something's wrong. I can feel it."

"So can I," Kayden agreed.

"Hazel took her job with my grandparents very seriously. There's no way she would have left until Nonno was fully recovered if something hadn't spooked her. She's running."

"Yeah. Well, we're going to run faster." Aldo could hear Kayden tapping keys on his computer. "There's a flight to Chicago that leaves in four hours. It'll put us in the Windy City by eight thirty tonight. We'll get a hotel for the evening, and then you and I are going to be at that bus station tomorrow morning at seven a.m. when Hazel gets off. It's way past time our girlfriend gave us some answers."

Aldo nodded, though Kayden couldn't see it. Leave it to his best friend to have a plan. Thank God.

"Okay. I'm going to clock out and head to my place to pack an overnight bag."

"I'll get the plane tickets now, then do the same. I'll swing by your place to pick you up in an hour or so."

"Sounds good." Then Aldo found himself asking the question that preyed on his mind. "Why do you think she left?"

"I don't know," Kayden said. "But we're going to get her back, Aldo. Hazel's days of running are over."

Aldo said goodbye, Kayden's words soothing the rough edges left behind by the thought of Hazel leaving them. He talked to his supervisor, requesting permission to leave work early. Luckily there were only three hours left on his shift. Not that it mattered. He would have used sick leave or vacation time if necessary.

Their girl was in trouble, and Aldo wouldn't rest easy until she was back in his arms again. Once they ran her down, things were changing.

Hazel was theirs.

And it was time she realized it.

* * *

Aldo rubbed his eyes wearily, his gut in knots. He and Kayden had gotten to Chicago later than they'd planned after a delayed take-off, due to rain. They'd dragged themselves into a hotel near the airport shortly before midnight, though neither of them had managed to get much sleep.

They'd shared a king-size bed, talking until nearly two a.m., unable to make sense of why she would leave or what the list of stolen items meant. Hazel wouldn't even keep the clothing his sister and friends had given her, so it seemed highly unlikely that she'd taken anything from Nonno and Nonna's house.

Kayden could have done some investigating, could have put her name in the database to see if anything pinged, but he refused. Hazel's story was hers to tell. And Aldo had genuinely thought they'd been earning her trust, getting her to the place where she would feel safe enough to share her secrets.

The fact that she ran...

It cut deep. And he wasn't the only one feeling the sting. Kayden sighed again as he made the turn onto his street.

They'd been at the station when the bus from Philadelphia arrived. Hazel hadn't been on it. Kayden was able to confirm that she had boarded it in Philly, but according to the clerk at the ticketing station, she could have gotten off at any of the nine stops along the way. It was something they hadn't considered, which—in hindsight—perhaps they should have.

So she'd bought the ticket to Chicago as a way to truly make her escape. They'd foolishly thought she'd been running from something in her past, whoever put that bruise on her cheek. It hadn't occurred to them that she was running from *them*. That she wouldn't want them to find her.

"Fuck," Aldo muttered, not for the first time. They'd left the bus station, frustrated and not entirely sure where to go from there. They didn't have a clue where she'd disembarked, and enough time had passed that she could have disappeared into any of those nine cities. Hell, she could have gotten on another bus, under another name, and gone somewhere completely different.

So they'd headed back to the airport, caught the first plane to Philadelphia, and now—eighteen hours later—they were home again. Without Hazel.

"What now?" Aldo asked.

Kayden shrugged. "I'm not sure. I could do some investigating, look her up, see what we can find out, but if she doesn't want to be found..."

That was the part that was killing Aldo.

Kayden pulled into the driveway. "Son of a bitch."

Aldo glanced at his best friend, his attention turning to whatever had caught Kayden's eye.

Then, he cursed too. "Thank fucking God!"

Hazel was sitting on the porch swing. Even from the car, he could see exhaustion written in her posture, on her face.

They both got out of the car, approaching the porch at a normal pace. Aldo wanted to run, but he was too afraid of spooking her.

"Hi," she said quietly, lifting her hand in a limp wave.

The circles under her eyes were dark as bruises, her hair was in a messy ponytail, her clothing wrinkled. At her feet was her backpack. Considering she'd returned all the clothing she'd been given, he'd guess there was nothing inside but the few outfits she'd bought herself.

"Where the hell have you been?" Kayden asked, his voice gruff.

Aldo reached over, placing his hand on Kayden's forearm, a weak attempt at calming him down.

They'd both been out of their minds with worry, imagining the worst. Kayden used to do the same whenever Keeley missed curfew. The cop was capable of drawing up some of the worst-case scenarios Aldo had ever heard. A skill he'd obviously taught Aldo, because he'd spent every hour since Nonna told him Hazel was gone worried that someone from her past had taken her, that she'd been hurt or—worse—killed. He'd spent most of the return flight home terrified he'd never see her again and trying to figure out how in the hell he could survive that.

"It's okay," Hazel said to Aldo. "You *should* be angry at me."

There was something off in Hazel's tone. Exhaustion was there, but it was more than that. Or maybe the word was *less*. Because there was no inflection, no emotion, nothing.

"We're not angry," Aldo said.

Kayden's head spun toward him. "The hell we're not." He looked back at her. "Hazel, we've been worried sick!"

"I shouldn't have run," she said, still in that dead voice that Aldo hated.

"Why did you?" Aldo asked.

There would be time to discuss their feelings later. Right now, he just needed to know what was going on. The fact she ran told him it was bad. But she'd come back, so while Kayden might still be annoyed, Aldo only felt relief...and hope.

Hazel wrapped her arms around her middle, and Aldo realized she was cold. While the frigid temperatures of winter had given way to spring, it was still chilly, and Hazel must have returned the coat. She was wearing the same tatty jeans and hoodie she'd had on the night they met.

Aldo stepped toward her and held out his hand. "Let's go inside where it's warmer."

Hazel rose, somewhat stiffly, and it occurred to him, she'd obviously been sitting there for some time. Her hand was like a block of ice.

"How long have you been here?" he asked, as he led her to the front door.

Kayden was already there, unlocking it, his scowl gone, replaced by a look of concern.

Hazel shrugged. "I don't know. A few hours?"

Kayden growled. "Jesus, Fireball. You'll be lucky if you don't get pneumonia."

The second Kayden called her by their nickname, Aldo knew he was calmer.

The two of them led her to the living room. Kayden grabbed a blanket from the back of the couch, wrapping it around her shoulders and pulling it snuggly as Aldo took both her hands in his, rubbing to warm them.

"You didn't make it to Chicago," Kayden said, once he and Aldo were settled next to her, both tucked in close, trying to share their body heat.

Hazel blinked in surprise, but if she was shocked that they

knew where she'd been heading, she didn't show it. She wasn't showing them fucking anything.

She shook her head. "I only got as far as Columbus before... before I turned around." Hazel's hands were clenched together tightly on her lap, Aldo's covering them. She stared down at their fingers as she said, "I don't want to run anymore."

"You don't have to run." Kayden said it as if it was as simple as that, but Aldo could see Hazel didn't believe him.

Her gaze was still lowered, and he hated seeing the utter defeat that had settled on her shoulders. She took a deep, steadying breath, then she looked up, first at Aldo, then Kayden.

"I'm not from Springfield," she started. "I'm from Boston. I'm Hazel Walsh from Boston."

She said her name like it should mean something to them, but hell if he knew what. Aldo could tell from the expression on Kayden's face he didn't get it either.

"My father is Danny Walsh. Eighteen years ago, he robbed a bank. While he was attempting to escape, he killed two of the police officers in pursuit."

Hazel was looking at Kayden now, waiting for a response.

Kayden stared back at her, frowning. "That's a horrible thing, Hazel, but that's something your *dad* did. You didn't think I'd judge you for his actions, did you?"

She swallowed heavily, and he saw the first crack in her composure. "That night in the theater room, you said you hoped that one day I would trust you with my story."

Kayden nodded. "I did."

"This is," her voice quivered, "this is me, trusting you."

Aldo thought he'd be happy when she finally admitted she trusted them, but he couldn't summon the emotion. Maybe because Hazel looked so fucking destroyed.

"And I'm fucking terrified." She whispered the last word.

Kayden placed his hand on her knee. "Don't be."

Aldo squeezed the hands he still held. "You don't have to be afraid. We won't let you down."

She scoffed. "Everyone lets you down, Aldo."

It was probably the most real response Hazel had ever given them, and he realized just how much she'd been holding back. She'd shared her happiness with them, but she'd hidden this side —the bitter one that had been kicked down too many times in life.

"Not us," Kayden said, deep and sure.

If he meant the words to be reassuring, Kayden failed. Because Hazel's spine stiffened, her eyes narrowing as if she'd taken the words as a challenge. She was going to lay herself bare to them— one of the bravest things Aldo had ever seen—because in doing so, she was expecting them to walk away at the end of this.

So now he wasn't sure if this was trust or a test. Either way, he didn't intend to fail.

Hazel took a moment before speaking again. "My dad is serving a life sentence in prison. His brother, my uncle Dennis, was part of the bank robbery, but he wasn't charged with murder because he'd been caught before my dad pulled the trigger on those two cops. He was released about six months ago, and he came to stay with us. FYI, he's a complete asshole."

Suddenly, Aldo started to suspect who'd hit Hazel, and it appeared Kayden had come to the same conclusion.

"My mom and I share an apartment together. I should have moved out years ago, but Mom has trouble holding down jobs. She's got some serious anger issues, and when you add in the fact she's a total drunk, regular employment isn't something she's ever succeeded at. I'm the only one who's ever managed to hold down jobs, so paying the bills has always fallen to me."

"What made you leave Boston?" Aldo asked.

"For the past three years, I've been working as an in-house nurse for an elderly woman with dementia. Mrs. Maloney." She said the name with a sad smile that told Aldo she had cared for her last patient as much as she did his grandparents.

"I was fired a couple of days before I drove to Philadelphia."

Aldo frowned. "Why?"

"Mrs. Maloney's grandchildren, Jeremiah and Annabel, accused me of stealing from her. A lot of things had gone missing in the home, and I was the only person outside of the family with a key."

"Maybe someone in the family—" Kayden started.

"No. The Maloneys are as tight as the Morettis. None of them would have stolen from their grandmother. They adore her."

"Yes, but to accuse you—" Kayden continued.

"Mrs. Maloney was never alone. I was with her twelve hours a day, then someone in the family would come spend the night with her."

It was the same setup they'd arranged for Hazel as she cared for Nonno. "Twelve-hour days." It explained to Aldo why Hazel was such a hard worker. She was used to long hours.

"I didn't mind that. Mrs. Maloney's house was quiet and clean. I actually hated leaving at night because it meant going home to…God…hell on earth is probably too nice a description for the shithole I lived in back in Boston."

Aldo looked at Kayden, then back at Hazel. "Did the family give you a list of what was missing?"

This time, Hazel looked shocked. "How did you know that?"

"Nonna found a piece of paper on the floor of your bedroom," Aldo explained.

Hazel glanced over at her backpack. She obviously hadn't realized she'd lost it.

"It said Stolen Items on the top," Aldo added.

Hazel pressed her fingers to her mouth, her eyes wet with tears. "Oh my God. She must have thought I'd been stealing from *her*. Did she search the house? Looking for what was missing?"

Aldo frowned. "No. Of course not. Why the hell would she do that?"

"What did she think that list was?"

Aldo shrugged. "None of us had a clue, but we sure as hell didn't think it was your shopping list. Jesus, Hazel. You didn't even take the clothes that were given to you. Or the money you'd earned."

She shook her head. "I didn't earn that money. I left early."

Aldo rolled his eyes. "That's a debate for another time. And believe me, we're going to have it."

"None of this explains why you left Boston." Kayden put them back on track. "Or here."

"I discovered it was my uncle who'd been stealing from Mrs. Maloney. I found a bunch of her things in his bag. He knew my schedule, and he'd lifted her key one night, had a copy made. He knew when we'd be out of the house for appointments, so he broke in then. I confronted him about it." Her fingers subconsciously stroked the cheek that had been bruised.

"He hit you." Kayden's tone was dark, angry.

Hazel nodded. "He told me if I turned him in, he'd tell the police that we'd been working together, that I had been in on it from the beginning. No one in the Boston PD would believe a Walsh innocent of *anything*."

For the next few minutes, Hazel continued her story, explaining about the police showing up, her running in the night, her uncle setting her up to take the fall by stashing the jewelry in her room, and how he'd found her at the pharmacy two days earlier, demanding money and telling her that she was wanted by the cops.

"I'm supposed to meet him at some bar in South Philly with more money or something of value from your grandparents' house, or he'll turn me in to the police." She looked him straight in the eye. "Aldo, I would *never* steal from Nonno and Nonna. You have to believe me."

"I do."

She blinked a couple times, and it seemed as if she was trying to decide if she'd heard him correctly. "I ran because I thought it would take them off Dennis's radar, but then I realized I'd left them here, unprotected and unaware. I hadn't warned them or you that he was out there. That's when I got off the bus."

Aldo frowned. "Do you think they're in danger?" He pulled his phone from his back pocket.

"I don't," Hazel quickly reassured him. "He thinks he's scared me into committing the crime. He won't do anything until I fail to show up tomorrow. That's when," she shrugged, "he becomes a loose cannon. I have no idea what he'll do, but my fear was he'd go to their house looking for me, and I couldn't let him do that without making sure Nonna and Nonno are protected."

Aldo made a mental note to call the guys later, to set up a new schedule where one of them was always at the house until Hazel's uncle was caught. "We'll make sure they're safe."

"Thank you." She bowed her head once more. "I've spent the last month tracking down Mrs. Maloney's things at pawnshops. I would save up enough money to buy something back, then return it to them anonymously. I was hoping that with the return of their things, they wouldn't press charges, but I guess it wasn't enough. I..." Her knuckles had gone white from how tightly she squeezed them together. "I won't fight you, Kayden," she said softly. "I won't resist. Just...please don't handcuff me."

Kayden scowled, his brows low over narrowed eyes. "What the fuck are you talking about?"

"There's a warrant out for my arrest," she replied. "You *have* to arrest me."

Kayden rose from the couch. "The fuck I do. You didn't do anything wrong, Hazel."

"But the police found her things in my room."

Kayden shook his head, then reached out to her. She took his hand, allowing him to pull her up. "I'm not arresting you."

"But..." She kept shaking her head.

Aldo stood, standing next to Kayden, the two of them facing her. "We believe you, Hazel."

"You *can't*."

Kayden leaned down, his face close to Hazel's. "We. Believe. *You*."

Hazel stood there for the beat of one heart, then two, then...

she fell completely apart. Tears streamed down her cheeks as her chest heaved with heavy sobs, all the bad shit that had been pressing down on her for weeks finally giving way.

He and Kayden were both there to catch her. They wrapped her up in their arms, letting her cry out all the ugliness against them, swaying ever so gently.

"Shh," Aldo soothed her. "We've got you now."

"Give it all to us," Kayden said. "We'll fix it. Promise."

She shook her head, the sobs growing louder at his promise, and Aldo suspected this sorrow had been born a long, long time ago. It had been festering inside the heart of a little girl who'd never been shown real affection or love.

His heart broke, while simultaneously, it swelled.

Those days were over. From now until the end of her life, a day wouldn't pass where Hazel didn't know just how much they loved her.

They remained there for...God...he didn't know if minutes or hours had passed. They simply held her in their arms until the cries faded and her breathing calmed.

"Come on," Aldo said at last. "It looks like none of us got much sleep last night. Let's crawl into Kayden's big bed together and take a nap."

Hazel allowed them to drag her along to the bedroom, standing still as he and Kayden undressed her.

Aldo frowned when he saw the dark bruise on her upper arm.

"Uncle Dennis grabbed me," she explained, as Aldo softly stroked his fingers over the injury, hating that he hadn't been there to protect her.

"He's never laying a fucking finger on you again," Kayden swore.

Once she was naked, Kayden grabbed one of his soft cotton T-shirts and pulled it over her head, the large thing hanging almost to her knees, thanks to her petite frame.

Kayden drew down the covers, helping her into the middle of

the bed, then he and Aldo stripped down to their boxers and climbed in next to her, caging her between them.

When Aldo closed his eyes, sleep came quickly because he had the two most important people in the world with him, safe and sound.

For now.

Chapter Twenty-One

Kayden tried not to jar the bed too much as he climbed back in. He'd only managed to grab a couple hours of restless sleep before he packed it in and got out of bed. Aldo and Hazel hadn't been suffering the same fate, the two of them sleeping the sleep of the righteous.

"Kayden," Hazel whispered, turning toward him.

He wrapped his arm around her shoulder, loving the way she curled into his chest. He felt Aldo stir, glancing over to see his boyfriend had woken up as well. He might have felt guilty about waking them, but they'd been napping for close to six hours.

"Where did you go?" she asked.

"I needed to make a few calls."

Hazel went stiff in his arms, and he hastened to explain.

"Stop, Hazel. I told you I'm not arresting you. I'm not turning you in either. But I needed to see what we were up against."

"We," she whispered, trying it on for size.

It made him smile. Kayden tipped her face up to his and stole a quick kiss. "We. Always."

"How bad is it?" Despite the fact they'd assured her they planned to help, Hazel continued to struggle to truly believe it.

Not that he could blame her. She'd spent twenty-five years getting shit on by people who should have been there for her.

"Honestly, it's not bad at all."

Hazel hadn't been expecting that. She pushed up until she was sitting between them. Kayden and Aldo followed suit, both shifting until their backs rested against the headboard.

"There's no outstanding warrant for Hazel Walsh in Boston," Kayden said.

"But Uncle Dennis—"

"Lied," Kayden interjected. "He was trying to scare you so that you would have no choice but to cooperate."

Hazel sighed. "And I fell for it."

Aldo grasped her hand. "Don't look at it that way. Your uncle is obviously an unscrupulous asshole. Why wouldn't you believe that the fucker had set you up to take the fall for his crime?"

She gave him a grateful smile before looking at Kayden again.

"However, while there are no warrants for Hazel Walsh, there are *two* for Dennis Walsh. One for assault and one for car theft."

Hazel nodded. "He told me he'd come to Philadelphia to lay low because he'd punched some bouncer at a bar, who was pressing charges. He claimed to have borrowed the car from a friend."

"That's quite a family you have, Fireball," Aldo said with a grin.

For the first time since they found her on the porch, Hazel laughed, and the sound warmed Kayden to the soul. "Tell me about it."

Kayden appreciated Aldo's ability to lighten the heaviest of moods. "I told my chief at the precinct we had a lead on where Walsh would be, so plans have been made to intercept him at the bar and arrest him."

Hazel's smile faded. "If you arrest him there, he'll know it was me who turned him in. What if he follows through with his threat?"

"You can't be convicted of a crime that hasn't been reported,

Hazel," Kayden explained. "The Maloneys never reported a theft." Kayden gave her a moment before dropping the next bomb. "I called Jeremiah Maloney."

Hazel's eyes widened. "You did *what*?! Why?"

"Because we need to know exactly what we're up against. Do you want to keep living with that ax over your head? Wondering if this will be the day they decide to report the crime and point the finger at you?"

She shook her head slowly, but she didn't look wholly convinced. Probably because she'd spent weeks facing down the barrel of that gun. She'd gotten too used to living with the constant worry.

Kayden refused to let her do that anymore. "I told them exactly what you told us. That it was your uncle who'd stolen from them. Then I explained that we were close to making an arrest—not for the burglary but for two other crimes that would most likely put your uncle behind bars for the rest of his life. He isn't just facing a third strike, but a fourth as well."

"What did Jeremiah say?"

"He said he and Annabel had wanted to report the crime, but...well, apparently Mrs. Maloney has good days and bad days."

Hazel nodded. "That's true. I never really knew if she was going to know me from one day to the next."

"She had one of her good days shortly after you were fired, and it sounds like she rained holy hell down on her entire family, claiming you would never steal from her, and that she'd disown every last one of them if they tried to have you arrested for a crime you didn't commit."

Hazel sniffled, a single tear falling. "She said that?"

Aldo lifted her hand and kissed it. "You have very devoted patients, Nurse Hazel. Says a hell of a lot about who you are as a person, if you ask me."

Kayden wanted Hazel to hear the rest of the story because every word Aldo said was true. "Jeremiah went on to say they'd gotten over half of the stolen items back anonymously. I told them it was *you* who'd tracked the goods down and bought them back because you felt guilty about what your uncle had done. He asked me to tell you to stop doing that. And then he wanted to know if you might want your old job back. According to Jeremiah, he used to dread his grandmother's bad days, hating when she didn't remember him. He said her *good* days are far worse now because Mrs. Maloney reads them the riot act for letting you go."

Hazel's smile came with tears. "Oh my God. I love that woman so much."

Kayden pressed a kiss to her forehead. "So all that's left is to arrest your uncle and send him back to Boston to pay for his crimes. You never have to see him again, Hazel."

She sat there for a full minute as he and Aldo let the words sink in. He swore he saw half a dozen expressions cross her face in those sixty seconds. Everything from disbelief to relief, from uncertainty to happiness.

"It's over?" she finally asked, struggling to take it all in.

"It's all over," Kayden reassured her—then he watched Hazel come alive.

She leaned toward Aldo, initiating a kiss hot enough to melt the paint. As they kissed, she reached over, wrapping her hand around his neck, pulling him closer so that when she and Aldo broke apart, all she had to do was turn her head and give him the same scorching kiss. When they came up for air, Aldo grasped the nape of Kayden's neck, the two of them kissing as Hazel watched.

Well, she watched for a split second, then she hopped in, her lips sliding over Kayden's cheek before bouncing over to Aldo's, her hand sliding around Kayden's waist, her fingers drifting beneath the elastic of his boxers. He could only assume her other hand was doing the same to Aldo because, one, Kayden couldn't open his eyes—too blown away by Aldo's kiss—and two, Aldo's groan matched his when their sexy woman slid her fingers along the top crack of Kayden's ass.

"Fuck, Hazel." Kayden pulled back no more than an inch,

his and Aldo's foreheads pressed together as she continued to kiss their faces, nip at their earlobes, her fingers teasing their asses.

"Take off your boxers," she demanded.

He and Aldo had taken the lead on their sexual interludes thus far, the two of them issuing commands. Kayden would have expected her words to chafe, but instead, they pushed his arousal to a fever pitch.

"I was going to suggest dinner." His lips traveled from the side of Aldo's face, along his neck, making it clear food was the last thing on his mind.

"We can eat after," Hazel said.

"After." Aldo's smile matched Hazel's. His lovers had just one hunger at the moment.

"After sounds good." Kayden gripped Hazel's ankle and pulled until she fell to her back halfway down the mattress.

She giggled the entire time. Aldo reached down to strip the T-shirt, which had ridden above her breasts, off completely.

"Kayden." She wrapped her hands around his neck when he climbed over her, caging her beneath him. He resumed their kiss, his elbows braced on the mattress next to her shoulders. From the corner of his eye, he watched Aldo rise and strip off his boxers, his gaze glued to them.

Kayden broke the kiss, his lips and tongue sliding downward until he reached her breasts. Aldo liked a show, and Kayden intended to give him his money's worth.

Gripping her breast, he looked up, his gaze connected with Aldo's as he sucked her tight nipple into his mouth. Kayden held nothing back, the suction rough enough that Hazel moaned, her back arching.

Aldo remained next to the bed, his hand lazily stroking his thick erection. Kayden bared his teeth, biting just the tip of her nipple, applying enough pressure to provoke yet another moan.

Aldo's eyes, dark with lust, watched Kayden intently.

"She likes it rough," he said huskily.

"She does." Kayden gave the same treatment to her other nipple as Hazel's breaths grew ragged.

"Please," she said, her plea not specific enough.

Kayden lifted his head and gave her a look. Every time they came together, he'd made her ask for what she wanted. Exactly what she wanted. It had a twofold effect. It proved to Hazel that there was nothing she could ask for that they wouldn't give her. Plus, he and Aldo were big fans of dirty talk, and their woman's sexy requests were some of the sweetest words he'd ever heard.

"I want you to fuck me." Her voice was more confident than Kayden had ever heard it. Now that Hazel wasn't looking over her shoulder, wasn't waiting for them to cut and run, she was staking her claim.

No, he thought, it was better than that. She was accepting her place here, with them.

She looked over at Aldo. "And I want you to kneel over my face," she pointed with one finger, "so that Kayden can give you a blow job, while I play with your balls."

Mother.

Fucker.

Aldo looked as shocked and turned on as Kayden felt. Hazel had just taken their kinky play from beginner—they'd been easing her in—to holy fuck.

Aldo reached into the nightstand, pulling out a condom that he handed to Kayden. Kayden awkwardly shoved his boxers down with one hand, while propping himself above her with the other. He refused to move an inch away from her. Kicking them off when they reached his ankles, he opened the condom and rolled it on.

Aldo shifted into place, his knees straddling Hazel's face. It was close quarters for all of them, but once they adjusted their positions, it worked just fine.

Kayden ran one finger along Hazel's slit, aware that—apart from the kisses—they hadn't done any foreplay. Every time they'd come together in the past, they'd spent the better part of an hour driving each other insane with touches and kisses and strokes and bites until they were panting, desperate to fuck.

That wasn't going to happen tonight. The stress of the past twenty-four hours, combined with the knowledge that there was nothing between them anymore, left them with an unbearable need to consummate this now.

Right fucking now.

Hazel was drenched, her tight pussy hot. It clenched around his finger when he shoved one in, and she cried out when he removed it just as quickly.

Guiding his cock to her opening, he felt the weight of Aldo's gaze as he slid inside her, more slowly than he would have thought himself capable of.

Inch by inch.

Drawing out the sensation for him, for Hazel.

And Aldo, who muttered a curse. "Fucking hot."

Hazel's fingers ran up and down Aldo's thighs, gripping them when Kayden hit her G-spot. "Please, Kayden," she whispered. "Too slow."

He wasn't swayed, his pace unchanged until, at last—thank God—he was buried inside her.

Once there, he turned his attention to his other lover. Aldo was fisting his dick, maintaining his own easy pace. Aldo, like him, was probably worried about this ending way too quickly.

Kayden lowered his upper body until the head of Aldo's cock hovered right by his mouth. "Feed it to me," he demanded.

Aldo didn't have to be asked twice. He pushed the thick head of his cock inside as Kayden opened wider to accommodate him. They weren't new to blow jobs. Shit, it was one of the first things they'd perfected all those years ago, when they became lovers, the two of them going down on each other way too often to probably be normal.

There was something addictive about sucking Aldo off and having him return the gesture. The two of them had become experts when it came to giving each other head, and as Aldo gripped the back of Kayden's neck, pushing forward until he reached the back of his throat, he realized again just how much he'd missed this closeness between them.

When Aldo was fully seated, he held there, cutting off Kayden's air for just a few seconds before withdrawing again.

Kayden realized the choreography of this, fucking Hazel while sucking Aldo, was going to fall to him.

Or so he thought. Until he thrust into Hazel as Aldo repeated the same in his mouth, and he recalled the night he'd taught Hazel how to give a blow job, remembered teaching her the difference between that and...

Aldo fucking his mouth.

When Hazel wrapped her legs around Kayden's hips, lifting up to claim more of him, Kayden stopped worrying about taking control and simply lost himself in the rhythm.

The three of them came together like feral beasts.

Aldo pushed into his mouth deeper—more deeply than Kayden would have thought possible—cutting off his air for a second longer each time.

Hazel writhed beneath him, rising and falling in time with his hard, almost brutal pounding.

Aldo jerked, then cursed, drawing Kayden's attention.

Looking down, he realized Hazel wasn't just driving him to the brink. She'd cupped Aldo's balls and she was squeezing them, applying enough pressure that Kayden wasn't sure if he was grateful or jealous he wasn't in Aldo's place.

The temperature in the room spiked, the air humid, more wet than that of the rainforest.

Their thrusts took on a life of their own as they created a symphony of moans, groans, cries, grunts, and curses.

Aldo fell over first, his fingers digging into Kayden's shoulders as he came, coating his throat. Kayden stilled, buried deep inside Hazel as he drew his tongue along the underside of Aldo's dick, swallowing down the thick load.

Aldo pulled away, falling back on his haunches, his chest

rising and falling, his face red from exertion. He leaned forward, giving Kayden a quick, hard kiss, then he shifted back once more, one eyebrow raised as if telling Kayden to get on with it.

Kayden began fucking Hazel in earnest, his own climax hovering right there. Reaching down, he stroked her clit, determined to push her across the finish line first.

Her back arched, her eyes closed as she called out his name. Her pussy clenched so tightly—too tightly—around his dick, and Kayden was a goner.

Unable to hold himself up, he dropped to his elbows, thrusting inside her just two times more before his balls emptied, filling the condom.

Hazel wasn't on birth control. Yet. One night after they'd slept together, they'd discussed whether she should start. Condoms weren't one hundred percent effective.

Now...

Now he was tempted to tell her not to.

Because he wasn't just fast-forwarding them toward moving in together. In his mind, they were making this thing a hell of a lot more permanent, complete with vows and babies and maybe even a dog.

He didn't realize he was grinning like an unhinged fool until Hazel tilted her head, giving him a funny look.

"Okay?" she asked, clearly confused by his extreme giddiness.

Kayden didn't bother to hide his thoughts. "Yep. Just wondering if it's too soon to start planning a wedding and making babies."

Hazel giggled. "Jesus. I'm still trying to wrap my head around the fact you want us to move in together after dating for all of a hot minute."

"Moving in together is a done deal." Kayden was aware she hadn't agreed, but he was also aware—given her own overblown grin—that she wasn't going to say no. "So it's time to start settling the rest."

Kayden pulled out of her body, dropping down to the bed next to her.

Aldo had already claimed the other side, so Hazel turned toward him, clearly expecting him to be the more reasonable.

She was destined for disappointment because Kayden knew if he—the king of overthinking things—had made this giant-ass leap, Aldo had gotten there way ahead of him.

"Don't look at me." Aldo confirmed Kayden's suspicions. "I'm thinking a fall wedding. And I'm partial to the name Francesca if we have a girl. Her nickname would be Frankie. How adorable would that be for our little curly redheaded daughter?"

Kayden laughed. Aldo had blown him out of the water, not only dreaming of kids but giving them nicknames as well.

Hazel rolled her eyes and shook her head. "You're both insane. And...this is not me agreeing to anything, but hypothetically speaking...a fall wedding *would* be cool."

Chapter Twenty-Two

Hazel sat in the passenger seat of Aldo's truck, parked outside the Happy Tap. She pointed when the door of the bar opened. Kayden and another police officer walked outside with her uncle—his hands cuffed behind his back. Her uncle had a black eye and a bloody nose, his dirty white T-shirt stained red.

Kayden opened the back door of the cruiser, his hand on Uncle Dennis's head, guiding him into the backseat as her uncle cussed a blue streak, loud enough that she could hear every word, even though the windows of the truck were rolled up.

Uncle Dennis insisted he'd been set up, protested he was innocent, then basically told Kayden he was a sick pervert, fucking his niece with another man.

She realized she hadn't warned Kayden that her uncle knew about her relationship with him and Aldo.

"Shit," she whispered.

"He's been watching you," Aldo said, unconcerned. "We haven't exactly been hiding our relationship, stealing good-night kisses on Nonna's front porch, picking you up together for dates."

"Yeah, but I should have told Kayden. That other police officer—"

"Has been Kayden's partner since the day he started on the force. Seth is a good friend, who's been invited to more than a few Moretti parties and nights out with the guys. He knows about both Tony's and Gio's threesomes, and he won't blink an eye when he finds out Kayden, you, and I are together."

"You're sure?" Hazel asked.

"Hazel, you found out Gio, Keeley, and Rafe were in a three-some relationship the first night you met them. What did you think when you heard that? What did you *really* think?"

"Honestly? That Keeley was one lucky bitch. Gio and Rafe are super-hot." She exaggeratedly fanned herself.

Aldo burst into loud laughter. "Walked right into that one, didn't I? Shit. Don't hold back, Fireball."

Hazel laughed too, jumping when she heard a tap on her window. She hadn't even seen Kayden cross the street and approach the truck.

She rolled down the window.

Kayden noticed their laughter but didn't ask about it. "I'm going to ride to the station with Seth, and we're going to book Walsh. The Boston PD is sending someone down to transport him back there tomorrow."

"Did he put up a fight?" Hazel recalled her uncle's injuries.

Kayden stared at her hard for a moment. "Sure."

She narrowed her eyes. "Kayden Gallo. You just lied to me."

He showed no remorse for it. "That fucker had it coming. Nobody hurts our girl and gets away with it. When I told Seth everything he'd done to you, the two of us agreed he was going to resist arrest."

"Even if he didn't," she pointed out.

Kayden shrugged, unconcerned. "Asshole was already drunk as a skunk. He won't remember he didn't put up a fight."

Hazel blinked, trying to fight back tears. She was moved by his defense of her. She'd never had anyone stand up for her the way

Aldo and Kayden did, so it was going to take her some time to get used to it without tearing up.

Kayden, of course, noticed, but he didn't say anything. Instead, he just cupped her cheek, stroking it gently with his thumb, his affectionate look doing nothing to help her stem the tears.

"Once we book him, I'm off duty for the rest of the day. Meet the two of you in our bedroom?" Kayden asked.

Hazel grinned. "Are we still on that? I don't remember agreeing to move in. Or get married."

"But you will." Kayden acted cocky enough that she considered knocking him down a peg or two, just for fun.

"I don't know about that," Aldo chimed in. "Apparently, Hazel finds Rafe and Gio very hot. We might have some competition."

Kayden scowled. "What the fuck are you talking about?"

Aldo and Hazel laughed, but neither bothered to put Kayden out of his misery because his jealous expression was too funny.

"We'll meet you back at your place in a couple of hours. I promised to take Hazel by Nonno and Nonna's. Apparently, they need visual confirmation that she's okay."

After hearing that, Hazel gave up beating back the tears, swiping them away as they fell, fighting to believe that all of these amazing, loving, kind people genuinely cared about her.

HER.

There was still that tiny part of her that couldn't accept this was real, something she'd confessed last night after she, Aldo, and Kayden managed to pull themselves out of bed for a *very* late dinner of grilled cheese sandwiches.

They'd promised her they would spend every day for the rest of their lives proving to her just how real this was.

She'd never received a greater vow.

Kayden crossed the street, returning to the cruiser, as Aldo drove them to the Morettis' house.

* * *

Hazel looked up when she heard the front door open. She and Aldo had returned to Kayden's house—or "home," as Aldo referred to it to his Nonna, when they were saying their goodbyes half an hour ago. She and Aldo had explained to the older couple why she'd run, Nonna wiping away tears as she hugged Hazel like she'd never let her go. Then Nonno insisted she come back to work as his nurse, swearing he'd relapse without her.

Hazel had been moved by their offer, their support, and their belief in her. She'd accepted the job, even though she knew as well as the Morettis did that Nonno didn't really need her anymore. Regardless, Nonna had demanded she work the full eight weeks they'd hired her for, which meant she was still employed for three more weeks. Aldo had changed one detail of her nursing duties, saying Hazel wouldn't be needing the guest room anymore, since she'd spend her nights with him and Kayden at "home."

His pronouncement had Nonna crying and hugging her again, welcoming her to the family and rattling off at least a year's worth of events where Hazel's presence would be expected—birthday parties, a Fourth of July picnic, the viewing party planned for when Joey's show premiered, as well as Thanksgiving and Christmas.

Nonno, the shameless joker, had hugged her as well, loudly whispering that she should run again while she had the chance.

Hazel was certain her feet hadn't touched the ground as she and Aldo said goodbye, and she promised to report back to work bright and early the next day.

They'd plopped down onto the couch together upon their arrival here, cuddling and talking about a bunch of nothing while they waited for Kayden. She had her shoes off, her feet tucked under her, and all she could think was she'd never felt this comfortable in the apartment she'd grown up in. Then it occurred to her there were a lot of things that were going to take some getting used to.

Kayden smiled when he walked into the living room and spotted them. "That looks cozy. Give me a minute to get out of uniform and I'll join you."

"Or..." Aldo said, standing. "We could help you change, and you could join us another way. And by change, I mean strip you naked, and by join us, I mean sexually."

Kayden crooked his finger at her, still sitting on the couch. "I like Aldo's idea better."

Hazel popped up so quickly, she almost tripped, Aldo steadying her as he chuckled.

"Last one there goes down on the other two," Aldo joked, setting off at a mad dash down the hallway, both cheating and laughing uncontrollably. Hazel hopped on Kayden's back in an attempt to slow him down as he cut Aldo off every time he managed to pass him. Aldo grabbed Kayden's belt, tugging him backward, while he used his other hand to tickle Hazel. Her squirming on Kayden's back threw him off-balance, and in the end, all three of them essentially fell into the bedroom at the same time.

She was laughing so hard, Hazel had tears running down her face. "Competitive much?"

Kayden snorted as he stripped off his police belt. "You're one to talk. You were climbing me like a spider monkey, trying to slow me down."

Aldo stepped in front of Kayden, unbuttoning the shirt of his uniform, adding a quick, brushing kiss to his jaw. Hazel never failed to get turned on by their genuine affection for each other. She'd been shocked when they had confessed to going cold turkey for almost a year. They were both very sexual men, and there was no denying the chemistry between them. She couldn't believe they'd resisted each other for so long.

Kayden toed off his shoes, then shrugged off his shirt once it was unbuttoned. He drew the T-shirt he wore beneath off as well. His pants were the next to go.

Hazel took a second to admire the bulge in his boxer briefs

and the way Aldo ran his hand over Kayden's hard cock, fondling it through the soft cotton.

"Mmm," Aldo hummed appreciatively.

"Am I the only one losing clothes?" Kayden reached out to cup Aldo's erection as well.

"So sexy," she whispered.

Both men turned to look at her, and once again, Kayden crooked his finger. "Get over here, Hazel."

She stepped close, the three of them sharing the same personal space. Aldo kept one hand on Kayden's dick while he wrapped the other around her waist, tucking her even closer before his fingers drifted south, stroking her ass.

Kayden used his free hand to grasp the nape of her neck, drawing her in, stealing a long, hot kiss. Kayden and Aldo were strong men, but they never used that strength to overpower her. When Kayden placed his hand on her like this, all Hazel felt was safe, protected.

When the two of them parted, Aldo leaned in, claiming Kayden's lips, their kisses rougher than the ones they gave to her. Their lips came together in a way that looked almost brutal, their passion burning so bright, Hazel imagined she could feel the heat of it.

Aldo turned to kiss her next, those lips that had looked so hard when they touched Kayden's feeling softer now. It was as if he was worshiping her mouth. She'd never been kissed so tenderly or with such affection.

They remained there for a long time, doing nothing more than kissing and touching. When she and Kayden separated after their thirtieth or fortieth kiss—she'd lost track—she cupped his face, overwhelmed by an emotion she had very little experience with. Perhaps that was why the words fell out of her.

"I love you," she whispered, before her gaze slid to Aldo. "Both of you."

Time froze as Hazel realized what she'd said. She'd never spoken those words aloud to anyone. Not once in her entire life.

Her own shock over speaking them now must have shone on her face as she stumbled back a step, wondering if she should take them back. None of them had mentioned love. Not yet.

Hazel shook her head, internally chastising herself. She'd been giving them shit for moving too fast, yet here she was, jumping the gun on expressing her feelings.

She started to take another step back, but neither man allowed it. Aldo gripping her waist. Kayden wrapping his arm around her shoulders.

"I shouldn't have—" she started.

"We love you too," Kayden replied.

"Don't you know that?" Aldo asked.

"We haven't...you never..." Hazel hated it when she got flustered because her ability to string words together in a coherent sentence always flew out the window.

"We haven't said it out loud because, up until yesterday, you were a flight risk," Kayden joked.

Hazel smirked. "So you were afraid I'd freak out if you said you loved me, but you didn't think making plans for us to move in together, get married, and have kids would do the same?"

Aldo shrugged. "No one's ever accused us of being too bright."

She wanted to laugh, but that stupid asshole Boston Hazel was back, trying once again to convince her that none of this could last.

"You love me?" she asked, wincing at the slight quiver in her voice.

"So much it hurts." Kayden kissed her on the cheek before glancing at Aldo. "And just in case you have any doubts, I love you too."

Aldo's eyes twinkled with pure mischief. "You think I have doubts? Jesus, man, what's *not* to love? I mean, look at me. I'm sex-on-a-stick fine."

"Cocky son of a bitch." Kayden closed his eyes and pinched the bridge of his nose, pretending to be annoyed.

Hazel laughed, then she shouldered Aldo. "Maybe you should tell Kayden you love him too, before he changes his mind about his feelings for you."

Aldo grinned, gripping Kayden's shoulder with strong fingers. The two of them stared at each other, neither one saying the words aloud. They didn't need to. Hazel had never seen love laid so bare before.

They leaned toward each other then, their foreheads touching —just for a moment—before parting and drawing her back into their embrace. It was the best hug of her life.

The kisses resumed, and soon, clothes began falling away. Once they were all naked, Kayden drew back the duvet, the three of them climbing onto the bed. She'd fallen asleep between them last night, Aldo's chest her pillow, Kayden's arm bracketing her waist as he spooned her.

She lifted her arms as Aldo lay down next to her, his hand finding her breast immediately. He had a thing for her tits, not that she was complaining. Especially when his lips followed, and he sucked her nipple into his mouth.

Hazel sighed blissfully. "That feels so good."

Kayden joined them, treating her other nipple to the same. Every so often, they'd lift their heads, sharing a kiss over her chest as Hazel's fingers tangled in their hair.

After a few minutes, Kayden gave Aldo's shoulder a slight push. "Roll onto your back, Al. Our pretty Hazel is going for a ride."

Hazel didn't have a problem with that at all. Aldo shifted, gripping her hips to pull her over him. She bent low so that she could kiss him.

The bed shifted behind her, and she heard Kayden open the nightstand drawer. At some point, she needed to make a doctor's appointment to get on birth control. She'd never bothered before because there had never been a need. She'd always made sure her past lovers wore condoms, and since none of her relationships lasted that long, she'd never made the leap to taking contraceptives herself.

The way she, Kayden, and Aldo couldn't be in the same room for more than an hour or so without ripping each other's clothes off told her she'd be smart to call and set up that appointment tomorrow, or the baby-name discussion might happen *before* the fall wedding.

She broke off the kiss when she felt Kayden's hand stroke along her ass. She shivered with arousal. Kayden ran his fingers through her hair, wrapping it up in his fist, using that grip to pull her up until she was kneeling over Aldo. His erection was nestled between her legs, the head resting against his stomach.

Kayden slipped a condom in her hand. "Put this on him."

She tore the wrapper open with her teeth, Aldo's eyes going dark with lust. Pulling out the condom, she shifted down his thighs a few inches, taking his dick in her hand.

Aldo hissed when she closed her fist around it, stroking it up and down a few times.

"Have mercy, Fireball," he pleaded.

She reveled in this newfound power, this ability to make two of the sexiest men she'd ever met weak in the knees.

She gave him a seductive grin, then shook her head. "No mercy." She pushed herself even lower, her thighs straddling his knees so she could run her tongue around his head, stealing a taste of precum.

Aldo groaned. "Jesus, baby."

Hazel suspected Kayden had a plan. One that she'd fucked with, because he shifted until he was kneeling next to them, lowering his own head. "Give me a taste."

Aldo grunted when Hazel released him with a pop, Kayden right there to take his place.

"Fuck. This is the opposite of mercy." Aldo's fingers white-knuckled the sheets, but he wasn't exactly fighting them. Actually, he was meeting them halfway, lifting his hips in an attempt to push deeper into Kayden's mouth, and then—when they switched places again—Hazel's.

Hazel reached between his legs, cupping his balls, squeezing them. With that touch, Aldo thrust his hips higher, faster, his cock brushing the back of her throat. She hummed, so ready to ramp up their play.

Unfortunately, Kayden cut her off. His hand tugged at her hair, pulling her off Aldo's dick, completely ignoring both of their complaints.

"Kayden," she started.

He twisted her face to his. "What did I tell you to do?"

What the hell was it about that tone that sent electrical sparks shimmering throughout her body? Hazel couldn't understand how he had this effect on her. She'd never—ever—given up control, so certain doing so would be her downfall.

But Kayden only had to give a command in that deep, dark voice, look at her with those stern but oh-so-sexy brown eyes, and she was ready to fall to her knees and call him master.

Trust.

The word popped into her head. That was the difference. That was why she was willing to put herself in their hands. It had taken her too much time to realize, to admit it—to them and to herself—but the truth was, she trusted them.

With her body.

With her heart.

Hell, with her life.

"You told me to put the condom on him. To ride him," she replied.

Kayden raised one eyebrow, making it clear she'd yet to do either of those.

She turned her attention back to the condom she'd dropped in favor of stroking Aldo's dick, picking it up and pulling it on him.

Aldo's hips shifted slightly, his eyes drifting closed, and she got the sense he was trying to regain his own control.

Hazel rose up, intent on taking Aldo into her body, but Kayden's hand landed on her shoulder, holding her down.

His lips brushed her shoulder, then slid along her neck, finding that perfect spot just below her ear that had her pussy clenching.

His breath tickled when he whispered in her ear, "I want to take your ass while Aldo claims your pussy."

Hazel's heart stopped for a split second as she let that request soak in. They'd come together countless ways—missionary, doggie style, blow jobs, Aldo taking Kayden's ass, Kayden taking Aldo's—but they hadn't explored anal sex from her perspective.

Kayden gave her a kiss on the cheek. "If you don't want that, Hazel, all you have to say is no."

She'd spent weeks fantasizing about these men, and what Kayden wanted was the one fantasy she had played over and over in her mind.

"I want to," she admitted. "It's just like I told you before…that area is sort of uncharted territory."

Aldo chuckled, but Kayden—always the more serious of the two—took what she said to heart.

"So you've never had anal sex before?" he clarified. "Not even with fingers?"

She shook her head. "Nothing. It's always felt like something that…well, I've never really been with anyone I trusted enough to make sure it didn't hurt. Before you two," she hastened to add.

"We would make sure we didn't hurt you." Aldo offered her reassurance she didn't need.

"I know that." She glanced back at Kayden. "I'd like you to be my first."

Kayden lifted her hand, placing her palm on his chest, right over his heart. "I love you."

Those words would always set Hazel free. She gave Kayden a quick, hard kiss, then she lifted her ass, grasped Aldo's cock, and pushed down—one fast, hard motion that left him seated to the hilt in seconds.

Her quick action took Aldo by surprise, his fingers digging into her hips, a guttural groan falling from his lips.

"Fuuuuuck." Tightening his hold, Aldo held her steady, tilting her hips, until the head of his cock hit her G-spot.

"God!" she cried on a gasp.

"Come here, Fireball." Aldo reached up, drawing her down until their chests were touching. "Lay your head on my shoulder while Kayden gets you ready."

Ready.

She did as Aldo said, loving the sweet kisses he pressed to the top of her head, the soothing words he murmured as Kayden knelt behind her, his hands drawing the globes of her ass apart.

He must have grabbed lube at the same time as the condom because his finger was slick when it slid inside.

She'd been right to trust these men, because Kayden was taking his time. Hazel lost track of the minutes as he slowly fucked her with one finger, then two, then more lube, then three. She'd expected pain, but apart from the slight pinch that accompanied each added finger, there was nothing but pleasure.

That was the part that surprised her. She hadn't anticipated this act making her feel so hot and bothered and needy. Her breathing grew more labored with each thrust, and soon Hazel was anticipating Kayden's rhythm, matching it. She wasn't moving much, but it was enough to keep Aldo on edge.

"Goddammit," Aldo said to Kayden, through gritted teeth. "It's like you're stroking my cock. I can feel everything you're doing."

Kayden continued stretching her until Hazel was dripping with sweat, trembling with need.

"Please," she said at last. "God, Kayden, please. I need you. Now."

Kayden's fingers withdrew slowly, and she sighed with relief when she heard the rustle of the condom wrapper.

Then...he was there. His cock was thicker than his fingers, but he'd prepared her well.

A low moan escaped as he pushed the head of his dick inside, that pinch back again. But that was all it was. And once the mushroom head was in, the rest of him slid in easier.

Like her, Aldo and Kayden were struggling for breath, all of them panting. Kayden was moving excruciatingly slow, taking her by degrees, giving her time to adjust or, if necessary, ask him to stop.

As if.

Once he was fully inside, she rested her forehead on Aldo's shoulder.

"Okay?" Aldo cupped the nape of her neck.

"So full," she murmured. "Love it. Love you."

"Thank God," Aldo whispered. "How did we ever live without you, Hazel?"

She couldn't reply to that because, fuck, what could she say? She'd spent a lifetime alone, even when she was surrounded by people.

"Ready for more?" Kayden asked.

"So ready."

"Don't move," Kayden demanded. "Just hold on. Let us make this good for you."

Hazel's fingers dug into Aldo's shoulders as Kayden gripped her hips, pulling out before driving back in again. For the first few thrusts, he paused between, giving her time she didn't need to adjust. Beneath her, Aldo alternated with Kayden, giving her a series of shallower thrusts that rubbed against Kayden's dick in her ass.

Hazel's eyes closed, bliss coursing through her veins. "More. More," she demanded. "Don't stop. Please."

Kayden, as always, maintained the control she'd lost. Her body no longer felt like hers, her mind drifting to a place she'd never been. Somewhere peaceful and wonderful, somewhere warm and soft and safe.

So safe.

She reveled in their arms, floating there between them, as Kayden and Aldo began to take her harder, faster, hotter, heavier.

Everything around her faded away, sound muted, as she lost touch with reality, aware only of the almost unbearable pleasure flooding every inch of her body.

She was vaguely aware of Aldo calling out her name, his body jerking roughly beneath her as he came. She could feel the pulsing beat of his climax.

Kayden's hand slipped around her waist, his fingertip stroking her clit, the last nail in her coffin. She'd been hovering right there, teetering on the edge.

"Come for us," Kayden murmured in her ear.

Free. He set her free.

With those three words.

While Aldo set her on fire with three more. "We love you."

Hazel exploded, a giant white ball detonating inside her, shattering her in the best possible way.

Kayden came with her, her orgasm triggering his. His fingers dug deep into her hips, and she suspected she'd wear his bruises there tomorrow.

"Hazel," Kayden said on a gasp that morphed into a moan of pure pleasure.

Hazel's bones melted, every ounce of strength in her body sapped. Aldo wrapped his arms around her, holding her steady for minutes—hours—until she finally managed to land.

When she opened her eyes, she had to blink a few times to focus. She lifted her head, surprised to discover Kayden lying next to her and Aldo. She hadn't even felt him leave her.

"There she is." Aldo's large hand stroked her hair.

She tried to make sense of his words, then she frowned. "Oh my God. Did I pass out?"

Kayden smiled and shook his head. "Not exactly. I don't think you lost consciousness, but you weren't exactly here with us either."

"I've never experienced anything like that. Jesus...I'll chase that high for the rest of my life."

Her admission had both Aldo and Kayden chuckling.

"You aren't the only one," Aldo said.

She twisted, aware all her weight rested on his body. He turned with her, placing her on the bed between them. The two of them faced each other, as Kayden wrapped his arm around her stomach.

"By the way, Kay." Aldo propped himself up on his elbow. "You owe me twenty bucks."

"What for?" Kayden asked.

Aldo grinned. "I bet you at Penny and Gage's wedding we'd be the next to find our girl. It only took a burglary, a fire, a heart bypass, and a flight to Chicago, but by God, we got her."

Hazel shrugged playfully. "Piece of cake."

The three of them laughed, the sound growing louder when Kayden reached for his wallet and slapped the twenty in Aldo's hand.

It might have taken her twenty-five years, but she'd finally found it...a home.

And she realized it had nothing to do with Kayden's house and everything to do with the men lying next to her.

With them...she was home.

Two months later...

Liza stood next to Gianna, holding two bouquets, hers and the bride's. She and Gianna had been friends for years, but now they were trading up, grabbing an even better relationship.

Sisters.

She smiled as Gianna stood facing Liza's brother, Elio, the two holding hands as they said their vows to each other. They'd written their own, and damn if there wasn't a dry eye in the place.

Gianna and Elio had opted for a smallish—nothing was truly small with the entire Moretti family in attendance—ceremony with just two attendants, Liza as maid of honor, and Aldo standing next to their brother as best man.

The wedding was taking place in the garden behind the haunted inn. It was a beautiful June day. Blue sky, warm—but not hot—weather, the flowers in full, colorful bloom, birds singing.

They'd set up a tent with tables and a dance floor for after the ceremony, with plans to serve picnic fare for the reception dinner.

In addition to her flowing white dress and blindingly happy smile, Gianna was also sporting a baby bump, she and Elio taking the entire family by surprise when they announced at the end of April that they were expecting a child in early September.

She was going to be an aunt...again. And she couldn't wait.

"I promise to laugh at most of your jokes," Gianna said, as everyone chuckled. "I promise to be there for you on your best days, your boring days, and your worst days."

As Gianna continued her vows, Liza studied Elio's face. She wasn't sure she'd even seen someone so genuinely happy. Then she reconsidered as she looked around. Aldo was looking toward the second row, smiling at Hazel and Kayden, the three of them had been floating in their own little bubble of bliss for almost two months now.

Gage lifted Penny's hand and kissed it as they watched the ceremony. Tony's arm was wrapped around Jess's shoulders as she and Rhys held hands. Rafe, Gio, and Keeley could probably have gotten by with one damn chair, given how closely the three of them were sitting.

Liza knew she should be happy for all of them—and deep down, she was. It was just difficult to watch everyone else around her finding their dreams, while she...well, she'd been treading water so long, she was getting leg cramps. At some point, she couldn't help but think she was going to drown in the loneliness.

Her attention was drawn back to Elio, who was now saying his vows. "As we grow into different versions of ourselves—as a couple and as parents—I promise to put in the work. I promise that whatever you dream up, I'll do my best to make it a reality. And I promise to sweep you off your feet as often as I keep you grounded."

Liza blinked several times, but there was no holding back the tears. It was all too wonderful and touching. After that, rings were exchanged as well as a super-hot kiss.

They all cheered, then slowly made their way to the tent, ready for the speeches and food and dancing.

Nonno, the shameless joker, had of course stolen the show when he'd asked everyone to lift a glass, offering advice with his toast. "Elio, my boy, you can be right, or you can be happy. But you can't be both. Here's to being happy."

Nonna had laughed even as she slapped Nonno on the shoulder, something they'd all seen her do no less than a million times.

The dancing went well into the night, no one ready to pack it in.

By midnight, Liza had lost her heels, consumed one—okay, three—too many glasses of wine, and was sitting in a chair, trying to catch her second wind.

"Quite a night." Gage dropped down next to her. "I have to admit, you and your friends know how to throw one hell of a wedding."

Liza grinned, nodding her head to acknowledge the compliment. She and her girlfriends had spent months helping Penny plan her Valentine's Day wedding to Gage. "It really has been a great night."

"You trying to recover from the dancing?"

Liza nodded, then added a shrug. "That, and maybe feeling a little bit sorry for myself. Always a bridesmaid," she said, trying to infuse a lightness to her tone that she didn't feel.

She wasn't sure why she'd said anything at all. Though in the past few months, it felt like she and Gage had been starting up a real friendship, instead of holding steady with the "person in common, aka Penny" relationship they'd begun with.

"I have two single brothers," he joked, wiggling his eyebrows.

"Hell will freeze over," she muttered.

Gage laughed. "I know he drives you crazy, but I think you and Matt have a lot more in common than you realize."

Liza narrowed her eyes. "Bite your tongue. And scrub that thought from your brain. I'm nothing like that asshole."

Gage lifted one shoulder casually, refusing to take back his words. "Well, if not Matt, how about Conor?"

"Thanks for the offer. Let me strike out on Hinge for another decade or four, and then we can revisit the conversation."

Gage gave her a wink. "It's a date."

Penny walked up as a slow song came on, dragging her husband out onto the floor for the last dance.

Liza remained where she was, watching all the happy people in love, vowing to herself that by this time next year...she would be one of them.

Ready for more Italian Stallions?
Down and Dirty
Hard and Fast
Rough and Ready
Wild and Wicked
Hot and Heavy
Naughty and Nice (a holiday novella)
Tempted and Taken
Steady and Strong
Kiss and Tell

Want to see how Layla Moretti met her guys, Finn and Miguel? Want to see how the Moretti brothers got their Italian Stallions nickname? Check out these books, standalone within the Wilder Irish series!
Wild Side
Wild Dreams
Wild Chance

Calling all fans of Mari Carr AND Facebook! There's a group for you. Come join the Mari Carr's Facebook group for sneak peaks, cover reveals, contests and more! Join now.

And be sure to join Mari's mailing list to receive a **FREE** sexy novella, Midnight Wild.

About the Author

Virginia native Mari Carr is a New York Times and USA TODAY bestseller of contemporary romance novels. With over two million copies of her books sold, Mari was the winner of the Romance Writers of America's Passionate Plume award for her novella, Erotic Research. She has over a hundred published works, including her popular Wild Irish and Compass books, along with the Trinity Masters series she writes with Lila Dubois.

Follow Mari:
www.maricarr.com
mari@maricarr.com

Join her newsletter so you don't miss new releases and for exclusive subscriber-only content.

www.ingramcontent.com/pod-product-compliance
Lightning Source LLC
Chambersburg PA
CBHW051247210726
48287CB00002B/391